The Apocalypse Outcasts

The Undead World: Novel 3

By Peter Meredith

Jilly bean lives !

Fictional works by Peter Meredith:

Chapter 1

David Wolf

New York City

In the month since Yuri Petrovich had perfected and demonstrated his vaccine, the *Nordic Star* had come to resemble, both in smell and appearance, the Grand Bazaar of Marrakesh. Vibrantly colored stalls lined both sides of the new pier where the cruise ship was docked while nearly every cabin onboard had been converted into a storefront of one sort or another.

Crowds bickered and bartered over every conceivable item, from the obvious: ammunition, food, and fuel—to the exotic: heroin, helicopters and even humans.

In her hatred, Cassie Mason had opened a door to the Seventeenth Century and now a new slave trade had sprung up. These poor creatures, their necks encircled in steel, were exclusively women.

David Wolf had his sights on one in particular, an Irish-looking girl with abundant red hair. She was small and pale with the fine bone structure of a sparrow. Her eyes were large and green and showed every single emotion that turned in her mind. Mostly it was fear that sat in those pretty eyes.

Wolf could see that she feared him, but there was little he could do about that and less that he wanted to do about it. He was an easy man to fear. His own eyes were grey and empty. They were flat, just like his every expression. Even when he felt an emotion beyond contempt, no one could tell.

He seemed to be the kind of man who could kill without the least qualm, which was exactly the kind of man he was. He was a sociopath and no longer bothered to hide it. Now, his lack of moral underpinnings was a distinct advantage in this new post-apocalyptic age.

"Let me smell that one," Wolf said, lifting his scruffy chin to indicate the Irish-looking girl.

Along with six slaves, there were two small, rat-like and swarthy men in the ship's cabin. Unlike the pale girl, they didn't fear David Wolf in the least. They had noted his size and his rough exterior, and that the knuckles of both his hands were crisscrossed with old scars, but they knew *Nordic Star* security would defend them if he turned nasty.

There weren't many laws onboard the Nordic Star, but if one of the few was ever broken, justice was blindingly swift, and the penalties savage. Yuri Petrovich had learned his lesson. Before his two ferry boats had been sunk by a six-year-old girl, he had tried to skimp on security. Now his black garbed thugs lurked everywhere, ready to crack skulls at the first hint of trouble.

"You wanna smell her?" one of the two men asked. "What? Her pussy? Naw. Not until I see your tally sheet."

Wolf didn't twitch a muscle. His tally sheet would remain in his jacket pocket. He wasn't about to divulge how much he was worth, not at this stage of the bargaining. "How much is she?" he asked.

"Eight thousand," the man replied, setting the price ridiculously high in preparation for the haggling that he hoped would commence. Wolf had come by every day for the last week to ogle the redhead and now his obsession couldn't be suppressed. Still, his willpower was formidable. He stared at the man, allowing an uncomfortable silence to come between them. "What?" the man asked after a minute. "I said eight thousand. You got nothing to say to that?"

According to his tally sheet, David Wolf was worth in gas, food, and other miscellaneous items, fourteen hundred 9mm bullets. The 9mm cartridge, also going by the names: 9x19mm, 9mm Luger, 9mm Parabellum, and 9mm NATO, all described the same cartridge and was the most abundant bullet currently available. It was basically the

5

"Dollar" of the new undead world. Fourteen hundred was a goodly sum, but clearly not goodly enough.

"You got an hourly on her?" David asked, testing. If there was an hourly he wouldn't bother. He wasn't interested in a rental with the option to buy, and he definitely wasn't interested in someone else's leftovers.

The man who had, up to now, done all the talking rolled his eyes and threw up his hands. His partner, working a tag team shook his head in a display of sadness, still trying to hook a sale. "No way, my main man," he said with a foreign accent. "These aren't those kind of girls. No one's going to pony up eight large for a used-up girl. Am I right? Here, tell me, how much ya got? Maybe we can work a deal for another girl. What about this one? Her name's Jennifer. She's sweet and not that bad to look at. And she can cook. You can cook, right Jen?"

The woman in question was long in the face and reminded Wolf of an aunt of his who was very likely dead. She nodded timidly at the question and kept her eyes down at the carpet. Wolf barely gave her a glance. His main focus was on the Irish girl. She had caught his attention. She was the one for him. She had that certain something that stirred *want* in him. It was a rare feeling for him.

"No. I want the other one," he said. There it was spoken aloud: *want*. He understood *have* better.

"Oh, my main man," the salesman said in a sad tone. "You can't afford her. I can see that."

"I can do five thousand." Though his tally sheet said fourteen hundred, he had another two-thousand—mostly in fuel—squirreled away in a shed in some crappy New Jersey town. The remainder he would scrounge up. The girl was very much like the first car he had ever purchased: shiny, sleek, and hot. The car, a 2002 Mitsubishi Eclipse Spyder, had been way out of his price range but he knew he had to have it and when David Wolf put his mind to something he was extremely focused.

"Let's not play around," the salesman said with a laugh. "Look at her. Have you seen anyone like her since the apocalypse? She is a natural redhead. Oh, yes, my main man, the collar matches the cuffs with this one. She is perfect. Skin as soft as silk and clear as marble. And," he laughed again and gave Wolf a wink, "she's virtually untouched."

"Virtually?"

"Come on. Do you expect her to be a virgin, in this day and age? Please. If you want a virgin, go see my cousin Sami three doors down. He's got a couple of twelve-year olds with skinny legs and no ass. Who wants that? Not you, my main man. You want a woman who knows her way around things, you just don't want her all used and up and flapping. Am I right? I am right. Ok, ok. For you, I'll do seventy five hundred."

Wolf stepped closer and gazed down at the Irish girl. She was on her knees, holding a light summer dress tight to her thighs as though she feared he would yank her dress up to check to see if she really was a natural redhead. He squatted down next to her. She was clean, smelling of shampoo and a light perfume.

"Let me see your teeth," he ordered.

After swallowing once she opened her mouth hesitantly sticking out a soft pink tongue. Her teeth were small, even, and white. Her breath was warm. He took one of her tiny hands in his and turned it this way and that. He then checked her ears; they were small with a single piercing in each. It was good.

"Seven thousand," Wolf said. "Fourteen hundred today. Two thousand tomorrow. The rest in a couple of weeks."

The salesman considered this while running his hands through his greasy, thinning hair. "I could go as low as seven if you had the full amount now. But you want me to also pay for her room and board for another couple of weeks? No way, my main man. We have quick turnover here. I can't afford to have a girl hanging around, and what happens if you come back without the rest of the payment?"

"You keep what I've given you," Wolf replied. "Give me three weeks from tomorrow to get you the rest of the money. Plus, I'll throw in another hundred for storage, but

I want her in one piece. If she's been pawed over…" He didn't need to finish his sentence. The cold message of death in his eyes was enough.

"Three weeks?" the salesman said to himself quietly. He screwed up his small eyes in thought, looked at the carpet, at the girl, and then shrewdly he examined David Wolf. "Ok. You have until noon, three weeks from tomorrow. Not a minute later."

Wolf turned to leave, but then paused and asked the girl, "What's your name?"

Again, she had to swallow audibly before she could answer: "Brandee."

His lip curled. "Sounds like a stripper's name. From now on your name is Erin. I like that better."

When he left the slave deck, as the lowest deck of the Nordic Star had become known, he went straight to the message boards on display on the top deck. His grey eyes scanned the notices, looking for the telltale pistols in the corners that were the universal symbol for a gunman for hire. There were only a few: people looking for armed escorts into one *Black* zone or another. These interested him, but the timing was off. Either the expeditions had already occurred or were coming up weeks out.

His eyes then fell on the bounties. There were over a dozen, most for piddling amounts and for trifling reasons, however two were for substantially more:

Reward!
Dead or Alive
Sadie Walcott
Female Caucasian
Age: 17-20—Height: 64"—Weight:100lbs
Black hair, brown/dark eyes

Nico Grekov
Male Caucasian
Age: 26—Height: 71"—Weight:180lbs
Blonde, blue eyes

^5000 reward will be paid upon receipt of either
fugitive aboard the *Nordic Star*.
The pair is thought to be traveling with a 36 year old
woman; *Sarah Rivers: Blonde, Blue eyes, 64" 105lbs
*No bounty is to be paid for any person or persons
traveling with wanted fugitives.
*Bounty hunters will not be reimbursed for any expenses
incurred.

His eyes bugged at seeing the number ^5000. For a
bounty, it was astronomical and suggested that Yuri was
less interested in getting the two fugitives than he was in
sending a message. The message was obvious: Don't fuck
with Yuri.

Wolf took the notice, folding it into his pocket. Like
everybody else he had heard the story of the vaccine
demonstration and what had happened in its aftermath.
The story had grown and warped with each telling. In one
version the teenage girl, Sadie, was actually a master ninja
who had killed a dozen men with her bare hands. In
another, it was Nico, her Russian boyfriend, who had
planted bombs on the ferry boats in a botched attempt to
free one of the prisoners.

Wolf didn't really care what the real story was. He had
money to make fast. There were hundreds of eyewitnesses
who had seen the ships go up in flames and the fight in the
water afterwards, but only one who saw what happened on
the bottom deck of *Nordic Star*, just before that.

He left to find a woman named Donna Rice. She lived
on a barge just upstream. Rumor had it she was reluctant
to tell her tale; unfortunately for her David Wolf could be
extremely persuasive when he needed to be.

Chapter 2

Sarah Rivers

Philadelphia, Pennsylvania

With her muscles tensely bunched and spring-loaded, Sarah swept into the kitchen holding her shotgun steady despite the sweat slicking her hands. Her denim blue eyes, sharp and quick, flicked all around the room. The fact that it was clear of zombies did not cause her to relax much at all. Instead, her breathing picked up in tempo: the cupboard doors were unexpectedly and amazingly closed. A closed door meant that perhaps, just perhaps, no other forager had been here before her.

The room was still, with a frozen quality, as if the oxygen in the air hung in sheets. The floor was layered in eight month's worth of fine grey dust. It was perfectly even and Sarah ran tracks right through it, hurrying to the first cabinet, her long blonde hair swinging gently behind.

The cabinet held glasses, mugs, champagne flutes, brandy snifters, tall plastic gas station giveaways. She went to the next cupboard finding plates, bowls, saucers... "Shit," she crabbed, going to the next in line.

From the front stairs, Nico called out in his accented voice, "You is find something?"

Before she answered, she swung back the cupboard door that was closest to the refrigerator. Before the apocalypse, this would have been the territory of spices and cooking oil, and odds and ends such as dry white wine and molasses. In every other house they had been through in the last few days this cupboard was generally strewn with a confusion of toothpicks, muffin sleeves, and grey, green, and white particles—the remnants of what used to be.

This particular cupboard was wonderfully different. The spices were faultlessly arranged like soldiers on parade and ordered alphabetically: Allspice leading the front left column, Tarragon heading up the last on the right.

"Nope, there's nothing here," Sarah lied as her eyes ran up the fully stocked shelves. At the sight of the cornmeal, the tin of flour, and the bag of sugar, her stomach rumbled. Then she saw something that really got her going.

"Oh my God," she said in a whisper, touching the feet of a five-inch tall bear filled with golden honey. It was a struggle not to pop its top right there and pour it down her throat.

From the second floor, Nico cursed their luck, causing Sarah to blink—the honey had mesmerized her. "Let's try the next house," she called out. In a hurry she left the kitchen, making sure to shut the door to her prize behind her and trying her best to appear disappointed.

The Russian came slowly down the stairs. "Maybe we should try garage. The door is not open. That is usual good sign."

Shaking her head, Sarah began walking to the front door. "No. Let's not waste our time. We'll go to the next one." Nico viewed her as almost his "mother-in-law" and was usually quick to knuckle-under when she made demands. Not this time.

"I suppose nothing in kitchen must mean rest of house empty." Russians were generally ham-handed in their approach to sarcasm, they always over did it. Nico even added a tremendous eye-roll to his windy sigh.

"Yep, let's go," Sarah replied. She was out the door before he could work up a second sigh; his usual when he didn't get his way. Once outside she glanced at the house and began repeating its number under her breath: "One-forty-two Clermont. One-forty-two Clermont."

Nico came out, keeping his chiseled features neutral. "So next place, da?" he asked, making sure to walk in a wide circle around her. As a matter of habit in spite of its rudeness, she stepped away from him as though he had something catchy.

Nico was her daughter's boyfriend and a fine man in Sarah's eyes, but she could not bear to be near him, or any man for that matter, not after her experience aboard the *Nordic Star*. Even in the car she would practically lean on her door, and she always kept her Beretta close. Even then she could feel it warm against her hip, as if it were alive—the opposite of her heart. That organ was ice cold, and frequently felt odd, as though it were foreign to her, like it didn't belong.

When a man was near, even a gentle man such as Nico, her heart seemed to swell. It would balloon inside as if it could take up her entire chest and it would pump so violently she could see the pulse in her wrist jumping like there was something beneath her skin fighting to get out.

If there wasn't a man nearby, her heart was a little, rotten thing. What should have aroused it, such as Neil being sweet, Jillybean being cute, Sadie cracking her jokes and then holding her hand, did nothing whatsoever to stir emotion within it. Sarah was dead inside.

"Yeah, let's check out the next one," she said, while in her mind she repeated the words, *one-forty-two Clermont*. The house had been the first fully intact home they had chanced upon in days. The moping willows hanging over a dirt drive and the chaotic overgrown shrubbery were the likely reasons why; it was practically hidden from sight, even when they were standing on the sidewalk.

Heading to the next house, a boxy, ranch-style home that had clearly been broken into already, Sarah whispered: "One-forty-two Clermont," and felt something new: guilt. Her family needed whatever supplies had been in that last house. The five of them had burned through the stores Nico had stolen from his former employer, Yuri Petrovich, and now they were down to a couple of days' worth of food. They were getting so low that Jillybean had set a clear pitcher of water filled with chopped pine needles in the morning sun just the day before.

"They'll be fine," Sarah said, under her breath, trying to convince herself. They should be fine, but she wouldn't be. She would need everything in that house and more.

She would need it to feed herself and to barter with. "Besides, they have each other."

Sadie was in good hands with Nico, and Neil was at the height of happiness raising seven-year-old Jillybean. All that Sarah had was the memory of being repeatedly raped and the hope that she would be strong enough to go to New Eden and fight Abraham and his sick cult for her baby daughter, Eve, no matter what the cost.

At this, she barked out a little laugh that went unnoticed by Nico who was poking his head in one of the low windows of the ranch house.

What would be the cost? Her life? It didn't seem worth all that much to her or to anyone. What value was there in a wife who shivered and felt sick at the least touch of her husband? Or what was the worth of a mother who couldn't protect her children? Even her enemies thought Sarah Rivers was worthless. Cassie had felt Sarah wasn't worth even a gallon of gas, while the colonel had treated her with all the consideration of a sheet of used toilet paper.

As always when the colonel, came to mind, a crawling shudder racked her as she recalled the rapes and the beating. The shudder ran right to her soul, making her lips sneer and her jaw clench. After the last few weeks the muscles of her jaw were hard knots and she had begun to look a little like Jillybean who habitually stored acorns in her puffed cheeks.

Sarah didn't care what she looked like. All she cared about was protecting Eve and that her pistol had a full load. Without even noticing she brought the gun up to her lips and kissed it.

"What are you looking at?" she growled at Nico.

The Russian had seen the odd kiss and his eyes widened. "Nothing, I think. But we cannot skip many more house. Sadie is not well and I do not wish to be gone as so long."

Although Neil had finally thrown off the infection on his forearm, Sadie's pneumonia was persistent and very hardy. So far it had resisted the antibiotics they had given her, and if she was getting better it was at a rate that wasn't obvious. Still she wasn't getting any worse and everyone figured that as long as she stayed in bed and didn't exert herself, she would get better eventually.

"We won't be gone much longer," Sarah said, stepping into the ranch-style home and knowing right away it would be a bust. "She'll be fine…I hope."

Chapter 3

Jillybean

Philadelphia, Pennsylvania

With her scabbed knees jutting out of her floral print sundress, Jillybean squatted over the low mound of tiny particles which had been laboriously created by jillions of black ants. These weren't the big "Army" ants. These were their itsy-bitsy cousins. They went about all over the place, seemingly in confusion, however, according to Ipes it was a well coordinated system that allowed them to survive.

As almost any seven-year-old would, she was about to upset the system. In her hand was a stem of long grass that had gone to seed. Stripping off its little branches, she dipped the long smooth end into the ant hole and watched as the ants went up it exploring to the tip.

"How long can two people nap?" Jillybean said with a sigh. With Sarah and Nico foraging, and Neil and Sadie napping, the little girl was bored, bored, bored.

They need their rest, Ipes said. *They're sick and when you're sick, you need to rest.*

"I guess, but why can't they rest and play *Candyland* at the same time? I told them I'd move the pieces for them and everything. It's not that hard."

It was muggy out, the sort of lazy, gloomy afternoon when Ipes couldn't do more than just shrug. After another sigh, she lapsed into silence as a falcon glided by. It turned a circle over the pair until Jilly pulled Ipes closer.

Thanks, the zebra said after a shiver quivered the tips of his spiky Mohawk of a mane. *Oh hey, your ants are starting to go back down. Are you sure you want to do this?*

"I think so," Jillybean said, squinting at the ants. "Sarah's out scrounging. You ever notice that she's not really very good at scrounging? Whenever she goes out they never bring anything good back."

Yeah, I've noticed, the zebra said, dryly. *Maybe some people are better finders than others. Just like some people are better at focusing on what they're doing and completing the tasks at hand. If you're going to do it, just do it already and get it over with.*

"I am focusing. Don't rush me," she shot back. After a shaky breath, Jillybean spat out the acorns in her cheeks, withdrew the blade of grass from the mound, and, without any further hesitation, she opened her mouth and ran the ant-coated stem across her tongue. The insects squirmed in her saliva and wiggled along the swells of her taste buds. She swallowed, made a face, and then swallowed again, making the same face afterwards.

Still there were ants hanging on to her tongue for dear life.

Try some water, Ipes suggested.

Jillybean drank from her water bottle and then ran her tongue along her teeth, finding a few strays. She swallowed them.

Well? Ipes asked. *How were they? What did they taste like?*

She shrugged and had to think about the answer. "They didn't taste like anything, really, though they were awfully crawly."

Ipes glanced down at the mound, which was in a state of frenzy. *They're ants,* he reasoned. *What do you expect?*

"I wonder how many ants make a proper meal?" she asked, sticking the stem back into the hole. This time the ants were much more reluctant to crawl up. They would go halfway up and then rush back down again.

The zebra bent closer to assess the situation. *I think you got it all slobbery. You can't expect them to walk in your spittle; I know I wouldn't. Try getting another stem.*

Since there were a few of the critters on the first stem she wiped it clean with her tongue; scraping them to the back of her throat with her teeth before attempting to swallow—they went down much easier in this manner.

After snapping off a new blade of grass, she speared the hole with it and watched as the ants went about exploring it.

Jillybean and her zebra spent the early part of the afternoon gobbling a few thousand ants. When that first mound stopped producing a steady flow she went on to another and then another. There were always more ant hills in the world.

As Jillybean ate she and Ipes kept up a steady conversation on a multitude of topics: monsters, honeybees, if butterflies ever had a destination in mind, and Sadie's new haircut: she had somehow cut her hair to exaggerate the points that went in all directions.

Trying to emulate me, no doubt, Ipes conjectured, touching his spiky Mohawk.

Although the pair always seemed deep in their conversation they actually possessed an awareness of their surroundings equal to any of the forest creatures around them. Jillybean saw the red squirrel as it leapt from tree to tree; the chipmunk as it nosed about among the leaves; the sleepy owl high in a branch who eyed her right back, wondering about this lone human. She heard the buzz of insects and saw the periodic flow of bees going left to right. Bees meant a hive and a hive meant...

"Honey would make these ants taste better," she said, "that's for sure." The day had begun in fine May fashion, with the skies a gentle blue. Now, there were grey clouds brewing up. There would be rain, but not for a while yet. "I know what April showers bring, but what do May showers bring?" she asked. "Anything cool?"

Ipes yawned and said, *You know, the usual, mosquitoes and weeds and flowers and long grass. Speaking of which, it's gonna be a jungle around here soon.* He wasn't wrong. The lawns of the suburban streets down below her were beginning to show the first signs that a trimming was in order: everything was green and leafy. Above, the sun had thickened the air, and, with her belly full of ants, Jillybean was getting sleepy, but sleepy or not, there was no way she could miss a walking bush even in all that green.

17

The little girl and her zebra were on *The Sledding Hill*, which was little more than a gentle slope, sitting above her old neighborhood. With its array of trees, it had the feel of limited wilderness to it and she liked to go there to watch the day pass by. From its rounded, woody peak she could see most of her suburban kingdom, including the man got up like a bush.

Stealthy, Ipes commented. The man crept along, staying close to either the rusting cars or the hedges that marked the borders of people's homes. *He is good. You could learn a thing or two from watching him. See that? In the open he's as slow and methodical as you could want but watch how he picks up speed when he has cover. That's...wait! He might be heading this way. Maybe you should...*

He didn't need to finish his warning to get out of sight. Jillybean hunkered down, watching the man from just above the tips of the tall grass. She was fascinated by the way he moved, the way he stalked, the way he dressed. Over his "army" clothes he wore a mesh layer which had been strung with a quilt of leaves and long grasses. When he was right next to the hedge, he practically disappeared.

With barely a thought, she began imitating the style. She pulled up handfuls of heather and garbed herself as best she could. Within a minute her hair was virtually thatched.

Don't forget your face, Ipes said, giving her a good look. The man's hands and face were striped in green and black. Jilly only had dirt and water to work with; happily she applied one to the other. When her face had been darkened by the daubed mud, she reached for Ipes.

Hey! No! I'm naturally camouflaged and besides I'm too pretty to get muddy.

Jillybean put her hands on her hips and demanded, "And I'm not pretty?"

No one told you to put mud on your face, Ipes replied. *You could've...shush! He's coming.* The shrub-man was nearing the base of *The Sledding Hill* and had only one street left to cross.

"He's gonna see us," she whispered, anxiously. Perhaps because the man was so exceptionally stealthy, his presence gave a nervous tremor to her ant-filled belly. "Should I use a magic marble?"

Ipes raised up the slightest. *No. Someone else is coming. Look, its Squatty.* The zebra pointed at one of the neighborhood stragglers.

Squatty was a toad-like zombie. She was round-faced and toothless. Her fingers were mostly gone and she was so gimpy that Jillybean could walk away from her without fear of being caught. Her eyesight was also so poor that it was probably just a coincidence that she happened to be crossing the path of the man/shrub.

From a crouched position, the man watched Squatty go by. His eyes were hard, grey and flinty and they made Jilly even more anxious. In the minute or so it took for Squatty to amble away, Jillybean took off down the back end of the hill and ran to hide herself among the neighborhood houses. When she finally looked back, the man was either not on the hill or was invisible in his shrub outfit. This last thought led to an idea.

"I think we should test my new camel-flodge," she announced. Ipes had long since given up trying to teach her that particular word and let it go as is. "That mean-ole bat Mrs. Bennett should do." Where Jillybean had a soft spot in her heart for Squatty, she thoroughly despised Mrs. Bennett and rarely passed up an opportunity to goad her in some manner.

The little girl slunk along the street keeping herself hidden from Mrs. Bennett, who was on all fours, eating the heads off the dandelions that had gone wild, taking over much of her property. Jillybean crouched down next to a blue Volvo on the opposite side of the street. "Hey! Mrs. Bennett!" she called out and then scrunched lower and went rabbit-still.

It took a few moments for the lady-monster to lurch to Jillybean's side of the street, but then the stupid thing just stood there gazing in the wrong direction.

19

"Over here, dummy," Jillybean prompted. That did the trick.

With a growly moan of anger, Mrs. Bennett went right for the little girl. The monster was pretty slow and Jillybean scootched around the Volvo and then booked it to her house before Mrs. Bennett understood where she had gone.

"That wasn't good at all," Jilly said, as she locked the heavy deadbolt behind her. "Was I moving too much?"

I didn't think so, Ipes put in. *Maybe you should go see what you look like in the bathroom mirror. Maybe you don't look anything like a shrub.*

In the second floor bathroom, she gave her reflection a sour look. She looked like she belonged in a first grade performance of *The Wizard of Oz* as the Scarecrow. "I need more grass. It's got to come up out of my shirt, and all up through my backpack, you know?"

"What's this about grass and a backpack?" Neil asked, suddenly, hopping into the bathroom. He had tried, and failed, to creep up on the little girl. He was far too loud and she was far too in tune with her surroundings to be caught unaware. Now he was the one who was surprised. He stood there with his mouth open, staring at Jillybean with all her mud and grass, looking as though he was doing an impression of Mrs. Bennett.

"Hi Mister Neil," she said as a greeting before going into her explanation: "There was this guy outside who was all got up like a bush. I mean more than just camel-flodge clothes like a normal army-man. He was like a moving bush. It was pretty cool and old Squatty walked right by him, but she can't see none all that great anyway, but still he was hard to see, so that I couldn't barely see him, you see?"

"There was a man outside?" Neil asked, his face tightening as worry lines creased his forehead. "Where?"

"Up on the sledding hill. You know the one just up the street? There were ants and I was going to…" she paused as a small sound came to her. Someone had rustled the leaves just below the bathroom window. By instinct, Jillybean knew it was a "someone" and not a "something".

"What was that?" Neil asked. "Was that a person?" When Jillybean nodded, he whispered, "Wait here."

She didn't.

He scampered down the stairs and foolishly went to the front door. The sound she had heard had been moving front to back. From a crouch on the stairs, she gave a low whistle and pointed to the back of the house, but by the time he got back there it was too late.

The shrub-man was standing full in their kitchen, pointing a gun at Neil's chest. "I'm looking for a girl named Sadie," he said. "And you're going to tell me where she is."

Chapter 4

Neil Martin

Philadelphia, Pennsylvania

The sound outside the window had failed to trigger much of an alarm in Neil Martin. He had credited the noise to a stray cat or the wind blowing, or some such inconsequential thing. However, the way Jillybean's face went white beneath her mud camouflage, and the way she subconsciously crouched smaller while at the same time her muscles bunched, these things awakened a fear in him.

Unfortunately, he wasn't afraid enough. He walked down the stairs as though he were about to scare away a potential burglar and not a ruthless bounty hunter.

The gun pointed at his chest disabused him of the notion.

"I'm looking for a girl named Sadie," the man said. "There's a bounty on her head and I've come to collect." He was dressed as Jillybean had described: very much like a bush, only Neil knew better. The ghillie suit was high quality and his face paint wasn't just slopped on; an experienced hand had applied it.

"S-Sadie?" Neil squawked. "I-I don't...is that a girl?" All Neil could see of the man beneath the foliage of his ghillie suit were flat, expressionless, grey eyes. Those eyes were so altogether pitiless that his insides started to quiver at the sight of them. The man did not bother to answer Neil's foolish question; he only continued to stare, which, even without the gun, was practically a threat itself.

Neil could hardly think straight with the man staring like he was. "I...I...Sadie? That's not a, uh, familiar name. I...I mean it's not a name you hear in a normal sort of day. You know?"

Now the eyes showed emotion: anger. The man exuded the feeling. Even his M4 assault rifle seemed to grow in menace because of it, something Neil didn't think possible.

"I...I...mean Sadie is..." Neil began, but just then, Jillybean interrupted him.

Stepping down the stairs she said, with more force than Neil had managed, "There's no one named Sadie here." With Sadie napping almost directly above their heads, Neil couldn't believe how calmly the little girl had lied. She went on, "My name is Jillybean, not Sadie. I saw you creeping around out at *The Sledding Hill*."

The bounty hunter took his eye off of Neil for all the time it took to blink and his reaction to the sight of Jillybean caused Neil to grow even more afraid—the man didn't react at all. The little girl couldn't have looked any cuter with her muddy cheeks and her thatched head, but the man only looked at her as if she were nothing more than a rock.

"Anyone else up there?" he asked. "Tell me the truth and no one will get hurt. You don't want to be the reason someone gets hurt do you?"

"Ipes says I can't trust you. And he says that if anyone gets hurt you will be to blame. And before you ask, this is Ipes. He's a zebra not a person. How did you know where I lived? Did you follow me?"

He cast another glance at Jillybean and the zebra, taking them in like a snapshot.

"I saw movement on the top of the hill," the bounty hunter recounted in his quiet, dry voice. "At the top I saw grass had been recently torn up. Then I saw where you had made mud and lastly, I saw your tracks down to the street. You walk in the same rut every time you go up and down. It's obvious. On the street I saw a female zombie searching about, a clear sign you had been through there and lastly, this is the only house on the block with a lived-in look."

"Oh," Jillybean replied.

"Yeah, oh," the bounty hunter retorted. "Now, I ask again, anyone upstairs?"

"No, I'm the only one."

"Get over here," the man growled, low. He then turned his attention back to Neil and asked, "Where is she?"

"Who? Sadie?" Neil asked, breathlessly. With the man staring so hard it felt like the bones in his legs were turning soft as warming butter. "I don't know anyone named Sadie. It's just Jilly and me here."

"Turn around."

Though it made him that much more vulnerable, Neil actually breathed easier facing away from the man and his cruel eyes. Jillybean came to stand next to him. She watched as Neil was frisked and then suffered the man's painted hands running over her own body.

"If it's just the two of you, where's your car?" the man asked.

The group was still using the Dodge Ram that Nico had stolen from Yuri, which now seemed to Neil like a huge mistake. Thankfully, the truck was with Sarah and Nico and they had not come back from foraging yet. Still, this did not help him answer the man's question. It made no sense for the pair to be without a car. "Our car? It's, uh, out front. It's uh a..."

"It's the white car," Jillybean said when Neil began to flap his lips uselessly. "It's a Toyota. I think that's what it's called."

"Yeah. The Toyota is ours," Neil said in a rush, thankful that a seven-year-old was leading him through the interrogation.

Behind him, Neil heard the bounty hunter give a short, bark of laughter. He spun Neil around and jabbed his M4 up under his chin. "You mean the white Toyota with its gas cap hanging out? Is that the Toyota you're talking about?"

Neil tried to swallow, but the gun was so hard against his throat that he could only make a gurgling sound. He opted for a little wiggling nod.

Jillybean was watching what was happening, her big eyes wide in her mud-stained face, yet her voice was exceedingly calm. "Someone took the gas," she said. "A stealer-man is what Ipes says."

The gun came down from Neil's neck as the bounty hunter appraised Jillybean closer. "Ipes said that? Interesting." He then stuck out his grease-painted hand and asked, "May I?"

Reluctantly, Jillybean handed over the zebra.

With a hard look at Ipes, the man said, "I got a problem here, little girl. You and this guy are telling me different stories."

"I don't think we are," she replied.

"You are with your eyes," the man explained. "His eyes are telling me there's someone upstairs, and, since the car out front isn't yours, that's telling me you have friends who have gone somewhere. But you, Jillybean seem much more truthful. All except your eyes...they're guarded."

"That's what means careful, right?"

"Did Ipes tell you that?" When she nodded, he nearly smiled. Just the edge of one of his lips cracked upward. "Ipes clearly means a lot to you, and I'm betting you don't want to see him get hurt."

She shook her head slowly, fear settling on her face like a shadow. "I don't."

"That's what I thought. Now tell me the truth. Is there anyone upstairs?" As he asked this he very slowly began twisting the zebra's head around on his thin shoulders.

With a cry, Jillybean rushed forward, only to be pushed roughly down to the linoleum by the bounty hunter. Neil grabbed her and held her behind him. "There's no one here, but us!" he yelled, hitting the peak of his courage.

The man glared so fiercely that Neil took a step back. The hunter then gazed down at Jillybean and said, "I'm just trying to keep anyone from getting hurt unnecessarily. There's someone up there and when they try to get all heroic I'm going to start shooting. You don't want Mister Sweater Vest here to get hurt do you?"

"No," she said in a breathy whisper.

"And you don't want Ipes to get hurt either I bet, so tell me, who's up there? Is it Sadie?" As he asked he started to twist the zebra's head around again.

Neil thought for sure Jillybean would crack and he prepared to launch himself on the bounty hunter, but the little girl held firm. "There's nobody," she whispered.

"Who's out with the truck?" The bounty hunter demanded, twisting harder, and now a seam opened up at Ipes' shoulder. Neil held the trembling girl back.

"We only have the Toyota. The keys are hanging by the door." Jillybean spoke as if from far away, or maybe from a dream. It reminded Neil of the time she had saved him on the ferry. Even threatened with a gun as he was, looking at Jillybean was unnerving to Neil. It was as if he were holding a possessed child.

The twist on the zebra's neck lessened by degrees until the man held the stuffed animal in only one hand. Ipes looked dead; like a turkey with its neck wrung.

How Jillybean could even stand, Neil didn't know. She trembled from head to toe and now her eyes rained tears. With callous indifference, the bounty hunter tossed her the zebra. "For your sake, you had better be telling the truth. We're going upstairs and if there are any surprises I'm going to shoot first and not bother with any questions. Do you understand?"

Jillybean nodded. Neil looked horrified, thinking about what was going to happen when they got up to the second floor and found Sadie probably crouched in her closet, hiding. The bounty hunter pushed them on with the barrel of his M4.

The seven-year-old went first, cradling Ipes like he was a murdered infant. Then came Neil, trying to fight the urge to pee, and then came the hunter. He was slow and methodical. The gun shoved into Neil's spine never budged even an inch. There wouldn't be a chance at getting the jump on him.

The first room on the second floor was pink with flowers on the walls and a unicorn on the ceiling. It had been Jillybean's back when she had lived there with her family. Now it was the room Sadie shared with Nico. Jillybean walked in with her chin cast down in sadness, but also with her eyes playing about alertly—the bed was rumpled but empty.

"This your room?" the bounty hunter asked Jillybean. Though she now slept in the attic in a nest of pillows and blankets and stuffed animals, the girl nodded, semi-lying with the motion.

There were only two places to hide in the small room: under the bed and in the closet. Sadie was in neither, which was a shock to Neil. She must have heard them talking and had hidden, but where? If anyone knew, it was Jillybean. The little girl loved hide-and-seek and, due to her size, she was exceptional at the game. He tried to catch her eye to get some sort of hint, however she refused to look his way. Instead she followed the man's instructions. He had her pull down the bedspread, swish the clothes back and forth in the closet, and open the curtains.

When the man was satisfied, they moved on to the room Neil shared with Sarah. "This is my room," Neil said. Unlike Sadie's room, which was clearly a little girl's room, this room was obviously a guest room. Thanks to Neil's fickle and fastidious ways it barely looked lived in, something that the bounty hunter remarked upon.

"Just the two of you and you choose this room?" he asked. "Not the master bedroom? I find that hard to believe." As proof, Neil went to the dresser and pulled out a sweater vest that was almost identical to the one he was wearing. "The closet, open it slowly," the man demanded.

Neil did, fearing that this was where Sadie was hiding. She wasn't there. Nor was she under the bed, in the hall closet, or in the hall bathroom. They all turned to the master bedroom at the end of the hall. The hunter took a firmer grip of his weapon and asked, "Who sleeps in there?"

"My mom," Jillybean replied in an empty way, as though she was beyond caring about anything. She opened the door to show him. This was the darkest room. Although it was a bright afternoon, the curtains were drawn, and everything seemed grey and stale and lifeless, especially the long human-shaped bulge under the covers.

27

The bounty hunter finally trained the bore of his weapon away from Neil's spine. "Come on out, nice and easy," he said, speaking to the lump. It didn't respond, nor would it ever.

As tired and hurt and exhausted as Neil's group had been when they fled from New York, no one had the stomach or the heart to move Jillybean's mom, and so she had stayed, tucked up in her bed. No one gave her much thought, except for Jillybean, who would sit outside the door talking to her quietly in the evenings before bed.

"She's dead, Mister," Jillybean told the man. "But don't shoot her. She's not a monster. She's just normal dead." The little girl went to the bed and touched the edge of the top quilt. "She got sick and then went to heaven."

"Really?" the man asked dryly. "I'm sure. Now, stand back."

Jillybean walked away from the bed and stood next to the closet door which had been flung back. Neil was pushed into the room to stand next to the dresser and there he practically jumped. Sadie, looking frail and sick, was flat against the wall, barely hidden by the chin-high dresser. Her tremulous breath came out of her soft and low, with a phlegmy rumble to it like a cat's purr.

Neil tried to hide her with his body, but knew that if the bounty hunter took two more steps into the room, nothing would stop him from seeing his target. At that moment, Neil regretted his warm sweater vest and comfortable Crocs. They made him feel soft and weak, especially in contrast to the hunter who was lean, tough, and merciless. Neil wished he could trade in his Crocs for combat boots and war paint, and that he had done something, anything to prepare for this moment. He couldn't fight a lick. But he would try.

And so would Jillybean.

The little girl had seen Sadie and hadn't reacted at all other than to go stand by the closet door. Now, Neil could see her leaning forward, readying herself to attack. She had done it before. According to Ram, Jillybean, using only a shirt, had attacked a stranger wielding a shotgun.

This would be different, Neil was sure. This would be a blood bath.

"No sudden moves," the bounty hunter warned the room in general. He stepped forward and prodded the corpse in the bed with his gun. "Hey. Let's go. Get up."

"She can't," Jillybean said. "She's dead. Want me to show you?"

"Yeah, pull back the covers nice and easy."

Jillybean pulled back the many blankets and revealed the long dead body of her mother. "She used to be prettier," Jillybean said sadly. "She was the prettiest mommy in the whole world."

The man only grunted at this.

"I told you this Sadie person wasn't here," Neil said. "See? Look under the bed and in the closet."

When he realized that if the hunter checked the closet himself he was sure to see Sadie, Neil practically jumped to the closet and swung the hanging clothes back and forth. He then showed the bounty hunter that no one was behind the closet door either.

"See?"

This time the man didn't even grunt. Slowly he went down to one knee and checked beneath the bed. When he stood up, his expression was a mixture of confusion and disappointment.

"Downstairs," he growled.

Jillybean paused to cover her mother, taking her time and tucking in the edges of the blankets as they had been. Neil wanted out of that room very badly. The phlegm noise Sadie was making seemed to be picking up and it triggered an emphatic response in him. Desperately, he wanted to clear his throat and cough, but was afraid that would trigger the same desire in Sadie.

Only when they were safely downstairs did he start coughing loudly. This had the bounty hunter eyeing him. "I'm not trying to signal anyone, honest," Neil said. "It was the smell."

Again a grunt from the hunter was all Neil received.

They slowly made their way through the rest of the house, finishing up in the kitchen where Neil's family kept their meager supplies. It added up to a few cans of food, a couple of candles and lighters, two guns, and the greatest item of value they possessed: the sixty-odd rounds of ammo that went with the guns.

The hunter picked over the pile and made a noise of disgust. "I don't know what to think. Half of what I see tells me you're lying, but the other half tells me that it's just the two of you living here."

Neil shrugged, not knowing what to say. He was sure that if he did say something it would only come out sounding like a lie.

Jillybean wasn't hampered in that regard, or any regard, judging by what she said next. "You could stay for dinner. Ipes hates you and so do I, but if you think we're lying then that's the best way to tell. Do you have any good food? We don't. All we have is this right here and pine-needle soup. It's on the back porch. I can get it if you want some."

This suggestion so shocked Neil that he knew his mouth had flapped open and his eyes had gone wide, but try as he might he couldn't seem to change his expression. There was no doubt the bounty hunter saw the look and read all sorts of meaning into it, however, Jillybean was so earnest in her invitation that the man couldn't help but be even more confused.

He stood for nearly a minute before making up his mind. "No. I can't stay."

Neil was a second away from breathing a sigh of relief, except the man started pocketing their ammo. He even unloaded the guns. "You can't leave us defenseless," Neil said. "We need that ammunition."

"So do I," was all the man said. After giving only a single glance to the remaining cans of food, he left without bothering to take any.

Stunned, Neil and Jillybean watched from the window as the man went up the walkway and then out onto the street, heading back the way he had come. When he was well up the block, Neil finally turned on Jillybean. "Why on earth did you ask him to stay for dinner?"

She was on her knees examining the extent of Ipes' injuries and didn't look up to answer. "I asked him to stay so he would go. Ipes says it's called reverse sy-ken-olgy, or something like that." She then took a shaky breath and said, "Look at poor Ipes. He's really, really hurt. We have to fix him."

"Sarah can help him," Neil said. "She can sew. It's going to be ok, Jillybean. Ipes needs to hold on until she comes home." Neil could sew as well, but just then he was experiencing such a bad case of the shakes that he was sure he would end up sewing Ipes' ear to his hoof.

Sadie appeared at the top of the stairs wearing her heaviest coat. It was deep black, making her face seem translucent in contrast. "Sarah can't come home," she said. "We've been too lax or someone saw us coming and going in the truck. If she and Nico come back, that bounty hunter will follow them right back here. You see? I gotta go out to the highway and stop them."

"No, I'll do it," Neil said. "You're too sick. Now get back in bed."

"Uh-uh," Sadie replied shaking her head. This caused her to stagger, and she clutched the railing for support. "You have to be here just in case that guy comes back. So that means I gotta go."

"No," Neil said. He was about to go on, but Jillybean raised her hand.

"Ipes says if one of us goes, we all have to go. We can't risk getting separated. And besides, this house is no longer safe."

31

Chapter 5

Sadie

Philadelphia, Pennsylvania

As was so frequent, when the zebra wasn't being a smartass, they took his suggestion. In their haste to leave, almost everything was abandoned. Ipes, in spite of his injuries, was vocal in his insistence that they leave within the minute. Through Jillybean, he explained that the man was more than likely heading back to *The Sledding Hill*, and from its peak he would be able see nearly their entire neighborhood, meaning he would see them if they didn't hurry.

Since there was little in the house that she was attached to, Sadie was at the front door within the zebra's time frame. Neil, who couldn't leave without his axe, and a change of shoes, and Sarah's make-up bag, and the rest of the food, was there a minute later, huffing and puffing.

A minute for Jillybean turned out to be an impossible time frame. Ipes had to be placed into a shoebox to keep him safe. Her magic marbles had to be bagged. Her dollhouse had to be lingered over and her tiny fingers had to trace its gabled roof once more, and finally her mother had to be kissed one last time.

The little girl came downstairs, much changed. She alternated between tears and a grim silence that was disturbing to see in such an angel-faced little thing.

"Not the front door," Jillybean said. "It will be watched for sure. We can go out the back. There's a break in the fence we can use to get to the next street over."

She led the way, stopping only a second to look up at the sky. The rain that had been threatening had finally come, though thankfully it was barely above a misting. No one paid too much attention to it, except Sadie who, almost immediately felt her lungs swell up and it seemed as though she were trying to breathe through a pair of sponges.

Jillybean took no notice. She was fully focused on escape and evade. She had them scampering around the edge of the yard to keep as much cover as she could between them and the hill. At the opening in the fence they crouched behind an overgrown rose bush as each wiggled into the next yard. Neil had to shrug off the backpack he was carrying, and Sadie had to pull off her coat in order to slip through.

She lay in the tall grass on the other side, coughing. "Take your medicine," Neil told her. "It's after four."

Sadie, who could only suppress her cough by breathing through her shirt, nodded to the suggestion, the useless suggestion, in her eyes. The penicillin wasn't cutting it. She had been taking it for a month now and at best it mitigated the worst of her symptoms. Her cough persisted, her fever lingered, and the sensation that there was a little less of her everyday continued unabated. She felt as thin and weak as a fog on a summer's morning, and she knew it was only a matter of time before the antibiotics failed completely and the pneumonia-driven fever would come on full force and burn the last of her away.

"We have to hurry," Jillybean pressed, as Sadie lethargically dug through her pack for her pills. "If he isn't already, the bad man will be up at the top of the hill anytime, and if he has those bino-thingies to see through, he'll catch us for certain."

Once Sadie had dry-swallowed two of her pills, they hurried through the neighbor's yard and then to the street beyond. Jillybean pushed them on as fast as Sadie could go. Unfortunately they were seen by a small horde of about forty zombies. From all around the neighborhood, they came at the trio, attracted by the human movement.

"We've got to get off the street," Neil said, looking with concern at Sadie who was swaying in place. "Here, this house looks sturdy. We can hole up…"

"No," Jillybean said. She looked hard and stern like an army sergeant, in other words not at all like herself. Sadie didn't like the sudden change, it was very unnerving. "We can't stop," Jillybean said. "The situation has changed. Although we probably haven't been seen, Ipes is sure the bad man has noted all the monsters. He's smart, he'll know humans are around here and he'll come investigate. If we hide, we'll be trapped."

"Then what do we do?" Neil asked, glancing back the way they came at the string of undead shuffling along in their wake. His eyes fell on a manhole cover. "What about the sewers? You've used them before."

Jillybean gave Neil an odd look. It was a partial smile, one that was as fake as Sadie had ever seen on the little girl's face. "We should only go that way for an emergency," Jillybean said.

"It sure feels like an emergency," Sadie said. "We can't stay here, and we can't…" She had to stop because a fit of coughing overtook her.

"That's why we can't go in the sewers," Jillybean explained. "You'll attract every monster down there right to us."

"There can't be very many down there," Neil said. "At least not compared to all of these. Either way we had better come to a decision right now." The zombies were closing very quickly now.

"Come on," Jillybean ordered as though she was in charge, which, in reality she was. Sadie's head was pounding and Neil seemed out of ideas beyond hiding in the house and slinking around in the sewers. The seven-year-old led the way up to the house Neil had pointed out as being sturdy.

Neil began spluttering, "But you just said we shouldn't go in…"

"Just go with it," Sadie said. The drizzle was getting worse and so was her phlegm rattle and her head ached.

The initial appearance of the house was deceiving. Though the front door was still standing, the side door to the kitchen was hanging off its hinge. Jillybean went right for it. They found that the kitchen had been ransacked, which was just as well since they made it in only a few steps ahead of the first zombies and didn't have time to scrounge around.

"Use your axe to hold them off for a bit, Mister Neil," Jillybean directed. To Sadie she asked, "Can you push the table over here to act as a…blocking thing…right, I mean a barricade?"

Neil hewed down the first two zombies that came up and then darted inside to help shove the table up against the door. "This is not going to hold very well," he said from the far end of the table. "They'll be able to push it back unless we get something to prop up against it. We could use the chairs."

"Yeah, do that," Jillybean said, walking out of the kitchen with her head cocked as if she had heard her mother calling.

"What the hell?" Neil asked. "Where's she going?"

Sadie's cough had advanced to such a degree that she was practically speechless. She only shrugged her shoulders as she held the table against the door, something that she wasn't going to do for much longer as the zombies stacked up outside. The beasts were also at the front door, hammering on it, and at the windows. Breaking glass was Neil's background music as he tried to pile up chairs in such a way as to hold the table in place.

"This wasn't a good idea," he remarked when he had the chairs positioned.

Sadie had to agree with him. It wasn't long before the door began to bow inward and groan under the force of the zombies. A grey arm crashed through the kitchen window ripping itself across the shards and sending black blood spraying.

"It was your idea…in the first…place," she said between coughs.

"I know," Neil said testily. "But you'd think that Jillybean would take into account…what is that? Is that smoke?" he asked. With a look of surprise they ran into the next room. The look expanded on his face as he found Jillybean building a fire with newspapers and old books on the living room sofa.

35

"How is this going to help in any way?" Neil cried. "Not only will you attract every zombie in miles you're definitely going to attract the bounty hunter."

"Yes," Jillybean replied. She puffed out her cheeks and blew gently at the base of the fire as Nico had taught her weeks before. When the paper began to go up in flames, she stored her lighter back into her *I'm A Belieber* backpack which she slung over her shoulder.

"The bad man is a noticing kind of person," she said. "Like I said, he may not have seen us, but he has to have seen the zombies. Ipes says he's on his way. But he's slow and careful, and we won't be. Come on."

Again, they followed after the little girl and, as they slipped through the house to the back door, Neil asked, "But what's with the fire?"

"The fire will keep the monsters' attention, and the monsters will keep the bounty man's attention. And, since he stolded all of our bullets he'll probably think we are using the fire to fight the monsters. Now we gotta be mousses...I mean mice, and be quiet."

As the front door came crashing down and the chairs in the kitchen were finally thrust aside and the zombies came storming in ready to kill, the three humans scooted out into the back yard, which was zombie free, and, after climbing a six-foot security fence, they made their way stealthily to the next street over. Though they weren't made up to look like zombies, at Jillybean's suggestion, they adopted the odd shambling gait of zombies.

"From far away we'll look like monsters," she explained. "Right. Ipes says we can't be all bunchy. They don't walk bunchy so spread out."

Neil had to let go of Sadie and she fell hard against a truck. "I'll be alright," she lied. Her head was like a room filled with banging hammers and all the strength seemed to have seeped out of her body. At some point she had begun shaking. Though the day wasn't exactly cold she shivered uncontrollably. Still she fought on.

They crossed the street and then went south, hugging the houses, killing stray zombies if they happened to get too close. After a half-hour they managed to put nearly a mile between them and the bounty hunter. The fire that Jillybean had started appeared now to be only a brown smidge in the air.

Sadie was done in. She found that walking like a zombie was the only way she could move. She staggered, barely able to keep her head straight on her shoulders. "Can we take a rest? I can't go on."

"Uh-uh," Jillybean said shaking her head. She was totally fixated on her mission of escaping. "Miss Sarah could be passing the highway at any time. If we miss her she'll be in big trouble."

Neil was torn. He stared south toward I-476 for a few seconds before turning to look at Sadie, who was glassy-eyed and only remained upright because she was slumped up against a Subaru. She tried to rally enough to stand, but she didn't have the strength.

"I'll go alone," Neil said, finally. When Jillybean opened her mouth to argue, he put up a finger. "I know what you're going to say about separating, but if we don't separate here and now, purposefully, then we'll end up separating by accident later and with dire consequences. That fire you set won't hold the bounty hunter's attention much longer. You two get up in this house and don't draw any attention to yourselves. No more fires, Jillybean."

She shrugged suggesting that she couldn't promise anything along those lines.

After divesting himself of everything except his axe, Neil ran off for the highway that Sarah and Nico would use on their way back home. Sadie watched for only a moment before heading straight for the front door of the house. Jillybean held her back. "Not yet. Let me go in first and check it out. There could be monsters and you don't look so good."

How long the little girl was gone, Sadie couldn't tell. She rested her head on the cool metal of the Subaru and, in what felt like a second, Jillybean was back shaking her and saying, "Wake up, Sadie. The house is clear." She said more than just that, but the words were drowned out by the thumping in Sadie's head as she staggered inside to fall down on a soft leather couch. The last thing she remembered was Jillybean covering her with a blanket.

Chapter 6

Jillybean

Philadelphia, Pennsylvania

The shoebox that contained Ipes' broken body was set down on the coffee table next to the couch where Sadie slept fitfully, wheezing in a scary manner. She glistened with a fever-sweat and her skin seemed even whiter than normal, except for her face which had turned a hot red. When she moaned, Jillybean began to pace in fear.

"Is there anything we can do for her?" Jillybean asked.

Let me see her medicine, Ipes said after a glance at the girl. Jillybean looked at the bottle first, trying to reason out all the long words, and failing. She then held it in front of the zebra. *It's expired, but not by very long. Maybe it's like milk and goes bad after a while. Sniff the bottle. Does it smell yucky to you?*

The pills didn't smell like much of anything to Jillybean.

Hold the bottle higher, I can barely read all of it, Ipes ordered. After mumbling his way from the top of the label to the bottom, the zebra laid back and sighed. *She's taking the correct dosage and at the right times. I'm sorry. I don't know what the problem is. This should be working.*

"Maybe I should look around," Jillybean said.

Maybe you should also consider fortifying this place. It'll be dark soon and we'll need a place to hole up.

"Yeah," Jillybean said softly. She was already home sick. She missed her mom, and she missed her friend Todd the Turtle, and her dollhouse, and her pillow fort in the attic. She was also afraid for Sadie. She had never known anyone to be sick for as long as she had been.

Shake it off, Jilly, Ipes said in his Daddy voice. *Do what you need to do to live.*

"Yes, Daddy," she said reflexively, and then went to take stock of what she had to work with.

There was little to the house to recommend it in the way of safety—thin doors, low windows, a poorly situated rear entrance. As well, the creature comforts were few—no fireplace, only two bedrooms, and it stank of mildew.

"Perfect," Jillybean whispered. If the bounty hunter came by he would likely just keep on going.

On the plus side of things, she found a portable grill, which she rolled into the kitchen. In a caddy next to the grill was a bag of charcoal, which she brought in as well. In the closets she dug out blankets, pillows, and sheets. In the garage she found a hammer and nails; mentally she assigned the task of covering the windows to Nico, because he was so much taller than Neil.

The kitchen had long before been ransacked, but things had been missed. In a drawer right next to the sink, Jillybean found a smorgasbord of seasonings in little packets: taco, fajita, guacamole. Among them she found packets of dried soup.

"Now all I need is water."

The toilets were bone dry. The rain was only an annoying mist and so the gutters were simply damp. She slunk about in the backyard looking for anything that held water, even dirty water. Two doors down, in the backyard of the only bi-level on the block, she found a little plastic pool that held a fair amount of brackish water. Back and forth she scurried with pots and pans each holding about a gallon of water, which was the most she could lift.

On her third trip she happened to glance into the yard of the bi-level and wandered over to an area of thick greenery. Her mind tried to place what she was looking at, but it wasn't until she squatted down that she found she was looking at a garden. The wet spring had caused the plants to go crazy.

Among the weeds that were threatening to take over, she found all sorts of vegetables: little tomatoes, carrots, strangely shaped potatoes and turnips. Although she was only interested in the potatoes, she harvested as much of everything as she could. Neil seemed like the kind of guy who would go into a tizzy over turnips and Sarah was good at glomping odd things together to make a decent meal.

Within thirty minutes of arriving at the house, Jillybean had set things ready. She would wait on nightfall to start the charcoal and hang the blankets. In the meantime she found a potato peeler and went to work skinning the carrots and the potatoes. These last were strangely orange beneath the brown skin.

She took one to Ipes.

Maybe it's a sweet potato. Give it a nibble.

Before she did she sniffed at it skeptically. "Do I like sweet potatoes?" From what she could remember she used to think they were weird.

Taste buds change over time, Jillybean. By the way, how are you going to get anything done when it gets dark?

Right. With the light already beginning to fade she set aside the question of potatoes and took to hunting about for candles. She found nothing in "their" house, but in the third up the block, next to the bed in the largest room she found candles and a lighter. And something that made her eyes go wide—it was a tiny gun.

It was silver and stubby. Though it looked like toy, it was a real gun. She could tell by the weight of it; for something so small it was as heavy as a good stone. It was a revolver, which her mind associated with a policeman, however it didn't look like a man's gun. Because of its stubby barrel and short grip, it looked more like a woman's gun. With a shaking hand Jillybean picked it up out of the drawer and had the illogical fear that it would simply explode without her doing anything. Hurriedly she put it back.

Just that simple act allowed her to breathe easier.

What good would such a tiny gun do? She wondered. Could it actually kill one of the monsters? It didn't seem like it could. And how loud would it be? Would it be quieter than a normal gun because it was so small? And

41

how was it loaded? How did she get the round part to open…

Just then she heard a vehicle approaching. "Oh thank God," she whispered. Mister Neil had come through for them. He had found Miss Sarah and Nico!

What if that's not Neil? Ipes asked. The question was so unnerving that Jillybean didn't realize the zebra wasn't even in the same house. His voice just registered in her mind.

What if it wasn't Neil? What if it was the bounty hunter coming after defenseless Sadie? Jilly's eyes went to the drawer she had just shut. In a flash, she had it open again and grabbed the gun. It was big for her hand, but not all that big when she held it with both hands. Quickly she snatched up the box of ammo that had been sitting next to the gun and then ran for the back door. Keeping low, but holding the gun out away from her body—she couldn't be too careful with the frightful thing—she sped back to the low ranch-style house where she had left Sadie lying in a sweat.

Thankfully, it was Mister Neil and Miss Sarah and Nico in the truck.

Before entering the back door, Jillybean stowed the gun in her backpack and wrapped the rattling bullets in her spare shirt. She came in wearing a big, guilty grin. "Hi," she said.

Sarah barely gave her a glance. She was standing over Sadie trying to hold back tears. Neil smiled wanly and looked sick himself, but he rallied and tried to pretend everything was ok. "Look at all this you did, Jillybean!" he said with a big fake smile. "Just incredible. I can't wait to have some sweet potatoes. I've never had them grilled, but I bet they'll be awesome. Thanks."

"We should wait until after dark," Sarah said, over her shoulder. She bent down over Sadie and touched her damp brow. The young woman didn't stir which was enough to bring the tears Sarah had been fighting against.

"What should we do for her?" Jillybean asked, coming to stand next to Sarah. "Ipes doesn't know how to fix her and neither do I."

Sarah shook her head. "I don't know…maybe she needs a new medicine. Something stronger. The only problem is that every pharmacy we have come across has been looted down to the last aspirin."

"Can we get them anywhere else?" Jillybean asked. "Like at a factory? I saw a cartoon once…"

"Do you mind?" Sarah asked, interrupting. "I want to spend some time with Sadie, quietly. Do you understand? So she can rest. Maybe you can help Neil with the barbeque. He's not so good with mechanical things and I don't want him killing us. Or you can play with Ipes."

Jillybean nodded and went to pick up the shoebox with Ipes, but was so preoccupied with what she carried in her backpack that she couldn't think about playing at that moment. She scooted by Neil who was in the kitchen messing with a hunk of blue tarp and went out into the yard. There she went to stash the gun in the tall grass that bordered the house.

Maybe you should keep that, Ipes said. This was so unlike the zebra that Jillybean didn't know what to say. Normally he was all about safety. He seemed to read her mind. *But you remember what Mister Ram said: Everything's dangerous now,* Ipes said. *I think you should keep it.*

Jilly didn't think she could. She worried she'd have nightmares about it. "It's making me be freaked out," Jillybean hissed. "And asides, you know what all the grode-ups would say, that I'm too young for a gun."

I know…but, never mind, he said. *You were right to get rid of it.*

Now Jillybean was doubly surprised: she had never won an argument with Ipes so easily. There was a first time for everything, she figured as she pulled back the grass and gently placed the gun in the dirt before covering it.

Relieved of the menace and the weight of the thing, she went into the kitchen and said to Neil, "Hi, can I help?"

He appeared to be in the process of building some sort of shroud to channel the smoke from the grill out an open window. She saw it would be messy, and the smoke would permeate the house to some degree, but it would work. If she had her way, Jillybean would've used the hood from the stove, which was held in place with only a couple of screws and she would've added some venting from above the now useless water heater. But she didn't want to seem like a know-it-all so she kept her mouth shut and held the tarp in place as Neil spun duct tape all over the room.

Jillybean liked Neil a lot, but in some areas he made her nervous. Sarah was right about his mechanical inaptitude, however his inability as a warrior was shockingly worse. It was why she hadn't wanted to venture down into the sewers with him, especially armed as he was with only an axe. An axe was no sort of weapon for fighting in a tunnel.

"You were very brave today," Neil said, "And Ipes, too. Just as soon as we can, I'll get Sarah to look at him."

"Thanks," Jillybean said. She didn't think there was much chance that Sarah was going to help. Jillybean couldn't help but notice the wall the lady had set up between them. It had been very hurtful until Ipes had explained Sarah's problems as a mother: she didn't think she was a good one. Her real daughter, missing and likely dead, her baby had been kidnapped and now Sadie was on the verge of dying from pneumonia.

This was going through Jillybean's head when Sarah rushed into the kitchen in a state of excitement. "Jillybean may have been right. Maybe we can get antibiotics somewhere else. I just need a phone book! Practically every veterinarian should carry some sort of antibiotic, right? I just need a phonebook."

The three spread out, searching. Neil found a phonebook in the hall closet and by the time Nico came in from hiding the truck, Sarah had ripped out ten pages from it and was dragging him back out again.

They were gone for hours and in the end came back with only a bag of dog treats to show for their troubles. In all that time, Sadie remained in a deep sleep. She could be awakened with great effort, however she was so out of it that it didn't seem worth it. Her breathing grew worse with every passing hour.

"Someone beat us to every veterinarian clinic. Every single one," Sarah said in a hollow whisper as she saw Sadie. "What are we going to do? She's going to die, Neil. We can't let her die!"

"We'll take her to the *Whites,*" Neil said. Although the race war of Philadelphia had ended, the groups had yet to intermingle and so the people in the walled off country club were still known as the *Whites.* "If I know John, he'll take her in."

Nico shook his head. "Nyet. I know Yuri. He has spies in *White* group. They will kill my Sadie."

"Damn it!" Sarah seethed. She pounded her fist on the phone book and then shoved it away. "Sadie…Sadie is going to die either way if we don't do something. Do you understand, Nico? She's going to die unless we can get her some medicine or something. This is my fault. I've been too preoccupied worrying about Eve. I just thought Sadie would get better."

"I did too," Nico said.

Sarah went to the wall and slumped down it and stared glassily at the floor. After a while she covered her face and said, "I don't have any more ideas. Can you help her, Jillybean? Or Ipes? Does Ipes have any ideas? Please think of something!"

Jillybean was in the process of picking up the phonebook, but now she froze at the request. "You want me to figure out how to fix her? I don't think I can. I don't know anything about medicine."

"You can try," Sarah said. "Just figure something out. Go on."

"No, Sarah," Neil said, shaking his head. "We can't lay this on a seven-year-old. Jillybean is smart, but she doesn't have magic powers. She can't heal people and it's wrong to even ask. We need antibiotics and we know where to get them. We're going to have to take our chances with the *Whites*. I say we leave at first light."

This seemed the only logical choice and the house went quiet as each realized that they were going to be exposing themselves to who-knew-how-many bounty hunters. It stood to reason that if there was one after them, there could be a dozen, or more.

In a pensive silence, broken only by Sadie's wheeze, Neil barbequed the vegetables turning the house hazy just as Jillybean had predicted. The veggies were good, yet no one seemed to enjoy them at all. Neil sat in with Sadie and fanned her with a newspaper as her fever spiked.

As a child of the digital age who had grown up with Google only a click away, Jillybean was intrigued by the phonebook. She thumbed through the yellow pages, looking at all the advertisements and then out of curiosity she looked up her own phone number. It wasn't there. She found the *Shaws,* but neither of her parents was listed. Her father's name was William Shaw, and the names in the book went from Wilhelm Shaw to Whythers Shaw.

She thought it an odd name and she pointed it out to Ipes. "What's that mean after his name? The D and the R?" she asked in a low voice.

It means he's a doctor, Ipes replied. There were a few seconds of silence between them as the repercussions of those two letters sunk in.

"I think I know where we might maybe get some medicine," Jillybean said. She pointed at the name she had discovered. "There are doctors in this phonebook. It lists their houses, where they live, you know? They might have pills in them. There are leftover pills, like aspirin, in almost all the houses but a doctor's house might have the right kind of pills we need."

"Maybe," Sarah said, gazing down at the hundreds of names on the page. "They could, but that might mean a whole lot of running around for nothing. I mean, I don't think doctors generally keep medicine at their houses."

"What about veterinarians?" Neil asked, standing up in excitement. "Doctors don't make house calls, but there are a lot of vets who still do…or I mean they used to. They gotta have meds." In his excitement he snatched the phone book from Jillybean and began running his fingers down the column on his side, while Sarah did the same thing on the other page.

"Which are doctors and which are vets?" she asked.

"I don't know," Neil said. "They're both technically doctors. But, wait! The yellow pages that you took. We can just do a reverse look up. We get the names from the ads and look them up in the white pages."

Not every advertisement came with a vet's name, but four did and two had lived relatively close by before the apocalypse.

Neil and Nico left in a great rush, in spite of the fact that it was deep night and dangerous. Nico went armed with the twelve-gauge, while Neil borrowed Sarah's Beretta.

When they were gone, driving slowly away, going without lights to keep their location secret from any bounty hunters that might be nearby, Sarah smiled at Jillybean. "This is going to work. I know it. It's going to work because of you, Jillybean. Tell me…can you promise me something?"

Never make blind promises, Ipes warned. *You don't know what you're getting into. There could be strings attached. There could be repercussions.*

"I guess so," Jillybean said, cautiously. "Maybe."

Sarah seemed to take that as a yes. "Promise me you'll always stay with Neil and Sadie."

This seemed like an odd promise, but also one that was going to be easy to live by, or so she thought. She was about to tell Sarah that she would, but Ipes stopped her. *Tell her you have provisions of your own. Tell her you want something out of the deal.*

"Only if you help Ipes," Jillybean said, holding up the shoebox to show the abused little zebra. "He got hurted."

Sarah took the shoebox and with surprising tenderness touched Ipes on his broad cheek. Amazingly she began to cry, something that Jillybean wasn't at all prepared for. "I heard," Sarah said. "Neil told us. He told us you were very brave."

"Ipes was the brave one," Jillybean said, trying to deflect the compliment. She didn't know how to deal with a crying adult and felt a strange sense of embarrassment for the woman. "Ipes told me not to say anything about Sadie no matter what."

Sarah swallowed hard and looked on the verge of saying something, but then she gently took the zebra from the shoebox. When his head fell to the side in an awful manner she cried even harder.

"You can fix him, right?" Jillybean asked, as fresh anxiety coursed through her. What would happen if Sarah couldn't fix Ipes' neck? Could Jillybean make him a neck brace? Or fit him with a collar or a napkin ring, like the fancy ones her mom used when they had company for dinner back in the old days?

"I need thread and a sewing needle," Sarah said. "And I'll need one of those little pillows on the couch. Hopefully they have fluff in them instead of foam."

It was fluff. Jillybean couldn't watch the operation. She had to leave the room after Ipes fainted early on and stayed in the kitchen with her ear pressed against the door and a feeling that her stomach was in her throat.

Sarah called her a little later. Jilly came into the living room with small steps. "He's ready," Sarah said. She held up the zebra and like a miracle his neck was stiff again.

"You did it?" Jillybean asked, blinking and feeling odd in the guts. "That fast? And look! His stomach is fat again, like it used to be when…"

Her words trailed off as a memory woke in her: she had been three years old. There was pain in her head…no, in her ears that wouldn't go away. She was in the hospital sitting on her Daddy's lap, waiting to have an operation. She was very scared and clung to him fiercely.

Her Daddy had held out Ipes to her and he was very new-looking. His white stripes were just that, white, not the dingy grey they had become and his mane had stood up tall but soft and his belly was so fat it was round like a little pumpkin.

That's where he keeps his cookies, her Daddy had told her. *He loves cookies and as long as you keep him filled up with cookies he'll always be your friend and he'll always protect you.*

Even in the osceration? Jillybean had asked.

Yes, even in the osceration, her Daddy had told her in the wise manner he used sometimes when he thought something was very important for Jilly to know. *So what are you going to name him?*

Stripes, she said without thinking. Not thinking was something her Daddy did not approve of and he gave her a look that hinted she try again.

Stripes? he scoffed. *Do you want someone to mistake him for a common raccoon or, heaven forbid, a skunk?*

How about Ipes?

Her Daddy had looked at Ipes and nodded his approval. *Ipes is a great name.*

"Thank you," Jillybean said, right there in the living room, feeling her eyes begin to water.

Mistaking that the little girl was talking to her, Sarah replied, "You're welcome."

Chapter 7

Neil Martin

Philadelphia, Pennsylvania

Neil drove without the headlights on for only about a mile before turning onto the highway. Once there, due to the ghastly figures that he frequently plowed into and over, he could go only a little further before he was forced to chance the lights.

Treading zombies beneath the wheels of the Dodge pickup always made him feel queasy. Beside him, Nico was mature enough not to comment on Neil's groaning. Nico was a good man; a fine combination of courage and caution, and quiet contemplation. Neil suspected Nico was so quiet because he wasn't the smartest of people. And that was fine too, because it showed what he lacked in raw intelligence, he made up for it in common sense.

With the headlights raking the night, Neil picked up speed, hoping to get to the first house on the list, find the right kind of medicine, and get home again as soon as possible. He hated being out at night. The zombies seemed to multiply when the sun went down. Even on the highway they were everywhere, making for a ghastly trip.

"I think light is make worse," Nico said.

Neil had to agree. He was swerving back and forth attempting to miss the beasts that flung themselves at the truck. It was perilous driving at such speeds; if he happened to hit one the wrong way it could conceivably come up and smash in his windshield. A prospect that left him even queasier. Regardless, he didn't slow a whit. Sadie was in deep trouble. Neil was sure her life hung in the balance and that the next twenty-four hours would decide things one way or another.

"This is exit," Nico said pointing them off the highway. On the side streets, the zombies came thick as flies, and

Neil was forced to turn off the headlights. Because of the dark, and the frequent obstructions, they slowed to a speed that was only slightly faster than a walk and it was a quarter after eleven before they found the first house. Even from the street, it was clear that it had been ransacked. In fact, few houses looked as purposefully destroyed as the three stories of brick and ivy which had once been the home of Evan Addison VMD. Every window was broken and every door leveled. Its front yard was strewn with clothes and trash.

"We go to next," Nico said, squinting up at it. "We spend all night to look in house and we find nothing since people is been here already."

"No," Neil said, shaking his head. "We look, but only in his study or office. A place like this, the guy had to have an office. And we'll look in the garage. That's it. We'll be done in ten minutes."

It took twelve. The house was not only zombie free, it was also medicine free, and it didn't take long to hurry through it with their flashlights slicing up the night. Their truck was still warm when they slid back in. Neil was about to start it when Nico grabbed his hand. In the dark his eyes looked huge.

"What?" Neil whispered.

Nico put his finger to his lips and turned to look out the front window. Neil saw nothing and heard only the moans of the dead. Slowly he began to run his window down and when he did he caught the low sound of a car's engine.

"Bounty hunter?" Nico asked in a whisper. Neil slunk down low in his seat. The Russian did the same

"Who else would be out for a drive at night?" Neil asked. "He must have followed us."

"Da. It was car light of ours. Is easy to see at night."

Neil bit back the words: *No shit.* Instead, he flicked the dome light in the roof of the cab to off. He then slid out of the truck with axe in hand. Pausing only to try to fix the sound of the bounty hunter's car with a position—generally east of them—he went to the rear of the vehicle and, as quietly as he could, smashed in the taillights.

When he got back in, he started the engine and then checked for any useless lights, even going so far as to dim the dashboard lights.

"Is good and dark," Nico said, stretching the limits of his conversational ability.

"Yeah," Neil agreed. "Roll down your window so we can hear that other car if it approaches. Also, no using the flashlight. If you need to check the map, get under the blankets, capisce?"

"Da, except what is word, ca-peesh? What is that?"

As Neil pulled away from the curb, he explained, "It's slang from the Italian: to understand. It's what all the Jersey *eye-talians* say. I'm sure the tense is never taken into account."

"Then, da, I ca-peesh."

"Good," Neil said.

He drove even slower now, worried far more about the bounty hunter than the zombies. Eventually the sound of the other car died away and Neil made it back to the highway without incident. He went south at a snail's pace, chugging along as the minutes went by, each one bringing Sadie closer to death. He was so caught up in his worry over his daughter that he let one precious second slip by when headlights suddenly flicked on behind them. They were at least a mile back, but still their very presence sent a ripple of panic through Neil.

"The bounty hunter!" Neil cried. "What do I do?"

"What? Go fast," Nico urged pointing at the zombie-filled highway.

Neil stomped on the gas and then when a different thought struck him, he hit the brake, jolting the two of them. The Dodge truck wasn't a vehicle that lent itself to fast getaways and car chases. The hunter was still far enough away that Neil thought it would be better to hide the truck, and what better way to hide it than in plain sight?

Stalled vehicles were a dime-a-dozen on the highway. Neil pulled in behind one and at first was simply going to park behind it. Instead he crashed into it. They weren't going fast, but still Nico let out a string of Russian curses.

"Get your gun," Neil shouted over him. He pulled out the keys and then leapt from the vehicle, running to a drainage ditch on the side of the road where he laid down in the tall grass. A second later Nico joined him. As any good soldier would, he trained his shotgun outwards, but Neil pulled him low.

"We're outgunned," he told Nico. "If he gets out of his car and heads this way, then we'll shoot, but not before." Neil's Beretta was in his hands and he didn't remember drawing it. As the lights came closer, he clicked off the safety.

"Neil!" the Russian, hissed, pulling at his sleeve.

A zombie was heading right at them. It wasn't much more than a rag-covered half-person, but under the circumstances it was as deadly as any. With the vehicle approaching and the zombie practically on top of them, there was only one thing to do. "Play dead," Neil whispered. He then half-closed his eyes. From the cracks of his lids he could see Nico fighting the idea.

Neil kicked him.

Then the bounty hunter was there. He slowed his Jeep at the sight of the Dodge Ram crushing in the rear hatch of a VW Bus. There was silence save for the moans of the dead and the purr of the Jeep. A second later a beam of light swept the Dodge. Next, the light ran over the drainage ditch passing over the tips of the grass and across the toes of Nico's boots. It kept going and then swung back.

The light was right over Neil's midsection. It was like a movie projector; he could see particles in the air floating gently. The light moved up; he thought it a strange direction until the zombie stepped full onto his stomach.

A grunt escaped him, which, in any other setting would have doomed him. However the zombie was fully focused on the light and the sound of the engine. After stumbling for a step or two it went at the Jeep, going faster as the ground flattened. The bounty hunter did not waste a bullet.

53

He scanned the ditch one more time and then drove off, speeding in the direction Neil had to go.

"Crap," Neil said, jumping up. The zombie had been watching the Jeep drive off, now it began to turn, but before it could, Neil kicked its legs out from under it. Since he had been vaccinated, small or skinny zombies didn't scare him. He stood on its neck and beckoned Nico. "Let's go. We have to find another route."

In no time they were in the Dodge and racing back the way they had come from. Nico, who was under a blanket with a map in one hand and a flashlight in the other, asked, "He find us very simple. Does he know where we go?"

Neil shrugged, a move that Nico couldn't possibly see. "I doubt it. Jillybean said he was a 'noticing' kind of man. We know he saw our lights and followed us. After that, who knows? I can only guess that he watched how the zombies were reacting."

"Then he will do so again," Nico said.

There was that possibility. In order to foil it, Neil had slipped off the highway and was driving down a neighborhood street. He took the first right he came to and then the next, and the next after that, then one more turn had them going in the same direction and on the same street as they had been. A few blocks further on he pulled the same stunt except with left hand turns.

Behind them, they left hundreds of zombies going in every direction.

Nico, who was left slightly carsick from all the maneuvering, came out from beneath the blanket. "I know which way we go."

The house of this second veterinarian was in far better shape, though it too had been the sight of criminal activity.

The looting seemed absolutely normal, however the corpse of a man just inside the doorway wasn't. He had been human, and had died of a single gunshot to the chest. The body was about half-decayed and smelled sickly sweet. Nico, who wasn't over his carsickness clutched his throat and moved on.

Neil didn't. Human deaths bothered him on a level he hadn't experienced before the apocalypse. Back then he couldn't crack a newspaper without reading stories of murder after murder. It had inured him in a way that wasn't healthy. Now, he felt a loss for each person who died.

"Neil!" the Russian called urgently. "I find something."

He found Nico in what could only be the veterinarian's home office. It was a gorgeous room, one that Neil would've loved for his own. Its walls were covered with bookshelves, its carpet was navy in color and so soft that he left tracks as he walked. The best part was the high-backed chair that sat canted toward a stone fireplace. Neil could picture himself reading in that chair as Eve played on the carpet with Sadie.

Except Eve was gone and Sadie was dying.

"Look," Nico said. Next to a wide, elegant desk was a mess of pill bottles and an overturned black bag. The Russian held a white bottle out to Neil. "My reading of English is not so good. Is this what Sadie need?"

It read: Cefa-drops 50mg/mL Equivalent to Cefadroxil

"I don't know," Neil said, trying to read the tiny wording that wrapped itself around the bottle. It mostly contained warnings about different drug and allergic reactions. Nowhere on the bottle did it say what it was actually for. Nico had another bottle ready when Neil looked up. This one read: Cephalexin 500mg 100tabs. At the bottom of the bottle were the words: Broad Spectrum Anti-biotic.

"This is it!" Neil cried. He peered close, reading, trying to find what the dose would be. On the back he found the following: Dosage 10 to 15 mg per pound (22 to 30 mg/kg) every 12 hours orally for dogs and cats.

"But what about for people?" he wondered aloud. Would it make a difference? Not likely; not at this point. "Let's take all of this just in case," Neil said and began throwing pills into the black bag.

Chapter 8

Sadie

Philadelphia, Pennsylvania

From the deepest sleep of her life, Sadie was pushed and prodded until she looked blearily into Neil's worried face.

"Huh?" she asked. Even this had her coughing again and she nearly fainted as a result.

"No, you don't," Neil said, shaking her until her eyes refocused. "Come on, Sadie! Wake up, honey. We have medicine for you. New medicine that'll fix you for certain. Please, open your mouth." He had a glass of water in one hand and the other was held out to Sarah who dropped four large pills into it. Neil shook his head and said, "I think you did your math wrong. We only need two."

Sarah pushed his hand toward Sadie and said, "Trust me on this one, Neil. I was a pharmacy rep and a mother. When an infection is this far gone you need an initial dose to be pretty heavy. And we'll want to follow it up in six hours, not twelve."

Sadie took one look at the pills and made a face. "Horse pills, ugh."

"They're actually dog and cat pills," Jillybean said. She would have gone on further, but Sarah gave her a look and she slunk back.

"You are supposed to be asleep, young lady. It's way past your bedtime." Sarah pointed to the kitchen where Jillybean's pile of couch pillows had been arranged into a bed of sorts.

"Can't I see Sadie get better?" Jillybean asked as sweetly as she could. "Pleeease. Ipes says it will be a learning experience."

"Did he really?" Sarah asked, with a particularly close inspection of Jilly's eyes.

Jillybean toed the carpet and said in a little voice, "No. He says to leave him out of this. But...but I do want to see Sadie get better, and it could be a learning experience, even if Ipes doesn't think so."

Other than practically choking on the pills, and thinking that she was on the verge of suffocating from all the mucus in her lungs, this was all Sadie remembered of that night.

The next thing she knew it was morning and Nico was there with more pills. Thankfully there were only two this time. They both took turns getting caught sideways going down her throat, or at least that's what it felt like.

"Do you feel any better?" Nico asked.

All Sadie could say to that was, "I feel gross." Her clothes were cold and damp with sweat. When Nico and Sarah undressed her, she shivered under a blanket. When they left to get her fresh clothing, Jillybean snuck in with one of her little fingers pressed to her lips.

"I'm not aposed to be here, because I told a little white, fib. That's like a lie but for a good cause, you know?" Jillybean actually waited a full second for Sadie to respond, however she was still too groggy and feverish to do more than look at Jillybean through half-closed eyes.

"So, are you better yet?" Jillybean asked. "You don't look all that much better. When I asked about the pills they said they worked like magic. Ipes thought they were the ones fibbing and...wait...here they come. Get better quick so we can play. Bye!" She scooted out of the living room so fast that it seemed to occur between blinks.

Sadie coughed up something green and fell asleep again while she was being changed a second time.

The remainder of the day she spent in an awful state in which she had all the worst qualities of being both asleep and awake at the same time. Her eyes would be open, but they wouldn't focus. Nor could she close them and sleep satisfactorily. Her cough seemed to grow worse and she brought up more and more chunks of green and yellow/gray phlegm.

She spat into a frying pan that Nico dutifully cleaned every time. He was also there for everything she could ask for, which really didn't amount to anything but water. All they had was gritty water, which was usually warm from having been boiled. It didn't matter though; her mouth was so dry she sipped at it nonetheless.

In the evening came more pills which she took with red Kool-Aid this time. Jillybean made sure to point out that she had found it especially for Sadie. Sarah was quick to add that Jilly had been grounded at the time and shouldn't have left the house at all. Though it was still gritty with flecks of bark and leaves in it, the Kool-Aid gave flavor to the water and Sadie secretly thanked Jillybean when Sarah was out of the room. She even asked for seconds.

"First we go for walk," Nico said. "Sarah does say that you must walk three times in day. More when you get strong."

"I don't feel like it," Sadie said and then coughed up more of the green stuff. Everyone but Jillybean, who was immensely interested in everything, turned away when she spat it out. Sarah pulled the seven-year-old back from the pan before she could find out if the green stuff was as gooey as it looked.

"It doesn't matter if you feel like it or not," Sarah told Sadie. "Neil went to the library this morning and did some research about pneumonia. Your sickness has settled in your chest. You have to get up as much as possible to help clear it out. Now come on, stand up."

With Nico on one side and Sarah on the other, and Jillybean coming behind with the frying pan for Sadie to spit into, they progressed back and forth across the room until Sadie couldn't feel below her knees and was practically being carried. When they finally let her lie back down she had only the strength to ask one question, "Where's Neil now?"

"He's looking for a new car," Sarah said, her face etched with worry lines. "We should never have kept the Dodge. It was a dead giveaway. I'm sure he'll be back soon. Don't worry." As far as Sadie knew, Neil had been gone almost all day and now it was night. That was always something to worry about.

He was back in the morning. His face scratched and one eye blackened, yet still his cheerful self. "Just a few zombies," he explained. "Nothing a warrior like me can't handle. Now, it's time for more pills. Yea!"

Sadie actually smiled at her adoptive father. There wasn't much energy behind it, however it was genuine. "Any more Kool-Aid?"

"Sorry, we're all out, but I have something better," Neil said, producing a six pack of *Sprite*. "Do you want some? It's hot as all get out since I found it in the back seat of a car, but it should still be good."

After the gritty water and the gritty Kool-Aid, soda seemed like a treat. Jillybean thought so too. She stood nearby rocking back and forth on her heels, while entwining her arms and braiding her fingers together, trying, and failing, not to let her longing be too noticeable.

"Yes please," Sadie said to the offering of *Sprite*. "What about you, Jillybean? You want some?"

The little girl nodded, but contradicted the movement by saying, "I can't. Ipes says you need rest and fluids." She then sighed. "And *Sprite* is the very best fluids, except strawberry milk, but there ain't any more cows...right. There aren't any more cows. Not cows that got milk inside their unders at least."

"I'm sure you can have a little *Sprite*," Sadie insisted.

Jillybean turned her head slightly as though listening for something that didn't come as expected. "I guess I can. Maybe just a little bit," she said in a whisper, perhaps trying not to wake Ipes' consciousness in her mind. She ended up sipping on a can until it was gone. This was a process that lasted forty minutes simply because she had so much to say. Mostly this concerned Ipes and Sarah, the two individuals Jilly spent all of her free time with—free time meaning the time she wasn't sneaking out and exploring the new neighborhood, bringing back odds and ends.

Sometime in the long and rambling and physically active speech—Jillybean rarely stood or sat when speaking, instead she would pirouette or climb on a chair or wander around the room touching things as she spoke—sometime during all of that, Sadie fell asleep again.

This marked the beginning of a day and a half stretch that basically consisted of a series of naps and walks and sweats and baths. It was full dark again when soft lips on her cheek brought her around. It was Sarah, leaning over her and whispering words that didn't filter through to her conscious until it was too late.

"You're going to be fine," Sarah said. "I know it. You'll all be fine. Watch over Jillybean and Neil for me. Stay safe and remember I love you."

"Huh?" Sadie asked coming awake slowly. "What... what's happening? Are you going somewhere?" It was dark. No one went out in the dark except in emergencies. "Is there something wrong?"

"No, honey," Sarah said, giving her another kiss. "Go back to sleep."

That Sarah was wearing her coat didn't register, nor did the fact that her backpack, stuffed as though for traveling was only feet away. Missing these little cues and crushed beneath the burden of her illness, Sadie fell back asleep, only to waken again when a dull grey morning light sneaked passed the blankets over the windows and Neil rushing around the house like a crazy man.

"Sarah! Sarah!" he cried. In his madness, he opened doors that didn't make sense to open: a hall closet, the stairs to the basement, a kitchen cabinet. "Has anyone seen Sarah? Jilly, have you seen her? Nico?"

"Nyet," Nico said, standing quickly and going to the door. Carefully he cracked it and glanced out and then gradually he eased it back far enough to slip out. He was only gone for a minute. "Car was down street. Now is gone. She take car," he said, his face grim. "Why she take new car I find in night when everyone sleep?"

Everyone looked to Neil, while he stood, open-mouthed, staring at a piece of paper that sat on a dusty TV.

It had been folded, but now the top leaned out at an angle and there was something apparently on it that kept Neil from blinking.

"What is it?" Sadie asked despite knowing already what was written on the piece of paper. She knew what was on there by Neil's expression; there were very few things that could impact a man like being dumped.

"Nothing. I don't know. I'll be right back," he said. He took the paper with him into the room he had been sharing with Sarah and was gone for a long time; twenty minutes at least. When he came back, Sadie thought him remarkably composed.

"Sarah has left us," he stated in such flat tones he might have been talking from the depths of a coma. "She doesn't love me. So that's that. She also says we should take care of each other and there might be some food for us at this address...142 Clermont Avenue."

"What the fuck?" Sadie cried out in anger, she then began coughing, making a sound like a seal's bark.

Neil didn't berate her for cursing in front of Jillybean. He heaved out what seemed like the world's heaviest sigh and did the same: "Yeah, what the fuck?"

For once, Jillybean didn't seem to notice the cursing. Either that or she didn't care. With Ipes cradled under her arm, she went and sat on the edge of the couch next to Sadie's feet. In Sadie's mind, she too seemed remarkably composed.

Nico was angry enough for everyone. He stormed out of the room, shaking the floor with his heavy, stomping feet, only to return with a map. "Here is Clermont. She make us skip house. Say it is empty, but it is not. Suchka! She plans this for days. Come, we go, Neil. Clermont is only four kilometers. We be there in twenty minutes. Come..."

Neil appeared very small just then, little taller than a child. He stood in the doorway with his shoulders hunched as if Sarah's leaving had crushed him physically as well as emotionally. He shook his head.

"What?" Nico cried, pointing at the map. "She is traitor. She steal from family. This is not right!"

"Yeah, it's not right, but when has anything ever been right?" Neil asked. "Nothing has ever been right. Ever. I didn't deserve her. That's what the problem was. You know? She was out of my league."

"She wasn't," Sadie said. "Especially, if this is the way she thanks you for everything you've done for her. Sarah was beneath you." She had finally been able to control her coughing but these few words brought it back, rendering her incapable of argument. It hardly seemed to matter; there was little that was going to get through to Neil just then.

"That's not how things work for me, Sadie," he said. "I don't need to be coddled. I know what I am and I know what I have to offer, which just happens to be not much. I guess she thought I would do when I was basically the last man left that wasn't taken. We both know she would've went for Ram if he hadn't already been with Julia..."

Neil paused and then snapped his fingers, his face finally showing more than a manikin's plastic features. "Son of a bitch!" he exclaimed. "She hung around me because of him. That's all I was, an excuse. She was always trying to keep him around. And when he died, she didn't see the need to stay."

Sadie had been fuming at Sarah, but Neil was going so far astray in his despair that she tried to bring him back. "Neil, you don't know what you're talking about."

Next to her, Nico snorted. "In Russia, woman leave man like these, she is whore. Sorry Jolly-bin for blunt words, but, it is true." Jillybean looked confused perhaps at the word whore or maybe at Jolly-bin. It was hard to tell.

That someone would agree with him deflated Neil so much that he couldn't stand. He flopped to the shag carpet and began shaking his head. "She's been pulling away for weeks now. I could feel it happening and...and I tried everything but she didn't want me near her. Did she meet someone in New York? Do you think that's what happened, Nico? Maybe one of the colonel's men who might have…"

"Stop it!" Sadie cried, daring her cough to come back. "Both of you stop it. You don't know what you're talking about. She was raped was what happened. The colonel raped her and beat her. That's why she's been behaving so odd."

Neil's mouth started flapping until he finally spat out, "Then…then…all that she said about hiding with the *Whites* wasn't true? What about…is that where she got all the bruising from?" Neil leapt to his feet. "It wasn't from the fight with Cassie?"

"No," Sadie said.

"Oh, son of a bitch! I'm gonna kill him. Where's my gun?" He raced out of the room only to come back with his head wagging from side to side, looking for the Baretta as if it would have been casually thrown on the floor. "Where is it?"

"Maybe she take it," Nico suggested. "Maybe she take gun to kill colonel."

"You think so?" Neil asked. He had gone from stunned sadness, to self-loathing, to violent anger in a matter of minutes, and now he was on to fear. "She can't take on the colonel, not alone. He'll kill her. Doesn't she know that? She wouldn't throw away her life for revenge, would she?"

With all the excitement, Sadie began to fade. There was little strength left in her voice when she answered, "It's possible. If something happened to you guys, I know I would have done something. But this is Sarah, the same woman who just left you…hell, she left all of us high and dry. She even took our car."

Neil didn't seem to hear her. He had marched to the window and was staring out. Blankly, he whispered, "She's going to kill the colonel. She's crazy. It is crazy, right? Or it's depression…it's probably depression." He started wandering around the room touching the strange knick-knacks of the stranger's house. With everyone watching him he circled the entire room before stopping in front of Sadie. "It doesn't matter if she doesn't love me," he told his daughter. "I still love her. So I can't let her go after the colonel," he said. "We have to stop her somehow. So here's what we're going to do: Jilly will watch over Sadie until she's better, while Nico and I go after Sarah."

This didn't sit well with anyone. Sadie wanted to go with Neil in spite of the fact she could barely stand. Nico didn't think anyone should go, but definitely didn't want Sadie to go until she was better, nor did he want her watched over by a seven-year-old. Jillybean was quiet, however everyone could see what she was thinking: she wasn't going to be left behind even if she had to teach herself how to drive, something that none of them thought was beyond her.

"Then we all go," Neil said after a draining argument. "We'll give Sadie three days to heal up with this new medicine. In the meantime Nico and I will scrounge. There's like a million homes and buildings in Philadelphia. We'll get more guns and more fuel and another car, then we'll go after Sarah. We'll find her, hopefully, and see what happens after that. Maybe she'll be thinking straight by then."

Jillybean raised her hand to be called on. When Neil nodded to her she said, "Ipes thinks we're all jumping on conclusions, that's what means…well, I'm not really sure what that means. Except, maybe we don't know if Miss Sarah is really going to go kill some bad army man. Does her letter say anything about the colonel? Or does it just say she doesn't like you anymore?"

The air went out of Neil and he couldn't bring himself to answer. Sadie asked, "Can I read the letter?"

Like a child, he held it behind his back. "No, I don't want you to. It doesn't say anything about the colonel. It just says that she doesn't love me and never did."

Sadie tried to get up, but Nico pushed her gently down. She craned her pale face around the Russian and said, "Neil, that's not true. I don't know what's going on with her now, but she did love you. I know it. She told me all the time how she thought she was lucky to have you."

"Then why did she wr-write it?"

It was something Sadie couldn't understand. It made no sense whatsoever, though just then, with her fever starting to drain away the last of her energy, deciphering and comprehending motivations was basically beyond her. Heart-broken, Neil wasn't much better, while Nico, who hardly understood American men, found their women beautiful but baffling in the extreme.

This left Jillybean to interpret.

"I have an idea," she said and then immediately made a face and held her zebra out at arm's length. "No, I'm not gonna hush up," she said to Ipes in surprise. After a second she blew out in exasperation and told the adults, "Hold on."

She went to the far corner of the room and plopped the round-bottomed zebra there before coming back. "Sorry. Sometimes, Ipes doesn't know who is the boss of who. He thinks because he's older in zebra years that I have to listen to him, but I'm older in regular years, that's what means he gots to do what I say. I think it's different with mongooses. Don't they live to be like a hundred? They're sort of like an owl in that way. Wise and…"

Neil held up his hand to her, stopping her running mouth with the gesture. "Weren't you going to tell us something else? About what we were just discussing?"

"Oh right. My guess why Miss Sarah would say those rotten things was because she knows you guys pretty good. She knows that if she just ran away to go fight the army, you'd follow her. But if you thought that she didn't love you anymore that you'd let her go."

Neil replied with a simple, guarded: "Maybe."

Jillybean wasn't done. "She knows Sadie, too. She knows that Sadie is like a German Shepherd." Sadie raised an eyebrow at this and Jillybean was quick to add, "A pretty German Shepherd, I mean. But you are loyal to Neil more than to anyone. That's what means you will think bad thoughts of anyone who thinks bad thoughts of Neil. You see? And you will protect Neil even from himself, which he needs doing sometimes. Miss Sarah also knows

Nico. She knows that he will go along with whatever Sadie says."

Neil had his mouth open as he listened to the odd pattern of words coming from Jillybean's mouth. When she was done he jumped in: "So she does love me? Is that what you're saying?"

"I think so," Jillybean answered, nodding and shrugging simultaneously.

"But she's just trying to protect me and all of us, so we don't get hurt," Neil said thinking aloud. "That's good. That's a relief, except we still need to stop her before she gets herself killed. So I guess our plan is still in place. We leave in three days. Hopefully we can travel faster as a group than she can alone. She can't have that much gas. She'll have to forage alone; that'll slow her up."

To this Jillybean said, "You're still in the corner."

"Huh?" Neil asked.

"It's just Ipes," Jillybean explained. "He still thinks we're jumping on the conclusions. Even though he knows better about talking in timeout he says we still don't know if Sarah is really traveling to *The Island*."

"You know about *The Island*?" Sadie asked. The small, fortified island where the colonel ruled was not something any of them spoke of regularly and none had thought it a good subject for a seven-year old.

"Are you talking to me?" Jillybean wondered. "I know about lots of islands. Australia is an island that's upside down. There's another island called Madagascar which they named after a cartoon. But Ipes is the only one of me and him who knows about this *other* island that you guys think Sarah's going to."

Sadie lacked the energy to deal with Jillybean and closed her eyes. Neil took up the questioning. "Where does Ipes thinks she's going if not to *The Island*?"

After a second she answered, "He doesn't know."

"What's his guess?" Neil went on relentlessly.

Jillybean shrugged. "He says he doesn't have one."

This roused Sadie, who cracked an eye to stare accusingly at the stuffed zebra as if it were really alive.

"That's strange. Don't you guys think that's strange? I've never known that zebra not to have too much to say about anything."

"It's not real," Neil said in a low tone to Sadie.

"You know what I mean," she replied out of the corner of her mouth.

Jillybean didn't hear. She was staring at the zebra, intently with her brow furrowed. "I think it's strange also too. What do you know, Ipes?"

Neil looked at the stuffed animal. "Well? What does he know?" he demanded, when there was a long silence.

"He won't say," Jillybean replied. "Except he says that Sarah's not going to *The Island*. Oh! He's so in trouble. I am very disappointed in him."

"This is weird even for me," Sadie commented with another seal bark. She thought it was fine that Jillybean had an imaginary playmate, but they were crossing into dangerous territory by pretending Ipes was real. Unfortunately, they needed answers sooner rather than later. "Maybe we are asking the wrong question," Sadie tried. "Will he tell you why he won't answer you?"

"Maybe because he does not know anything and can't really talk," Nico suggested. "Maybe little girl is like attention."

Neil shook his head at this. "No. It's because he's trying to protect Jillybean. I'd like to think he was trying to protect us or Sarah, but it's Jillybean that he's really invested in. Ipes didn't say one word until we started talking about going to *The Island*. Only then did he start advising us against it."

"He says that protecting me is his *only* job," Jillybean said, her lips drawn in and her eyes sparking at the zebra. "We're supposed to be a family, Ipes, and families protect each other. Tell me right now, Mister! How long did you know Sarah was planning on leav…that long! Where is she going? Tell me this instant or so help me, it'll be a spanking for you."

Sadie watched the eerie battle of wills until her eyes started to droop. "You don't need him, Jillybean," Sadie told her. "You know everything he knows. You just have to remember it."

Jilly scratched the side of her nose and said, "Normally that's true. Normally, I remember things the second he reminds me of them, but I don't know this secret. It's a little crazy feeling in my head," she put her fingers in her hair and pulled gently. "It's like there's something just on the tip of my tongue; like the memory is just out of reach."

"You know that's not good, right?" Sadie asked.

"Of course it's not good," Jillybean agreed. "That's why he's in so much trouble. He should be telling me."

Neil suddenly let out a groan. "We're getting nowhere with this." He stood and began pacing, thinking. "If I was Sarah, where would I go? Would she go after the colonel for revenge? I wonder. That doesn't seem like her, not with Eve down…that's it! Ipes you pain in the ass. Sarah's going after Eve, isn't she? You're trying to keep us from going to New Eden."

Jillybean began to nod, slowly, her face troubled by what she was hearing. "Yes, Sarah is going to try to rescue Eve. That's what Ipes says. He also says sorry."

"He should be sorry," Neil griped. "Making us jump through hoops just to get a question answered."

"No," Jillybean said. "He's says he's sorry because Sarah doesn't think she's going to live through the attempt, and neither does Ipes."

Chapter 9

Sarah Rivers

Philadelphia, Pennsylvania

By the time Ipes confessed what he knew, the house on Clermont Avenue had already been picked over by Sarah and abandoned. Yet, there were many choice items still available. It had been her idea to take as much as she could south in order to bribe or buy her way into New Eden, but guilt over having left Neil and Sadie kept her from taking half as much as she felt she needed.

There were other houses that she visited later, which filled the gaps. During her scrounging with Nico she had managed to stash quite a few items away when he wasn't looking. She had a list of addresses memorized, and these she hit in turn, one after another, going methodically along, pausing only when the zombie menace forced her to hide.

She wasn't a warrior and, before that day, never had a pretense in that area. She wore the Beretta on her hip and used it reluctantly. On a long string slung diagonally across her back, she carried a hand axe—it was the last thing in the world she wanted to use, at least on a zombie. Frequently, she dreamed of splitting human skulls with it. She had a memorized list of those names as well.

"Petrovich, Williams, Abraham," she whispered.

Her words were quiet, barely slipping from the hollow of her cheeks. Across the street, just next door to a home on her list, was a pair of zombies. They had come stumbling from the back yard when she pulled up and she hadn't seen them until she had gotten out of the Honda that Nico had brought back a few days before.

Were they stragglers, or part of a larger horde? Did she dare to make a dash for the house? Or did she try one of crazy Jillybean's magic marbles. Sometimes the marbles distracted the beasts and sometimes they brought more out of the woodwork. It was a crap shoot, one that Sarah didn't have time for.

There was a bounty hunter out there who was probably even then up in some water tower with a high powered rifle. Perhaps he was looking down his scope at her. The thought made the spot between her shoulders twitch, and in homage to her paranoia she looked up to the skyline. The fact that there wasn't a water tower anywhere in sight didn't ease her worries in the least. In her mind, perhaps due to the influence of Hollywood, the capability of sharpshooters was exaggerated to a point that was well beyond simple physics and into the realm of the magical.

She wished she knew how to work a rifle like a Navy Seal. "Petrovich, Williams, Abraham," she whispered again, picturing herself with a nasty black rifle that could hit a target dead between the eyes from a mile away. "Bam, bam, bam. The lady is a winner. What's it gonna be? The kewpie doll or the necklace of teeth?"

Just then she felt slightly ill, because in her mind she wanted the necklace of teeth. Once, *she* had been the kewpie doll; the prize men had showed off for. What had she ever gotten out of that? A lot of promises, a lot of empty talk about finding the right woman and settling down to start a family, a roll in the sack, and then a bunch of unreturned phone calls. That had been true misogyny, on a national scale.

Colonel Williams? He wasn't a misogynist. He was evil, pure and simple and Sarah wanted his teeth to wear on a necklace. She hadn't known that she wanted such a horrible thing until that moment on the street. It gave her a sick feeling of desire. It was an evil feeling, one that couldn't be denied, mainly because she did nothing at all to stop it. For a long time she had felt hollow inside, except for the parts that felt rotten and useless that is, but now there was something she could latch onto. She could kill. She had once before and could again, this time with a little more desire.

Before she could come to grips with this new feeling she stepped out from behind the Honda and lifted the string of the hand axe from across her shoulder. One of the zombies came at her. It was quiet. Strangely the entire world was quiet. No moaning, no wind, no chatter of squirrels or piping of birds, no shifting sounds of her clothes as she rushed at the zombie.

There was only the axe. She crushed it into the head of the zombie with such force that it sunk in four inches deep before stopping with a jarring sensation that ran right up to her shoulder. The zombie, still in a perfectly soundless state, crumbled to the ground with the axe embedded, pulling it from her grip.

She gave it a half-hearted tug and distantly she heard the echo of her own voice in her mind as she let out an apathetic, "Shit."

A second later, the other zombie was there, reaching for her with long fingers on even longer arms. It had been a man once; tall and maybe even handsome. It still wore the shreds of a suit and on one foot was a Bruno Magli loafer —apparently, he'd been a clotheshorse once, her type of man. Perhaps he had even been one of the men she had dated, one of the men who had pretended to care, who had pretended to be interested in what she had to say, who had been quite willing to lie his way into her bed.

As the zombie reached out towards her, there came a point where the evil in her soul intensified like a white fire as she remembered how Cassie had reached for her in the same way. Her dark hands had come at Sarah's throat and it had felt so natural and easy to kill Cassie. It was as though Sarah had been born to kill her; as though it was her destiny.

Now, it was the same with the zombie. Its hands reached, and without effort, Sarah took hold of the outer one at the wrist and forced it across its body. The zombie's momentum changed direction at once. She further complicated its desire to kill her by stepping behind and kicking it in the back of the knee. It went down so easily that the entire sequence of events felt choreographed.

71

There was only one question: for the coup de grâce would it be the gun or the knife? In other words, the old Sarah Rivers or the new? The old Sarah didn't like things messy; she liked them neat. She didn't care for things that were hard; she liked things that were easy. She didn't want confrontation; she wanted team building and consensus.

There was no choice, not really. The knife was hard and messy and it was the epitome of confrontation. A knife was personal in a way a gun could never be—you could feel a man's dying pulse through the blade of knife. A knife knew evil like nothing else. It was comfortable with death and it bathed in blood like no other tool made by man.

Sarah didn't hesitate in making up her mind.

In a flash of steel the hunting knife cut a line in the morning air as it streaked down to embed itself in the top of the zombie's cranium. Like the other zombie, it wanted to tumble over leaving her empty-handed, but Sarah wasn't going to give up this new part of her. She planted a foot on the zombie's back and, like a modern day King Arthur, withdrew her blade with a flourish.

She even went so far as to brandish it at the imaginary sniper staring down his imaginary scope and, for just a second, she envied Neil for being vaccinated. He could kill like this all day long. He didn't have to worry about scratches or bites. He could just kill and kill in any manner he chose. It all seemed so great for Neil, but then she remembered how he had come to be vaccinated and who'd had to die for it to have happened.

This cast a pall over her moment and that heady, evil feeling that had flared in her abated, leaving only the hollow and the rot behind.

Kneeling, she cleaned off her knife and then retrieved her axe. Next she went into the house to the hall closet where she found the six cans of assorted soup and the two boxes of mac-n-cheese she had hidden two weeks earlier. She hefted them into a cardboard box which went into the rear of the Honda and then she whisked out of there, making sure to take a different route out of the neighborhood than the one she had entered from.

Total time on Third Avenue, even with killing two zombies: one minute and four seconds. If the bounty hunter had spotted her from some far away vantage, he would have an awfully hard time catching up.

She hit two more houses in the same speedy way: in and out, quick. At the last one she parked the Honda out front, making sure to open the gas cap to give it that empty look, and took an hour for lunch, sitting in an upper floor bedroom. She sipped on candle-warmed soup and kept watch.

If there was a bounty hunter curious over her, he never showed. What that meant, she didn't know. Had he moved on to another city searching for Sadie and Nico? Or was he just confused at the apparently random movements of the little Honda skipping around the south-west suburbs of Philadelphia.

"Or maybe he was taking a nap and missed me driving around," Sarah said to herself. "Or maybe he got eaten by a zombie."

There was no way of knowing what was going on. For all she knew there were a dozen bounty hunters running amok in Philly, killing everything that moved, perhaps even each other.

Who knew?

Certainly not Sarah, and especially not a minute later when she was sleeping in a comfy chair that sat propped near the window. She had not slept all the night before, and this was on top of the little she had been sleeping for the past month.

Detailed and dreadful nightmares came every time she closed her eyes. They were always the same four horrible events that she was forced to live over and over. In one, she was held down and endless raped by men she could not recognize. She was raped until something ripped open inside her and her guts rushed out in a smell of copper and filth. At the end of that dream, she always came awake in tears, clutching herself.

Then there was the nightmare of fighting Cassie in the dark river where the only thing Sarah could see were sharp white teeth in a grinning mouth and Cassie's evil eyes glowing. In it, Cassie, with her dreadlocks floating like a squid's tentacles, seemed like a water creature herself. She pulled Sarah deeper and deeper, laughing without bubbles, as Sarah fought to free herself and fought to hold her breath one second longer. She always came awake gasping for air and clawing at her own throat.

Perhaps the worst was the one where she couldn't save Sadie. In that nightmare Sarah would pull her daughter to shore to begin CPR, but each time she went to do the chest compressions she would push Sadie deeper into the earth until the girl was lying at the bottom of an open pit that was six feet deep and six long. Whenever that dream struck, she would go to stand over Sadie and stare, reeling in guilt until the sun rose.

The last of her routine nightmares dealt with the ferry boat and the fire. In that one Ram was always alive. He and Neil and Sadie sat chained to the deck waiting for Sarah to come and rescue them. She always tried. She tried to push through an endless throng of men wearing the camouflage of the army, but they weren't soldiers; they were devils holding her back. She was always weak and slow and couldn't get away to save her friends. Neil and Sadie would call out *Sarah! Sarah!* Over and over they would call and the more they called the harder she fought to get to them, but she was always too slow. Then the fire would start and Jillybean would dance on the deck and then when the boat would begin to tip she would walk on its highest edge without fear. Jillybean had no fear because she had started the fire. She was a destroyer. Everything she touched burned and crumbled.

But on that day Sarah slept soundly in the comfortable chair in the empty house. She was exhausted, and for once the dreams didn't come. She slept without stirring, even when a black Jeep crept down the street.

Chapter 10

Neil Martin

Philadelphia, Pennsylvania

Neil carried Sarah's letter everywhere he went. It sat folded in his shirt pocket beneath his ever-present sweater vest, where it felt strangely heavy. At all the wrong times he would take it out and reread the line that counted for everything: ...*You're not what I want. I thought I loved you but I was wrong*...

All the wrong times to read that line consisted of anytime of the day. He could be smiling at some crazy antic of Jillybean's and then look at the sentence and feel his heart go numb. Or he could be sitting alone in his room with his heart numb and look at the note and sense a blackness eating away his soul. Or he could be sitting on the edge of the tub resting his head on the shotgun wondering what the blackness in his soul would feel like if he pulled the trigger.

He was on the verge of finding out.

At some point, seemingly by itself, the barrel of the gun had slipped up under his chin. It was cool and not particularly uncomfortable. It felt good, actually. The shotgun was something real. It was something that he could understand and trust. It would do its job no matter what. No one could question the loyalty of the...

"Hey, Mister Neil?" Jillybean called through the bathroom door. "Are you in there?"

Neil jumped and the trigger he'd been caressing jerked slightly. He coughed and cleared his throat. "Yeah, I mean yes. I mean you can come in."

"Ipes said you'd be in here," Jillybean said walking in. Without asking she pulled the shotgun away from him and set it in the corner. "You don't need to be afraid of the dark in here, Mister Neil. I have candles you know. In my backpack if you want one." She slid the pack off and was about to open it up when she paused to look at the image on the front. "Tell me, who is this guy, Belieber? This guy on my bag. He's got the biggest head I've ever seen."

"He was a singer...sort of."

"And he made backpacks, too?" Jillybean asked in surprise. "He must've been real busy."

Forgetting the candle, she stepped around Neil and into the empty bathtub, laying down as if there were water in it. "Did you want something in particular?" Neil asked.

"I'm bored," she griped. "Sadie is taking a nap and Nico is out."

"And I'm last on your list?" Neil said with a note that was part accusation and part pathetic whine. He immediately shook his head, wishing he hadn't said anything. "Sorry, I didn't mean that. If you're so bored, why don't you and Ipes go exploring."

It would seem strange to suggest that it was ok for a seven-year-old to go out by herself in an undead world, however, everyone had long since stopped trying to put a limit on Jillybean. She was sort of like a stray cat that had adopted them, but was still mostly wild. She came back to the house for food or companionship, however she was just as much at home in the dangerous zombie-filled streets as she was being tucked in at bedtime.

Neil would have taken a more active role in parenting her, but he had been sick for weeks, while Sarah had been crushed with the loss of Eve, as well as trying to secretly cope with being raped. Jillybean had just sort of been around; always cheerful, but also almost always alone.

Now, strangely, she had barely left the house in the two days since Sarah had disappeared.

At the suggestion of exploring, she sighed and said, "I don't know." For a while the bathroom was quiet. Jillybean just looked at him as she walked her fingers, insect-like around the edge of the tub. Neil wasn't in the mood to play any of the games she liked. He was about to ask her more forcefully to go do something else when she most unexpectedly asked, "Were you going to use the gun?"

"Huh?" Neil blurted.

"You know, for suiciding yourself. I know what is suicide means. My mom did that, you know. I told you, remember? Not with a gun. She stopped eating on purpose and that is what means she killed herself on purpose. I think she was sad, just like you, because my dad left. So? Were you going to do it?"

For a minute Neil didn't know if he was going to answer her, mainly because he didn't know the answer, at least not completely. His heart still stung over the loss of Ram, and there was a bitter hole where the love for Eve had once been. Now, on top of all of that, he had been shaken to his foundation by Sarah leaving him.

And Neil was just plain tired of this new world. He was tired of zombies and the bad food. He was tired of fighting for his life and drinking crummy water that tasted too much like dirt. He was tired of being afraid.

"I wasn't going to do it," Neil concluded. "I think I was just fantasizing of all the hard parts of life being over. It all seems hard these days. But I still have to hope that what you said about Sarah is true. That she's just trying to protect us. And there's Sadie to worry about, and you, Jillybean. I worry about you."

She looked at him as if that was a surprise to her. "Well, I think that's all kinds of funny because Ipes is making me hang around because he's worried about you. He says I have to be extra good so you won't suicide yourself."

"Tell Ipes that I'm tougher than I look," Neil said as a way of reassuring her.

"With that black eye you look pretty tough," Jillybean said, pointing at his face. "Tougher than normal, which is like librarian tough."

His shoulders twitched at the mention of his black eye. A single second of carelessness had nearly been enough to mean his death. One moment he was checking under the hood of a fine old Ford truck that had been refurbished to appear as if it had been newly minted, and the next a zombie was on top of him, biting into his shoulder. Neil counted himself lucky that the sixty pound hood had dropped on both of them. He had gotten a few scratches and the shiner, while the zombie had part of its skull caved in.

Jillybean hadn't noticed the shiver and had gone on, piping in her little girl voice about toughness in general, but when she brought it back to Neil he had to smile.

"Were you tougher as a pirate?" she asked. "Sadie says you used to be a pirate. Ipes says there's probably no such things, but isn't sure. Did you have a bird? Pirates have birds and eye patches and peglegs. Peglegs is what means you wear a wood thing down here of your leg." She pointed at her own shin and then waited expectantly for Neil to answer.

"I wasn't that kind of pirate," Neil told her. "I was a… never mind. You don't want to hear about that kind of thing. It was business stuff, only. There weren't cannons or treasure or anything cool."

"I still want to hear about it," she assured him.

He gave her such a keen look she shifted her eyes down. "Why do you want to hear about it?" he quizzed her.

She sighed again and said, "Ok, I don't. Ipes says suicider people should talk a lot. He says I should keep you talking and then you'll get all better. My mom never said anything and she died. That's what it's all about. I don't want you to die, Mister Neil. I like you a lots. So that's why I wanted to hear about you being a fake pirate and all. You can still tell me, but can we also play a game at the same time?"

Neil had come in to take a break from his seemingly endless scrounging and, since they were scheduled to leave in the morning, he should've gone back at it, however he agreed to her request. They played *Go-Fish*, though Jillybean called it "Gold-Fish," a mistake he allowed because it was innocent. Neil needed a hefty dose of innocent just then.

As he had expected, she did almost all of the talking. That was ok with him. He wasn't in the mood to talk. Still it helped a little. The game kept his mind off the letter, and the little girl filled the numb void in his heart which had once belonged to baby Eve.

Neil had long ago given up on ever getting Eve back. At first, when they had fled from New York and settled in Philadelphia, Sarah had pushed for them to do something, to come up with a plan to invade New Eden, to make preparations to take on Abraham. However no one had. Neil and Sadie had been sick, Nico didn't have the brains to be a strategist and Jillybean had been playing herself a game of *Jenga* during the talk since no one would play with her.

"We don't need a plan to storm the underground fortress, and battle Abraham's fanatical followers," Neil had said at the time. *"What we need is a way to grieve and cope and try to go on with our lives."*

"That's our child you're talking about giving up on," Sarah had replied. She hadn't been angry. She was rarely angry after New York; she was always just there, more or less living in bland, neutrality.

"I'm not talking about giving up on anyone. I'm talking about trading lives. You know we won't be able to just walk in there and walk out again with Eve. People are going to die. Some of us are going to die. As much as I love her, I couldn't trade any one of you for Eve."

It was still true. Other than Nico, they weren't warriors. They were just people: a mom, who on her best day was only an average shot, a Goth girl who was fresh off being dead, a Wall Street guy who knew his way around a wine list better than he knew any weapon, and a little girl whose sanity was daily fretted over.

To take on New Eden was clearly suicide, making Sarah clearly suicidal.

Neil blew out in a noisy sigh, not happy about how dark his thoughts had become. "Do you have any eights?" he asked.

Jillybean gave him a look before picking out the eight of Clubs from her hand. "Can you see my cards?" Before he could answer, she glared at Ipes, who sat propped up in the corner of the bathtub. "I'm not being a sore loser. I just asked a question."

"Don't worry, I can't see your cards," Neil told her. In order to throw the match, Neil then asked for a jack, a card he had only just asked for the round before. Jillybean's lips went white.

"I just pulled that one," she said and handed over her jack reluctantly. "Can you read minds or something? What am I thinking now?"

He was about to blurt out *cookies*, only for some reason he stopped and actually thought about it. What was she thinking? If there was ever a girl of two minds this was it.

"My guess is that you're thinking about all sorts of stuff. You were worried about me, and I know you are worried about Sadie. And I think you're afraid. You're probably afraid to leave this house, and probably afraid to go on another crazy trip. I'd bet you're definitely afraid that the bounty hunter is out there tracking us. And maybe you're afraid of what we will find if we have to go to New Eden. Am I close to what you were thinking?"

She shook her head, arrayed her cards better in her hand and said, "No. I was thinking about cookies. Ipes started going on about Oreos, which are his favorite and it got my stomach rumbling. But you were right about all the rest, even though I wasn't really thinking about those things just then. You were right about everything 'cept being ascared of leaving this house. This really isn't a good house at all. The only thing it's good for is fooling the bounty hunter man."

"I almost said cookies," Neil told her. "Ipes had that look in his eye. It's the look a lion get when it sees a gazelle."

"Yeah," agreed Jillybean. "He's worse than the monsters if you put a plate of cookies in front of him. He'll go crazy!"

"Then I guess it's good we don't have any cookies," Neil said. He had meant it to be a joke, but Jillybean's smile disappeared. Clearly, in her mind, there was never a good time to be out of cookies.

Neil was about to apologize, but just then there came a tap at the door. Sadie peeked in, showing surprise on her pale face. "Cards in a darkened room? Is this a high-stakes game?"

"We aren't playing for steak," Jillybean said. "It's free. You can play if you want. It's gold-fish. But be careful, Neil is hard to beat."

"I'd like to play, but I was just coming to tell Neil that I'm ready to travel. Those pills have done wonders. We should leave as soon as Nico gets back. I'll start getting my stuff together."

She started to go, but Neil took her soft hand and held her back. "I told you, tomorrow. And that's if you pass the breathing test. You can try it now, but I still hear the rattle in your lungs. Go ahead and prove it to yourself. Put your arms over your head and now, take a deep, deep breath."

"I'll be fine," Sadie insisted. "The new medicine is working great and all I'm gonna be doing is sitting in a car. That's not exactly a strenuous activity."

"You don't know what will happen out there," Neil said. "No one does. What happens if we run into one of the giant hordes? Can you sit in a truck all night without heat? What happens if the bounty hunter finds us? Can you run away? What happens…"

"None of that matters!" Sadie interrupted. "Sarah could be practically at New Eden right now and you're just sitting here worrying about me. You shouldn't be. You should be worrying about her."

"I am," Neil told her. "I'm worried sick. I'm worried that we won't find her in time, but I'm more worried that we will, and that she'll refuse to come back home with us. What do we do then? Do we go on with her and try to attack a city of over three hundred people?"

Sadie began to cough. It was a wet sound, but still infinitely better than it had been. "Maybe," she managed to reply after a minute.

"With two guns shared by the four of us? How far do you think we'll get before they shoot us like dogs, or heaven forbid, burn us at the stake?"

"I don't want to be burned like a steak," Jillybean stated, trying to be helpful. "Do they eat you when you're done, do you think? Is that what steak is? People? That's gross…oh. Ipes just told me it's cow meat. That's better because my dad used to like steak a lot and I didn't like the idea of him being a cannonball."

"It's pronounced cannibal, and it's really not a good subject to discuss," Neil told her. He stood and stretched, kneading his knuckles into the small of his back. To Sadie he said in his strictest, *I'm the Dad around here so no back-talking*, tone, "We're leaving tomorrow and that's if you can draw a proper breath." Inwardly he added: *And if we find more gas*.

So far, in two very long and challenging days, he and Nico had only managed to scrounge up four gallons of gas. It would barely get them out of the suburbs of Philly if they took the Ford Expedition that Neil had found intact and drivable. There were smaller cars available that would get them further, but these offered nothing in the way of protection from the zombies, nor did they have off-road capability, a feature that was becoming a must.

"I have to go," he told them. "Jillybean, take care of Sadie. And Sadie, get back on the couch.

Chapter 11

Sarah Rivers

South of Philadelphia

A run of delays kept Sarah pinned in place for longer than she could have believed. First there had been the catnap. She had wanted to get in a quick snooze to energize herself, but somehow the nap had turned into an all-day slumber. By the time she cracked a bleary eye and ran a dry tongue around the inside of an even drier mouth, the sun was dipping down below the horizon. Much to her annoyance, she was forced to spend the night in the lonely house.

The next day's delay was due to an influx of zombies on a terrific scale. They came marching out of the morning mist just as she was rolling up her sleeping bag. Strangely they appeared to be moving in formation, schlepping down the suburban street in a vile imitation of a parade. Sarah waited patiently, watching from her chair on the second floor, but abruptly, something stopped the lead contingent and so row upon row of dead people stood waiting as if for a command from an undead drill sergeant which never came. Eventually most of them began to graze in the front yards of the neighborhood houses; eating flowers and wild grasses. Unfortunately, there were still too many left in the street for Sarah to try to get away in the little Honda.

The day dragged and she grew sleepy. Sarah lolled in the chair and at some point in the early afternoon, she fell asleep. Time wore away and as it did the zombies dissipated, meandering toward their uncertain future. At about the moment Neil slipped the shotgun barrel beneath his chin, Sarah was awoken by the sound of an engine.

It was a black Jeep, the same sort of vehicle that had chased after Neil two nights before when he was searching for Sadie's medicine, and, unbeknownst to Sarah, the same

83

vehicle that had been creeping around searching for her. This time it did not creep up the street, it went at a steady thirty miles per hour heading in the exact direction Sarah needed to go.

When it passed, she hopped up and went to the window to watch its progress, however, because of the angle, she lost sight of the Jeep after only a minute.

Had it turned east? She had been planning on going east, but now she didn't know what to do. Hurriedly, she unfolded the map she had picked up at a gas station and stared at it intently. Perhaps it was stereotypical, but she wasn't good with maps. Just finding her present location took a minute and then she painstakingly oriented the map to the real world so that she could conceptualize directions better.

She was two miles west of I95 in the very southernmost portion of Philadelphia. It had been her plan to join the highway at Madison Street and then make a dash south before Neil could catch up—in her heart she knew he wouldn't be stopped by the nasty words she had written, and she knew he would figure out her destination eventually. It wasn't like she had many options.

Brittany or Eve were the only choices left in her life, or so it seemed to Sarah. Search for one or save the other. A vain hope or a certain death, that's what her children meant to her, and even then she didn't know what the right choice was.

With depression threatening once again to cloud her mind, she put her finger down on the map. "I'm here...and I want to go there." She began tracing a new route to the highway, one that was out of the way, but not by more than a few miles. With fuel being so short, she couldn't spare the miles, however she couldn't spare getting caught by a bounty hunter either.

She left as soon as she got the map folded. The Honda was packed with all the gear needed for a trip, including, food, water, and diapers—she may have been a bad mother, but she was still a mother.

Sarah drove with the windows down, listening for the bounty hunter's Jeep. On the seat next to her was the Beretta, cold and black. It was the great equalizer. With it she didn't need to fear rape or robbery. With it she was every bit as tough as a man. She touched it at odd times as if to reassure herself that it was real, and when she took a turn she instinctively put her hand out to keep it from sliding.

The detour, characterized by Sarah being extra vigilant and jumping at every sound, lasted an hour longer than she had planned. On the way, she discovered a man dangling from the limb of a tree by his neck. He swayed gently, pushed by a soft breeze. She pulled over and looked at him, wondering if he had killed himself or if had he had done something to deserve being strung up like that?

Taking the Beretta in hand, she climbed out of the Honda and advanced on the dead man. He was so purple in the face as to appear black and his tongue seemed to stick out of his mouth by a foot. Next to the tree was a deer rifle with a round chambered and a few feet away from that she found a backpack with some canned food and twenty more rounds for the rifle.

"Suicide," Sarah concluded with a sigh, giving a last glance to the corpse. The sight gave her a nasty feeling that was part-nausea and part-surrender. "I'm right there with you, buddy," she said, as she took the rifle and the pack and wandered back to the Honda.

She had always known her mission was suicidal, but it really struck home when she saw the dead man. In a way he was lucky. Abraham had threatened her with death by fire. Whenever she remembered that, she involuntarily touched her long blonde hair. She hadn't had a proper cut in so long that her hair was like a lion's mane and it hung down well past the middle of her back. It would go up in flames splendidly when the time came.

The image of her hair burning like an inferno unfounded her mind, and inexplicably, she pulled out her hunting knife and began to saw at her hair, hacking off foot-long chunks of her golden tresses. After a minute, and after quite a bit of pain, she realized that cutting her hair in that manner wouldn't do. As though Abraham were chasing her with a lit torch, she jumped into the Honda and drove through the sprawling suburbs until she found a hair salon in a little strip mall. *Cute Cuts & Color* the sign read.

The salon was basically intact. Someone had prowled through the drawers at one time, perhaps looking for stashes of food, but of the hair products, and cutting tools nothing had been touched. It was all Sarah's. There was plenty of light left to the late afternoon and she went right to work with a pair of shears that were still wonderfully sharp. In minutes she had butched her hair, cutting it unevenly with lengths ranging from a half-inch to two inches. For some reason it felt wonderfully liberating. It was as if she were cutting herself out of her own life with each snip of the scissors.

There was only one thing left to make the transformation complete: black hair dye. She chuckled as she began the dye job—Sarah Rivers was disappearing right before her eyes. Almost too late she remembered that she would have to wash the excess dye out. In a giddy panic, she grabbed a bottle of shampoo, some towels, and a mirror and ran back to the Honda.

Finding water on the east coast wasn't an issue; very quickly she passed over a creek. Giddy or not, she kept her wits about her and exited the Honda slowly keeping an ear out for zombies. Streams like this could be deadly. Greenery was thick on the banks and the splashing water could mask the approach of what would normally be a loud zombie.

Sarah eased down to the water and was slow to begin rinsing out the dye; she had time, there was no sense hurrying when it wasn't needed. In this instance her caution was for naught and she was able to wash her hair in the chilly water without incident. When she got back to the car she found it impossible to keep from staring at herself in disbelief.

"It doesn't even look like me," she said, touching her face. Without the golden mane, her head seemed small, and her blue eyes fairly blazed in contrast to the black hair. "Will Eve recognize me?" she wondered aloud. It was then that an idea formed. "Would Abraham recognize me?"

Probably not, she decided, especially if she were to make a few more changes to her appearance. Before going back to the highway Sarah Rivers went shopping. Next to a gas station just down the block was a *Goodwill* and in it she found a patchwork of different sized clothes that, when safety-pinned in place, gave her a whole new wardrobe. Gone were the casual jeans and the soft sweaters. Her slim figure was disguised beneath layers and in her mind she looked like a gypsy, in other words absolutely nothing like her old self.

"Interesting," she remarked as she gazed at her reflection in a mirror.

Suddenly her mission didn't seem so suicidal. "I'll become one of those daft *Believers*," she said with a grin. "Oh, praise God for allowing Abraham to build a stupid underground fort instead of stopping the zombie virus! And bless his great, God-like hair and, oops, so sorry, Mr. Abraham fell on a knife six or seven times." The grin turned into a wicked smile that faltered as she caught sight of something. She went closer to the mirror and looked at herself from different angles. Though the smile was wicked, beneath it she could see hints of the old Sarah Rivers.

Without effort, she replaced the smile with a sneer and stuck it in place. "Good bye, Sarah." Her old self disappeared from the mirror and in a second her new self was climbing back into the Honda, sneer in place.

She drove for the highway and once on it found her progress slower than on the side streets, due for the most part, because of the many zombies who seemed trapped on it. The roadway was bordered by fencing that stymied every effort of the zombies to get away. Some found their way off exit ramps, but an equal number seemed to come on as replacements.

Sarah, not only had to dodge the zombies, she also had to weave her way around all the stalled-out cars. It was a tedious and mind-numbing way to drive. With not much sunlight left to the late afternoon, she found nearly her entire side of the road blocked by cars. They seemed unnaturally placed. Fearing an ambush, she stopped well back and brought out the deer rifle.

It had a good scope and she was able to see every detail of the cars as if she were standing twenty feet away. At first nothing moved, which had the adverse effect of making her more anxious over the situation. Then she saw a flicker of blue behind one of the cars.

"Now I got you sucker," she whispered, thumbing the switch from *safe* to *fire*. She had no qualms about killing first and asking questions later. What sort of person would set up an ambush on a highway? The only answer that came to mind was quite simple: a bad person. "Now just show yourself so I can get this little episode behind me and find a place to hole up for the night."

More slow minutes crept by before the flash of blue formed up better on her scope and she saw that it was only a zombie. "Fuck," she swore. It was the bounty hunter she had expected to see, not some stupid zombie.

She still couldn't relax. Something wasn't right. Just in case she had missed something, she waited another ten minutes, staring down the scope at the cars and up along the fencing. There was nothing to see but a few zombies and, with the scope, she was certain of their authenticity.

That odd feeling of something no being right remained, but she had to move. She hurried to get her car past the obstruction, riding up onto the grassy shoulder. She was so nervous that she actually drove with her left hand out the window, training her Beretta outward, ready to shoot the first thing that moved. With her attention divided, and the grass on the side of the road grown thick, she did not see the spike strip that had been purposely placed there until her front tires went over it.

Both tires exploded like twin shotguns going off, while at the same time the car seemed to rise in the front a few inches before dropping as if settling into a ditch. The Honda ground to a halt.

"What the hell?"

At first, Sarah didn't recognize that she was in serious trouble. She figured she had run over something, glass or a piece of metal, in other words, something innocent. With more swearing, she climbed out and looked down at the damage to the front left tire. It was only then that she saw the rows of sharpened spikes jutting from a long rectangular mat.

She had never seen a police spike strip before and a part of her still clung to the idea that it was there by mistake. *Perhaps it fell from a passing truck*, she rationalized. It wasn't until an electronic chirp sounded behind her that her fear began to ramp up.

It had come from the piled cars that stretched across the highway, and it repeated every couple of seconds. Sarah swung her Beretta to point at the source of the sound: a little black...

"What is that?" she asked as she came closer. It looked like a thick black phone sitting under a brick. It chirped again. The sound was a catalyst for her memory and she suddenly knew what she was looking at: a walkie-talkie. It was a two way radio, but what was the brick for? And why was there fishing wire wrapped around it? And why was there a small twig between the brick and the walkie-talkie. It sat squarely on a button that read: *Push-To-Talk*.

"Oh shit," Sarah whispered. She grabbed the fishing line and followed it from the brick to around the axel of the closest car and then right back to the spike strip where her car had severed it. Seeing the simple trap she had stumbled across had her going cold, and expecting to be attacked at that very instant she brought the Beretta up again and trained it all around her, prepared to fight for her life. She progressed in a slow circle, but no attack occurred; there were only a few zombies which she ignored.

The walkie-talkie chirped again, sending out its poisonous signal. From what she knew of them they could broadcast on different channels and she could imagine the bounty hunter sitting in his Jeep, waiting for signals, each one corresponding to a different area he had trapped.

In a panic she leapt into the car and stomped the gas. A second later, her rear tires exploded as they passed over the spikes. She let out a little scream, but kept her heel hard to the floorboard. Behind her she left chunks of black, vulcanized rubber—a little at first, however as she swerved back onto the road, a lot!

The Honda shrieked and rumbled and shook beneath her. The steering was "soft" at first, and then it became chaotic. The car would slide like it was running over butter, then it would hitch and jump as it corrected itself. It stank of burning rubber. She could see smoke in her rearview mirror. She watched the mirror more than she did the road, afraid that at any moment she would see the black Jeep.

It showed up just about the time the last bit of rubber left her tires and the Honda began making a horrific squealing. The sound could be heard for miles and upwards of a thousand zombies began to head toward it. On a certain level, Sarah knew this, however on a far more overriding level she didn't care. The bounty hunter had spotted her and was blazing straight down the highway.

He was far in the distance, just a tiny spec, but that wouldn't last, not at his speed. She figured she had two minutes before he was on her. Sarah hauled the Honda over to the shoulder of the road where it shuddered to a stop after barely twenty feet. Leaving the keys still in the ignition, she grabbed her Beretta, the backpack that had belonged to the hanged man and the deer rifle. Her eyes fell on the package of diapers and she hesitated.

"No," she whispered. At the rate people were having babies, diapers would not be in short supply for many years.

She left the car and all the possessions she had managed to scrounge and ran for the fence. Zombies ran with her and more ran at her. It was the ones right on the other side of the fence that she worried about. Three quick shots from the Beretta felled the closest of them.

"Petrovich, Williams, Abraham," she whispered, pulling her trigger with deliberate cool. By now the black Jeep was at the trap half-a-mile away. She saw a man in camo hop out and drag the spike strip out of the way.

Sarah had thirty seconds before he would be on her. There weren't many options left to her: a gun battle that she would likely lose or running away from the bounty hunter and into the arms of a host of undead.

On the other side of the fence, there was a gentle slope of green that tilted down to the edge of more suburbs. As far as suburbia went, it was at the low end of the spectrum. The houses were tiny, box-like and one step up from mobile homes. There were many hundreds of them crammed into a few acres land. The little town was alive with the undead.

Sarah chose the dead.

Chapter 12

Jillybean

South of Philadelphia

At about the time Sarah was scaling a fence with a jeep roaring down on her and a whole throng of zombies converging on her desperate to kill, Neil climbed on his bike and rode away from the little house to continue to scrounge. Bikes were slow and dangerous, especially for Nico who wasn't vaccinated, however fuel was simply too precious to waste looking for more fuel.

Sadie was anxious for Neil, and she was afraid in general girlfriend-terms for Nico, however it was her fear for Sarah that occupied her to the greatest extent. *How could she do this to us? What was she thinking? Is she trying to kill herself?* These three questions Sadie asked aloud over and over. With all her stress, combining with her slowly fading pneumonia she made a poor companion for Jillybean. If she wasn't worrying, she slept a lot.

When Jillybean felt Sadie had snoozed long enough, she tried sighing loudly, but the girl didn't budge. She then did a tap-dance routine that she had learned two years previously. It didn't have the same flair when performed on linoleum and all Sadie did was roll over.

"Can't I go yet?" she asked Ipes when she had finished in a lunge, jazz hands extended and quivering.

Not yet, he said, shooting her a look. *You heard Mister Neil. We have to watch out for her.*

"I don't thinks that's what he said exactly," Jillybean replied. "He said to take care of her. And he told Sadie to stay on the couch. She's on the couch and she looks taken care of if you ask me. I don't see what more we can do here. I say we go find that cat we saw before. I'm sure if she's already in the car, Mister Neil will let us keep her."

This nearly did the trick of getting them out of the house. Ipes completely forgot Neil's instructions and jumped into the planning stage involved in capturing a stray cat and getting it into a car without getting scratched to death. The strategies devised were so in depth that Jillybean also forgot what her main goal was and in the end they stayed indoors, somehow transitioning from building a cat trap to having a tea party.

"I thought you were supposed to get me up for my evening pills," Sadie asked a few hours later.

To this Jilly replied, "Huh? Oh hey, the sun went down."

Sadie went to the window and looked out. "It's been down for a while. Did Nico stop by? He should be back by now, or at the very least he should have stopped by to check in. Did he? No, of course he didn't. He would've woken me up. So what do you think happened?"

"Nothing, probably. He should be ok," Jillybean assured her. "He is big even for a grode-up."

The Goth girl didn't find this very reassuring and she stayed at the window long after she should have. Now that Jillybean was aware of the time, she began the steps involved in securing the house: dark sheets went over the windows, she checked the perimeter, and then lit candles for both light and heat.

Eventually she had to pull Sadie back. "The candles, Sadie. I lit the candles, you can't be there. And you look all weird. Are you hungry? We have one more box of mac-n-cheese."

"Gross," Sadie said, allowing herself to be pulled back from the window. "Without milk and butter that ain't mac-n-cheese. It's orange crap."

Well, how do you like that? Ipes said sharply. *We go out of our way to help her and this is how she acts? How ungrateful!*

"Is that what means not saying thank you?" Jillybean asked under her breath. Ipes declared it was. "She's been sick," Jilly stated, making allowances for her idol.

Sadie refused all of Jillybean's food ideas. She sat on the couch coughing weakly and growing more pale by the second. When Nico came in at nine that evening Sadie launched herself on him and cried. "Sorry," she said a number of times. "It's being sick. Whenever I get sick I get extra emotional."

Nico didn't seem to mind. He caught her tears and then laid her down on the couch. When he made the mac-n-cheese she didn't complain though in Jillybean's eyes hers was better. The Russian's mind wasn't on the task at hand. He alternated between fixating on Sadie and griping about how poorly equipped they were to go on a long journey.

"Look," he said, holding up a two quart bottle. It was a little less than half full. "Is all gas that I find. Is not good. And these gun? I have fourteen rounds. What is this good for? Nothing! We should not be in hurry to find Sarah. She has make her decision."

"I don't know what the right thing to do is," Sadie admitted.

Jillybean and Ipes looked at each other but neither said anything. It wasn't Jillybean's place to as far as she was concerned. She was seven and deferred, generally, to the wishes of grownups. Sadie was different.

You ever notice that Sadie doesn't like to make too many decisions, Ipes remarked.

"Whatcha mean?" Jillybean asked. She had slipped away and was now pulling items out of her pockets that she had collected over the course of the day and setting them next to her bed. Already she had a gold pen, two C batteries that she had tested on her tongue, a handful of crabapples, and a seven-inch rubber band. Currently she was wondering if she could use the rubber band to shoot the crabapples across the room.

She folds to the dominant personality around her. Remember the night we set those boats on fire? Neil had told her to run away and she did, but you told her to go back and she did that too.

"So?" Jillybean asked. She stuck a crabapple in one end of the loop and drew the rubber band far back. "Is that a bad thing?"

No. It's just a thing worth noting...he paused as she let the crabapple fly. It plinked up against the stove, square in the little pane of glass in its door. *Nice shot. Who do you think she will side with? The man she loves or the man she's accepted as her father?*

"Does it have to be a man?"

No, Ipes replied. *Sadie will listen to you if you come up with a good idea, and you're just a kid. She also used to listen to Sarah. What are you trying to hit?*

Jillybean had settled down in her nest and was now aiming the rubber band: one loop over her outstretched thumb. "I'm aiming at whatever I hit," she replied. The band stretched nearly the length of her arm, and the idea of it slipping made her nervous. She could lose an eye as her mom had always warned. But she didn't slip and the rubber band zipped from her fingers to smack the wall next to the stove. She'd been aiming at the saltshaker that sat on the edge of the oven, two feet over.

I guess you were aiming at the house, Ipes said. *You're a regular Robin Hood.*

"Stupid zebra," she grumbled under her breath. She then picked up one of the crabapples. "You think these are any good?"

I wouldn't try it; you just brushed your teeth.

"So? I won't get a cavity from one little apple-thing." Without waiting for a response she popped it into her mouth and began chewing. She stopped after two seconds as her face twisted.

Pretty sour, isn't it?

The apple was so fantastically sour that her face continued to turn and torque and she made the noise: "Ooooh." Normal speech was, for the moment, impossible.

I bet it's worse since you just brushed your teeth. Too bad you weren't warned ahead of time.

She was still in a state of facial contortion when Neil came into the kitchen. "Are you ok?" he asked going down on one knee. "Is there something wrong?"

"Crabapple," she managed to say as her eyes started twitching. "Ooooh."

"Oh. Those suckers are tart." She offered him one and he shook his head. "We still have people food. We don't have to eat like squirrels just yet. Tell me, are you ready for tomorrow? I want to leave first thing." With the zombie menace being what it was, first thing meant about nine in the morning depending if it was cloudy or not.

"So you found enough gas?" Jillybean asked. Neil's face dropped which she read correctly. "But Nico said we shouldn't go unprepared. You know, without enough gas and stuff."

Neil offered her a toothy grin. "We're ready enough, don't you worry." He then gave her a kiss goodnight and tucked her in.

Jillybean wasn't fooled in the least by Neil's demeanor. "He didn't get any more gas."

Not a drop, Ipes shot right back.

"Do you think they're going to fight?" she asked. Neil had gone into the living room and his voice was very low.

Not with their fists, if that's what you mean, Ipes said with a note of disappointment. In order to hear better, Jilly crept to the edge of the living room and listened.

"Then you are feeling better, good," Neil was saying to Sadie. "I want to get as early a start as possible. Make sure you're all packed."

"Da, but first we find fuel," Nico suggested. "Then we go on journey. We would not want to waste time to go so short way with little fuel we have."

"It's not a waste of time," Neil said, just off the edge of calm. "We've checked everywhere around here for gas and have come up empty. So I think it'd be smart to check somewhere else. The gas we have should get us eighty miles down the road. Who knows what we'll find there? Greener pastures I hope."

"Green pasture?" Nico asked. "What does this mean? In farms?"

"It's a saying we have. It means somewhere newer and nicer," Sadie explained. "And maybe somewhere with more gas."

Nico nodded his approval of this. "Da, finding gas is good. Finding Sarah is nyet, not good. She is looking for one-way trip, not to come back. That is her decision. My decision is we should not be go to New Eden. Especially my Sadie. She is nonbeliever. She tell me what this means. Is not good."

"We're all nonbelievers," Neil said. "It's dangerous for all of us."

The Russian let out a weary, theatrical sigh before saying, "Da, that is all the more reason to stay away. Neil, you give up on baby because of so much great danger and that was smart. I think is smart to give up on Sarah, too."

Jillybean could sense Neil's emotion through the wall. His facial expressions seemed to be shifting with his feelings: denial, anger, self-hatred. "I gave up on her...on Eve, because I knew that to get her back meant one or more of us would die. When I was sick I would lie in bed and I couldn't decide who I wanted that to be. You know? Who would you choose if you had to trade one life for another?"

Nico faltered over this question, but Sadie was quick to say, "Myself."

Neil smiled at her answer at first, but then he became grim. "Who would you choose other than yourself?"

The question was met with silence, which only increased Jillybean's instant fear. She was sure her name was on the top of everyone's list. It only made sense. Sadie loved Nico and Neil. No one had ever said they loved Jillybean. Neil had adopted Sadie, but no one had mentioned a thing about adopting Jillybean. That left Nico who rarely even looked in Jillybean's direction and couldn't even pronounce her name right. He would not vote for his girlfriend, or another grown up, especially one who didn't have to be worried about being bitten by the monsters.

Don't forget, they tried to trade you before, Ipes said, adding to her fears.

They certainly had. It was something no one ever talked about however, being traded like a fish at the market wasn't something she would ever forget. The incident had been brushed under the rug and Jillybean had hoped it was a one-time lunacy on Neil's part, only now the concept of trading people one for another had arisen again, sending a cold shiver down her back.

You should pack your stuff and get out of here, pronto, Ipes suggested.

Before she could respond or react, or question the word *pronto*, Neil spoke, "You see? You can't choose anyone else and neither could I."

"But that was with baby," Nico said. "Now with Sarah you change your minds. You trade us all for one person. It makes no sense. There is too much great danger."

"I can't keep letting people go without trying," Neil said. "I can't keep making excuses for not doing the right thing."

There seemed to Jillybean to be a balance in the room: safety versus holding a family together. Nico versus Neil, with Sadie the deciding vote. As Ipes had pointed out, Sadie didn't like being put on the spot and there came such a long silence that Jillybean could hardly stand it.

Finally, Sadie gave a half-shrug and committed, somewhat halfheartedly, to both men. "I think actually trying to get into New Eden may be just too dangerous. It won't be one or two of us getting killed, it'll be all of us. On the other hand I think we should go after Sarah. It's the right thing to do to try to stop her from killing herself."

"That's right," Neil agreed. "That's why I want to get going early. I want to be able to cut her off before she gets too far south. We should all have out bags packed and..."

He went on, but Jillybean tuned him out. "They aren't going to trade me," she said, feeling slightly giddy and then suddenly very tired.

I wouldn't have let them, Ipes assured.

"And what would a little zebra like you have done?" Jillybean asked, climbing into her nest of pillows and blankets. She was warm and so very comfy that she was on the slip edge of consciousness when Ipes answered:

You'd be surprised what I can do.

Chapter 13

Sarah

Northern Maryland

With the late afternoon light striking her dead in the face, Sarah hit the highway fence and went up it like a lion. The lion isn't known as the best climbers in the cat kingdom. When they have to climb they aren't in the least graceful; they generally "muscle" it up and Sarah did the same thing. It didn't help that she climbed the fence almost midway between the supporting posts. The fence yawed inward at an odd angle and then as she got to the top, it rocked back the other way, almost making her lose her grip.

"Mother fucker!" she cried.

With that same lioness strength she clung to the wire until she was able to swing a leg over. Then it was just a matter of jumping and listening as cloth tore. She had on a floral shawl that had snagged somewhere and was now in two pieces. In truth, she couldn't have cared less about her gypsy attire.

The hundreds of zombies in front of her, and the racing black Jeep behind, kept her focused on what was important: living beyond the next two minutes.

Sarah ran at the zombies. They were strung out, coming up from the white-trash neighborhood in a long grey wave. She ran at them before they could coalesce into a dense mob. Strung out as they were she hoped to rupture their lines with a few well placed head shots and zip through.

Her first two shots missed completely and her third only wounded. Sarah realized she had begun shooting from too far away. Now, she ran up until she could see the yellow pus running from their eyes. At this range heads exploded and black blood vaporized, creating a dark mist that hung over the corpses.

Twelve shots in ten seconds blasted a big enough gap. She raced through the converging mob and into the warren-like neighborhood. The houses here were low rent: paint peeling off the clapboard siding in long strips, shutters hanging askew, window screens held together with duct tape. Dotted among them were little gems, homes where people actually cared, but for the most part the crumbling neighborhood seemed ready made to spawn zombies.

Out of every home the undead came, on and on; there seemed to be an endless number of them. Sarah shot her Beretta only when she had to. The definition of "when she had to" gradually narrowed as she went through bullets faster than she could reload. Soon she shot only when a zombie was right in her path. The streets were so crammed with the beasts that this happened at every turn.

She had hoped to be able to dash through the town and into the woods beyond, however there were just too many zombies. Eventually she was forced into one of the little ranch houses, where she spent a futile minute barricading the door only to have zombies blast in the front window.

Without wasting a moment on thought, she ran for the back door, smashing through it with a bang, like a kid on the first day of summer, eager to see the unfettered world. Sarah's world was hardly unfettered. There were zombies in the backyard too, and more came spilling around the sides of the house. They were being drawn by the sharp crack her Beretta made when she was forced to kill. But what could she to do? Not to fire it meant being dragged down and eaten.

The question would have to be answered some other time, possibly when she ran out of bullets. Sarah took off through the weeds and the year-old dog crap that lay crumbling in the sun. She ran for a waist-high, chainlink fence that separated one ill-kept backyard from another, and vaulted it awkwardly, landing on her hands and knees, drawing blood from one of her palms.

Still, she had put a barrier between her and the greatest portion of her pursuers. The zombies crushed up against the fence but few could find a way over it. Those that did were more or less pushed over the top to go face first into the grass of the next yard.

Sarah had been gasping for breath and backing away from the horde but as the first fell into the yard she turned and ran. With her heavy pack swaying, and the rifle banging against her shoulder bones, and the split shawl flapping, she was a slow runner and only just made it to the next dinky little house ahead of the zombies.

Thankfully, she found the back door unlocked, a situation she remedied the moment she rushed into the house. The lock was flimsy and the door had a hollow core —it wouldn't last, but neither would Sarah, at this rate. Desperate to catch her breath and reload, she pushed a chair in front of the door and dropped onto it. Almost immediately the door was attacked with great thumps and splintery crashes.

As she fumbled out a box of ammo and began sliding bullets, one after another into the Beretta's clip she hummed quietly, nervously, trying to match the cadence of the sound of the battering. She paused as the she slapped the clip back in place. Next she took the empty clip that she had automatically pocketed and began refilling it.

"*Mother, mother, mother, what's going on?*" she sang the old Marvin Gaye song, the words quivering as they left her throat. Behind her the door began to come apart under the assault. With forced calm, she willed the bullets into place. To her right, in one of the back bedrooms, glass shattered. "Shit!" she cried. She then began to rock as she worked and sang: "*What's going on? What's going on? What's…*" Her song faltered as a section of the flimsy door just behind her back broke away and a grey, scabbed-over hand reached in.

Leaning forward to stay out of reach, Sarah finished topping off her clip and then, after taking a deep breath, she fast walked to the front door and flung it open. A zombie fell inside. It had apparently been pushing on the door to get in and now it was sprawled at Sarah's feet. She didn't waste a bullet.

Instead she stepped around it and went outside to squint into the low, raking light of the dying afternoon. She found herself in someone's front yard. There was a street, some cars, a broken bike, and many, many zombies. They stared at her for all of a second before she was at it again, once more, running for her life.

There was no going back. She plowed ahead, using cars and hedges and now another house as a means to keep out of reach of the throngs of dead. She left one street behind, only to find another just like it. And then a third where she couldn't run fast enough and she had to resort to using the Beretta again.

When it went off she noted how it seemed to spit flame —the sunlight was fading rapidly and when it was gone out of the sky...

"Shit," Sarah cursed. She had to find shelter, a place to hide, or fortify, or anything, before the dark came to claim her. It was unquestioned: the undead ruled the night. Her fear spurred her on and she passed two more streets the hard way, climbing fences and dodging the dead.

Then she came to the edge of the subdivision, where the houses ended and the woods began. There was a stretch of rodent prairie a hundred yards wide between the two. It was blessedly empty. There wasn't a single zombie to be seen in the gathering evening before her.

Normally, the woods were not a place she would consider safe, but it appeared that all the shooting she had done had drawn them into the little subdivision.

"The woods couldn't be worse than this," she said under her breath. She was wrong. After only a few steps she saw the last light of the afternoon glint off of something in the woods. It was something darker than the coming shadows. It was the black Jeep. As she had wasted time fighting her way through the neighborhood, the bounty hunter had just skirted it altogether to wait for her on the other side.

The thought of the bounty hunter struck a dirty chord in her heart. Zombies were evil, inherently so. It was fundamental to their nature; in other words they couldn't help what they were. It was impossible for them to try. On the other hand, Sarah knew the bounty hunter to be purposefully, thoughtfully cruel. He was also fearfully determined. Sarah didn't want to find out what lengths he would go to in order to discover Sadie and Nico's location.

Turning on her heel, she ran back to the subdivision, though not in a straight line. In the few seconds she had spent in the field, zombies had closed in on her. There weren't more than a dozen which, after the masses she had escaped from earlier, seemed like child's play to escape from. She dodged to her right and made for the nearest house while behind, an engine's roar sent a fresh wave of adrenaline through her.

Although she told herself not to look back, she did anyway, just in time to see the Jeep break from the tree line and make right for her. It covered the hundred yards of the little prairie belt in twenty seconds. By then Sarah was racing once again through the neighborhood. She kept off the streets and went yard to yard.

Zombies seemed to be going in every direction and by ill-luck Sarah ducked into a house that wasn't a house any longer. It had scorched walls, part of a roof, a few feet of blackened flooring and the front door. She took one step in, saw the sky through a gaping, charred wound in the ceiling and stopped, inches from a drop into a pit that had once been a basement, but was now an ash-filled crag.

Just then, the Jeep turned down the street and came tooling along very slowly. In haste, Sarah shut the door. Even this little movement was too much for the weakened structure to bear; the floor beneath her gave way and she dropped. The Beretta went flying as she flung out her hands to catch hold of anything that would keep her from impaling herself on the debris below. Her hand caught what had once been part of a stud, but was now only a piece of wood unconnected to anything.

She and the stud dropped into the grey gloom. There were sharp pains in her back and legs as her fall was arrested by splintery boards and the blackened remains of furniture. She was cut and scraped up and down her body, yet somehow she managed to keep her lips pressed shut.

Holding in a whimper she peered through the gloom all about her with a feeling of surrender growing inside. Nearly ninety percent of the house had burned up in some months-old fire and had fallen into the basement. All she knew was that the gun was somewhere in the gloom to her right where there was wreckage of twisted metal and ash ten feet deep. She had no time to look for it. Outside, the Jeep had stopped, while inside, something was clawing its way toward her. There was a zombie in the pit with her.

Chapter 14

Sarah Rivers

Northern Maryland

The zombie advancing on Sarah was charbroiled. There was no other way to describe it. Its skin, which should have been a repulsive grey, had been blackened like a piece of chicken left too long over the coals. Its hair had been seared away leaving a cracking and blistered pate and, to make matters worse, it was frightfully naked, showing to the world the crispy curled flesh where its manhood had once been.

Sarah felt her lunch coming up. It went right to the back of her throat and threatened to come heaving out of her just as the first of the gun shots rang out. For just a moment she felt wild elation, thinking that it wasn't the bounty hunter at all, but someone there to rescue her. The elation was short lived.

"Come on out, Sadie! I won't hurt you. We'll just talk." It was the bounty hunter, who was obviously confused over who it was he had managed to corner. With her new haircut, Sarah clearly resembled Sadie more than she thought. "You might be able to hide from me, but there's a thousand stiffs heading right for us. They'll get you…"

He paused to shoot a few more times. As he did, Sarah glanced back toward the zombie. It had clawed its way closer. With its lips and tongue burned away, it was silent for a zombie, strangely making it even more menacing than normal. Sarah picked up the stud that had fallen in the pit with her and poked at it, hoping to fend it off. It didn't work. The zombie grabbed the board and tried to pull it away. They fought in silence over the piece of wood as the shooting stopped.

"Don't be like this, Sadie," the bounty hunter yelled. "I get paid even if I bring you back as a zombie. Is that what you want?"

Something shifted beneath Sarah and the zombie and they both dropped deeper. Sarah's head was practically covered by the ash and the wreckage. The wooden stud was gone. She tried to get the rifle off her back, but it was hopelessly caught on something unseen behind her.

"I hear you, Sadie," the bounty hunter said.

Practically above her, the door opened and Sarah froze in place as the bounty hunter took a single step onto the rickety floor. The man wasn't at all as Neil had described: *dressed exactly like a bush.* In the dark night, the ghillie suit the hunter wore rippled and flared in a light wind and from below he looked demonic; a living shadow without true form or substance beneath.

In one hand he held a flashlight which he beamed all over the pit before him. Though it was not yet full dark out, the pit was arrayed in shades of grey and black shadows. The hunter saw the zombie, which thankfully, turned its attention upwards. He also should have seen Sarah. As the beam came at her she closed her eyes and remained stalk still. For a second the light ran right over her, and then whisked away again to take in the edges of the pit.

"Shit," the hunter griped after a moment. "Fine, get eaten by the zombies. That's alright with me. I'll be back in the morning to get your sorry, grey ass."

Just like that he was gone, shooting a few zombies that got between him and his Jeep. When the engine faded away, Sarah and the zombie looked at each other. For half a moment it looked as though the beast would turn away. Was she so covered in soot as to be unrecognizable?

The answer was no. It took a bit of staring and more than a bit of pondering on its part, but the zombie finally concluded or perhaps remembered that she was a human. He began to claw at her again. For her part, she tried to push away from it, only to slide deeper. She was standing on something that gave no leverage; every time she tried to push off she'd slip further into the quagmire.

Somehow the zombie was able to find a sturdy footing and lurched at her. It got within three feet before it got snagged in the springs of what might have once been a couch. Up to that point Sarah had been basically stuck in place. With a huge effort she forced herself away from the beast only to sink again, but now her foot hit something solid and reaching down she felt the edge of a bathtub.

A question slipped through her mind: How the hell did that get by the front door? The question went unanswered. It didn't matter. All that mattered was that it gave her purchase enough to push herself halfway out of the bog of cinder and waste. From halfway she was able to grab the edge of a joist above her. The next move required a real struggle: she had to pull herself, the rifle and the backpack up using only the muscles in her arms.

She lacked the upper body strength and succeeded only in exhausting herself before she sagged back down into the pit. Behind and below her, the creature was not stopped by exhaustion. Somehow it pulled itself off the springs of the couch. There was a sucking sound and when Sarah looked back she saw that the zombie had left behind the blackened husk of its own skin.

At the sight of the skinless creature, Sarah went dizzy and wondered, in a disconcertingly calm way, if she was about to faint. Her body felt disconnected from her brain, as though her head were floating. She sagged in what she could only describe as a "pre-faint" and as she sunk back into the buried bathtub her shifting weight caused part of the structure around her to crumble. This exposed a fire-warped hunk of plastic and metal which after a moment of confusion, she recognized as what had once been a vacuum cleaner.

Pick it up! Her mind screamed in a distant sort of way. It was like the command of some outside force and she did as she was told, hefting it above her head, holding it there with shaking arms until the fleshless zombie was almost in range. Grunting like a cave-woman she dashed it down with all her force and watched, still in a fainting mood, as the zombie's head came apart.

"Ok...ok...that's done," she said in a breathy whisper, before leaning back into the dangerous remains of the fire to relax for a moment. It wasn't comfortable, but she needed to collect herself before she turned her full attention to getting out of the pit.

She saw that getting out was going to be simply a matter of dragging up the sturdier chunks of wood and heavy crap and building a ramp of sorts. It was a fantastically dirty and very dangerous undertaking, and the entire time she worked at it she just knew that if Jillybean had been there she would have said something like: Why don't you just do this simple thing, or take that easy way?

Unfortunately for her, Sarah could not think of the easier way and when she finally made it to the little lip of foyer which was all that was left of the inside of the house, she whispered, "I did it all by myself," and felt silly doing so.

She then dragged open the front door to the house and came, literally, face-to-face with a zombie. It had been a woman at one point and the two of them were of equal height. The zombie leaned in, staring, trying to fathom out the dreadful apparition that Sarah had become.

This time, Sarah didn't wait for the zombie to come to any conclusion. She simply grabbed the zombie by the arm and yanked it across the threshold of the door, sending it face first into the pit.

There were more zombies in the street. Most gazed at her in their stupid manner before turning to go about their business, however a few were curious enough about her to start heading her way.

Now the first thought in Sarah's mind was: *What would Jillybean do?* The answer came quick: act like a zombie. Jillybean had told the story of Ram; of how he had infiltrated the zombies by pretending to be one of them. The little girl had even demonstrated how to do it, complete with make-up and moans.

Sarah wasn't going to need the make-up. She was head-to-toe, black as night and looked more like something that had just dragged its way from hell than an actual person. She sort of felt that way, too. The fall into the pit made it so that she didn't have to fake either the limp Jillybean had suggested, or the groan. They were very real.

Sarah went into zombie-mode and passed inspection with flying colors. No one and no thing bothered her as she gimped back to her car. It turned out to be a waste of a trip through the deadly little town. Before she even got to the fence, she saw the Honda had its doors flung and its trunk sprung.

The bounty hunter had already been through it taking everything of actual value. Sarah still had her clothes and her sleeping bag, but she lost her food, her fuel and her common sense. For some reason she didn't find it the least bit foolish to climb into the Honda, lock the doors and fall straight away to sleep.

She was fortunate that the bounty hunter had other traps to set and that he didn't come back along that stretch of highway. It was for certain he would have noticed the Honda's doors shut, and the person sleeping inside.

Fortune was on her side and she slept peacefully, especially when a light rain came to patter among her dream of Eve and Neil. It was a long, in-depth dream that she never wanted to end, but Jillybean woke her. In her dream the little girl came to her and shook her, saying: *The early bird catches the worm.*

It was not early when she woke, however with the clouds and the mist hanging low over the earth it seemed early. Sarah fell back to sleep, but immediately resumed the dream of Jillybean: *Get up early bird, Neil is making pancakes.*

"I'm up, Jilly," Sarah mumbled. "Give it a rest." She ran her hand over her face, but stopped in shock as she saw the color of her palm. Sitting up she gave herself a quick look in the mirror. "Whoa! Look at me."

Somehow she had managed to cover the entire interior of the car in black ash without losing even a shade of it on her own skin. "No one will recognize me now," she said, noting how brilliantly white her smile was compared to the black. The smile disappeared when a thought struck her: "But they'll try to recognize me."

The Believers wouldn't let her into New Eden without a thorough scrubbing and then they'd be keen to see who it was under all that ash. There was a possibility that they would recognize her then. No, she couldn't go in looking like a chimney sweep. She'd go in looking like her new self and no one would be the wiser.

Sarah poked around in the backpack she had taken from the swinging dead man in the tree and found a can of pineapple chunks that would do for breakfast. After she ate, she added some extra clothes to the pack and roped her sleeping bag on top. When she was done she stared at the pack until a little voice in her mind said: *That doesn't look like a monster's backpack, that looks like a people pack.*

"That's because it is a people pack, Jillybean," Sarah said. Sighing, she tore off the sleeping bag, and then dumped out everything. She looked at the array: clothes, food, utensils, can openers, candles, flashlight, and sleeping bag. She needed all of it, but what would Jillybean take?

The question just popped into her head. "What the hell is my deal? Who knows what Jilly would take?" Her *I'm a Belieber* backpack was always filled with so many oddities that it was enough to make a person's head spin.

But this was different.

"I don't need a sleeping bag," Sarah said, pushing it aside. There were blankets in every house. "And I don't need any more clothes than what I have on my back." There were also clothes in every house. She packed the food, the can opener, a lighter, and a single fork. Everything else she left on the side of the road. *This was a one way trip*, she reminded herself. It wasn't a scrounging expedition.

She took off the torn and tattered shawl, but did not cast it aside. With a grunt she slung the pack on her shoulders. The rifle went across the top of it, running through the straps to stay in place. It was a weak weapon against zombies, but there was still the bounty hunter to worry about. Finally, she took the tattered shawl and draped it across herself where it hung oddly.

Once she was decked out, she began her limping way back toward the ratty neighborhood. This she skirted to the south, making sure to keep to the woods. These weren't the thick stands of the Appalachians where the greenery was sometimes a solid, impassable wall and the likelihood of getting lost increased with every step, these woods were thin, little more than surviving trees crowded on one side by the strip of I95 and on the other by suburbia.

Eventually, in another ten miles or so, the neighborhoods would give way to little self-sufficient towns, which in turn would lose their cohesion and become homesteads and farms. However that wouldn't last either. Baltimore lay directly along her path, and no amount of ash or zombie make-up would get her to walk through that city. It had a bad reputation even when humans lived there.

At first, Sarah kept to the forest. This was in spite of the zombies, which stood about, unmoving, looking like stunted trees. For the most part they seemed asleep on their feet and did not bother her unless she came too close. If they noticed her, she went deeper into her acting which always fooled them.

She kept to the woods because they were safe. The forest concealed her from the bounty hunter. It was her hope that she was leaving him behind with every step; that he had gone back to the low rent neighborhood hoping to catch sight of a zombie that matched Sadie's description. However, she didn't believe the man would sit around there for too long. He wasn't a "hanging around" type of guy. In her gut she knew he was searching…hunting really.

He had Sarah's scent and was now after her. This was why, instead of looking for fuel and transportation, she walked through the mists and the trees for hours, slowly heading on a parallel path to the highway. She tromped under the green canopy where everything was damp and as she walked she thought about the family she had left behind.

Were they still in the ranch house she had abandoned them in? Or had they found gas and a car and were already at New Eden? It was possible. With enough gas it was only a fourteen hour trip and this was the third day she had been gone. But it wasn't likely. Neil, who was very cautious, wouldn't chance moving Sadie until her pneumonia was almost cured, which was today according to Sarah's calculations.

"At least they didn't have the bounty hunter to worry about," Sarah said to herself. The thought was reassuring until she began speculating on the tenacity of the hunter. What if he had reset his tire-blowing, radio trap?

"Damn," Sarah whispered, looking back the way she had come. She had put ten miles between her and the spot on the highway where she had been ambushed the day before. If Neil had figured out which way she was going it would mean he would come barreling into the trap any minute.

"Damn, damn, damn," Sarah hissed, feeling real emotion inside her for the first time in weeks. Yes, she had felt fear when she'd been stuck in the ash pit with the zombie, however that had been her body's reaction to outside stimulus. This was a reaction from the soul: her loved ones were in real, immediate danger.

"What do I do? How do I warn Neil?" Should she go back and see if the hunter had reset the trap? That would mean another three hour hike. Her only other option seemed to be to find a working car and drive back, which, though it sounded great, was something far easier said than done. She could be all day looking for a car.

Which way to go?

She decided to pin her hopes on finding a car. In a fever of worry, Sarah raced due west where she saw the top of a distant building. It wasn't a long run, not upwards of two miles, yet her head was dizzy when she burst out of the woods and into the strewn remains of a proper America town. There was a main street where everything was brick or painted stark white. There was a grocery store, a school, a quaint little park, and all the rest that would make people nostalgic for summer days and apple pie.

Sarah ignored all that. She hurried to the nearest car—some little foreign thing that she didn't make any attempt at recognizing. To her it was nothing more than a car and the only question was, did it have gas?

It didn't. Neither did the next one or the next. She ran down the street, so focused on the cars that she didn't see the first of the zombies come staggering at her. If it hadn't accidentally kicked a rock it probably would have came right up and ate her.

She saw the thing just in time. There were others, of course, but this one had a bead on Sarah and bore down on her at its greatest speed. Nimbly, she stepped aside at the last moment and she even had the presence of mind to leave an outstretched leg in the zombie's path. It fell hard, but wasted no time getting up in spite of the fact that its nose was now turned sideways on its face.

Sarah barely noticed. She ran for the nearest building which turned out to be a junk shop of sorts. Though the sign above the door read "Consignments" it looked like someone had walled in a garage sale. It hardly mattered what the building was for. Sarah used it to get away from the zombies that were bull rushing her. Through the front door she went and after zig-zagging through the not so carefully stacked merchandise, she was out the back, slamming the door behind her.

She found herself in a wide alley that looked like it hadn't known there'd even been an apocalypse. It seemed like any alley she had ever stepped foot in: trash in the corners, weeds sprouting in the seams of the cement, a little graffiti, a bum…

It was a real bum. Not a zombie in rags, but a man, dirty and smelling of urine. His hair was eight months long, matted in parts, and stuck up in an electrified manner in others. His beard was a demonstration of his insanity: under his chin on the right side it was burned away while on the left it was a tangled jungle, home to a bottle cap, assorted fluff, and a paperclip.

"Go away, fucker," the bum seethed. "This is mine. All of this." He waved his arms expansively at the dirty alley. "Go away or you'll get the pipe."

At first she thought "the pipe" was a sexual reference, but then the bum picked up a length of pipe the size of a baseball bat. He brandished it over his head, but only waited. Sarah wasn't going to wait. With a great deal of fumbling, she wrestled the rifle from her back and aimed it at the bum.

"What the fuck" he asked in a tone of awe. "Are you guys starting to remember? Are you seeing again? Can you see me? I'm Artie, remember? Me and Beth always did those block parties? I bowled on Wednesdays at the *King's Pin*? Remember that? And on Thursdays we'd stay home because Beth always liked her shows. But on Fridays we'd go out to the Megaplex. Do you remember the Megaplex?"

"I don't know the Megaplex," Sarah answered when it became clear that Artie was looking for a real answer. "I'm Sarah Rivers. I need gas. Do you have any? Or do you have a car I can borrow?"

"Sarah Rivers? Did you just call yourself Sarah Rivers?"

"Yes. Have you heard of me?" She was worried he had. It would mean the bounty hunter had been through there asking questions, and, judging by the man's loose mental state, it must have been recently.

"Have I heard of you?" the bum asked theatrically. "Have I heard of Sarah Rivers? No. And do you want to know why? Because there isn't anybody named Sarah Rivers in Easton. I'd know if there was and there isn't, so that makes you an imposter. A zombie imposter who talks! What will they think of next?"

"But I'm not a zombie," Sarah said. With the rains from the night before there were plenty of puddles. She knelt over one and splashed the soot from her face. "You see? I'm a person."

The bum only laughed at her as though he thought she was still trying to trick him. "Oh no, that won't help at all. There isn't a person named Sarah Rivers in Easton. I was on the yearbook committee! You see? I would know. I would know if you existed and you don't. You're not a person and you're not a zombie. You're nothing. That's what you are. So go away, nothing. Go away or you'll get the pipe."

"Sure thing, psycho," Sarah said, backing away, keeping the rifle trained on the bum. When she hit the edge of the alley she asked, "What about gas? Do you know where any is?"

"Nothings don't get gas," the bum said.

"It's for the mayor," Sarah countered. "He asked me to look around for some."

This caused the bum to begin a mad cackling. In response, Sarah stepped even further away. "Why lie, Sarah Nothings?" the man demanded. "Don't you know I'm the mayor? If you were a part of this town, you'd know. Elections were held on New Year's Day and I won by a single vote! I ran a good clean campaign. I didn't stoop to lies like you did, Sarah Liars. That's your new name: Sarah Liars."

"Whatever," Sarah said. The alley had ended at a narrow, two-lane street. In one direction was a run of cars, parked neatly. In the other direction: zombies. She flung the gun over her shoulder and went into her zombie routine, heading for the parked cars in a slow stumble, making sure to keep her semi-cleaned face pointed down, but ready to sprint away if she was discovered.

There was little chance of that. Behind her, the mayor of Easton continued to call her names in a high voice. Next he took to berating the zombies for coming into "his area." Sarah didn't look back.

The cars were all dry. In desperation, she went to the main street and after checking each of the cars there she went to a row of bikes that were chained to a rack. All their tires were flat and the rubber appeared to be degrading faster than she thought was physically possible.

"What am I going to do?" she asked. But then another question struck her: What would Jillybean do? The answer was as obvious as it was useless. "She'd start a fucking fire. That's what she'd do. Fires seemed to be her answer to every little prob…"

As she was complaining she was picturing a fire: huge, roaring, and billowing black smoke. Jilly would have started it in the *Kinkos* across from the City hall, because of all the paper. Without gas, she'd need something readily flammable. However all that paper would mean the smoke would be seen for miles and it would surely attract the bounty hunter. He would have to leave his trap if he was going to come investigate.

Sarah smiled at where her train of thought had gone. "Thanks, Jillybean," she whispered, heading for the *Kinkos*. The fire would indeed be glorious. It would smoke like a volcano and Sarah was sure it would attract the hunter. But he wouldn't be the hunter any longer; not when Sarah had a high-powered rifle and a great location to shoot from.

Atop the city hall was a clock tower. In her eyes, there was no more fitting location than a clock tower to turn hunter into prey. But first the fire!

Chapter 15

Neil Martin

Northern Maryland

It was still dark when Neil woke. His first awareness was loneliness, then sadness, then began the biting nervousness that would sit in his gut until he got his first taste of action. He always seemed to be nervous over something. That morning it was the zombies he would have to fight, and the bounty hunter who was after them, and the idea that he was already far too late to catch up to Sarah, and of course, he was afraid of the unknown.

The unknown had always bothered him more than almost anything. Neil was a man of routine. It was his defining characteristic and had been since he could remember. In his old life, people who knew him could count on his routine almost to the minute. He was always fifteen minutes early for work. On Fridays, his numbers would be in by eleven sharp. He had lunch at his desk every day but Wednesdays when he would treat himself to one of three restaurants. Every night he was home by six and by seven he had more than likely trounced the featured contestants on *Jeopardy* while he ate his carefully prepared dinner

Now, he had to wonder where his next meal would come from, and he didn't even want to think about their fuel situation. That was a sure-fire way to an ulcer.

To keep from thinking about that or the fact that a light rain was falling—meaning they would be delayed again—Neil crept to the kitchen to prepare breakfast. Though he moved with all the stealth of a mouse, Jillybean still cracked an eye and watched him from her nest of blankets.

"Good morning," he whispered.

After a glance to the window she asked, "Is it really morning? It's awful dark."

"Oh yes, it's morning," Neil assured her. "It's just a dark morning because of the heavy clouds. You want to help with breakfast? I have a surprise."

When it came to routines, Jillybean was the opposite of Neil. In her mind, new was, in all ways, better than old. The idea of not knowing where or when her next meal would come from, not only didn't bother her, it was far preferable to eating the same thing every day.

Clearly, she enjoyed surprises, even gastronomical ones.

"Yes, please," she said. "What kind of surprise?"

"We're having pancakes," he said. Her smile turned false. Pancakes weren't much of a surprise since he had made two attempts at them already both times with poor results. With the first try all he had to work with was the boxed mix and some grainy water. He added vegetable oil to the second attempt which helped only a little. This time would be different. "I know they haven't been all that good in the past, but look at what I found yesterday."

With a flourish, he produced an egg in each hand. Again her look was one of disappointment.

"Ipes says to be careful, because eggs go rotten and you can't tell until you open them up. We saw that on a cartoon once."

"Does Ipes know that these are fresh eggs?" Neil asked, partially talking to the stuffed toy. "I saw the chicken myself! It was a wild chicken just walking across the road."

"You did?" Jilly said, jumping out of her covers and rushing over to inspect the eggs.

Neil bent to start a fire in the barbeque and after gently blowing on the flames to get the coals going, he turned back to Jillybean. "Yep. The chicken just sort of pecked about and then went back across the road for a few minutes and then it re-crossed. It did this for over fifteen minutes going back and forth. Finally, I went to see if it had a nest and sure enough there was a little burrowed out area in the tall grass next to this one house and in it were these two eggs."

119

"Cool," Jillybean said.

She was eager to help and he allowed her to do all the measuring and stirring, but since he was worried about egg shell fragments winding up in the pancakes, he reserved the honor of cracking them himself. Right before he did, she dropped this little bombshell on what he thought was going to be the perfect breakfast to travel on: "You know there might be a baby chicken in that egg."

He hadn't thought about that. His hand stopped halfway to the mixing bowl as he felt a sudden queasiness strike.

"What do you think it looks like?" Jillybean asked. Clearly the idea of him plopping a dead baby chicken into the pancake batter wasn't nearly as unpleasant in her mind as it was in his. "I bet it's all squishy. I think they come out icky, but then they get like a blow dryer on them that makes their fur stand up."

Neil figured the baby chicken would be both dead and icky. It turned him off pancakes altogether, but since Jillybean was still looking hopeful, he glanced at the egg in his hand. "I wonder how you can tell if there's a chicken in there," he said.

"I dunno," Jillybean said, picking up the second egg and putting it to her ear. "I don't hear any peeps or any chicken noises." She gave it a vigorous shake. "It seems juicy inside."

Juicy, Neil didn't like the sound of that. His stomach liked it less. "Maybe I should just chip off the top and see."

Jillybean gave him a look. "Ipes says this is an all or nothing kind of deal. If there's a chicken in there you just can't put the top of the egg back on and think it'll be alright."

"So what do we do?"

This struck her as a strange question. "Crack it open in a different bowl if you're worried. If it's just an egg then we'll have pancakes that might taste good for once. If it's a chicken, then we'll put the other egg back in the nest...Or we keep it! I can grow it up big and fat and it'll be all white with a red booger on its beak! We can have eggs every day."

"Having a chicken would be kind of cool," Neil said. "Here goes nothing." He made a cringy face and cracked the egg on the edge of a bowl. It turned out that the egg was only an egg much to Jillybean's disappointment.

"Do you remember where you got these?" Jilly asked. "I'd like to capture that chicken. I could get a leash and train it to do tricks. Not just laying eggs. I mean, like dancing or counting to twelve, stuff like that."

"I'm sorry, but we don't have time," Neil said. "I want to leave after breakfast if the zombie numbers aren't bad. But if everything goes ok, I think it'll be alright to come back and look for that chicken. Maybe chicken farming will be our calling if we can ever get to a place where we can settle down."

"I'd like to farm cats, too," Jillybean said.

As Neil cooked, the little girl went on about all of her favorite animals which included just about every animal she could name. Eventually, Sadie came in and listened. Neil noticed that she had put on make-up, a first since she had been dragged out of the East River. He didn't ask how she was feeling, knowing that she would lie.

The pancakes were actually quite good, needing only butter to make them perfect. Neil kept at the grill until everyone was full, something that hadn't happened in a long while. They took their time since it was zombie-weather outside. Zombies liked the cool mists and the streets were filled with the beasts. It made just running for the Ford Expedition a challenge that could mean an avoidable death.

For two hours they sat in the living room in silence, watching to see if something would draw off the zombies. Eventually the sun got a firmer grip of the day and the mists started to retreat. The second it did the zombies drifted away.

"Everyone ready to go?" Neil asked. "All packed up?" This was a silly question. They hadn't managed to scrounge enough to fill the back packs they each carried.

121

No one said anything, but when Sadie gave her half-shrug, Neil said, "Then let's go."

Axe at the ready, Neil left the house first checking all around. With the coast clear, he gave a low whistle. Out of the house hurried the other three, Nico bringing up the rear.

"So far so good," Neil said, cheerily, the second the car doors were locked.

"I hope we see another chicken," Jillybean said eagerly. Nico was quiet and nervous, while Sadie pretended she wasn't still sick, doing her best not to cough.

Without being aware of it, Neil followed Sarah's winding route out to the highway and tooled along at an easy pace, doing his best to avoid the many zombies wandering around. He was going slowly enough that he had plenty of time to see the cars draped across the roadway exactly as Sarah had only the evening before. He stopped the Expedition well back.

"Is trap?" Nico asked.

"That's what I was thinking," Neil said.

"What do we do?" Sadie asked from the back seat. "We can't fight our way through if it's an ambush and we can't go back at the first hint of danger. We could take that other highway to the west, but that's pretty far out of our way and we'd lose a third of our gas just getting there."

This was a succinct description of how screwed they were. None of the choices appealed to Neil. "I have an idea," he said. "We'll go back a bit. Over that hill where we'll be out of sight and then I'll get out and circle around to see if there's anyone hiding in those cars ready to ambush us." He felt ill over his own plan.

"You want I come?" Nico asked.

Desperately, Neil did, however he shook his head. "No. Two people will only draw more attention. I'll go by myself."

"You should go as a monster," Jillybean suggested. "I know we don't have the make-up anymore, but we could cover you in mud. That should do the trick."

Despite Sadie's endorsement of dressing like a zombie, Neil didn't trust the concept, especially the part where he couldn't run or scream or any of things he usually did when confronted by a zombie.

"I have my axe," he told her. "And I don't see any monsters hanging around. I'll be ok."

They went back and parked on the lee side of the hill, out of sight of the cars. Neil scampered up the embankment easily enough, but the fence was a bit of a trial, not made any easier when Sadie began snorting with laughter as Neil's pants got caught at the top.

"I'm not a commando, you know," he said, grimacing. The fence was biting into his unmentionables.

"And that's not the face of a cliff," she called back. "That's a fence." Her laugh turned into a cough which she had trouble suppressing.

"Serves you right," he said of her cough. "Making fun of an old man." At thirty-five he wasn't exactly old but to him, the challenge of fence climbing was practically an Olympic event.

Once on the other side, he left them with a wave and went to brave the forest, and for him it was very much an act of bravery. He gripped the axe with sweating hands, jumped at every sound, and frequently found himself freezing in place if a zombie got within a hundred yards of him. It took him half-an-hour to circle the few hundred yards to where the cars were arranged on the road.

Neil let out a sigh of relief when he saw there wasn't anyone near the cars. They were abandoned completely. On a whim he decided to get a closer look at them and climbed the fence right there; this time like a pro.

"No one around to see my triumphs," he said, moseying up to the highway. He saw the spike strip hidden in the tall grass right away. "What the hell is this?" he asked, pulling it up. It was a moment before he understood what he was seeing and another before its ramifications sunk in. When he realized that he was indeed standing in a trap, Neil crouched down next to the closest vehicle, gripping the axe even harder than before.

He stared all around, fully expecting an attack to occur with ear-shattering rapidity, but nothing out of the ordinary happened and the only thing of note that he saw was a column of smoke rising far away to the south west.

"Maybe it's an old trap," he said to himself. "Or maybe they come by and check it every once in a while." Strangely, Neil didn't equate the bounty hunter with the trap. The "they" in his mind, was a faceless group of dirty, bandit looking men who hid behind bandanas and large, military style weapons.

The image was enough to get Neil moving, although he almost immediately tripped over something and spilled onto the grass. Tripping wasn't a new occurrence for him and so he was up in a flash and didn't even hear the walkie-talkie begin to chirp as he started to jog up the road.

By the time he reached the top of the hill, Neil was blowing hard and waving his free hand at the Expedition parked down the road. They didn't see him, however a pair of zombies did.

"Oh balls!" Neil cried. "Hey! Nico, Sadie. Hey!" He began waving his arms frantically now, but still the Expedition just sat there.

The zombies were between him and the SUV and what was worse they were equal in speed, meaning they would get to Neil at just about the same time. He stopped in his tracks and stood leaning on his axe, puffing out air. If he was going to fight he would at least do it without being exhausted. In spite of the two-to-one odds, Neil wasn't exactly scared.

With his axe he held a huge advantage on the offense against zombies and on defense his immunity to their bites and scratches meant they would have to wrestle him to the ground and actually tear out his neck to do real harm. The very notion always made his throat tighten.

Still, he was a thinking creature and they were not. He cast about and found a hunk of asphalt from the edge of a growing pothole. It was good-sized so that Neil had to lay aside his axe in order to pick it up; he stepped forward ten feet and waited. After a minute the zombies were close enough for Neil to act. Grunting with the effort, Neil smashed the larger of the two in the face with the asphalt.

He didn't pause to see how the blow fared. Instead he ran back to his axe and scooped it up. The rock did not kill the zombie. It crushed the side of its face and slowed it down enough for Neil to use his axe properly. Two wide-arced swings later, Neil stood gloating over his enemies as they lay at his feet.

"Ta-duh!" he said, taking a bow toward the Expedition. There was no reaction from the vehicle. It just sat there, sixty yards off, idling. "Idling! What the hell?"

He ran up to it and saw that only Jillybean was awake. She was playing with Ipes in the back seat. "Hi, Mister Neil. Was it a trap? You have a little black blood on your face. Right by your nose. Did you battle a monster? Sadie was coughing a lot, but she said not to talk about it so I guess I shouldn't have said nothing. I mean anything."

Sadie cracked a bleary eye. "I'm fine," she said in a voice that rumbled with phlegm. "Just a little tired."

"We'll let you rest in a little bit," Neil said, climbing in and staring at the gas gauge. The indicator rested on the tip of the E. "You might get more rest than you want. We're going to run out of gas soon, because you guys left the engine running."

"Oh my God!" Sadie cried when she saw how low they were. "I'm so sorry. I fell asleep, I didn't know." Nico, who had been in the driver's seat, grunted an apology as well.

"We were going to run out anyway," Neil said with a sigh. "I was hoping for later rather than sooner, but what can you do? Oh, by the way, that bunch of cars ahead was a trap. There isn't anyone there now so we better get past it before they come back."

They cleared the trap and saw nothing of the bounty hunter all that day. With the gas they had left they were able to go fourteen more miles before the Expedition began to hitch and chug as its tank ran dry. Thankfully, they were on a nice downward slope near an exit ramp when it happened. Neil was able to coast the beast of a machine for more than a mile, all the way to the edge of a little group of homes and businesses that could barely be called a hamlet.

Sadie got all the rest she wanted as Neil and Nico spent hours hunting in vain for fuel. "Everything close to highway is searched time and again," Nico said, wiping sweat out of his eyes. "We must go away further from road."

Neil agreed but with only an hour of daylight left he was stuck with a tough decision: did he try to go searching by himself? He wouldn't make it back before dark and that was a truly scary prospect. But taking Nico with him would mean leaving the girls to fend for themselves.

"Do you think you can walk for a mile or two?" he asked Sadie. "There was a sign for some place called Pinedale. It's just down the road. Maybe we can find gas there."

Pretending she was feeling better than she was, Sadie agreed she could indeed walk such a short distance. They hitched their packs and gathered their weapons: Neil had his axe; Nico had an aluminum bat, and Sadie toted the shotgun. Jillybean had Ipes.

The walk was pleasant for Neil, but a strain for Sadie. She hung on Nico's arm and her face grew more pale with every step. After only a few minutes Nico took her pack and the shotgun so that she wouldn't be burdened. She could barely hold her head steady; the only time she looked up for more than a minute was when they got to the edge of the little town of Pinedale and walked past a McDonald's.

"Can we go look to see if they have any ham-buggers?" Jillybean asked in a pleading voice. There was no way that it would, but she and Sadie had stared at the dark building and its yellow arches with such longing that Neil agreed. All she found were fourteen packets of ketchup—thirteen since Jillybean had one open and had sucked down the contents in a second.

"Shouldn't you save those for French fries?" he asked her.

"We don't have French fries," she replied. For her it wasn't enough to suck out the ketchup, she peeled back the package and licked it clean.

Neil shrugged. "We have a little bit of oil left. If any of these houses has a garden like the one you found before, we could have fries in a snap."

Jillybean's eyes went huge and she clasped her hands together and begged: "Can I look? Please, please, please? I'll take Nico with me if you want."

The town wasn't more than a wide spot in the road. There was a mile long "commercial district" down the center, with the McDonald's, a Sears, and a Walgreens as the anchor stores. Everything else was strictly mom and pop. Fanning out from the main strip was the residential section. There were all manner of homes in it: little rickety ranches, a smattering of sixties era bi-levels, duplexes, some nice three story homes and in the back of the town bordering on field and forest was a flock of mobile homes on cinder blocks.

There were few zombies in evidence, which was why Neil agreed to Jillybean's request. Nico gave him a dark look as Jillybean took his big hand in hers and dragged him off chattering about the need for French fries in their diet.

"Is that in retaliation for him leaving the Expedition running?" Sadie asked.

"What?" Neil asked in fake outrage. "Never!"

Sadie gave him a lukewarm smile that faded to lukecold. "I need to lie down. I don't feel so good."

"Of course," Neil replied, taking her arm.

One of the closest homes was two stories of rambling wood and shingle. It had two separate garages, something Neil had never seen before, and four dog houses chained to slowly strangling poplars. Its yard was packed dirt overlaid by long-dried dog crap. Beyond the crap there was nothing else to be seen of the dogs.

Neil went into the dim home first and, after seeing what shape the yard was in, was not at all shocked at the mess that greeted him. He was sure a family of packrats had lived here and he was certain it retained much of the same look it had from before the apocalypse. The cleanest room was an upstairs guest room. It was here he laid Sadie down and gave her a canteen of water to sip on.

She fell asleep quickly.

While she snored, he busied himself with a fire and then explored the house. The next nicest room was a little girl's room; its theme was pink. Nothing went with anything else, but by God it was all pink. In this girlie maelstrom he uncovered a Barbie doll in good condition and a Velveteen Rabbit. Also a little stack of clean panties that he figured would fit Jillybean, who had been making do with three pairs which were thinning after so much use.

"This is just what the doctor ordered," Neil said as he came down the stairs. He stopped at the last step and stared, his mouth hanging open.

There was a man in the living room. He had a gun and he was dressed in green camouflage, after that Neil couldn't describe him. He was far too focused on the gun and how it pointed straight at his face. Too late Neil tried to hide the Barbie and the panties.

"You're one of them perverts, aren't you?" the man asked in a cold tone.

What could Neil say, but, "Yes. I guess I am."

Chapter 16

Sarah Rivers

Northern Maryland

Sarah very nearly set the *Kinkos* alight without first checking it for a hidden cache of food or weapons. It was a bust, however upon reflection that was alright with her. She wasn't there to scrounge, she had to remind herself. She was setting her own trap.

The paper turned out harder to get going than she thought it would. Individual pieces lit without an issue, it was the thick reams that didn't want to burn in the way she had imagined they would. After several tries, she decided to break them open and spread the paper out everywhere. When the floor was carpeted to the depth of a foot, she went about lighting everything within reach, working her way from back to front. By the time she stepped out onto the sidewalk the interior of the store was a solid wall of gray.

"Maybe too much gray," she said. What would happen if the flames were smothered by the smoke? Easy, the fire would go out. "I can't have that." Her hand axe was a simple solution. Enjoying the rebellious nature of her actions, she broke every window.

This sudden influx of oxygen turned the smoking storefront into a five alarm beast that would eventually consume every building on the block. Sarah smiled at her handiwork. Soon the fire attracted a throng of undead, who came to stand in an arc around the building just like normal people might. They stared at the dancing flames just as Sarah did, something she hadn't expected. Adopting a zombie shuffle, she left them to their entertainment and headed for the clock tower.

The city hall, a sturdy brick affair was horrible in a way few places were. The people of Easton, Maryland, with a one-time population of over five thousand souls had used it as a morgue during the apocalypse. In nearly every meeting room, hallway and office on the main floor, bodies were stacked like cordwood. The ones at the bottom of the piles were properly sheeted and tied against the misadventures of rigor mortis. The ones on top were not. They were open for all to see.

The full ugliness of death was on display—the rotting, fly-covered flesh, the draining ribbons of fat, the pudding-like black blood which pooled in the low spots of every room—was of such magnitude that it left even a veteran survivor like Sarah stunned. Making a retching sound in her throat she staggered for the stairs as behind her in the hall, one of the piles teetered and fell over. There was a zombie among the dead. Unlike the cadavers all around her that seemed extra-skinny and deflated, the zombie was morbidly obese. It had been feeding on the dead like a pig at an endless trough.

Even then as it stared at her with deep set, piggy eyes, it was chewing on greasy flesh.

Like a bull, it bellowed, sending out flecks of diseased meat, and then it charged. Sarah fled up the stairs, taking them two at a time, easily outdistancing her attacker. Eventually the stairs ended at an open landing in the middle of a long hallway on the third floor. It had been her hope that the stairs would have a door that she could block.

"This won't do. Fuck! This won't do at all," she hissed. The zombie would have trouble on the stairs, but it wasn't going to have any trouble wandering the halls until it found her. Even the narrow stairs leading to the clock tower weren't barricaded by anything more challenging than a red velvet rope.

"I'm being silly," she said to herself. The zombie was going to forget about her any second and go back to eating. It wasn't going to climb all these stairs to get at her, or so she hoped. Doing her best to put the foul creature out of her mind, she went up the narrow, spiraling stairs and found a door at the very top. It was flimsy to begin with, but when she shouldered it in, it became useless.

"It won't come up here," she said to reassure herself about the fearsome zombie. "Never going to…happen. Whoa." The *Kinkos* and the city hall building were only separated by the main street and a pretty green lawn of some sixty yards in width. She was close enough to feel the staggering heat being thrown off by the fire. It was a massive thing now. It had fully engulfed the *Kinkos* so that only edges of brick could be seen in all the smoke. She craned her head back and saw that the smoke had risen beyond her ability to judge. It could be a mile high, or ten, for all she knew.

Perfect.

"Now to get comfortable," she said, figuring it would be a while before the bounty hunter showed up. That meant going back into the municipal building to get a chair. With the height of the railing, a barstool would serve her needs best. "But who's going to have a barstool here?"

The mayor—not the bum who had claimed to be mayor, but the real mayor that is—had one. He also had a bar and good Belvedere vodka. Sarah pocketed the alcohol and then dragged the chair up the stairs. Propping her feet on the rail, she took a slug of the vodka. "That's for the bounty hunter." She took another. "And that's for the stink."

The odor of rotting flesh from below, seemed to channel up the stairs to hover around the clock tower like an invisible cloud. She tried not to think about it. Instead she set her eye to the rifle's scope and slowly worked the gun among the zombies in the street. She then scoped the other ways into the town and saw only more zombies.

Almost beneath her feet came a crash. Sarah sank another drink. "And this is for you, fat-boy."

She sat on her perch above the town for an hour and only had one more drink. It occurred when the crazy "new mayor" arrived at the scene of the fire. He went among the zombies in a rage, blaming each for the fire and vowing retribution. Those that attacked him he struck down with his heavy pipe. Those that were mesmerized by the fire only got an earful of his constant diatribe.

After that fourth drink, Sarah was close to telling the crazy man to shut the hell up. She even went so far as to put the cross-hairs of her scope dead on his chest. "Shut the hell up," she whispered, touching the trigger. The Belvedere had put her in a mood, but not in a mood to commit murder.

It put her in the mood to right at least one wrong.

Sarah slid off the bar stool and then grabbed the railing as her head went light. The alcohol had gone down smoothly and four shots made the earth seem to tilt. "I'll be ok," she said. After a couple of seconds of deep breathing she felt good enough to go on. She went down the stairs, listening to the fat zombie wheeze and moan. It was trying to get through a door on the third floor, bashing at it with its ham-sized fists.

Sarah took aim. At thirty yards, its head looked to be the size of a pumpkin. She almost didn't need the scope. Almost. Thinking she couldn't possibly miss, she thumbed off the safety and fired. The gun kicked like a mule and sounded like a cannon. The bullet passed through the zombie from cheek to cheek taking with it a number of teeth and spraying the hall with black blood.

It was close as to which of them recovered from the gun's blast first. Sarah had fully expected the zombie to be dead and was working her shoulder in circles, while wearing a look of pain. The zombie stood looking at the door as if it had attacked him. It then spat out its own tongue before turning and locking eyes with Sarah.

Sarah ran. She took off down the stairs, trying to reload and manage the steps at the same time.

The zombie chugged to the stairs and immediately fell. The fat beast was faster this way and it came tumbling to the second level to land practically at Sarah's feet. She backed up as the zombie struggled to stand. It was sort of comical in a sickening way. Its belly was so distended from its constant feast that it outshot its arms. It had to use the stairs to stand and by the time it did, Sarah had reloaded and was again drawing a bead.

Her one problem was that she was so close that the zombie filled the entire scope and she couldn't tell what part of it she was aiming at. She could have backed further away, but she chose instead to sight down the side of the barrel. When she pulled the trigger, and the gun deafened her a second time, she was pleased to see the top of the thing's head shoot upwards. The rest of it fell forward with a slap and a squish, his fat body seeming to ooze outward in death.

"Wow, that's so gross," Sarah said, feeling her stomach turn over in a slow roll. Wearing a light sheen of sweat, she went back to the clock tower and considered another drink of the vodka, but held off as the new mayor of Easton came marching across the street. "Go away," she yelled at him.

"Who's doing all that shooting? You? What are you... hey! That's my tower you're in," he cried, shaking his pipe at her. Her response was to chamber another round. Either he didn't notice or he didn't understand the significance of the move. "Get down from there," he went on. "That's mine not yours. I'm the mayor, remember? You're nothing but a pretender to the throne."

"Go the fuck away," she yelled back. "I'm warning you." When he began to jaw at her again she chucked the bottle at him, missing wide.

"You can't do that," he said in disbelief. "I am the mayor! Don't you get it? The mayor!"

"Well, good for you," Sarah yelled back. "But I'm the bloomin' Queen of England which means I outrank you." The "logic" of this statement so upset the threads holding together the man's fantasy that he could not quite recover. Sarah went on in a truly wretched British accent: "Thas right. Be gone with ye or it'll be the tower for you. Go back to your alley until it be the 'morrow."

Perplexed, he stumbled away out of her sight, presumably back to his alley. Sarah didn't really care where he went as long as he stopped his ranting.

133

Time clicked slowly by. The fire began to consume the building next to the *Kinkos* and now there were easily a hundred zombies taking in the spectacle. It was interesting in its way, but more and more she grew bored. She looked down her scope periodically and wondered if she had lit a fire for nothing.

After a few more minutes she let out a sigh and leaned over the rail to search for the bottle of vodka. It was intact. She groaned, wanting another drink and wishing she hadn't thrown it at the deranged man. More than anything she wanted to run down and get the bottle and zip back, however, by her "calculations" the bounty hunter should have been there already.

The fire had been going for almost two hours. If he was anywhere within twenty miles he had to have seen the smoke by now and should've been sneaking around trying to find the human amongst the zombies.

For the twentieth time, she checked her watch. It was just after two in the afternoon. Miles to the south of her Neil and Nico were searching in vain for gas for the stranded Expedition, and six feet behind her the bounty hunter took another step closer—like a cat playing with his food.

Another groan from Sarah meant she was just about to sight down the rifle again. It was a habit that she wasn't at all aware of. The hunter had seen this particular tell of hers three times in the last ten minutes so he knew he was perfectly safe to take one more large step closer.

"Where are you?" Sarah asked, rhetorically.

When the bounty hunter answered, "I'm right here," from directly behind her she screamed and tried to turn, but he stuck a pistol right to the back of her neck and she froze. "I've been looking for you everywhere, Sadie."

At the name she jerked.

Chapter 17

Sadie

Pinedale, Maryland

The long day spent in the car, topped off by the late afternoon two mile hike had sapped all of Sadie's strength. She even lacked the energy to cough properly and with every breath she could feel the phlegm settle deeper in her lungs. Even before Neil left the room Sadie knew she would sleep the evening and night straight through.

In fact, she had already begun to snore lightly when she heard a strange voice in the house. The sound penetrated right to her consciousness and she was fully awake when Neil admitted to being a pervert. There was only one reason a good man like Neil would ever say something like that: he was protecting her.

That was her first thought. Her second was: *Hide! It's the bounty hunter!* Somehow, they'd been found again, although to be honest, they hadn't been exactly sneaking down the highway in their big green Expedition, nor had their hike to the little town been anything but a stroll right down the middle of the road with the two men killing the occasional zombie and foolishly leaving their bodies where they fell. They'd been obvious and now they were caught.

Without a real weapon, hiding was Sadie's only option. Luckily, the house seemed ready-made for hiding. The place was a maze of junk and trash. Newspapers, take-out boxes, clothes, engine parts; it sat everywhere in piles or stacks, in bags and boxes or strewn about—everywhere except the room she was in, of course. Though it wasn't exactly sparkling with polish, it was the least messy room in the house. In all the other bedrooms someone had dumped the contents of the dresser drawers into piles, here the drawers had only been yanked open and prowled through.

She contemplated trying to sneak into another room, but she didn't know the house at all. If it was a house full of squeaks any movement would be a dead giveaway. That meant she was stuck hiding in the room she found herself in. Under the bed was silly and obvious. The closet was too open; she'd be seen easily. If there had been piles of clothes like in the other bedrooms she could hide in them; after all she was very slim and small, but unfortunately the clothes were still in the drawers.

Duh! She could pull the clothes out herself.

She slid out of bed and tip-toed to the dresser and started chucking clothes in every direction, all except the dark colored clothes which she piled in the corner next to where the dresser hit the wall. As she did this, she caught the words from downstairs she dreaded to hear:

"I'm looking for a young woman named Sadie Walcott," the unfamiliar voice said. "She's about your height. Dark hair, dark eyes. She's with a Russian, Nico Grekov. You know them?"

"A Ruh...Ruh...Russian?" Neil asked, choking on the words. "No, I don't think I know any Russians. Have we been invaded? Ha-ha."

The joke fell flat and seemed to arouse even more suspicion. "What's your name?"

"Me? It's Ne—Ni—Nor, uh, Norman. I'm Norman. What's this all about? Why are you after a Russian and some girl?"

"There's a bounty on their heads," the man replied. Sadie's muscles began to quiver. Even with all the clothes she was piling over herself she felt cold at the idea of being caught. Yuri would do things to her before she died, she knew it.

"How much is the bounty?" Neil asked, trying to keep the anxiety out of his voice, and failing. "I could use the money. Right? Who couldn't use more..."

"Shut up," the man barked at Neil. He then issued orders to two other men who had been so silent that Sadie hadn't even known they were there. "Search the place. Mac upstairs. Bull take this floor and outside."

"There's no one here but me," Neil said very loudly. Sadie cringed at how obvious he was being.

"I told you to shut up."

Neil stopped talking abruptly and was so quiet that Sadie could practically hear him listening for her. She wished that he would just act normal but for Neil there was no "normal" setting when he was as nervous as he was.

Sadie could hear footsteps approaching. She could hear them stop at every door; there would be a pause and then the steps would go around the room hurriedly before moving to the next. Then the footsteps came to her room. Sadie went still beneath her mish-mash of clothes. She tried to will herself into being smaller, less noticeable, just another clump of clothes, just like all the rest.

The man stomped to the bed. With a light grunt he bent to peek under it. Next he went to the closet and then, miraculously, he left, heading for the next room. Very quickly, or so it seemed to Sadie, the man had checked every room and was heading back downstairs.

"All clear."

The man named "Bull" announced the same thing not a minute later. Neil's sigh of relief couldn't have been more obvious than if he had said: *Thank God you didn't find her*. Luckily, the men seemed to have forgotten him.

"Someone needs to tell the colonel that this is a waste of our freaking time," one of the men, either Bull or Mac, said.

"Next time we see him, I'll let you do the honors," the man who had first spoken replied. "And you, *Norman*, give me those! If I ever find you with girl's panties again I'll cut your balls off. That's not a threat. I will do it. Are we clear on this, you sick fuck."

"Yes sir," Neil replied. "You won't have to worry about…"

"Shut up," the man demanded. Sadie heard footsteps going towards the front door but they stopped just at the threshold. "And Norman? One more thing, forget about any bounties. Forget you ever even heard of it. I don't need a crap weasel like you messing where you shouldn't be messing. Am I clear?"

"Yes. No bounties and no panties. Got it. Sorry about…"

"Shut up," the man said a final time before leaving. The moment he did, Sadie climbed out of the clothes she had piled over herself. Since the window in the guest bedroom faced the backyard, she hurried to the room across the hall and snuck to the corner of the window.

Three men were walking across the street in the direction of the McDonald's. They were clearly soldiers; Sadie could tell by their gear and their bearing. They walked noiselessly despite their heavy packs and their eyes scanned constantly.

"Sadie?" Neil called from the first floor.

She popped her head out into the hall and answered, "I'm just making sure they're really leaving. You should see if Nico and Jillybean are wandering around. We don't want them to accidentally run into the soldiers."

Neil went from window to window, looking for the pair, but there was no sign of them. He came back to where Sadie was looking out. "Can you still see the soldiers?"

"Barely."

"They were the colonel's men."

"I heard."

This seemed to shake Neil. "You heard all of it? Then…then…those panties weren't mine, you know. They were for Jillybean, I swear."

Sadie snorted laughter at him—it was all she had strength for. "For Jillybean? Like that Barbie?"

He seemed unaware that he had been running around carrying a doll and a soft, brown rabbit. He blinked at them in surprise and now Sadie actually laughed. It turned into a cough in rapid fashion.

"I'm glad you can laugh," Neil said. "You should have seen those guys. They were scary. Even scarier than the bounty hunter."

"Then they must have been the scariest guys ever," Sadie said. The few seconds of laughter coupled with the stress and fright of the last few minutes had Sadie feeling like she about to swoon. Neil saw her begin to blink uncertainly.

"You should go lay down," he said. "I don't think they're going to come back. They're thoroughly convinced that I'm a freaky perv. It's probably why they didn't do a very good job searching and why they were so quick to leave."

"It's the sweater vests, Neil. Only child molesters still wear sweater vests." She meant it as a joke, however she appeared so drained and listless that he barely cracked a smile. Instead he wore a look of worry as he led her back to the bed where she was asleep in seconds.

It was the dark of late evening when she was gently shaken from sleep by Nico. He held out her pills and a glass of water. The water had a metallic tang to it that was unpleasant. He made her drink it regardless and as she did, he ran one of his heavy hands through her short hair.

"Kiss better," he said, touching his warm lips to hers.

This earned him a smile. "That was nice. I must be cured," she said.

"It will take more than just one kiss to make my Sadie better. You is must rest."

"If she needs more kisses I can kiss her, too," Jillybean said. She'd been standing by the door watching and because the house was so dark, Sadie hadn't seen her. Now she came forward like a pale angel.

"One more kiss should do the trick," Sadie said.

Jillybean puckered her lips to the size of a penny and when she pulled back she left a little spot of wet on Sadie's cheek. "I can go get Ipes if you need another kiss. Right now he's in timeout for being mean to the Velveeta Rabbit."

Despite her weariness, Sadie grinned at the word velveeta. "No, it'll be ok. I just need more sleep."

"What of food?" Nico asked. "Are you hungry?" Behind him Jillybean's eyes shot wide and she began to shake her head in a clear warning.

"No, thank you," Sadie told Nico. "Just sleep."

After a final kiss he left her. Jillybean made as if to leave as well, but she turned away from the door and tiptoed back to Sadie. "You don't want what we had for dinner. It was fried carrots." She made a face at the memory. "It was really blechy tasting, specially when Neil promised they would taste as good as French fries."

"At least he tries."

"Yeah, sometimes too hard. Hey, do you want to sleep with the Velveeta Rabbit? He's super soft. Here, feel."

Sadie's first inclination was to decline the heartfelt offer, but the rabbit was incredibly soft, and Jillybean seemed to really want her to take it, and she was practically asleep anyway. The Goth girl fell deeply asleep with the rabbit tucked just under her chin.

Hours later, she and the sun stirred the morning at about the same time. Sadie stretched and yawned, still clutching the rabbit, and it was a second before she realized that her yawn had been full; her mouth wide and gaping, and that her lungs had expanded in their old manner. Excited, she took a deep breath in, coughed once, more from a tickle in her throat than from phlegm, and then breathed out in a rush.

She did it again and this time there wasn't even the little cough. "I'm getting better," she said with a smile. Still holding the smile to her face, she went down to the kitchen and discovered Neil eyeing the eleven cans that constituted their main source of food. On the counter were a few wiggly, unappealing carrots, an onion with spots that were so deep they looked more like veggie-cancer, and six packets of ketchup.

"Good morning," she said brightly.

He replied in kind, adding: "Since you're up first, you get first crack at the vittles. Sorry, there isn't much to choose from."

"What about you?" she asked. "You were up before me. You should get to choose first."

He waved her words away. "I already ate. I had the leftovers from last night. Fried carrots aren't that bad." As he spoke, his hand stole to his stomach and began rubbing it as if the carrots weren't sitting well; he didn't seem to notice he was doing it.

"I'll have the cream of corn if you don't mind. Do we have any salt?"

He nodded and said, "And pepper, courtesy of our local *McDonald's*. Sit down while I get the fire going again."

Neil had banked the fire the night before—it was a simple process of pushing the hottest coals and glowing logs to the corner of the fireplace and gently covering them with a layer of ash to hold in their heat. When he tapped away the ash and gently blew on the coals they glowed orange even after six hours. He then began adding paper and kindling, then larger hunks of wood and in two minutes the fire was going merrily.

Sadie was blowing on her hot corn when Jillybean came down sporting the latest style of bed-head: the *tornado*. She smacked her lips and blinked blearily until she saw the rabbit next to Sadie's bowl.

"Are you, uh, all done with the Velveeta Rabbit?" the little girl asked. "Can I have her back? Ipes is lonely you see. He might be in love."

"I won't get in the way of love," Sadie said, handing the rabbit over. "By the way she was very soft, and I think she might have curative powers. I feel so much better today than yesterday."

Once Ipes explained the word "curative" to her, Jillybean was pleased to no end. "The Velveeta Rabbit is magic? Maybe she was a magician's rabbit? Maybe there's a magic hat around here somewhere. And maybe there's a wand! That'd be cool." She began to dash off but remembered she was hungry just in time. At the doorway to the kitchen she turned and asked, "Mister Neil, can I please have that squiggly pasta in the can for breakfast?"

141

"It's rigatoni, and yes, you may." She was gone in swirl of brown hair and flashing heels.

"Are you ever going to tell her that the rabbit's name isn't the Velveeta Rabbit?" Sadie asked around a mouthful of corn.

"Not if I can help it," Neil replied, popping the lid off the rigatoni. "I think it's darling. It's too bad Sarah…" He stopped in midsentence, his face squinching up.

Sadie patted his hand and said, "She'll warm up to Jillybean. We just have to find her before she gets to New Eden, and knock some sense into her."

"She has all the sense in the world," Neil said. "She has the sense of a mother protecting her baby."

"At the expense of everyone around her?" Sadie asked, pointedly.

"Yeah," Neil replied, turning quiet. "I can't blame her for trying to rescue Eve, even if it kills her. I'm not going to pass judgment, because in this there are no good choices, only hard choices. We got screwed. Somewhere along the way we got screwed or we messed up."

"I don't think we messed up. Is there anything you would have done different?" Sadie asked. "Would you have stopped Sarah from going to New York? Could you have?" To this Neil shook his head. Sadie had to agree. Sarah had demanded to go in an attempt to find one daughter, only to have another taken from her.

"I'm afraid it's going to be more of the same," Sadie said. "Even if we find her before she gets to New Eden, she won't listen to reason. She'll go regardless and…" She didn't want to finish the sentence and didn't really need to.

Neil emptied the rigatoni into a sauce pan and set it over the fire. With his back to Sadie he said, "We don't know what will happen when we find her, but we have to try."

"We have to get gas first," Sadie said.

More than food, fuel was dictating their lives. It had always been scarce however lately it had become nearly impossible to find. The town they found themselves in didn't seem like it would produce more than a few ounces.

Every single car, truck, and tractor had its gas cap off. The group tried garages for spare fuel cans. They checked lawn mowers and weed-whackers and even the single snow-blower possessed by the town. All were dry.

It was midday and they had progressed from one end of the town to the other and each of them was getting hot and irritable. All save Jillybean. She had her cheeks puffed by a pair of acorns and she went here and there with all the forethought and care of a butterfly. Eventually, she decided to turn her thoughts to what the grownups were getting all grumpy over.

She went to the closest car, a sad little Volkswagen Beetle sitting on saggy tires, and poked the vapor gasket back to the gas tank and looked in the dark hole. She gave it a sniff. "Ew! There's gas in this one. It stinks."

Neil was too tired to entertain the girl's notions. "You're just smelling the fumes. All the cars have fumes. That doesn't mean there is any gas in there."

"Ipes say it should. He says that gas fumes come from gas."

"In this case Ipes is wrong," Neil said. "Even empty gas tanks smell like that. It's a residual odor."

"What would gas tanks smell like if they had fuel in them?" she asked.

Sadie, who had parked herself in the shade of tree, had to laugh in spite of the fact that she was dragging worse than any of them. She was getting better, but she wasn't all the way there yet. "I don't think she'll stop until you give her a demonstration."

"Fine," Neil said, though clearly it was not fine. He worked his siphon hose into the tank until it struck bottom. Then, after taking a few deep breaths he began to suck. There was a moment when he pulled enough fluid into the hose to create a touch of suction, but then he hit nasty fuel-tasting air and wound up with nothing more than a bad taste in his mouth. He stood bent over at the waist, spitting onto the street.

143

"You see?" Neil said, wiping his lips and looking more pale than usual. "These cars have all been siphoned to the point where there's too little to bring up."

"Maybe we try next town," Nico said. He pointed at a distant water tower. "Is that direction, three miles according to map."

Sadie heaved herself up. The euphoric sensation she had experienced when she had first woken up was long gone. Still, she vowed not to slow the group down.

That would be Jillybean's job. The group shouldered their packs and started walking, all save the little girl. She raised her hand, and when that went unnoticed she called, "Mister Neil?"

A weary sigh escaped him and he stopped. He didn't turn around. Sadie saw Jillybean's pursed lips and said, "Maybe Ipes has an idea." This caused everyone to turn expectantly, but Jillybean dashed their hopes.

"No, Ipes is being a butt," she said. "He says he won't help because he doesn't want me to go to New Eden. But I have a question. You say there's too little gas to suck up. How much is too little?"

Neil rubbed his head, clearly feeling the effects of the fumes he had breathed in. "A few ounces, I don't know. It doesn't matter because, like I already said, we can't get it up."

"What about getting it down?" She squatted on her haunches and pointed under the vehicle at the gas tank. "I had a fish tank once with goldfish but it gotted a leak and all the water came out and the goldfish died, which was very sad and I cried, but if we can make a hole in the tank on purpose we can get the gas."

Without saying a word, Neil rushed back to the Beetle and stared at the tank. "I need a rock! Or a brick." As Nico ran for a rock, Neil pulled out a Swiss Army knife from his pocket and worked the inch long screw driver from where it sat snuggly in with the other tools.

When he had his rock, he sat down cross-legged as close to the back of the beetle as he could and then hammered the screw driver into the tank. It took a dozen strikes from the rock before he got through the metal but, when he did, gasoline began pouring out over his hands. He jabbed his thumb onto the hole and cried: "I need something! A pan or a pot or anything to catch this." Even with the spilled amount they collected close to half a gallon.

"It's not that much," Jillybean said as Neil began to laugh out loud.

He grinned at her. "You're right, but look at all these cars." He waved his hand. They were at the edge of the town and still there were thirty-two cars in view. "I think you solved our fuel problem, Jillybean."

Chapter 18

Sarah Rivers

Easton, Maryland

Inwardly she swore at her own stupidity. First, she had allowed this guy to sneak up on her and then, by flinching, she probably gave away the fact that she knew the name Sadie. Lying in any manner wasn't something she was good at, and now lives depended on it. She would have to convince this evil beast of a man that not only did he have the wrong person, but that he wasn't even close.

"How'd you know it was me?" she asked, making sure to keep her face turned away. She also tried to add a little toughness to her voice, something the four shots of vodka helped with. "You a mind reader?"

"Yeah, I'm a mind reader. I know when people lie. It's a gift." He reached around and took the rifle from her hands; she didn't struggle. He had her at too much of a disadvantage. She would struggle eventually, that she promised herself, but only when the time was ripe.

"So how'd you know it was me?" she asked. "You didn't answer my question."

He turned the barstool so that she faced him, however she kept her chin down so that he couldn't get a good look at her face. "Lucky I guess," he answered. "I knew it was you on the highway. You're not exactly traveling incognito. Though with all this crap on you it wasn't easy. What is this, soot? Is that how you got away last night? Were you in that burned up house?"

"Yep," she answered. "You were right above me and you didn't even know. Not much of a mind reader if you ask me. Just like now. You think you got me, but you don't got squat. I don't have anything left, since you took it all already. Sorry to break it to you, chum." For some reason, using the silly word "chum" threw off her train of thought.

It felt like a mistake, however the mistake came a second later when she glanced up at the bounty hunter.

"Stop playing games. You know why..." He stopped in midsentence when Sarah lifted her chin. Even with her face a filthy mess, it was obvious she wasn't seventeen years old. "What the...Who the hell are you?"

"I'm Sadie if it will get all my stuff back."

The bounty hunter was in his cammo which showed nothing of him save for his furious grey eyes. He grabbed her by the tattered shawl and lifted her off the barstool with one hand. Behind her the railing seemed no more substantial that a pile of kindling.

"I don't think you understand what's going on here," he said through gritted teeth. "I don't care if you're alive in five minutes. I really don't. In fact, I'm thinking about pitching you right off this tower."

He had her leaning well over the railing now, her ass resting only on air. "Please...please don't," she begged. Her tone was craven; his response was silence, yet somehow through it he conveyed his contempt. "Please, why? Why would you do that to me?" she asked. The terror in her voice wasn't fake and neither was the sincerity in her question. He was a bounty hunter and a thief. Why would he kill when he didn't have to?

"Because I don't have time for games," he said. "Tell me who the fuck you are or..." The "or" was obvious. He leaned her so far back that she couldn't do anything but grab his arm frantically.

She blurted out the first name that came to mind: "I'm Brit. My name is Brit. I don't know any Sadie! Please let me up. Please!"

Had they been sitting, calmly, eye-to-eye Sarah would never have been able to pull off the lie. Dangled off the edge of a building, her fear overrode everything but the lie. She knew she would either be Brit or she would die.

The bounty hunter didn't pull her back up, not yet. "And what the fuck is all this? What's with the gun and the fire?"

147

Lying about her name had been easy, since her daughter had been on her mind for weeks, but trying to come up with a lie about why she was in a clock tower with a high powered rifle was impossible. Without any choice she tried the truth.

"It was for you," she cried. "You took everything from me. I was trying to get it back."

"By setting a trap?" he asked, calmer. Traps and assassinations were things he seemed to understand. He pulled her back up so that the rail was once again shoved into the small of her back.

"Yes," she admitted. "I wanted to kill you, alright? You left me with nothing. What kind of asshole does that to a woman?"

His grip had been relaxing, and his eyes softening as her motivations came clearer, but something happened when she said the word woman. His suspicion flared; she saw it clearly in his eyes.

Without explanation, he pushed her to her knees and then pulled out his canteen. He began pouring water all over her face and in her hair. She spluttered and coughed, and tried to blink the soot/water combination out of her blue eyes. As she did, he stared intently at her. He even pushed her head this way and that, looking for something.

"What is it?" she asked. "What are you doing?" Of course she knew. If he knew the name Sadie, then he probably knew the name Sarah Rivers.

"Where are you from?" he demanded. Now he held her by her butched haircut in such a tight grip that she could barely blink.

Would it be smart to tell the truth? Did he know where Sarah Rivers was from? Or was he simply looking to see if she would lie. Again, eye-to-eye with this cold, reptile of a human she didn't think she could pull off a lie. Besides there were a lot of people from Iowa, at least there used to be.

"Iowa," she admitted after what she thought was only a minor pause.

His eyes went to slits, showing only a gleam of grey. "Where in Iowa?"

This time the pause was so long it was uncomfortable. "Danville," she answered. She had wanted to lie, however with him staring so hard, the names of other towns simply vanished from her memory. Now, somehow, his stare intensified. It was as though he was boring into her skull with his eyes to discover the truth.

"Really, I'm from Danville," she said. Was she digging her own grave by answering truthfully? It was true, he might really know Sarah Rivers was from Danville. It wasn't like she had kept her home town a secret from anyone.

In her mind she went down the list of people who had known she was from Danville. One name stood out from all the rest: Colonel Williams. Would he have told anyone something so insignificant? If he had, it would've been only in passing, after all, he found her insignificant, something to be used and thrown away. Something with no more value or use than the butt of a cigarette. She was nothing to him so why would he waste even a thought on her?

With her mind on the colonel, the bounty hunter didn't see what he was looking for in her eyes. She didn't notice. Goosebumps ran down her arms as they always did when Williams came to mind.

Then she jumped with a cry. The hunter had a hand on her left breast. He cupped it roughly and without any pretense toward subtlety, he then slid the hand beneath her armpit and then down her side. Once there, it went across her waist.

Only when he found her hunting knife did she understand he was frisking her and not trying anything more. She breathed a sigh of relief until he tossed the knife over the railing. "Hey! That was mine." His only response was to turn her around and kick her legs wide. Panic at the prospect of being raped again made her breath very light in her throat. She looked over her shoulder at him. "D-don't do anything to me, ok?" It came out as a whisper.

Again, he didn't answer. His hands were wide and rough as boards. They slid over every inch of her body, including right up between her legs, which elicited a whimper of fear that embarrassed her. For the last month she had been working a great hatred inside of her, one that would allow her to kill without a qualm, one that was supposed to overcome such a trifling thing as fear, but here she was whimpering!

The bounty hunter didn't care one way or the other. He shoved her to her knees and then picked up the pack she had set aside. After a second of digging, he found the box of ammo for the rifle. It went into a hidden pocket beneath his camouflaged outfit with a brassy jingle.

"No...no I need those," she said, the whimper still very apparent.

"So do I."

He stole the round she had chambered in the rifle as well. She watched this with her head shaking back and forth in denial. "But you'll leave me defenseless. You can't do that."

"I could kill you," he answered in a quiet voice. "Do you want me to do that? It might solve a lot of your problems."

"No, but..."

Just then he took out a clear plastic zip-tie, the kind police officers sometimes used in lieu of handcuffs. She began to stammer, "Ok, ok. You don't need those. I'll—I'll be good."

She didn't know what *good* entailed she only knew that she was utterly powerless compared to this sociopath and that she was totally freaked out by the way he alternated between seething anger and cold resolution. Nothing she said mattered to the man. He yanked her to her feet and stuck her hand hands high up the middle of her back and tied them there. He then pushed her down to her knees again and squatted right in front of her.

"I'm looking for a girl named Sadie. She looks like you but with dark eyes and she's much younger. Have you seen her?" Sarah didn't trust her mouth to lie properly so she shook her head. "What about a Russian man? Tall, blonde, speaks with an accent?" Again a head shake. The hunter started to get mad. "Have you see anyone in the last few weeks?"

"No, no one," she said a little too quickly. His eyes again peered hard at her and she felt her lip begin to quiver. "I mean yes, but I wasn't thinking you meant these people."

"Who do mean?"

"There wasn't a girl. I saw two people and they were both men." She paused thinking he would say something to that, but he only continued to evaluate her in nerve-wracking silence. She decided to go on. "There was a guy up the road, closer to Philly, only he was dead. He wasn't a zombie. I mean he had killed himself."

"What did he look like? Was he white? Black? Asian? What color were his eyes?"

"Um," Sarah said, picturing the corpse as it dangled from the tree branch. "He was white I think. White or Asian. It was hard to tell because he'd been dead for a couple of days. He had dark hair, but I didn't look to close at his face. Maybe if you…"

"Forget about him," the man said, cutting her off. "What about the second guy?"

"He lives here in this town. He thinks he's the mayor." She tried to picture the crazy man; in her mind he was rather formless and faceless. Sarah had never liked crazy people. The crazier one was, the less likely she would look him the face. "I don't know what he looks like. Except he's white. I know that because…"

She broke off remembering her first conversation with the bum. She had very clearly given her name out, and not just once. He had repeated it to her: …*there isn't anybody named Sarah Rivers in Easton*. What if he remembered the conversation? Or at least the name? What if it came up when the bounty hunter went to see him?

"Because why?" the hunter asked. He spoke so low that she had to lean in to hear, which made it feel like she was sticking her neck out for him to hack it off.

"He—he had rags and they moved a little so that I could see his face. But he really was a bum; he smelled like urine and everything." The hunter's eyes perked up at the word *urine* as if it rang false, which it might have with how she looked and had acted. Sarah tried to bury it. "I told him I was the Queen of England and he believed me that's how nuts he is. You aren't going to hurt him, are you? He really is just harmless."

"You should be more worried about yourself."

"I am," she insisted. "That's why I'm being so cooperative. You gotta let me go. You can have the bullets but please don't leave me tied up."

"You get tied up or dead. Those are your choices."

"Tied up," she said, dropping her chin. "Will you come back later after you talk to the bum? You'll see I wasn't lying. That should be worth something, right? Don't you think? Maybe untie me then?" This was the best acting she had done so far. She didn't want him to come back, ever. Not when she was unarmed and most certainly not when she was tied up.

"Like I said, tied up or dead, and that's me being generous. After all you were up here with the idea of killing me. I normally don't let that sort of thing pass so lightly."

"Yeah, that was a mistake," Sarah agreed. She let her body slump so that she had an excuse not to look at the bounty hunter anymore. "Sorry about that. You know I won't do it..." In the middle of her sentence he got up and left, trotting down the stairs lightly.

When his footsteps faded, Sarah growled, "Fuck you." A few seconds of grunting later she managed to get her feet under her body and push herself up. "Maybe it's fuck me," she said. Just standing up had been a chore and now that she was up she glanced down at her rifle, axe, and pack, wondering how the hell she was going pick all that stuff up with her hands tied behind her back.

Feeling like some sort of giant insect she lowered herself back down to her knees in front of her backpack and grabbed one of the shoulder straps between her teeth.

Gently, she lifted it so that it arced up away from the pack and then, with a squirming motion, stuck her head under the strap and sat up again.

Like a feed-bag the pack hung from her neck, the weight of it on her breasts made her lean slightly forward. "Well, this sucks," she whispered. Where the pack sat on her was ridiculous; she couldn't see a thing and it was as uncomfortable as hell. Her remedy, swinging her body out and to the side in order to shift the pack behind her, failed miserably.

Even when she was able to get the pack behind her, its full weight sat directly on her throat, choking her and worse, when she bent toward the hand axe and the rifle, the bag swung back wasting her efforts and completely obscuring her view. In order to see anything, she had to look over her shoulder rather than straight on. Whichever way she looked at it, she realized that, with her hands tied, she could only take one of the two.

The idea of leaving even a single item behind was gut-wrenching and yet a gun without bullets was useless. She went for the axe in about as awkward a manner as she could fathom—she basically had to lie on it in order get her hands within reach. Then came another grunting, swear-ridden attempt at standing.

She had just lost five minutes. Those were precious minutes. With all his ravings, the mayor would be found quickly by the bounty hunter. Even quicker he would talk. In her gut, Sarah knew the mayor of Easton would spill everything he knew, probably without even the threat of pain. The man couldn't seem to keep anything inside and although he didn't know much, what he did know was poison.

The bounty hunter would be back and this time he'd be far more thorough with Sarah, he'd take his time and there'd be blood and tears. And Sarah had just lost five minutes. She didn't have many left.

Chapter 19

Sarah Rivers

Easton, Maryland

Compared to just standing up, the stairs were easy to handle, and yet she couldn't speed down them with the backpack hanging just below her chin. It was in a side-stepping, tentative manner that she descended; she lost another three minutes getting to the main floor. Two more were spent getting outside where the afternoon was beginning to seem dim compared to the fire across the street. The heat of it made her blink and turn her head.

The fire mattered very little to her. Her stomach was a butterfly-filled mess as she thought about the bounty hunter and the crazy mayor and the fact the two had to have found each other by now. How long would it take for the mayor to let drop the two words that would have the hunter racing back? The two words being: *Sarah Rivers.*

If it hadn't happened already it was likely only minutes away. Despite being fully aware of this, Sarah didn't go running off. What she needed more than anything was her knife. With it she could free herself and make a proper get away—that is if one considered stumbling around the zombie-plagued country side armed with only six inches of steel a proper get away. There was only one problem with the plan: her knife was nowhere to be seen or felt.

"Where the hell is it," she asked, sensing her desperation grow with every useless second she spent kicking about in the grass. She went back and forth, letting precious seconds speed by as she searched. The backpack chaffed her neck and made it hard to see but she persevered. It should have been easy to find, after all, the hunter had casually tossed it straight out the window.

Sarah craned her head back to see if she was in the right spot. She was. The tower stood tall almost right above her. To see if the knife was on the steep angled roof she took a couple of steps back. It wasn't. More seconds drifted by as she scanned the gutter, looking for the telltale glint of metal. It wasn't there either, as far as she could tell.

She dropped her head, wondering how much time she had left and as she did a slight movement from far in her periphery caught her eye. It had been nothing more than a flicker of green, a breeze shaking a tree, a phantom of her imagination, a bounty hunter stealing behind the municipal building...

Had it been the hunter? Had he spotted her staring up at the building with her mouth hanging open like an idiot? From his point of view she probably looked no better than a zombie. Maybe she had looked like nothing more than a zombie! With the stupid pack around her neck and her body draped in filthy rags, she certainly didn't feel very much like a human. And who, but a zombie, would spend their time gaping at a building?

If that had been him, and he had been fooled, it meant Sarah only had a minute or two to get away. Her first impulse was to make a dash for the forests that edged in close to the town but she squashed the idea. The trees were hundreds of yards away and the clock tower afforded a great view of the entire town. He would see her and the hunt would last only minutes.

Since she couldn't run she had to hide. The most logical place to hide was exactly where no would want to: a building on fire. The *Kinkos* was out of the question, it wouldn't be anything but rubble soon. The same was true of the next couple of store fronts which were beginning to brew up in a fierce way, however the fourth only seemed to be venting smoke from its second floor windows while the main floor look fully intact. It was, she hoped, perfect: close enough to the fire to be considered a crazy place to hide, but not so close as to get incinerated.

A voice in her head warned: *Is this what Jillybean would do?*

The voice made Sarah's teeth grind together. Who knew what Jillybean would do? Sarah didn't and she couldn't spare even a second to consider it. She headed for the stores across the street, though not in a rush. Not only did she have the hunter to fool, there was a line of zombies that she would have to cross as well. Most were standing in the middle of the street, still captivated by the fire. They didn't seem to see her even when she moaned her way right through them.

That was more than fine with her; she had never felt more vulnerable than at that moment. However, the feeling grew when she had to turn to get the shop's door open; first she accidentally dropped the axe which clanged onto the sidewalk and then a shard of light shot into her eye from the direction of the tower.

It was her assumption that the hunter had the rifle she had left up there pressed to his cheek and was glassing the street and the buildings, searching for her. If she was in his crosshairs she would die, it was as simple as that. If not then she might escape without being seen at all. The image produced by the scope was wonderfully sharp, but also extremely narrow, meaning if she could get inside quickly he might not see her.

She entered the shop by the quickest way possible: she turned the doorknob with her bound hands and fell in backwards. Once inside she kicked the door shut and tried look around through a gathering smoke.

A sign above the counter read: *Earl's House of Vacuums*. It was a sad, lonely looking establishment, as if even in its heyday the bell above the door hadn't rung more than once or twice a week. There was even a TV on the counter with a canted chair in front, where Earl no doubt had sat with his feet propped up watching *Wheel Of Fortune* while waiting for his next customer.

How a shop like this made it, Sarah didn't know. America, whether for good or for bad, had become a nation that understood and embraced the concept of temporary. People didn't hold onto their jobs for thirty years anymore, they didn't stay in the same home their whole lives as their parents had. Half the time they didn't even keep the same spouse for more than a few years.

Before the apocalypse it was understood that things did not last, and that included vacuums.

A broken belt was about the limit most people would accept in way of repairs. Anything more meant a trip to Sears or Walmart for a new one.

Yet, somehow, Earl's had been in business right up to the eve of the Apocalypse. Though it wouldn't last much longer. Already the room had filled with smoke and the temperature was such that Sarah's pores had blossomed sweat the second the door had closed. Her eyes stung and she could barely open them even into a squint. She tried to cough, but she choked instead—beneath the super-heated air there were nasty fumes that she feared would kill her if she stayed there any longer. Clearly, Earl's was not the perfect place to hide from the bounty hunter.

She had to get out of there, but with the hunter possibly up in the tower, leaving by the front door was a gamble she didn't want to attempt. Instead she stumped forward on her knees towards a door that led to a rear area. Here the smoke roiled angrily and was so thick that she couldn't see the ceiling seven feet above her head and the sound of the nearby inferno was a roar that blotted out her thoughts.

What was worse was the temperature in the room. It seemed to slap her in the face. Even on her knees it had her head spinning. Her body rebelled against the intensity of the heat, it was as if her lungs and throat had shrunk and, when she fought to suck air in, it felt like she was breathing through a very long straw. Each breath was an ordeal.

Still she was without options and she persevered despite the pain. When she reached the back room, she saw it was where Earl had fixed the few vacuums that came his way—it was sparse in its tools and more so in its inventory of broken machines. There was little to it and even if she had wanted to hide in the room, which was out of the question because of the fantastic heat, there was nowhere she could take cover.

This meant pushing on. Twenty-five feet from her she could see the lower half of another door. It had to lead out.

157

If it didn't, she knew she would die. The wall to her right had begun shimmering in the past few seconds. It scared her badly, more than the smoke and the heat. She watched it as she plodded forward on her knees. She watched as the paint first turned liquid and ran down the wall. What remain bubbled and swelled; when these popped they did so with little gouts of flames. The wall was simply evaporating from the intense heat on the other side.

She tried to go faster as the wall began to crumble and the colors of flying orange and hideous black swept the entire room, but the air was no longer breathable. Her lungs shriveled and her throat was raw sandpaper and try as she might, the hellish air wouldn't pass. Seven feet from the rear exit she lost consciousness and fell flat on her face.

Sarah would've died right there, except that at almost the same time a wall came down in the adjacent store, collapsing the roof. This took out the wall that had been burning twenty feet from Sarah, which fell away from her with a great crash. Now, the smoke and flame that had been trapped shot upward, billowing into the late afternoon air adding to the tower of smoke that was already a mile high.

A hot wind—what would have been unpleasant on any other day—rushed in and breathed Sarah back to life. Barely.

The first thing she noticed was that half of her body, the side facing the fire, was so hot it couldn't be described, while the other side in comparison, was like the dark side of the moon. She rolled on her side, putting her back to the flames. This brought one second of relief and then it felt like her back was being peeled by searing whips.

A great part of her wanted to give up and die, however the lash of pain and heat forced her on. Standing seemed beyond her. Even kneeling was too much just then and so she undulated like an inch worm on its side to the door. There, she did her best to kick it open, stomping at the knob until she felt death closing in on her once more.

She would have to stand up where the heat doubled and the fumes were poison; standing was the only way out of the inferno that was quickly engulfing *Earl's House of Vacuums*. From her back, she rolled to her side and then, as if she had become used to moving with her hands tied behind her back, she went to her knees and then to a standing position in one fluid motion. Immediately, she swooned and fell face first into the door, held up simply because her knees had locked instead of buckling. The heat sapped her of every ounce of energy she possessed, while at the same time the smoke and the fumes made her so light-headed that her thoughts seemed to be coming to her from a tin can with a string attached. The string was very long and, the sound of her inner voice a tinny, weak thing.

Each thought oozed up from her mind as if it were bubbling up through thick molasses.

Turn around.

"Ok," she mumbled, twisting against the door, feeling like skewered meat over a fire.

Grab the door knob.

There was no speaking now. The fire had baked every drop of moisture from her mouth. Her tongue felt swollen and scratchy, like a hot sock balled in between her cheeks. Her lips had begun to crack and peel. Fighting to stay conscious, she turned the knob; nothing happened.

She was beyond the ability to panic or feel fear in any capacity; all she knew was pain. The door was locked or broken or she had forgotten how to work it or her hands...

Try the other way. Turn it the other way.

Compared to the great roar of the fire, the inner voice was the smallest sound in the universe and yet it could not be denied, no matter how much she wanted to let her knees come undone and fall to the side and be done with the pain.

In some fashion, the inner voice was connected to her hands. Sarah turned the knob the other way and the door swung out, opening onto an alley where a number of zombies stood watching the fire. They glanced at her but she didn't see them and even if she had she wouldn't have cared. In the few seconds of consciousness left to her she saw and understood only one thing: water.

Next to one of the zombies was a puddle left over from the previous day's rain. It was deep black with a blue-green oily sheen floating on top. Nothing had ever looked so inviting. She staggered to it, sagged to her knees and collapsed into it face first.

Sarah was unconscious in six inches of water and again she might have died if not for the strangest of fates. The zombie she had stumbled past saw her as a wild looking apparition; black with soot and grime, short hair smoldering from the heat and going in every direction, her body torqued with her hands behind her back and a bag across her neck, and yet something in her demeanor made the zombie curious as to her humanity.

With a growl it yanked her over and stood staring as water ran down her face, carving bizarre streaks through the mud and muck plastered to her soft skin. Had she moaned or spluttered or done anything other than just lie there as still as death, it would've attacked. But she did not and, after a moment, the zombie's natural inclination to destroy anything human faded back into what was left of its mind.

She went ignored until the sun dipped and the fire grew less and the moon strode to the middle of the heavens and lit her body with its pale light. Then she was shaken into a state that was close to consciousness. Even when water was splashed onto her face, the night was nothing but shadows in her mind.

Hands gripped her and she was flung across a broad shoulder. Then she remembered nothing more until sometime later water was again splashed into her face. It was clean and cold and she drank it even as she blinked trying to make sense of the world. Her first sense was of pain. The greatest was in her hands and shoulders, but there was also pain in her jaw as she drank and in her right eye as she tried to blink and see where she was.

She guessed she was in the basement of a home. It was hard to tell because the flickering candlelight created more shadow than understanding, and because the man she knew as the mayor of Easton stood directly in front of her blocking most of her view.

"You're a liar and a fake and you're not the queen of England," he said, when her blue eyes began to flutter. "I know! I know the truth about who you really are and what your mission is. He told me." When he spoke he would blink very hard, closing his eyes for most of a second and squeezing them tight before popping them open again.

"Who? Who told you?" she asked in a whisper. It hurt to talk. She was so thirsty that her lips and her throat crackled like dry leaves.

The mayor pointed away from himself toward a wall. The gesture was meaningless to Sarah and she shook her head. "The man from the government. The real government. He told me what you are, Sarah Rivers. He told me you are a spy!" He practically spat out the word, making a face of disgust as he did.

Again Sarah shook her head and after trying to coax the smallest amount of saliva into her mouth she asked, "The man in camouflage? Is he here?"

"No. He's left to hunt down the others spies. That's right, he knows what you are. He knows about the Shadow Government. He knows and now I know. I knew things weren't right. I knew the people had changed. I didn't always know. No, I didn't. He showed me the truth! Truth and lies! And now I can show him that I belong on the right side. I just have to call him."

"How?"

"Not by phone!" he cried in sudden anguish. "That uses beams. It's how it all started with satellites and cell phones and high frequency beams. We can't use those. He told me about what you did to them, how you sent coded messages. No, we can't use them. But I can use a CB. He gave me a CB. He told me to call if I found you and I did. He also said to be careful. You're the decoy. He said you tricked him so the other spies could slip around west. He knows and I knows."

Chapter 20

Jillybean

Pinedale, Maryland

"I think west is the only way," Neil said. His map was out, laid flat on the hood of a little red car. Though the car was little compared to the adults, it was still too tall for Jillybean to see what Neil was pointing at. "We should make for Hagerstown and then go south on I81."

Maps, especially road maps with all their squiggly lines, didn't interest Jillybean much and, since she was serving real tea in real tea cups at a real tea party, she was exceptionally disinterested. The ramble house they had spent the night in had provided a dusty can of Lipton's Iced Tea, and one of the many, many cars they had emptied of gas had two bags of months-old groceries in the back seat. Among the remains of long-rotten vegetables were some odds and ends: canned goods, pasta, spaghetti sauce and a package of Nutter-Butters.

Strictly speaking, store-bought, peanut butter flavored cookies were not acceptable tea party fare, with the sole exception being apocalyptic tea parties in which the rules were generally relaxed. Sadie, who didn't seem all that excited about the map either, nibbled at her cookies, sipped her tea, and sighed in weariness.

"Why do we want to go west?" she asked. "Just because the colonel's men walked off eastward? I'm sure they have cars. They could be anywhere."

"But you not think of trap," Nico said. He also held a cup of tea—Jillybean wouldn't be a proper hostess if she left him out just because he guzzled his tea more as an afterthought instead of taking proper sips with his pinky up as manners dictated. "It was most like the other bounty hunter who set spikes in our path. If he is in east then we go west as Neil says."

"Just not today," Sadie said. They had spent the second half of the day knocking holes in gas tanks, collecting almost forty gallons. After that, Nico, who was sound in his mechanics, worked elbow-deep in the guts of a dark blue Explorer getting it ready to travel.

"There's still a few hours of daylight left," Neil said. "We could probably get fifty miles further if we left right away."

"You don't understand," Sadie replied with another heavy sigh. "I'm beat."

"Maybe you could take a nap on the way," Neil suggested. Unlike Nico, he raised his teacup to the hostess before taking a modest drink.

Jillybean nodded in return, but quickly looked to Sadie to see what her reaction would be to Neil's deceptive remarks. Sadie wouldn't be able to sleep in the SUV unless they were very lucky.

First, there were the ever-present zombies; running over one was dreadful and waking up to see their black blood smeared across the windshield was the stuff that made nightmares. Then there would be the constant fear of the bounty hunter and the colonel's men coming after them. All day they had moved about like furtive squirrels. This was a natural state for Jillybean, but it had left the rest of them frazzled.

With a bit of a grimace, Sadie shook her head at Neil's idea. She then jutted her chin toward the smoke in the north-west sky. It had been a devil's cloud of billowing black the day before; now it was a haze of grey-brown on the horizon.

"Why haven't we considered checking that out?" she asked. "Smoke means fire and fire means people. Besides we could be there and back before dark."

"It may not mean the right kind of people," Neil replied. "It could be another trap."

"It could be Sarah sending out a signal for help," she countered. Neil continued to look skeptical and Nico joined him, so Sadie turned to Jillybean and asked, "What does Ipes think about the smoke?"

Rather than answering the question, Jillybean purposefully stuck a Nutter-Butter in her mouth and turned it sideways so her cheeks bulged. As she chewed she held up a small finger to forestall them further, hoping they would go on to another subject in the meantime.

Ipes was decidedly unhelpful on the subject of helping Sarah. It was disconcerting...no, it was a little frightening to Jillybean. Ipes had always helped her in everything. Sure, he would make his jokes or be stern like her father had been, but lately he would tell her things that weren't true or things that were partially true and partially lies. That wasn't how it was suppose to be.

"Well?" Sadie asked. Her smile held a reserve of worry that showed through even beyond the last of her sickness.

Jillybean finished chewing her cookie and then took a sip of her tea.

I don't think we should investigate the fire, Ipes said. *I agree with Mister Neil, it's probably a trap, and if it's not, then it's someone in trouble. As much as I'd like to help, we can't even help ourselves, Jillybean. The grode-ups have only the one gun between the three of them.*

The little girl turned slightly away from the grownups and whispered, "What if it's Miss Sarah who's in trouble?"

It's not, Ipes replied. *Miss Sarah wouldn't try to signal us in so blatant a manner because she knows it would also attract every bounty hunter within miles.*

That made sense. It was perfectly logical, however it wasn't the entire truth. Somehow she understood that either Ipes knew more than he was letting on, or he had a very good guess concerning the fire. "Anything else you want to add?" she asked, sounding cross and very much like her mommy used to when Jillybean had done something wrong. With the adults watching her she did not wait patiently and when half a minute passed, she tried something new: she attempted to read the zebra's mind.

It had always been the other way around. Ipes seemed able to read her mind at will. Now, she strove to find his thoughts in the thimble-full of fluff he used as a brain—

and was shut out. The zebra closed his mind in a way Jillybean couldn't.

It's for your own good, Ipes told her. *I'm sorry.*

Shaken, she turned to the adults. "Ipes says west is ok," she said, wearing a false smile.

"We wanted to know what he thought of the smoke," Sadie reminded her.

"Oh, that. It's a trap, one way or the other." Even as she said this, Jillybean didn't know quite what she meant by it. It was as if her words had come from a part of her mind she didn't normally use. Her blue eyes flicked to Ipes, however he pretended to be deep in conversation with the Velveeta Rabbit.

Before she could question anything more about what happened, Neil jumped on the statement as if it was all the proof they needed. "You see? It's a trap. I know Sarah... not as well as I thought, but I know she wouldn't set a fire like that. It would attract bounty hunters like crazy. It's probably where those army guys went."

"Then we head west?" Nico asked.

Sadie rubbed her head before answering: "Yes, tomorrow."

Only Neil chaffed at the delay. "She's been gone for five days," he said. "She could be in Atlanta by now and we've barely gone fifty miles!"

Nico dropped to one knee next to Sadie and then lifted her as if she was made of feathers and down. "We endanger Sadie too much as is," he said to Neil gruffly. "She will be strong enough to travel tomorrow." The Russian put her in the Explorer and drove her back to the ramble house, as Jillybean called the trashed out place they were staying in.

"Well, how do you like that?" Neil asked. "They just left us here."

"I don't know," Jillybean answered. "I think I'm ambigalus about it. That's what means I don't have an opinion. Which means I don't mind walking."

"I think you mean: ambiguous," Neil told her. He drank down the rest of his tea and stowed away the remains of the tea-party in his pack. As they started the trek back, he added, "That's a big word for a little girl."

"I know lots and lots of big words. Mostly thanks to Ipes. He usually helps me out, though he's being a pain today."

Neil seemed only partially focused on her; the other part watched all around them for zombies and he answered vaguely, "Oh, yeah? What words?"

"Like terrapin. That's what means turtle," Jillybean said. "Or a type of turtle. I know lots of kinds of turtles. There's a box turtle, and the snapper, and the red-eared slider, and the...

Ask him what he's going to do with Miss Sarah when he finds her, Ipes suggested, interrupting. Jillybean cleared her throat and, deciding to ignore the unruly and rude zebra, went on listing the turtles that fell within her ken. Neil always let her go on-and-on without judging, which was one of his best traits in her eyes.

"Isn't there one that sits in the mud?" Neil asked when she paused for a breath.

She giggled and said, "Yep. It's called the mud turtle. That reminds me there's also the sea turtle, but for some reason there isn't a flying turtle."

Before she could think of another type of turtle, Ipes asked, *What happens if he finds Sarah and she still wants to go after Abraham and the Believers? Did you ever wonder what's going to happen to you if that happens? We both know Neil won't let her go a second time. He'll try to help her break into New Eden and rescue Eve.*

With Ipes in her mind she couldn't think of any type of turtle or anything for that matter. "I like Eve," was all she could think to say. Neil heard this; only raising an eyebrow but not saying anything.

That's not what's important here, Ipes said. *We all love Eve, but she is beyond our help now, only they don't see that, especially Sarah. When we find her she's not going to stop and that means Neil is going to go with her and that means Sadie will also. And that's fine, but what isn't, is that they're going to want you to try to help them. I know it. In fact, they're going to make you help them.*

"Why shouldn't I?"

Because Eve is their daughter, and Sadie is her sister and you...you're nothing but a weird little girl. That's what Sarah thinks of you. She doesn't care about you and she doesn't love you.

"But what about..."

What about Neil? Is that what you were going to ask? Sure, Neil likes you. But we both know he loves Sarah and he loves Sadie and he loves Eve. Don't you get it? He loves them more because they are his family. Where do you fit in?

"I don't know," she said in a whisper.

You fit with me, Ipes said. *I'm your family. These other people don't love you like I do. They won't protect you. They'll use you because you're smart and resourceful and...*

A couple of little sounds behind them, a scuff and then a scrape, stopped the zebra's vile words. It was a monster; a townie as far as Jillybean could tell by its mullet haircut and the tattered remains of a Walmart wardrobe. It only had one arm.

"Mister Neil?" she said.

He smiled down at her. "You've been quiet for a long time. I take it you and Ipes had a lot to discuss."

"Yes, but..."

"You were so deep in conversation that you almost seemed to be sleep-walking," he said with a laugh. "I bet a zombie could've snuck right up on you and you wouldn't have even known."

"Yeah, maybe. Speaking of zombies, there's one behind us," she said.

Neil jumped and let out a squawk of fear, something Jillybean thought he did for her amusement. "Stay behind me," he ordered, brandishing his axe. "This is why you should be more careful. Daydreaming out here could get you killed."

167

As the zombie advanced, Neil took a step back, tripping on a branch and landing, hard on his butt. Without thinking, Jillybean leapt in front of him and waved her arms.

What are you doing? Ipes cried.

Since it was obvious she didn't answer, instead, as the monster was missing his left arm, she darted to her right. He turned slowly, reaching across his body with his one arm—in this way he had an effective reach of eight inches. It was nothing for the quick little girl to keep away from him until Neil came up and split its skull.

"Now that is how you kill a zombie," he said, working the axe out of the dead beast.

He thinks he was saving you, when it was you who was saving him, Ipes said. *You see? He can't protect you. It's only going to get worse when we get to New Eden.*

"Mister Neil? Can I put Ipes in your backpack? I don't feel like carrying him right now."

Chapter 21

Sarah

Easton, Maryland

"Don't," Sarah said, her lips cracking. The air coming up through her blistered throat was like acid. "Don't call."

The mayor of Easton sneered through his wild beard, "You would like that I bet. You would like to see my appointment with destiny canceled. But I can't trust you, liar. You're not the Queen of England and you're probably not even Sarah Rivers. You are a spy. I know a spy when I see one. You're a spy, a spy, a spy! A spy with the shadow-government. I know."

"Don't," she whispered. He didn't seem to hear. With his index finger pointing up, a gesture of some importance to him, he left the room.

Sarah almost swooned again, but she fought the sensation. She had to stay awake if she had any chance to talk the crazy man into letting her go. This led to a series of questions: How do you talk sense to the senseless? How do you reason with the unreasonable? Despair hit her like a truck as she realized she was doomed. This crazy person was crazier than most and crazy was the only language he spoke.

"Here it is," he called from somewhere in the house. There was the sound of footsteps banging down stairs, heavy breathing growing louder, and then the mayor was back in the room carrying a CB: a squat, rectangular box with dials and buttons and a small hand microphone. He plunked it on a table and left again.

"Need juice. Need electricity, but don't get it on me. Can't get any on me or they will know. I know." Seconds later, Sarah heard the whirring sound of a small generator. "Careful! Careful! Can't get it on me," he said in a carrying whisper. Now he came in holding an extension

169

cord near the end; he had it up in the air as if there was something fluid in it that he didn't want to spill. When he plugged it in he breathed a sigh of relief.

"I'm clean," he said happily. "No waves, no cells, no advanced alien technology. I know. He told me."

"He lied to you," Sarah said. It was clearly the truth, which meant the crazy mayor wouldn't believe it for a second. It almost felt like a waste of breath, but the statement triggered something in her mind. The bounty hunter had found a way to talk to this crazy man. He must have spoken the language of crazy to him.

"You are the liar," the mayor said matter-of-factly. He then flicked on the CB which instantly began to warble and scritch erratically with static.

"Turn it off before it's too late," Sarah cried. Just that little outburst had her seeing the world through a hazy filter. She was about to pass out. "They can hear you," she said before the world turned black.

Again she had water splashed in her face to revive her. This time she had the wit enough to keep her eyes closed so that he splashed her three times before he started to shake her. The water was wonderful, but the shaking sent waves of pain down her arms which were still tied behind her back.

"Who will hear?" he demanded. "Are you lying to me? Can someone hear? Don't you know this isn't cell technology. There aren't beams coating us, damn it. I know. That means you're lying...right? Answer me!"

"Water," she begged. "Can't talk."

He had a big plastic jug which he poured directly into her mouth. She drank until the jug was half-gone and then he grew angry again. "Who can hear? Who? That's a CB. That means *citizens band* and I'm a citizen! I'm the mayor of Easton. I won that election fair and square. And before that I was...Artie. Me and Beth always did those block parties on the Fourth...and I bowled on Wednesdays at the *King's Pin*? Remember that? I told you all about that. Remember on Thursdays we'd stay home because...

because Beth always liked her shows on Thursdays. That's right. On Fridays we'd go out to the Megaplex."

"I remember, Artie," she said.

"Yeah, so that makes me a citizen. I can use the CB. I should be allowed to....but not if someone can hear me. Who is it? Tell me, please, who can hear?"

"The, uh, the CIA." It was all she could come up with. Sarah Rivers wasn't exactly conversant in crazy.

Artie was confounded by the answer. He went to the CB and looked it over very closely. "It's not bugged. You're lying!"

"No, I'm not. You have to open it up," Sarah said. It was her hope that he would break it in the process. She was a little too transparent.

"You are sneaky," he said in an evil whisper, his eyes slits in his dirty face. "You want me to break it don't you? You think you'll be able to get away. You'll go back to the shadow-government and make your report. I won't let you, because I know the truth!"

He turned the CB back on and the static was loud. Within the heavy fuzz there were strange echoes and high pitched noises as if birds were using another CB somewhere close by. Every once in a while there was an eerie voice that spoke only a word or two; it barely seemed human.

"They can't hear," Artie said. He seemed to be trying to convince himself.

"Not only can they hear," Sarah whispered. "They can also…send out beams…to control your mind. Listen. Did you hear that? It's in the static. There it is again."

The mayor pulled his hands back from the CB in fright. "I-I heard that. It said *Cutter*. And that! Was that ice or eyes? Those are real words. Did you hear that too?"

She hadn't actually. There had been something that sounded like "nice" but that was about it. Still, she wasn't about to admit that. "Turn it off!" Sarah cried. "They want you to cut your eyes out. I heard it, too."

His face stricken by terror, Artie scrambled at the machine hitting every button and eventually turning it off.

171

He then just stood there in silence looking at the ceiling as if expecting, at any moment, that jack-booted thugs would burst into his home and drag him away. "Are they coming? Did they hear us?"

"I don't think so, but you better unplug it just in case."

This time his fear of the plug was so great that he ran and got a towel which he wrapped around his hands before pulling the extension out. He then hurried to where the generator was, sweating in his fear of the electricity. When he came back, he brought more water. Sarah's mouth came open thinking it was for her, but he didn't give her a drop. Instead he poured it on the CB.

"Gotta get rid of the residuals," he explained. "Everything has residuals but this is really dangerous. I bet the beams are all over us."

"There's some on me," Sarah said. "Can I have some more water?"

She groaned in pleasure as he doused her with water. Every part of her felt blistered and raw. "Thank you. Now, can you untie me? I'm afraid for my hands. I haven't felt them since the fire."

Artie took a step in her direction, but then his paranoia came back full force. "No. You're with the shadow-government! Obviously, I can't trust you. I can't trust anyone from either the government or the shadow government. You're all evil."

Sarah felt ten times better now that she had a belly full of water. Her head was finally clear enough to deal with one crazy person. "Think about it, Artie. Who gave you that CB? The man from the government, that's who. He's the one that's evil. Can you trust him? Can you trust his words?"

"No! He tried to control my mind. But I can't trust you either."

Sarah tried her best to give him a compassionate smile, however she could feel the blisters on her face begin to weep fluids and she had to wonder how horrible she looked. "You can't trust me, because you believe the man from the government," she stated.

"Yes…I mean, no."

"That's right. He told you a lie. I'm not from the shadow-government. I saved you from that CB. I kept your mind from being controlled. I'm on your side Artie."

"Who are you with?" he asked in a small voice.

Sarah could tell this was going to be the most delicate question she would have to face. The wrong answer would bring his crazy exploding out of him. "I'm all alone," she said, hoping the truth would suffice. His narrowing eyes told her it wasn't.

Who could she say she was with that sounded believable? The PTA? The Teamsters Union? The freaking Girl Scouts? It had to be someone that the "Government" would see as a possible enemy. Nothing sprang to mind at all except the image of little Jillybean. What would Jillybean do in this situation?

No answer came to her, only another question: How had she ever come to bastardize: *What would Jesus do?* into: *What would Jillybean do?*

The very question offered her the answer she was looking for. "I'm with…I mean, I'm a Christian. There's a prophet down south that supposedly had a vision of everything that has happened to us: the zombies and the black zones and all the death. His name is Abraham and he built himself a new civilization called New Eden. I think that's what that hunter was after. I think, maybe the government is trying to stop it."

Artie stared at her for a long time, trying to discern the truth in his addled mind. "Why would they be up here? If you say it's in the south why aren't they looking for it down there?"

"Because it's hidden," Sarah answered, the truth lending strength and conviction to her words. "Most of the buildings are underground. Only the fields of wheat and corn and all that are above ground."

He began nodding at this, but then his eyes flew open wide, and he ran from the room only to come back with a bible. "Here it is! It's in the gospel of Matthew: *That it might be fulfilled which was spoken through the prophet saying, I will open my mouth in parables; I will utter things hidden since the foundation of the world.* They're underground! I get it now."

"Are you a Christian," Sarah asked. The bible gave it away that he was, but she asked the question in a quiet tone, as if her great hope was countered only by her fear that he wasn't.

"Yes," he answered and there was awe in his voice.

Here was her salvation. Not only would he free her, she was sure he would accompany her south and in that way she would be able to pass the doors to *New Eden* and find her baby. All she had to do was play her cards right.

"Me too," she said, again truthfully. "I think the government has taken their war on Christmas and turned it into a war on Christianity."

"I know it has," Artie said, eagerly. "That's what this is all about! It's the beams and the cell towers of the government. It's turned the Christians into the undead. Wait, I got it!" he cried suddenly and raced a circle in the room with his hands in his hair. "It makes sense now! The government..." Here he came very close to Sarah and dropped his voice to a whisper, "...The government is in league with Satan. It's the only way this could have happened. The undead are his minions. I know."

"Yes, and now they're after us," Sarah said, adding fuel to the lunatic's fire. "They're after the only Christians left."

"By God, you're right," Artie said. He looked at her and for the first time seemed to notice that she was still trussed up. He produced a knife and began to saw at the ties that bound her. "You're not alone, now."

"Thank God," she said and again meant it. The relief at having her hands freed was glorious, fantastic, wonderful, and lasted only thirty-two seconds. Then the pins and needles of returning blood flow struck. It was torture. "Oh, jeeze. That hurts so bad!" Sarah cried. In seconds her agony was such that she was writhing on the floor.

Artie watched this with growing alarm and came to, what could only be considered, an insane conclusion:

"There must be a chip in you! It's probably going to self-destruct." Before these words could even register in her pain-stricken mind, Artie had his knife out and was bending down to her. "We got to cut it out of you."

The glittering edge of the blade focused her like nothing else could. "No," she gasped, between gritted teeth. "It's my circulation coming back. Rub my arms, please."

He recoiled at the idea. "I can't. Remember Beth? I have Beth. She'll get better and then she'll come back. You can't..."

"Uhhh!" Sarah cried.

Artie stepped further back and held the knife up in front of him. "Beth wouldn't want me to touch you. It's a chip. I know it. I had one, too but I cut it out. Look." He yanked off his hooded jacket; underneath he wore a stained and acid smelling grey t-shirt. He pulled up his left sleeve and showed a red-purple wound that couldn't be more than two weeks into the healing process.

"You probably have two chips," he added. "And maybe some wiring running between. We'll have to get it all. It's the only way. I know."

"No, no. It's passing," she said, forcing a fake smile onto her face and trying to ignore the pain induced nausea that was threatening to bring up the precious water in her belly. "I feel better now. It's just the circulation returning. I'm fine. Can I get some more water, p-please, and some Chapstick."

"Chapstick. Beth had some sort of balm for her lips," Artie said, growing calm and staring at a wall. "I always thought it was funny. She had such thin lips, like two pink lines that went around her mouth. That's all. But for some reason she always put on the balm. I used to joke that she had nothing to get chapped."

Sarah was barely holding it together. "Yeah, could you get that?"

When he left, she went back to groaning and rocking. Luckily for her, his search for lip balm took ten minutes and by the time he returned the worst of the pain in her hands and arms had subsided. The rest of her was another story. She had second degree burns on her face, neck, and hands. Even her scalp was blistered and bright red beneath her bad haircut.

She was also dehydrated to a degree she had never known before. This turned out to be a blessing in disguise. Artie was at his sanest when he was busy with a task, such as fetching water, or making a bed for her to sleep in. When he was idle, his mind went to bizarre and frightful places.

Frequently he would forget who she was. When that happened he would stalk about, threatening her with his pipe until she could convince him that she was Janice from down the block. Apparently there was some sort of physical resemblance between them, or at least there had been—Janice had become one of "them." Sarah made sure not to dwell on that.

Instead, she reinforced the name Janice at every opportunity. She dreaded the idea of getting to New Eden only to have Artie drop the name Sarah Rivers.

Sarah slept fitfully that night. This was due in part to the pain, but a larger part was due to Artie, who could not control his crazy. He ran about the house at the oddest times and would leave in a rage at others, and always he would mutter to himself.

He was an average-sized man, with the insanity-fueled strength of a giant. His mental state also made him altogether fearless; there wasn't a zombie he wouldn't crack over the head with his pipe if it got in his way. Strangely, perhaps because he was only barely human at this point with his wild beard and fiercely burning eyes, the zombies didn't go out of their way to attack him.

Thus Sarah was basically safe from everything but Artie. She slept with her door locked and the dresser pushed in front for added protection.

At dawn, when Neil was standing in the kitchen of the *ramble* house eight miles away, trying to swallow the left over fried carrots, making retching noises as he did, Artie left. He didn't give any indication of where he was going or when he would be back. He just left.

The four hours he was gone was the best sleep Sarah had. Despite the rest, she awoke in pain, was light-headed and thirsty as if all her drinking the night before had simply flowed right through her—and she had to pee very badly.

With the light of day, she discovered she was in a boxy, two-story home just off the main street, a few blocks from where the *Kinkos* fire was winding down. It wasn't much of a suburban house except for the kitchen which was bright and airy, and very clean; impossibly clean. It unnerved Sarah the way every chrome surface shone, and how every window was clear as the morning air and how not a speck of dust was visible to the naked eye.

The rest of the house was as ignored as the kitchen was cared for. "This must be Beth's place," Sarah surmised, standing in the doorway of the kitchen. She resisted every urge to find out if there was anything in the fridge to eat, fearing that Artie would know if she stepped one foot in the room. It would send him over the deep end, she was sure.

She nosed about the rest of the house until she found a jug of water in the master bedroom. In seconds she drank it down completely, and then went back to bed. When the sun was directly overhead, Artie came back in a foul mood. He stomped around the house complaining about the grass being too long in a neighbor's property. Sarah thought it best not to say anything until he calmed down.

"Hello? Artie?" she called when his yelling had been reduced to a low angry murmuring. "It's me, Janice."

He came flying up the stairs, three at a time and from the far end of the hall he pointed his pipe at her. "What are you doing in my house? Why aren't you home with Bob? If Beth knew…"

All at once his crazy eyes flew open and he began to nod at her. She nodded back, saying, "Remember the Prophet down south? You were going to come with me?"

"So he could fix all of this," he said. "So he could fix my Beth…and all the rest. Then the lawns will be right again. And the hedges. Paulson's hedge is too tall and it's hanging over the sidewalk. I tried to talk to him about it, but he is one of them. He got the beams, bad. They must be soaking into his skin."

"I bet they are, the poor guy," Sarah said, striking a note of compassion. "We have to hurry if we have any chance of saving someone that far gone. Do you have a car and some gas?"

He gave her a sharp look. "Why? Why do you want to know? I'm the mayor, not you, Janice. It's my responsibility to see that the resources of the community are used right and proper. It's a public-fucking-trust, Janice!"

With an effort she kept the smile on her face, though she couldn't help taking a step back. "Of course it is, Artie. But in order to save the community we're going to need to go south. We need a car or something."

"To save Beth," he said in a whisper. "Yeah, I have a car and lots of gas. The town hoarded everything in Chris Potter's storm shelter because of all the filthy thieves that came out of Baltimore. They were a plague, worse than the zombies. They were like locusts: eating and destroying everything in their path. I always thought Potter was crazy for being so afraid of storms, but he was right to be afraid of a storm of humans."

As Artie told it, Chris Potter had lived on what had once been the edge of town. He had owned farm property that he had sold in huge chunks to builders who had thrown together so many subdivisions that, in eight years he was no longer on the edge, but rather right in the middle of town. Potter had kept an acre for himself and under a portion of that was his "storm shelter." It was really a high-tech, multi-room man-cave that he used to get away from his constantly yammering wife.

It was large enough to throw fantastic Super Bowl parties in and, what was better as the town saw things, its doors were sod-covered and set into the ground. They were practically invisible unless one knew where to look.

The bunker held an astounding amount of fuel, both gasoline and diesel. In one back room there were fifteen huge barrels of the stuff. There were also stacks and stacks of crated weapons of all kinds, most of them completely useless. The only ammo left in the entire town was forty rounds of .38 caliber ammunition.

Sarah picked up a Smith & Wesson revolver and loaded it as Artie watched. "Just in case we run into that spy again," she explained. Since her companion was too unstable to look after the care and maintenance of his own beard, Sarah pocketed the remaining bullets.

There were many other items available: medicine, lanterns, candles, seeds, and tools. Of food there wasn't a single chip or can of corn.

The two of them worked at bringing up one of the drums of fuel from the bunker, and then about two in the afternoon they went for Artie's truck. It wouldn't start. The battery was dead with little possibility of revival.

Because of the "beams" and the supposed liquid and volatile nature of electricity, getting a new battery charged up on Artie's generator took far longer than it should have. The sun was dipping on a murky evening when they finally had everything ready to go, however with all of their tinkering and Artie's frequent cries of "Look out, the beams!" there was a sizable zombie problem around them.

Just like Neil, who was only a few miles away, Sarah decided to put off traveling at night and vowed to get an early start in the morning. The delay was nearly as painful as her blisters; she had been without her baby for thirty-eight days now and every second longer was a knife twisting in her heart.

Chapter 22

Sadie

Pinedale, Maryland

Sadie woke to birds outside her window doing their raucous Spring thing and making a racket fit to wake the dead. Cuddled up beside her, with a heavy arm thrown across her chest, Nico snored on, oblivious.

He was a log in the mornings, slow to stir, slower to get his mind in action, long in his urinating. The man was a river of pee first thing in the morning. This silly thought brought a smile to her face and stricken with love she hugged his arm.

A mumble of Russian escaped him which she took to mean: *Too early*. Taking his arm back, he rolled away.

"Da," she agreed, utilizing her mastery of the Russian language to its fullest.

Normally, she liked nothing better than to slumber the morning down to its dregs, but she judged by the bird activity that they were already late. She gave Nico a shove and when that didn't stir him in the least she slapped his bare bottom.

"*Nyet*," he growled. "*Mya Chopa bolit*."

"Whatever that means," Sadie replied.

He rolled onto his back to reply: "It mean, I have nice ass. So no hit."

She laughed fondly and smiled at the hunk of man. He began to snore again a second later. "I know one way to wake the pee-pee champion." Sticking out an elbow, she leaned her full weight upon his bladder. This brought a grunt and a Russian curse from him before he grabbed her and held her to the mattress, lying over the top of her, nose-to-nose. That he could pick her up effortlessly, or pin her with only a single one of his strong arms always sent a warm thrill through her.

He held her easily as she squirmed with all her strength. When she finally went limp, he kissed her and said, "Good morning." The view from the window: a bright sun and the sky the color of a robin's egg suggested it was.

"I hope so," she answered. Despite the pretty morning and his strong arms, she began to feel the hollow nervousness that had accompanied most mornings since she had died.

When Sadie was younger, even during the early part of the apocalypse, she had greeted each day as the beginning of an adventure. Then Ram had been killed right in front of her, and Eve had been sold as an infant bride, and Sarah had been beaten and raped. The worst, in Sadie's perspective was when she, herself had been killed.

Now, she woke up everyday worrying: what would happen next?

Would someone die that day? Would they be shot or would a zombie get in a lucky scratch? Would they get robbed again? Would they stumble on Sarah's dead body? Would the bounty hunter finally catch up to them? All these questions hit her just like they did every day since she had been held under the green water of the East River, but this time was different. Sadie didn't get the feeling that someone had just walked across her grave.

Maybe I'm better, she thought. *Or getting better*. There was still the nervousness in the pit of her stomach, after all.

Aloud she said, "There's no time for smooches. We were supposed to have an early start."

Wearing a wolf's smile, he leaned in and kissed her deeply. Jillybean interrupted with a knock on the door.

Sadie knew each of their knocks: Jillybean would tap from low on the door and the sound was so light that it would carry eight feet and no more. Neil would knock twice and then listen at the door. Sadie could practically hear him *hoping* that nothing sexual was going on. Nico was loud, hitting the door with his fist as if to punish it. When Sarah was with them she would knock once, say

181

Hello, and then wait exactly two seconds before coming in, whether she had been invited or not.

That had always bothered Sadie to no end—and just then she missed it terribly.

"Come in, Jilly," Sadie said when Nico had rolled off her. As usual, Jillybean entered the room slowly, her blue eyes hyperaware of everything. "I see Ipes is being good this morning."

She carried both the Velveteen rabbit and the zebra. The night before she had been glum and it had just been the rabbit. "He says he's learned his lesson and will try to be more helpful."

"That's good," Sadie said. "I miss the old Ipes coming up with crazy plans. Does he have one for getting down to Atlanta before Sarah?"

Jillybean shook her head. "Nope. He doesn't think it's possible since she's had such a long head start. That reminds me, Neil says to get you two sleepy-heads out of bed. We're apose to be leaving soon."

They had little to pack and thus were sitting in the Explorer fifteen minutes later. Neil drove, singing: "*On the road again. I can't wait to get on the road again…uh…on the road again…*I guess I don't really know that song all that well."

Next to him in the passenger seat, Nico smiled in a strained way. "It was good. But this is better. Is Russian song for travel. Is called *Into Dark Forest*."

He sang it all the way through and it was very long. Or at least it seemed that way. It wasn't a dark dirge as Sadie had expected, but it also wasn't peppy enough for an American girl raised on Lady Gaga and Pink.

Jillybean offered her rendition of *Old MacDonald* next and as expected her version of *Old MacDonald* featured a zebra and a rabbit. Unexpectedly it also had elephants, otters, and fish. She had them rolling with laughter as she sang in all seriousness: "…with a bloop, bloop here and a bloop, bloop there…"

"I think that's what fishes say," she said, not at all worried that they had laughed. "Ipes says they don't say anything because they are aquatic. That's what means living under water, but I can speak under water. It doesn't sound all that clear and I have to be careful not to breathe in but I can talk a little."

Neil had her sing it again as if she were underwater and that was even funnier than the first version because of her complete seriousness in the matter. This time it was the elephant's trumpet spraying spit that had Sadie crying with laughter.

It was Sadie's turn to sing next, but she refused, saying she was tone deaf. "I don't want to break the mirrors."

"Can that really happen?" Jillybean asked. Neil explained that it could but not because someone was a bad singer, only if someone was a very powerful singer. "You could use your secret voice," Jillybean suggested. "That won't break anything at all."

Sadie lifted a single shoulder in her version of a shrug. "I don't have a secret voice. Wait, what's a secret voice?"

Jillybean looked around as if there were spies that might overhear. "It's a voice no one knows about. The voice you only use when no one's around. Everyone has a...no, Ipes. I'm talking, now shush. Everyone has one, that's what my mom says. I mean she used to say."

"I'm afraid I don't," Sadie said.

Neil glanced in the mirror and agreed, "I don't have one either. Do you, Jillybean?"

"Yes. But I already sang." She turned pink and held the zebra in front of her face. "Though I guess I could again if you all didn't look right at me. It's sort of embarrassing."

"Don't be embarrassed," Sadie said, patting her knee. "What are you going to sing?"

She had expected another kiddie song, instead Jillybean sang *Yesterday* by the Beatles. It was absolutely haunting. Her voice held the accumulated grief of a lifetime of pain and as she sang the car went dead quiet. It stayed that way long after she hummed the very last bar.

Sadie had to blink back tears. "Could you sing it again?"

183

"Could I sing a different one?" Jillybean asked. "Something happier?" When everyone agreed she launched into a medley of Christmas songs that took them all the way west to Hagerstown.

It was an old town with lots of brick buildings, mature trees, and even more mature zombies. The narrow streets were crammed with toothless, balding, wrinkled, grey creatures. The sight of them stopped Jillybean's singing, cold.

"This is weird," Sadie said, flinching back as the first octogenarian zombie tried to gum her window. It left a long streak on the glass.

"Maybe this part of the state just had an older population," Neil said.

"But where are all the young zombies?" Sadie asked. "There should be some. Not that I want them around. I'm just curious." No one could answer the question adequately and all were glad when Neil was able to turn the Explorer south onto I81.

"Other than the zombies, that was a pretty little town, didn't you think?" Neil asked after a few minutes, as always trying to put a positive spin on everything. He didn't get any takers on his question. Everyone looked a little ill—Neil had been forced to run over a number of the aged zombies and their bones had cracked with the sound of someone stepping on a bag of pretzels.

"At least they…at least…" Neil paused, looking into the rearview mirror. His eyes went huge.

"What is it?" Sadie asked, whipping her head around. Hagerstown was quickly fading in the distance, but there was something moving and seeming to grow, far down the road. It was a black spec on the highway that soon was close enough for them to make out: it was the bounty hunter's black Jeep.

"Oh crap!" Neil cried, flooring the Explorer. It was fairly speedy for its size, however Neil wasn't the best driver; when an obstacle presented itself, he would hang on the brake a quarter second too long, and he was slower on turns than the Jeep. Neil also had an issue with running over zombies. Sometimes he was forced into plowing straight over them and sometimes he would slow down to get around them. Unintentionally, he was creating a lane behind him for the hunter zip right through. In no time it became obvious that the hunter would catch up.

"Neil, what are we going to do?" Sadie asked. In her mind the obvious thing to do would be to give herself up so no one else would get hurt. They had only a single shotgun between them and who knew what sort of weaponry the bounty hunter possessed. Likely a machine gun of some sort, but even if he had only a deer rifle he could shoot them down from a distance. Their shotgun was practically useless after about forty yards.

Neil knew all of this as well. His face was lined with misery and fear; he could only shrug. "I don't know."

"You keep drive fast," Nico said, pointing forward. "You drive and maybe we get lucky."

"No," Jillybean said. "That's stupid. Take the next exit, Neil. When we make the turn, Nico and I will switch places." Her tone was curt and her words clipped as if she didn't want to waste time or breath.

"Why?" Neil asked. "What good…"

"Exit in one mile," she said, snapping her little fingers and pointing. "Face forward or you will miss it."

Sadie eased back away from the little girl, looking at her blue eyes and not seeing Jillybean in them. She got a queer feeling being so close to her. "Hey, Jillybean? It's going to be ok."

"No. It's not ok," she snapped, turning to look back behind them. "You have us blundering about like idiots. Did it take any brains to realize that the bounty hunter could just sit up near the junction of I-70 and I-81 waiting for us to come by? He's like a spider and you had her singing her way right into his trap. You're going to get her killed, don't you see that?"

Now Sadie felt cold. This wasn't Jillybean. With a quick yank, she snatched the zebra from Jilly's stiff fingers. The little girl blinked slowly. "What are you doing with Ipes?" she asked, confused.

185

"Oh, honey, I think Ipes was sort of controlling you," Sadie said. "You were saying things that didn't sound like you."

"I was?" she asked, shaking her head gently. "I don't think I was."

"You were, trust me," Neil said, turning off the exit. "But maybe you should've waited to do that, Sadie because I don't know what I'm supposed to do next. Do you?"

"Uh-uh," Sadie replied. She glanced to Jillybean and asked, "Do you know what we're supposed to do next?"

"Next about what?" Jillybean replied, looking completely baffled.

"Give her back the zebra," Nico said. He was clearly nervous, frequently wiping his hands on his jeans so the shotgun he was holding wouldn't slip.

Sadie pulled the zebra away further. "I don't think so. That was too weird. And we don't need Ipes. You and Jillybean switch seats." After they did, everyone but Neil looked to Sadie for what to do next. The Jeep was half a mile back and just coming off the exit.

"What do I do?" Neil demanded. His knuckles were white on the steering wheel and his right foot alternated between stomping the gas and cramming down on the brake as he followed a winding secondary road.

"I don't know! Try to lose him." It was all Sadie could come up with and within a minute it was obviously the wrong choice. The Jeep gained a quarter of a mile as Neil took one turn after another. The land was green, hilly, and thick with trees, however there really wasn't any place to hide since they kicked up a fine trail of dust wherever they went.

In desperation, Sadie handed the zebra to Jillybean. "Don't let him take control, Jillybean! Just ask him what we do next."

Her eyes bugged. "He says to take the next turn and stop hard." This seemed like the craziest thing possible, but it had been ingrained into them to listen to Ipes. The little girl then turned to Nico as the car shuddered to a stop. "Get in the cargo area and break the glass with the end of the shotgun."

In a flash Nico was in the back hammering the glass until it rained sharp crystals. Jillybean surveyed the distances as the roar of the Jeep came closer. "Back up! We have to be closer."

Neil threw an arm over the seat and backed up until Jillybean grabbed him. Almost at the same time, the Jeep bounced around the corner; it was twenty feet away by the time it slammed on its brakes.

"Shoot the windshield!" cried Jillybean to Nico. Thunder shook the Explorer and then Jillybean was shaking Neil and screaming: "Drive! Drive!" Nico fired twice more and then the road took a turn. The air smelled of hot sulfur and their ears rang from the blasts.

"Where do I go?" Neil screamed as if the hunter were still right on their tail still. He was nowhere to be seen at the moment.

"Take your next left," Jillybean said. "We have to get off these back roads. Ipes thinks all the dust we're kicking up will allow the hunter to track us."

Sadie sat in her seat shaking, feeling the sweat of her fright cool on her neck. "Did you get him?" she asked Nico.

He shrugged. "Maybe. I shot windshield; now he cannot see so well. Maybe I got tire too, but I do not know."

They took the next left so that they were heading roughly parallel to the highway a few miles to the east. No more roads branched off of it and Jillybean began to get nervous. "Ipes says we can't stay on this road. He thinks the bounty hunter may try to get to the highway, drive ahead and cut us off. We have to get to the highway before him."

Neil gestured all around: farm country on the left, forest on the right, more of the same ahead of them, except a distant water tower suggesting a town a few miles away. "That's great but I don't see a sign for the highway."

Jillybean pointed to the left across a field. "It's that way. Go that way."

"Hold on!" he cried, before turning the wheel and taking down a wire fence. The ride was jarring. It felt like it was going to rattle the fillings right out of Sadie's teeth and all the shaking made her realize that she had to pee. There would be no stopping, however.

In minutes the highway was in front of them and Neil really had to speed up to crush through the heavier fencing there. He did so with a giddy smile. "Next stop: Atlanta!" he said.

No one believed his enthusiasm. They stared out the back window waiting for the return of the bounty hunter. Not a hundred yards past the Martinsburg exit they saw the black Jeep a good mile and a half behind. "Do I go back to that exit?" Neil asked, slowing slightly.

"No," Jillybean told him. The Jeep was missing its windshield. Paper and trash were whipping round the camouflaged driver. "We'll lose too much of our lead. Ipes thinks we should be able to outrun him if Mister Neil will stop using the brake so much."

The hunter was a very good driver and Neil hadn't improved in the last few minutes. Again the Jeep began to close. "He's got a gun!" Sadie screamed. The black barrel of an M4 came to rest on what remained of the windshield. When the Jeep closed to a quarter of a mile, fire seemed to leap from it and the Explorer shuddered and slewed to the left.

Nico returned fire, but a shotgun was useless at such a long range. Bullets thumped into the Explorer at a steady tok-tok-tok. Two traveled all the way through the vehicle to shatter the front windshield and more took out the mirrors and sent pieces of dash flying. Neil hollered for everyone to get down—Sadie threw herself into the footwell just in time as holes started appearing in the back of the seat she had just been in.

"Holy crap!" Neil screamed as a new sound erupted: Bam! Bam! Bam! This was coming from in front of them. In the face of logic, Sadie popped her head up in time to see an army Humvee sitting across the highway. It seemed to be spitting fire from every window and when the bullets passed, the air shrieked as if in pain.

Chapter 23

Sarah

Washington DC

With the knowledge that the bounty hunter was going west, Sarah and Mayor Artie cruised south on I-95. Artie drove for the first half hour. During those thirty minutes he proved as unsafe as anyone Sarah had ever driven with, and that included a number of falling-down-drunks and a sixteen-year-old who had been in four crashes before she had her license a full year.

His lunacy and paranoia made him see enemies in everything, from wire-guided robot-crows, to satellites and drones hidden in clouds. In order to avoid these mirages, he would swerve dangerously left and right, or he would speed up to "lose" his pursuers. She drew the line when he wanted her to use the .38 to shoot the clouds.

"How about I drive?" she said when she couldn't take it anymore. "*They* will never expect it."

As a passenger he was nearly as bad.

He wouldn't let them drive under power lines, period. This forced them into many annoying and time consuming detours. Telephone wires were easier to slip past; all he had to do was wrap his head in his coat. He became so difficult that she looked forward to the next set of telephone lines.

"Are they gone?" he asked, his voice muffled by a sweat-smelling winter parka.

"Not yet," she lied. "You better stay hidden." She had fifteen minutes of peace before the heat forced him to come up slowly. When he looked at her through slitted eyes, she said, "Drones," by way of explanation.

"Right. The drones know. We have to be careful with the drones. I vetoed all the drones when I was mayor. We were drone free. But we weren't chip free. You still have yours. We got to get it out of you before we get there. And the wires. You have the wires."

"We will, don't worry," she replied, trying to give him a smile. Smiling hurt her face so she kept it to a minimum. The mayor of Easton never smiled. His expressions only varied between the two poles of crazy and extra crazy. His wild hair and the abstract version of a beard he sported didn't help.

With a glance in the mirror, Sarah realized that she wasn't far behind him in the escaped-lunatic-looks department. Her own hair was singed frizzy in spots and, while the blisters on her face were healing, her skin had begun to peel in long sheets. "I look like a leper," she moaned.

Artie didn't disagree—a bad sign.

At the next set of power lines, Sarah wanted to make an excuse and stop at another salon, however they were on the outskirts of Washington and Artie wouldn't allow it.

"The government!" he hissed, holding his coat up to his face. "This is Washington for God's sake! They're here. Think of the beams. Can't you feel them peeling away your skin?"

"Yeah, I guess so."

"Then don't stop. Whatever you do, don't stop. You should see your face."

"Yeah," she said, glumly. A minute later she was forced to stop whether she wanted to or not. They were on the beltway trying to run the ring around the city when they came upon a horde of zombies; Sarah guessed there couldn't be less than ten-thousand of them. They had pulled down the highway fences and were migrating from the west, into the city.

"The beams!" Artie cried out. "See what they've done."

Sarah reached out and grabbed him. "I see and if you don't shut up they're going to see us as well."

Artie paid her no attention. He was focused on the thousands of slow-paced zombies stretching across their view. Before she knew it he had climbed out of the car.

191

"Go back," he yelled at the zombies. "Go back. You're heading right for the beams."

With the sun sending a fierce glare off the windshield, the zombies hadn't been aware that humans were in the car. Now that Artie was out of it and waving his arms, they couldn't help but notice. In a second, zombies by the thousands were charging right at the two of them.

"Get back in the car, Artie," Sarah said as calmly as she could. The zombies had a hundred yards to cover. There was still time. "Get in the car or I'll leave you. I swear to God."

He walked away from her flat-footed and stiff-legged as though his body was in rebellion against the lunacy. He turned his head as he walked and berated Sarah, "They need us. The beams, Janice, you never ever consider the beams. Can't you see that those people are coated with them?"

Her mouth fell open. He was going to die right in front of her, and it wasn't going to be an easy death either. The crowd of zombies roared and screamed in a manner Sarah hadn't seen before. *Do I leave him to die?* she wondered. The easy answer: *Hell yes*, came to her quickly and without actual thought on her part.

But what of New Eden? How was she going to get in without him? There was the Noah's Ark rule she had to consider. Coldly she rationalized that she had to save Artie because she needed him. He was there to serve a purpose. Yes, he would likely die, and that was just ok with Sarah, as long as he died for the right purpose—her purpose.

She gunned the truck, raced past Artie and yanked it hard over so that she was between him and the zombies. They were forty yards away.

"Get in!" she cried.

"No, the beams," he replied in proper lunatic fashion. He tried to go around the truck but she spurted it forward a few feet to cut him off.

She almost repeated her demand for him to get in, but then she realized they were speaking two different languages again. "Mayor," she called, trying to pitch her voice so that it could be believed that they had known each other longer than a day and a half. "You can't trust them, they're with the government."

This stopped Artie. He stared at the leading elements as they came closer. When they were twenty yards away he turned to Sarah and said, "Are you sure? They don't look like government."

Ten yards. Sarah tried to keep the fear out of her voice. "They're undercover, Mayor. The government never looks like the government, right?"

Five yards. "I see it now! That woman has a lab coat on..."

The zombies crashed up against the truck and it rocked. For a frantic second, Sarah feared that they would upend it. Instead, they beat at it with their hands and fists, and, in one case, a head. Some foul creature that had once been a perfectly ordinary woman repeatedly smashed her face against Sarah's window.

"Get in," Sarah screamed.

"They're scientists," Artie said, sounding dumfounded. He stood in the crook between the door and the truck body, but made no move to get in. "They must be controlling the rest somehow.

Sarah's window made a crackling sound that could be heard in spite of all the banging. "Jeeze!" she cried in a high voice. The window had cracked beneath the power of the fists. The zombies were pouring around the truck and out of desperation she jumped the vehicle forward three feet, dragging Artie along more by accident than by design.

It was a fortuitous accident. For some reason, the momentum of the truck and his body, prompted Artie to climb in and shut the door just as the beasts circled them completely. Now the truck truly began to rock. It felt like a dingy on a violent sea.

"You were right about the government," Artie said. Finally fear seemed to have seeped into his addled mind. He picked up his length of pipe and sat clutching it in both hands. "They were trying to coat us with the beams so that we would become like them. I know."

"You sure do," Sarah said. She hit the gas and began plowing through the undead. It was grisly beyond her experience, mostly because she decided to turn around. There were simply too many thousands of them in front to trust that their windows would hold up.

Since she couldn't gather any momentum, the turn was slow and sickening. Artie's truck wasn't one of the mega-cab, extended-bed, workhorse type of trucks. It was a Ford ranger and because of its small size it was having a tremendous time climbing over the grey bodies that fell beneath its tires. It wasn't long before she managed to high-center the truck on a particularly large mound of the undead.

"Not again!" Sarah cried, gunning the engine and hearing the tires spin in a high-pitched whine. The ranger rocked back and forth as more of the zombies got hold of the stranded truck, and Sarah realized that it was only a matter of time before the windows would come smashing in.

This understanding brought with it the cold-steel of panic lancing into her guts. It was a feeling that arced outwards—it clutched her throat, making breathing difficult; it ran down her hands, and they shook as though she were attached to a live wire.

Strangely, underneath all this fear, there was a single ray of calm within her. Its cause was simply the question that came to Sarah's mind: What would Jillybean do?

This wasn't the first time Sarah was in a high-centered vehicle, and Jillybean had been instrumental in getting that truck unstuck. That had been an easier situation. They'd had time on their side then. Now they had only seconds to work with.

So, what would Jillybean do?

"Does this have four-wheel drive?" Sarah asked Artie, as her eyes scanned the dash.

"No," Artie replied, simply.

"Of course not," Sarah said. "That would be too friggin' easy." She stared around trying to find something that would help, something, anything to get traction under the rear wheels. All she had was Artie's pipe, her backpack, a .38 and a thousand zombies. The panic began to overwhelm the slight sensation of calm, just as the zombies would soon overwhelm them both.

"Oh, Christ! What would Jillybean do?" She practically yelled this. Her breathing was now practically a dog's pant.

The answer came to her from that little pool of calm. *Jillybean wouldn't panic.* That was right. The little girl always seemed relatively detached, which probably allowed her to think straight. Sarah took a breath, deep and purposeful.

"I have to find a way to get something under the rear tires for traction or, I can do what Jillybean did, and weigh down the back." A small section of the rear window was on runners that would allow limited access to the bed. Sarah could squeeze through it if she wanted to, but since the bed was open it would be suicide. Nor was there anything in the cab with them that was remotely heavy enough that she could throw back there.

"Beams," Artie said, slinking lower in his seat. "They're coated with them. They're weighing them down and not just in the back. It's all over them. I don't like that. No to beams. Just say no."

His lunacy grated on Sarah's nerves, however she still had that Jillybean calm which kept her from lashing out uselessly. Instead she gazed at Artie with cold and calculating eyes. He was only a tool in those denim-blue eyes; the only question was how best to use him.

Not as sacrifice, not yet. Nor as a distraction—how would that get the truck unstuck? He was too big to fit through the back window to help and all that would do would attract more of them...

In a blink, Sarah saw a way to get the traction she needed. "I need this," she said, grabbing the four foot length of pole from Artie's hands. Normally his insanity lent him strength, now however he was cowering and his fear made him weak. He tried to grab the pole and at the same time he opened his mouth to complain.

Sarah smashed him in the face with the end of the pole, leaving his nose bent and bleeding. She said, "Sorry," despite not feeling sorry in the least. In fact she felt empowered. Her first thought at seeing the shocked and dazed look in his eyes was: *I wonder if this is how men feel when they win a fight...or rape a girl?*

The thought of rape caused the empowered feeling to diminish. "No time for dwelling on that crap," she said. Still crouched in the footwell, Artie began to splutter half-formed angry words. Sarah ignored him. Her backpack had been sitting on the console between their seats; she grabbed it, dumped everything out of it onto Artie's seat, and then stuck it on the pole. She slid back the little square of window behind her, and stuck the pole out.

Waving it around, she cried: "Come on zombies, you stupids! Come and get it."

Up to this point, the zombies had been focusing their rage on the cab where the two humans sat trapped. Now, a good number of them turned their attention on the pole and the pack. The shrieking words also helped to antagonize them. They seemed to go berserk, climbing over themselves in an effort to get to over the sidewall of the truck's bed.

Those that fell became stepping stones for the many hundreds of others pushing forward. Soon, a number of zombies were on the bed and even more were hanging off the end of the truck which began to tilt rearwards, just as she had hoped.

Sarah pulled the pole back inside, put the truck in gear and hit the gas. She had expectations of the truck mauling over the zombies, perhaps not in spectacular fashion, but in a steady way until they cleared this section of the herd. Reality was different.

The tires were slow to find traction seeing as they were basically driving over a carpet of human corpses. The truck jounced and lurched as the Ranger shredded up the zombies, spitting out slapping wet sheets of grey flesh and sending up gouts of black blood.

The undead weren't moaning as they usually did, they were practically shrieking. Next to her, Artie, concussed and cross-eyed, was ranting about his pole and the beams as he tried to climb up from the footwell. Blood poured from his nose like twin rivers. It ran into the thicket of his moustache where it disappeared, not even reddening his lips in the slightest.

Sarah couldn't spare a moment to worry where it was all going. Her world was all chaos and mayhem. She had managed to turn the Ranger around to point back the way they had come, but now there were so many of the beasts in her way, both in front of them and beneath the tread of her tires, that the truck seemed alive in her hands.

It bucked savagely and, when she least expected, would suddenly attempt to spin in place as one tire or the other would lose traction, slipping in guts. She found it impossible to keep the wheels aligned and, like a sailboat being driven by a crosswind, she found herself side-slipping toward the guard rail. Finally, she ran up against it with a shriek of metal.

"Hey!" Artie said, somehow finding, if only briefly, a moment of sanity. "Watch the paint."

"Doing my best," Sarah replied through gritted teeth. She fought the Ranger off the guard rail only to have its rear try to swing out. "No! We're not playing that game." She swung the wheel into the skid and just like that the tires bit on plain old asphalt and they leapt forward, gaining speed until at last they were clear of the zombies.

Clear except for the three in the bed that had managed to hang on and were banging on the glass of the rear window. She slowed way down, and then accelerated quickly. The zombies plodded backwards at the mercy of the momentum change until they hit the tailgate and fell out.

"Thank you, Jillybean," Sarah said, after a deep breath.

Artie thought she was talking to him. "I'm not that. I'm the mayor of Easton."

197

"Yes you are," Sarah told him. "And I'm Janice..." She realized just then that she didn't know her fake last name, or anything about this Janice-person she was pretending to be.

"Sills. You're Janice Sills," Artie told her. Whether from his case of the crazies or from the blow she had given him, he sat on the cans of food she had emptied from her backpack, blinking like an owl. "Where are we going? We've been this way already."

Could he have forgotten the zombie horde already? With him it was a distinct possibility. "The road was blocked, remember? We have to find a way around. While we drive, you can tell me everything you remember about me."

As mayor and year book president back in high school, he seemed to know a lot. He spoke until it was clear they weren't leaving the city that day. A tremendous west to east migration seemed to be occurring and every road out of the city was packed with zombies.

"Keep talking," Sarah said, pretending she wasn't the least bit afraid. "I want to hear all about me."

He nodded vacantly as Sarah took them into the heart of the deadest city in America.

Chapter 24

Jillybean

Western Maryland

Ipes was in her head yelling. Beside her Neil was hollering. Sadie was screaming and Nico was cursing. Guns were firing and bullets were passing each other, some going south, some going north. Some hit the Explorer, while others blazed by, looking like shooting stars.

Jillybean was petrified by all the commotion. At Ipes' suggestion she had dropped down into the footwell and now she held her arms tight around her knees, refusing to poke her head up to see what was happening. She was a little ball of very soft flesh and easily broken bones. Like a ball, she bounced when the SUV suddenly jumped.

It was the front tire exploding as a bullet struck it.

Neil screamed louder, uselessly crying: "Hold on!"

What was there to hold onto that couldn't be shot away? Despite the rhetorical question that had popped into her head, she looked around for something to grab, however it was too late. Neil swerved the Explorer straight off the highway.

Caught in a crossfire, it was his only choice. With an ear-shattering screech of twisting metal, they laid a fence full over and then went rushing down a steep embankment.

"Lookout for the trees!" yelled Sadie.

"I know," Neil said, fighting the SUV, and trying to turn it. He succeeded so that for a brief second, they were traveling parallel to the hill and not straight down it. Then the blown wheel colluded with gravity and the Explorer tipped onto its side, and then rolled over onto its roof.

Jillybean lost track of which way was up or how many times they spun. She was too busy bouncing like the little ball she was. Holding on was not an option for her, and it was likely a good thing that she didn't try. She simply went with the flow until the vehicle came to rest in an upright position and she found herself sitting in her seat and wondering how she got there.

Around her the Explorer had been transformed. Every window was broken; the roof was squished down and dented in all sorts of ways. They no longer had a hood covering the engine. It had simply disappeared, as had both side mirrors and the radio antennae.

Amazingly, the engine still ran. When their sideways revolutions had been checked, the engine made a sound that was half-growl, half- scream, like a cat in the middle of a fight. It then chugged and spluttered, again like a cat, this time one bringing up a fur ball, then, happily, it found a soft purring rhythm.

Behind Jillybean, Sadie was coughing and Nico was still cursing in a muttery sort of way. Next to Jillybean, Neil stared around as if surprised to find he was still alive. Up on the highway the sound of shooting went on.

"Go, Neil. Drive," Sadie said. She was feeling her face with the tips of her fingers and working her jaw around as she spoke, so the words came out warbly.

"Yeah," he replied. His hands shook and seemed unsure of themselves. He acted as though he had never driven before. First he touched the steering wheel, then the keys, and for some reason he looked at the pedals on the floor as if they might have become switched, gas for brake, with all the tumbling.

Finally, he gave the gas a press and they began to rattle away through a spare forest of pine. They made such a clamor that Jillybean looked back to see if they were leaving pieces of the Explorer behind.

"They do not follow yet," Nico said. He too had been looking behind them.

After they had progressed maybe a mile, Neil suddenly blinked and asked, "Is anyone hurt?"

Mumbles were the reply, except for Nico, who said, "I have scratch. Is nothing."

Sadie leaned over the seat to see about the scratch. In a remarkably calm voice she said, "He's been shot. In the arm. We'll need to stop in a little while as soon as we can." Her voice might have been calm, however her face was bloodless and her lip quivered.

"Ok...ok, we'll stop," Neil said. "Just not yet. Can anyone see them? Are they coming?"

"I said, they do not follow," Nico grunted. "They fight each other." The sound of the gun battle echoed among the trees, gradually growing fainter as they put more distance between them and the highway.

"Thank God," Sadie said.

"Thank you, God," Jillybean said, obediently. She knew what God was. Back in the *Before*, in the time of Mommies and Daddies, she had gone to Sunday School and to church. Not everybody did, but she did. She had worn a white dress with a yellow ribbon for a belt and she remembered the white shoes she had worn had to be cleaned a lot because she always scuffed them.

You also had a pink dress and a flowered one, remember? Ipes asked. She remembered. The pink had been worn on Easter, when they hunted for eggs. Ipes had sat in her basket with a lap full of jelly beans.

"Isn't it supposed to be Easter, now?" she asked. Her insides felt quivery from the accident and the shooting. She had supposed that the feeling would diminish, but it hadn't. Instead it had grown like a balloon that wanted to pop. Perhaps to counter this swelling sensation, she felt an overwhelming need to talk: "It's spring, right? So that means Easter and the Easter Bunny. When's he supposed to be here? Do you think he got turned into a monster? I don't think so since we don't see normal rabbits being monsters. Maybe I should ask the Velveeta Rabbit..."

Neil interrupted, "Shush."

The sound of the guns had ceased. Now Jillybean didn't feel swollen. She felt small and, wanting to get even smaller, she shrank down in her seat.

"Is this as fast as we can go?" Sadie asked. In spite of the shimmying and the shaking, and the clanking and the wheezing of the Explorer, they were making steady, though not spectacular progress.

Neil tried the gas and everything became worse. "I have to slow down. I'll shred the tire and who knows what else if I don't." He eased up on the gas, but the Explorer never recovered. A new thunking noise from within the engine heralded its doom and after a half-mile the engine seized up.

It had been their intention to jump out of the vehicle and put some distance between them and it before either the bounty hunter or the colonel's men found them, however not a single door still functioned. They were forced to climb, very carefully, through the broken windows to get out.

"I'll take the backpack with the food, and the axe, and one of the fuel cans," Neil said. "Sadie, if you'll carry the shotgun and some of the water."

"I can carry some things," Nico said. He was grey in the face, and held onto a tree to stay upright. His statement was ignored by everyone.

They're forgetting the battery, Ipes mentioned.

"That's what I was thinking," Jillybean said. "Hey, Mister Neil, you'll need the battery out of the car. Amember how long it took to find this one?" It had been a task of over an hour to cull through hundreds of cars to locate one that still had any juice left to it.

"We don't have time," Neil said.

"And it's too heavy," Sadie added.

Ipes blew out through both of his wide nostrils. *If they don't take the battery...*

"Then they should leave the gas," Jillybean finished the zebra's sentence. "How about if I help you guys?" she asked them.

"You're going to help?" Neil asked. "The battery weighs almost as much as you do. You'll never get it five feet and I don't think I could carry it more than a mile."

"I'm not gonna carry anything," Jillybean said. "That's silly. You and Sadie will carry it all, and it won't be that tough."

Their looks of incredulity were fascinating to her. Couldn't they see that everything they needed to transport their gear was right in front of them?

"Whatever we do, we must hurry," Nico said. "We don't have much of head start. Is not good."

Jillybean jumped right into action. She directed Neil to pull the battery out of the Explorer and then she picked out a good sapling for Sadie to chop down with the axe. When the sapling was hacked down and shorn of its branches it was essentially a rough pole. This they hung with the backpack, a gallon of water, a five gallon gas can, and the battery hanging by its strap.

It was a heavy load at ninety-five pounds, but when Neil took one side of the sapling, and Sadie the other, and settled it on their shoulders it wasn't bad at all.

Nico took the shotgun in his good hand and Jillybean hefted the axe to her shoulder like a continental soldier. "Let's go," the little girl said as though she was in charge. For lack of a better idea, they walked in the direction of the slope, letting gravity assist them. Even with the sapling distributing the weight, Sadie and Neil were soon sweating.

"We're lucky the battery had a strap," Neil said. "Otherwise we'd be screwed."

What does he mean by that? Ipes asked. *He was right there when Nico put it in the Explorer to begin with. Do you think he forgot? How can you forget about something so obvious?*

"I don't see how he could have," Jillybean answered in a whisper. "It hasn't even been a day. Maybe he's not good with observationing things. Grode-ups rarely are."

"Hey, Jillybean," Sadie said. "What are you whispering about?"

"Only stuff. I was just talking with Ipes."

"Wouldn't you rather talk with me?" Sadie asked in between large breaths. Jillybean, who was very much enamored with the older girl, slowed down to walk beside her, and looked up at her expectantly. Sadie shifted the pole to her other shoulder.

After a bit, Jillybean asked, "What do you want to talk about?"

"Me? Nothing really. I just like having you close, that's all. You really need to be around people more. If you ever feel like talking, you can come to me. Or if you're scared or...or confused about what's going on, I want you to find me and we'll talk it out."

Nico, who walked with ponderous steps on Sadie's other side, cleared his throat quietly and said, "Kraslvaya, you should not speak. We must listen for approach of enemies."

"Crazy-what?" Jillybean asked. "What does that..."

Sadie made a noise to quiet Jillybean, before answering in barely a whisper, "He calls me beautiful in Russian. But now we should be quiet like he says. That hunter could be breathing down our necks."

Jillybean walked backwards for a number of steps. The forest was quiet save for a couple of crows jawing at each other. *I don't think the bounty hunter is breathing down our necks,* Ipes said. *He can be stealthy or fast, but he can't be both at the same time. However, if he is tracking us, we are making it easy for him.*

"Yeah," agreed Jillybean. "We should go that way," she told the others pointing to the right—with her brains jumbled from the crash, she couldn't tell north from south. To the right the trees of the forest stood close to each other and there was a goodly amount of kudzu and other scrub that reduced visibility.

With Sadie and Neil lagging from their burden and Nico injured, they took Jillybean's advice without question. They walked with their feet forward, but with their heads turning back and their ears pricked for the slightest telltale sign of someone following. All they heard was the low moans of zombies from somewhere in the forest. The sound grew as they walked until even brave Sadie suggested they go in a different direction.

"But I thought we wanted to find another car or truck," Jillybean replied, confused. "Zombies stay near people places. Since we're hearing more of them it means we're close to being civilized."

"But..." Neil said, looking a little green. "But we're in no state to fight zombies."

"Yeah, that's why we gotta be real careful," Jillybean said. She left Sadie's side to scurry in front of the others by a dozen paces, leading the way through the bramble, where their ability to see and be seen dropped to a few yards. Zombies were a perpetual fear of hers, but they weren't her only fear.

"Ipes, what does poison ivy look like?" she asked under her breath.

He considered for a while, dredging her memories, until he found what he was looking for. *Clusters of three, let it be,* he recited. *Your Uncle Mitch said that once when he went with you and your daddy on a nature walk.*

"But what's it mean?"

You have to look out for plants with three leaves, I think.

Jillybean gazed about her and then shook her head. "That can't be right because there's a bajillion leaves on every plant. There's none with just three..."

Through a break in the trees she saw movement and instantly forgot her worry over the poison ivy. Instinctually she went bunny: slinking down and freezing in place; she also remembered to put a hand out to the others. They stopped and although Neil and Sadie tried to be quiet, easing their load down to the ground, the pole creaked and the water jug thumped in a human-sounding manner.

The sound attracted something no longer human. Jilly saw the zombie, a cranky-looking, snaggle-toothed, old hillbilly with grey skin that ran with yellow pus. Before she knew it, she had a magic marble in hand, and after kissing it she heaved well beyond the zombie where it plunked off a tree.

The zombie turned on the spot. She threw a second one and when the beast moved off to investigate the sound, Jillybean slunk through the brush after it to see what it was haunting. A little further on, the bramble gave way to open forest which ran right up to a few decrepit old "dwellings."

Two of the buildings were trailer-homes, one of which was cracked in two right in the middle, and the third was little more than a shack that looked to have been constructed of pure rust. Its walls and canted roof might have been sheet-metal at one time, now it was dull-orange and flaking. Hanging from a jagged shard of the rust was a *No Trespassing* sign.

There didn't seem to be any reason to trespass. Jillybean, after sounding the word out on the sign and deciphering its meaning, turned back to the others. "We should go around. There's no cars or anything."

She led them away from the hillbilly zombie and the hillbilly homestead, circling wide around it. They had been in the forest over an hour, in spite of this she made no more noise than a mouse; the others were loud and slow. Neil was out of breath and huffed constantly under the strain of his burden. Sadie kept switching the pole from shoulder-to-shoulder and stumbled over every root. Nico had to hang onto trees to keep himself up; he had begun to moan, zombie-like.

With their strength beginning to fail, Jillybean again led them straight downhill until finally they came upon a two-lane road. With sighs of relief the three adults collapsed and lay panting.

What are they doing? Ipes demanded. *They can't rest right here! Are they crazy?*

"Uh, Mister Neil?" Jillybean asked, with her hand in the air. "We can't stay here out in the open. Not even for a rest. We should at least hide behind those bushes."

Neil nodded and started to get up, but Sadie didn't budge. "We can't go any further," she said. "Look at Nico's arm. The bullet must have hit a vein or artery or something."

They all crowded round the ashen-faced Russian. He had been shot through the left bicep and the arm, below the wound, was dark and sopping wet with blood. When he mumbled something about being cold, even Jillybean knew the man was in deep trouble.

"Ok...Ok. It doesn't look so bad," Neil lied. "Here's what we'll do...uh, I'll go look for a car and you, Sadie, stay here and keep pressure on the wound. Jillybean, I want you to guard them."

She said she would, but eyed the axe with trepidation as soon as Neil left. It was one thing to let it bruise her shoulder as she walked through the forest, it was another thing entirely to try to use it against a real, "live" zombie.

You won't have to use it, Ipes told her. *Sadie is right here. I'm pretty sure it'll be ok if she releases pressure for a minute.*

Jilly wasn't keen on "pretty sure."

Thankfully Neil came back before Jillybean was put to the test. He came jogging up and said something in an overly-breathy way so that all anyone could really understand was the word car. Sadie questioned him, but he only shook his head before he hefted the battery up by its handle and left, walking leaned way over because of the weight of the thing. Soon, he was back for the gas can, and sooner, he was back in a teal-colored Tercel.

Even to Jillybean it looked frightfully small.

"It gets great mileage," Neil said, putting their meager belongings in the tiny trunk. "And its safety rating is better than you'd expect."

"Is it safe against zombies?" Sadie asked.

"It was our only choice," Neil told her. "Everything else sat on flat tires. Now, let's take a better look at that arm."

Interested in all things as she was, Jillybean squatted right next to Neil and watched as he tore away the bloody shirt. She started asking questions, which was ok, however, when she pointed out that the wound looked like raw hamburger, Neil went from sweaty and pale to sweaty and pale green. She was ordered to stand guard.

Her explanation that her guard was never down didn't help and she didn't get to see what a tourniquet was or how it would stop the bleeding. Even Ipes didn't know what it was.

It helped one way or the other and, after Nico was squished into the backseat, they left, heading as southward as Neil could manage on the winding mountain road. Their idea was to find a town and get a proper bandage on Nico's arm and maybe some medicine, if that was an option, however the road seemed laid out so as to avoid towns.

For three hours they drove, stopping at the ramshackle little houses they would find tucked up in the woods or sunk down in the hollers. They scrounged gas, a clean ace bandage, and bushels of wild fruit, but saw nothing bordering on civilization until the heat of the afternoon was at its height.

They rounded over the top of the one of the millions of hills that made up the Appalachians and saw the tiny town of Elkins, West Virginia, down below them. It was exactly what they were looking for, but they didn't take the turn that would lead directly into the town. From one of the many chimneys that poked up from one of the many houses, a little ribbon of grey smoke drifted into the air.

The same thoughts went through their minds: Was this a trap? Had the bounty hunter got there before them and set an innocuous cooking fire alight in order to lure them in? Maybe it was bandits, or slavers.

Without discussion, Neil kept to the high road and put Elkins in their rear view mirror.

This is crazy, Ipes said. *We're too afraid to stop, when we should be too afraid to go on. They are going to be waiting on us.*

"Who is they?" Jillybean asked. In her heart she knew, and that meant he knew that she knew.

The hunter or the colonel's men or maybe even Abraham; no one has even considered that he might have heard about the bounty, too. And that's why this is all so crazy. As always, we're being far too obvious. We keep traveling south.

"Which way should we be traveling to get to Georgia?" Jillybean asked, watching the trees as they drove; she had never seen such a beautiful, lush forest in all her seven years.

That's just it we shouldn't be going to Georgia. Practically everyone knows we came up from the CDC and everyone knows Abraham has Sarah's baby, thus everyone knows that's exactly where we'll be going.

"Sometimes you don't have a choice when…" she stopped, hoping Ipes wouldn't catch on to what she had been about to say.

When it comes to family? Ipes asked. *Oh, you poor girl. Please, don't get too attached. Look at them.* Obediently she glanced at the three adults and saw that they were as ragged a group as she had ever seen. *They aren't going to make it. They aren't survivors like you. They're going to die one-by-one and you'll be all alone once again.*

"I'm not afraid of being alone," she said, defensively.

Ipes sniffed derisively at this. *I know what you're afraid of. Deep down you're afraid of what Abraham will do to a little girl like you. And you're afraid of the slavers in New York who deal in virgins. Remember, I was there when we overheard Mister Neil talking about the rumors. What do you think will happen to you when all of your so-called family gets killed down in Georgia? What is…*

Just then Sadie, who had been watching Jillybean's side of the conversation with worry in her dark eyes, interrupted Ipes. "May I hold your zebra for a while?"

Ask her why she wants to? Ipes demanded. Jillybean fought the urge to ask. It wasn't easy because, really, why did Sadie want Ipes? What was she going to do with him? Keep him forever? Throw him out the window? Hurt him?

"Jilly?" Sadie asked. Her concern was now more evident.

Ipes ignored the look. *She's not your family, Jillybean. She's not your sister.*

She could be, Jillybean thought. The little girl handed the zebra over without a word and then passed the back of her hand across her brow—it came away damp.

"You look a little pale," Sadie said, putting Ipes out of sight.

"It's just hot in here is all," Jillybean said, failing to mention how her stomach had also been cramping during her talk with Ipes. It felt better to look out the window at the forest and not think about Ipes.

Chapter 25

Sarah

Washington DC

By the time Jillybean fell asleep in the Tercel with her forehead resting against the cool of the glass window, the muffler of Artie's Ranger finally let go. Immediately, the engine roared out BLAATTT!

Sarah looked into the rear view mirror and saw the muffler. The leading edge of it had sunk inches deep in the skull of the zombie she had just run over.

It was a wonder the muffler had lasted as long as it had. Only God knew how many zombies she had plowed over in the last five hours or how many curbs she had banged up onto, or how many medians she'd had to cut across in order to save their lives. Everywhere they turned, zombies came at them.

Though it had never been classified as *Black*, Washington DC was a hellhole of epic proportions and had been so from the beginning of the apocalypse. Even after weeks of mayhem, during which live people were slowly outnumbered by the undead, limp-wristed politicians had refused to admit the obvious: that the nation's capital had fallen, and thus the people were left to fend for themselves. Riots, street-fighting, and a last ditch effort to save the city by a doomed brigade of Marines, had left Washington in a state reminiscent of Stalingrad in '43.

More buildings had collapsed or burned to the ground than still stood, and the 2 X 2 Ranger proved a pathetic vehicle for such terrain. Sarah had already stopped twice for repairs. The first time was when a hunk of rebar from a mortared street had shredded one of her tires. The second time they had been nearly trapped by converging hordes when Sarah tried to blast through them. By then she had figured out that pure momentum was the only recourse when trying to get through so many bodies. She went heavy on the gas until they were clear, but then there came, from beneath the hood, a horrific shriek, as though the car had received some sort of mortal injury.

She kept going, simply because slowing wasn't an option. When she felt she was "safe", a term very loosely defined in Washington, she checked under the hood to find a stiffening, grey hand with a trail of stringy-looking veins caught up in the engine's belts. Using Artie's pipe she had pried it out and continued on her looping, circling, maddening way.

Now, with the muffler a useless hunk of metal in the road behind her and the engine roaring with even the slightest push of the gas, she felt it was time to get rid of the Ranger. It made such a racket that she knew she would attract unwanted attention from more than just the zombies.

Sarah found a row of burned out townhomes which had two things going for them: one, there weren't hundreds of zombies roaming in every direction as in the rest of the city and, two, although the residences were mostly ash, the carports directly across from them were, for the most part, undamaged.

"We have to ditch your truck," she said, nervously looking around. "Grab your stuff."

As usual Artie didn't go quietly. "I know this isn't right. None of it. We have to go back to Easton before it's too late!"

Sarah hoped her extreme irritation didn't show on her face when she said, "But you forget that the government is controlling Easton with beams." Normally the topic of beams would set him raving but in a harmless manner. She figured it was his way of coping.

"Beams, beams, beams!" Artie cried. "That's all I ever hear out of you. It's beams this and beams that. You know what? I don't want to hear about the beams anymore."

"I'm sorry. I won't talk about beams," Sarah said, as she got out of the truck, making sure to take the keys with her—she didn't want Artie to drive off in his lunacy. They were a man's set: they held four keys and nothing more. No bling, or extra keys to locks that were long gone, for the mayor of Easton. They reminded her of something that she had failed to take into account: "Here's a new subject, how do you hotwire a car?" She had seen Ram do it, but the mess of wires beneath the steering column was daunting.

"Hotwire a car? Me? You want to know if the true and properly elected mayor of Easton can hotwire a car?"

"Yeah," she replied without enthusiasm, already knowing the answer.

"It's against the law!" Artie cried. "This is entrapment. I know. You're trying to trap me, just like the government. You're with *them*, aren't you?"

Sarah turned away before rolling her eyes, but her groan was so loud he had to have heard. The day had been so trying that she didn't much care what he heard. He spluttered for a bit and ranted, however her mind was on a row of very nice, late-model cars that she had to choose from. Some were sporty, some fuel-efficient, and some were hefty SUVs. She tried the bigger vehicles first. All were locked and so she resorted to breaking one of the back windows to gain access to a honking big Lincoln Navigator that still had temp tags on it.

During this, Artie forgot about the possibly of her being part of the government and began a heated argument with an ash-covered zombie that had drifted out of the torched townhomes. He was screaming about private property rights and, once more, beams. Sarah didn't waste time concerning herself with his safety. She reasoned he had somehow made it this far without any help from her and thus should be safe enough against a stray zombie or two. After all, he had his pipe: four feet of heavy metal; it was a scary weapon when he was worked up.

Turning from him, she grabbed a chunk of sidewalk that had cracked from the heat of the nearby fire and used it to bash open the plastic that covered the steering column below the wheel. When it finally fractured and dropped to the floor she sat back with a grimace.

213

"Shit," she whispered at the sight of such elaborate and convoluted wiring. She had hoped that getting the engine going was simply a matter of exposing the wires and touching them, one to the other, until she had the right combination.

Fearful of getting shocked, she used her knife to strip away the least amount of the rubber coating from each. Gingerly, she began touching them to each other until eventually, the engine began to sputter. Pressing on the gas pedal, she fed it fuel and then giggled, feeling altogether clever when the engine turned over and began a fine humming.

In seconds she had thrown their gear into the SUV, next, she backed over the zombie pestering Artie and, while it squirmed and moaned with the weight of the Navigator crushing its legs, she asked Artie to join her.

"Only if we're going back to Easton," he said.

She lied easily, "Of course!"

By the time the sun set on that hellish day, she had finally left the city behind. Without regard to Artie's wish to go back to his hometown, she went south, as she had planned. He didn't notice as he spent most of the time hiding from beams beneath his coat.

She drove long after it was safe—meaning she drove after it was dark and the zombies were more energetic and seemed to multiply in numbers. Still, she managed to find a roadside bar outside of Aquia, Virginia that had, at one time, been fortified against the beasts. Its windows were boarded over and it possessed sturdy doors of oak. It even had a fireplace and a small amount of alcohol left on its shelves.

Artie did not partake in any of the alcohol, nor did he come to sit by the little fire Sarah had kindled. Instead, he stumped about, squinting through the cracks of the boarded windows until he had convinced himself they had traveled the wrong way. He confronted Sarah over this seemingly insurmountable fact, waving his pipe as he spoke.

When he was riled he made her nervous. When he was riled and swinging the pipe she was nervous enough to keep her hand on the grip of her .38. "It was the government, again," she explained, riffing off the top of her head. "They, uh, they switched the directions: north is now south. They're trying to confuse us, but don't worry, I got it covered."

Not only did he believe this, he fully endorsed the idea and couldn't wait to see the sun rise in the west or to see if the stars in the sky had been moved as well. He went back to the windows to watch. Sarah found a bottle of tequila and drank until he no longer seemed so crazy. It took a lot of tequila to get her there.

"Love you Eve," she whispered before closing her eyes. Then with them closed she added, "Love you Neil and Sadie and Brit..." her mind cast a fleeting glimpse of Jillybean across what was left of her conscious, but Sarah didn't add the little girl's name to her list.

"If I do, she'll die because of me," Sarah said, slurring the words that gradually dropped into less than a whisper. "Everyone I love has to die...unless I go first."

The next morning her hangover was intense. A warm shower would have helped but God had sent her a cool rain instead. It was better than nothing. She stood under a downspout with her .38 hanging on a nail within arm's reach. The water and the soap sloughed away a good deal of her peeling skin, and for the first time in days it didn't hurt to smile. When she was done she tried to get Artie to shower as well, which he refused to do on account of the beams of course.

"They can't get you in the rain," she said, as though she were an expert on the subject of nonexistent beams. "They wash right off." He began to shake his head at this and she tried: "What about Beth?"

"What about Beth?" he asked slowly, looking at her through partially slitted eyes.

"Don't you want to look good for her when she comes back? Remember New Eden and going to see the prophet? He can help us. He can...he can heal her."

"But she's in Easton. I know she is. We're supposed to be going back to Easton. Maybe we can get her and bring her with us. Does that sound good?"

Sarah's teeth ground together in frustration, but she did her best not to let it show. "Yes it does, but only if you get cleaned up first. You don't look like yourself anymore, that's why I didn't recognize you at first back in that alley in Easton. It's probably why you didn't recognize me, Janice, either." He started to look at her with his crazier-than-usual eyes so she added, "But, if you don't care enough to look good for your wife..."

He insisted that he did and when he went out in the rain armed with soap and shampoo, Sarah slid down the wall, wondering how she was going to fool him into thinking he was going to Easton, Maryland when every road sign they passed would be pointing them to Georgia. "He'll forget," she told herself. "He's so crazy he doesn't know which way up is. He will forget all about this in a few hours."

But he didn't forget. Artie latched onto the idea of seeing his wife. He even allowed Sarah to cut his hair and trim back his beard and, later when they passed an outlet mall, he was the one who suggested they stop and get him clothes that were presentable.

She tried her best to get him fixated on a new idea, such as beams or Area 51 and, for an hour, the Bermuda Triangle, and he would, for a little while, stop torturing himself with the vision of Beth. But he never forgot they were supposed to be going to Easton and he grew quickly suspicious with every road sign that pointed them to Richmond, or Charleston.

At first she stuck with the concept of the changing polarity of the earth's magnetic force and how that would work to deviate their perceptions. "It's all alien cell technology," she insisted.

This worked for the remainder of that day until in the evening when they slipped across the border from North Carolina into South Carolina.

"This is wrong," he said, pointing out the car window at the sun which hung just above the horizon far to the west. "That sun is wrong and this road is wrong. This is all wrong! You've been taking us south haven't you?" His pipe rested against the SUV's door. When he grabbed it she put her hand in her coat pocket, wrapping her fingers around the butt of the gun and slipping one around the trigger, ready to put a hole in her coat and in Artie.

She started to shake her head but then his eyes went wide and he pointed again out the window. "They've changed the poles back!" he cried. "That's what they did. North is north. That's what happened. I know." Unexpectedly, he opened the car door and she only just managed to stop before he jumped out.

He raved at the sky while Sarah seethed in fury. "How is this happening to me?" she demanded, punching the steering wheel. The answer slipped into her consciousness: *Because you are using this poor, crazy guy and you deserve everything you get.*

This was truth.

"Yeah, but…" she said as a hundred rationalizations sprang to mind. *Yeah, but nothing. You're as evil as all the rest.*

More painful truth.

With a sigh, she opened the door to the Navigator and slid out. With her mind so jumbled between sort-of right and sort-of wrong, she almost left the .38 behind. A charging zombie reminded her. She ran back for it and, displaying her growing confidence with weapons, she put a burning hunk of lead into the zombie's forehead from ten feet,

Before it was done flopping about, she went to talk to Artie.

"Did you hear the good news?" he asked her. "They've changed the poles back. We can go home to Easton. I'll be mayor and Beth can be deputy mayor. That's a new position, but I'm going to need her help. I know. But thank God about the poles, right?"

"It's not that simple," Sarah said, feeling her soul wrinkle and shrink within her.

Artie turned on her. "Why? What have you heard?"

217

"It's the gravity," she said. "It's been adjusted. We're being pulled south. We can't fight it."

Artie's knees buckled and he dropped to the grass at the edge of the road. He began to cry miserably. "Why would they do that? Why would anyone?"

"Because the world is evil now and people are evil," she said, admitting as much truth as either of them could handle at the moment. "I promise you, Artie, I'll do my best to get you home when this is all over."

He seemed like a little boy just then with his tears and his hair that he couldn't seem to overrule. "When will that be?"

Unless something went horribly wrong, they'd make it to New Eden the next day and she planned on stealing her baby back as soon as possible. "Very soon," Sarah said. She then pointed up at the darkening twilight. "We'd better find a place to sleep. They don't call them moonbeams for nothing."

It had meant to be a joke, but Artie no longer understood humor and so he hurried back to the Navigator, leaving Sarah alone with the greasy feel of evil coating her insides. She meant to keep her promise to Artie, *if* she lived, but she knew that was going to take a miracle.

That night they slept in a lonely farmhouse. It had a perfectly useable barn with a loft that would guarantee them protection, only Sarah couldn't force herself to go into it. Barns and haylofts had been hers and Neil's thing. It almost felt like cheating on him to use one.

So she stayed in the farmhouse with Artie and fell asleep to the moans of the undead in the pasture. By ten the next morning they crossed into Georgia and by two in the afternoon they were on the edge of a field looking up at a familiar silo. The air hung about them stiff and unmoving; the field was silent and empty; the corn was alive with the dead. Sarah wore a sheen of sweat, though the day was as nice a Georgia day as you could ask for.

"Are we here?" Artie asked.

"Yeah."

Chapter 26

Neil

Western Appalachians

The night Nico was shot they slept in a cabin deep in the backcountry of West Virginia. There didn't seem to be much more to the state than backcountry, Neil thought. It all seemed rather tree-ish and dirty, and there were far too many bugs in West Virginia for his tastes.

The cabin wasn't up to his refined sense of discrimination either. It was only slightly larger than the outhouse which sat at the edge of the backyard. What's more, the cabin was filthy in a manner that skeeved him out. Nothing looked to have been vacuumed or dusted in years. In the kitchen the walls were waterproofed and hermetically sealed by a quarter-inch of layered grease. A number of dead cockroaches lay, legs up, in the sink. Neil walked about with his hands pulled in and forbid Jillybean to touch anything.

The cabin did have one thing in its favor: it had running water. Not in the traditional sense with taps and a faucet, instead it had a well and a hand pump. There was even a garden hose that could stretch into the kitchen or to the little cube of a room right off of it. They called this the bathroom, though once again it was a most incomplete bathroom since it held only a claw-footed bath tub and a mirror.

Despite his exhaustion and the stress of the long day, Neil cleaned the bathtub, started a fire, heated round stones that Jillybean collected for him, and filled the tub three different times with warm water so everyone could bathe. Nico refused his opportunity. His arm pained him too much and he feared it would get infected if it got wet. It was only when Neil boiled water especially to clean the wound that he allowed them to touch his bandages.

The process turned out to be a mistake. The bandages, sodden and black with congealed blood were so bound to the wound that by taking them off, Neil accidently started Nico bleeding again. Regardless, Neil bathed the wound and wrapped it a second time. Unfortunately, it leaked blood in a steady manner despite everything Neil tried. By the time midnight rolled around, Neil had a mound of blood-soaked rags that sat higher than his knee.

Nico had either passed out or had fallen asleep at this point and Neil finally went to bed and was so exhausted that he didn't care his mattress was nothing more than piles of grass Sadie had tucked under a sheet.

Sadie came to him the next morning when he was picking ants out of his hair and looking around blearily. "I know you want to find Sarah," she said, "but we have to do something about Nico, first. We need new bandages and antibiotics and I don't know what else. He won't stop bleeding, so we'll need stitches probably. I don't know anything about stitches. Do you?"

"I think it's sort of like sewing," Neil replied, hoping the shiver that went down his back wasn't as noticeable as it felt. The idea of sewing real human flesh skeeved him out worse than seeing what had been left in the outhouse.

She hadn't noticed the shiver; she was staring blankly at the floor. "I can't sew at all," she whispered as if it were a personal failing on her part. "My mom never taught me and I didn't take *Home Economics* in school. Only the ugly girls took *Home-ec.*"

"Is that right?" Neil said. He had taken *Home-ec* for two years in high school. At the time it seemed more suitable for him than *Shop* class, which was chock full of bullies. "I think I could manage a stitch or two." *As long as I don't throw up in the process,* he thought.

Their main problem wasn't Neil's weak stomach; it was the fact that they were still being hunted. At midday, after many miles of driving, they had searched the offices of three small-town doctors and came away empty-handed. They decided to creep down out of the hills and see what the town of Edray, West Virginia had to offer.

"Pocahontas Memorial Hospital," read Neil from a phonebook he had liberated from a now defunct gas station.

"Pocahontas?" Jillybean asked. "Is that for reals?"

"Looks that way," Neil replied, tossing the book out the window and tuning south on route 55.

"Will it have that little dog?" Jillybean asked, staring all around at the remains of the dead town. "Or the raccoon? I can't believe this is for reals. Oh, my goodness! Look, there's a sign. That word is Pocahontas, I know it. It is for real."

"What are you talking about?" Neil's mind wasn't following the little girl's odd questions, it was consumed with the horrific images of what he would find in the hospital. How many zombies would there be roaming the halls or chained to beds? And what sort of state would they be in? And how hungry would they be? He began to sweat.

"Pocahontas," Jillybean said as way of explanation. "It was a movie with a dog and a raccoon and a hummingbird, and an Indian girl, and a guy from England, though he sounded like he was from Philly, like me. Ipes said it was true but I thought that he was being a jokester as always. But, wow, there really is a Pocahontas."

Neil, who had zero experience with children's movies, only grunted in reply. He was busy planning. "Jillybean, you're going to wait in the car with Nico. Make sure you don't draw attention to yourself, but if for some reason you get in trouble, honk the horn. Sadie, you take the shotgun. I'll have my axe…"

Sitting up high in her seat, Jillybean was watching ardently for the coming hospital with a hopeful expression on her face. This turned to bug-eyed fear the second the building came into view. "Stop! Stop the car. Look!"

There was a green-camouflaged Humvee parked square in front of the main entrance to the hospital. Neil hit the brakes so hard, everyone was flung forward.

"Please be careful," Sadie said as Nico grunted in pain.

"If we're still alive in five minutes, I'll be careful then," Neil shot back, turning the wheel sharply and

221

gunning the car around in a tight circle. He blazed down route 55, while behind him a soldier dashed into the hospital.

"They saw us," Sadie cried. "Hurry, Neil!"

He pushed the Tercel to its greatest speed which wasn't in any way blinding, however, by the time the soldier had rushed back out of the hospital and jumped in the Humvee, Neil had a four minute head start.

This he did not squander on a high-speed chase down the highway. Although the forest and hills was the terrain the Humvee had been created for, Neil took the little Toyota off-road as soon as he was out of sight. It was a completely unexpected move and they were able to breathe a sigh of relief a few minutes later as they saw, below them, the army vehicle continue on down the interstate.

"This isn't happening," Sadie said in disbelief. "How do they keep finding us like that?"

"Ipes says it's easy since they know where we are and where we're going," Jillybean said. "He also says we should…never mind. He's being bad again."

Neil wanted to know what the zebra had to say, but Sadie overruled him. "We need to stop relying on Jillybean and what she hears from…other sources." She gave Neil a pinched look which he took to mean he wasn't supposed to bring up Ipes anymore.

He gave her a shrug and asked, "Then what do we do and where do we turn? I'm almost out of ideas here."

Sadie dropped her head and said, "Maybe if I took Nico and left, you could…"

"Stop it," Neil said cutting her off. He started driving again, southwest just as he had all morning. "You're my family now, Sadie. We don't leave family behind. We'll keep going, is what we'll do. I'm sure we'll find another hospital or something."

They did find something, and just in time. In spite of Neil's care, or perhaps because of it, Nico's wound would not stop trickling blood at a steady rate. He grew sickly pale and drowsy in a worrisome way. As the afternoon faded he seemed confused about where they were going and he sometimes spoke Russian in angry tones. Sadie insisted they keep driving regardless of the night and the waking of the undead. She feared that if they waited until morning to find help he would be too far gone.

This fear had been planted in her head by none other than Ipes, who had earlier been placed in the trunk for an hour for misbehaving. According to Jillybean, he came out with a better attitude and described the nature of shock, what he worried was happening to Nico.

"I thought shock had to do with getting a bad fright," Sadie said. "You know, like if you see a ghost, you go into shock."

"No, it's what means he's doesn't have enough blood," the little girl explained in awed tones of fright. "Like a vampire got him, 'cept it's on account of his wound. We saw it on a show about doctors but it was for grode-ups and was sorta boring so I didn't pay attention so much."

Neil knew it was a real condition, so he ruled out Sadie's ghost theory. "Did the TV show explain what to do when someone's in shock?"

"Take him to the hospital?" Jillybean said with a shrug. "They also covered him up and put his feet in the air a little, but I don't really know what else."

Sadie moaned at this. "We have to do something. His heart's going really fast."

Neil promised that they would "figure something out" but all he knew to do was to keep driving and hoping. In the dark, the woods felt extremely close and the turns very tight. He was forced to drive slowly which made bumbling over zombies a queasy endeavor. Still he persevered until he rounded a twist in the road and not twenty feet away was another military Humvee. It had them dead to rights and Neil could do nothing but sit there waiting on the inevitable.

A soldier came at them and Neil forced a smile onto his face, while his mind tried desperately to come up with excuses and aliases, with elaborate back stories, and plausible reasons why they had a bleeding Russian

223

traveling with them. He blanked on everything including common sense.

He rolled down his window and said, "Hi. Can we get…"

With a cry, Jillybean pointed and grabbed his arm just as the soldier grabbed his other arm. Her hand was small and her nails were painted purple. The soldier's hand was large and grey. It was missing all of its finger nails and it smelled of rotting flesh.

Neil slammed the Tercel in reverse and spun them back, leaving the zombie standing there, holding nothing but a strip of shirt and a little of Neil's flesh.

"I would stop if I was you, Mister Neil," Jillybean informed him as he backed around one turn and then another.

"Yeah," agreed Sadie. "That was a soldier zombie. It could have guns we could take. Better guns than this stupid shotgun."

Jillybean agreed with an emphatic nod. "Also that was an amba-lance…I mean an am-bu-lance. Didn't you see the big red cross? That's what means amba-lance in the army."

"I guess I didn't," Neil said. He touched his neck where the zombie had scratched him, saying, "Ooh, that smarts."

"Thank God, you're immune," Sadie said. She smiled in a bittersweet manner, probably remembering Ram just as Neil was. Her look changed to one of mild alarm. "Oh crap, here comes that zombie. He's got a helmet on. Maybe you should use the shotgun."

"No, I don't want to draw everything else in the forest to us. It's bad enough with these lights on. I'll just give him something to think about." Neil revved the little four-cylinder engine and sent the Toyota buzzing at the onetime army medic. Since there wasn't a lot of room to gain speed he ended up crushing the thing's legs and dispatched it seconds later with a blow from his axe to the back of its neck as it crawled toward him.

Another zombie, this one in a green uniform as well came limping from behind the humvee. Sadly it looked like it had been mostly eaten before it *turned*. Since there wasn't much left to it, Neil put it out of its misery, stoutly swinging his axe like a woodsman.

"Wait here," he said, leaning down to look into the Tercel. "Hopefully, they have something of value."

Behind the boxy ambulance Neil found a dreadful number of bodies. They were the rotting, fly-covered corpses of soldiers. They were heaped in three great piles, each twice as tall as he was. The stench was overpowering and Neil turned away and dry-heaved. Had a zombie come by just then he would have been powerless to fight it.

When he stopped heaving and belching, Neil pulled his shirt up to cover his face and turned to investigate the ambulance.

He found guns without bullets, food in brown plastic that said: Meals Ready to Eat, gallon-jugs of fresh waters, and a saggy, half-empty med-kit. This he opened under the full light of the Tercel's headlamps.

"What's in there?" Sadie whispered. She stood with one leg out of the car and one leg in, ready to go in either direction quickly.

"Uh…some bandages," he said, squinting at the writing. "And uh, what does that say? Normal Saline? It's some sort of fluid for IVs. Here's a BP cuff, a tourniquet… oh, here are some pills." Neil held it up to the light and read aloud, "Narcan. Don't know what that is. I know what Naproxin is, it's a pain reliever. They also have Tylenol."

That was it for the med kit. He brought it all to Sadie. "Stay in the car. See if you can read the little print on the bottle that says Narcan. Maybe it will help."

Neil hurried back to the ambulance to search inside, and again felt the need to vomit, which he fought, but just barely. Inside the Humvee he started opening drawer after drawer, most of which were empty, however in one he found a gas mask and because of the smell he pulled it out of its handy little carrying case and forced his head into it. Now that the smell was diminished, he could breathe much better but his vision was severely compromised. The lenses in the mask were thick and slightly distorted, and the plastic hood that framed his face and draped over his shoulders gave him zero peripheral vision.

His lack of vision didn't really matter; there was nothing to find that would help Nico.

The last place he checked was in the front. The cab was layered with trash and the spent brass casings of rifle bullets. While pawing through it, hoping to find at least one actual bullet, he found an ammo box under the driver's seat. Excitedly he pulled it open but blinked behind his round lenses at what he saw: bottles of pills and among them were a few ampoules of clear liquid.

"I guess it's something," he said.

In three trips he transported the food and the water to the Tercel.

When he finally climbed in and pulled off his mask, Sadie held up the Narcan. "It's got something to do with morphine. Like it counteracts it or something. It's not what we need."

Neil showed her the ammo kit. "Look." They both reached in and started reading labels one after another until Neil found Amoxicillin. "Here we go. Take two by mouth three times daily until gone. This should help, don't you think?"

"It couldn't hurt," Sadie said.

After he swallowed his pills Nico passed out and Neil drove on until he found a suitable place to make camp: another of the classless hillbilly homes. This one they were forced to share it with a family of raccoons which lived under the porch.

They tried the tourniquet on Nico's arm, which turned his fingers blue, but slowed the rate of bleeding greatly. Neil then brought out the IV kit and the fluids but without instructions he didn't know what to do.

"The bleeding will stop on its own," he said to Sadie who was white with worry. "Don't you think?" She didn't know. Exhausted, they dropped off to sleep—Jilly happily sleeping with the Velveteen Rabbit and Ipes, snuggling up to Sadie on the lone mattress. Nico got the couch and Neil slept on more bundled grass. He woke frequently from the itching and the constant comings and goings of the raccoons.

His sleep was so awful that he slept half the next day away as Sadie drove them further south and west. Nico was neither better nor worse that day. He rallied after sipping on a gallon jug of water until the empty plastic rattled on the floorboards, but then relapsed when Neil tried to get circulation to the cold fingers of his wounded arm by undoing the tourniquet. It was hard, anxious day.

They made camp that night in northern Georgia near a town called Clayton. They were three hours from Atlanta and already they were seeing orange Xs on doors that denoted someone had been there and searched them.

Nico's sluggishness and rapid pulse had Sadie in a frantic state. "Should we give him four of the amoxicillin? Do you think that'll do anything?" This she asked of Neil but when he only shrugged, Jillybean answered.

"You want to know what Ipes thinks?" she asked sweetly enough.

"No!" Sadie practically screamed. "I don't. I want to know what *you* think. If you have an idea then spit it out, otherwise...I don't know what, but you need to stop listening to his voice in your head. It's not right."

The little girl's mouth came open and in a whisper she said, "He's just trying to help."

"I'm sure he is," Neil put in, taking her hand. "We're just worried about you. A make-believe friend is normal, but it can be unhealthy if you let it take over your personality."

"I don't think Ipes is doing that at all. I'm the boss of him. He can't boss me around if that's what you mean."

"Yeah, that's what we mean," Sadie said. "Look, I'm sorry, but you can't let him do your thinking, Jillybean. You are very smart. Now tell me what your idea is because I'm going out of my head. Nothing is working."

"Ipe...I mean, I think the pills and the bandages aren't working because we haven't gotten to the...what's the word, Ipes? Oh yeah, the root of the problem. That's what means he thinks part of the bullet may still be in Nico's arm. If it's sharp it'll keep being like a saw, you know what I mean? Every time he moves it'll cut open the old healed part. That's what Ipe...I mean that's what I think."

Neil and Sadie looked at each other. He could tell she was realizing the same thing as he was: one way or the other, somebody was going to have to operate on Nico.

"You do it, Neil," Sadie said in a rush. "I'll screw it up. I'll kill him, I know it."

The words made his head go light so he sat down on a chair. They were once again in gentlemen farm country where the houses sprawled out over the smooth hills and the homes retained their charm even though their owners had long ago died in great violence.

Neil couldn't see the charm just then. His mind was fixated on Nico's wound, on the idea of gouts of blood and maybe a great bubble of pus hidden in the black edges of the wound. Taking a deep breath he tried to order his thoughts. "I'm going to need some boiling water to sterilize everything, and Nico's going to want to have some of that morphine. And...and I need some towels to soak up the blood and...and I think I may throw-up. Jilly can you get me a bucket or something?"

He was able to hold down the MRE he had eaten for dinner, barely. When the feeling of nausea passed he took stock of what he had to work with and knew it wouldn't be enough. Their sharpest knife was a bowie-knife which was more of a stabbing instrument. It had a great point, and with it he could kill a zombie in one blow, however its edge was too dull to slice even paper.

A second problem confronting them was that they didn't have any surgical thread to sew up the wound when he was done and Neil feared that using anything else would only bring on more infection. The third issue Neil had was with their environment. The house was nice but it wasn't sterile, not even close.

"I can't do it," he said. "Not here, not with what I have to work with."

Sadie's hands crumpled into fists which shook in her anxiety. "But this is all we have. We've looked everywhere from here to West Virginia and this is it. You've seen the Xs. Who knows how far they've gone looting everything. So, you have to make do with what we have. Somehow."

"I might kill him," Neil said in a whisper. "There's an artery right in his arm, a big one. My knife is really dull, if it slips, that'll be it."

"Then don't slip!" Sadie cried.

"I know where there's stuff that might help him," Jillybean said with her hand in the air. Before she went on, her eyebrows shot up and she stared at her zebra in amazement. "Why are you talking like that? It's not too dangerous."

"What is it?" Neil asked. "What's dangerous?"

Jillybean went from confusion to cool assertiveness in the blink of an eye. "It's nothing. Just a mix up, but we've got it straightened out."

"Ipes?" Neil asked, feeling his stomach drop. "Is that you?"

Jillybean cleared her throat and said, "Yes."

Sadie's dark eyes were round circles of black fear in her head. She knelt down in front of the little girl and said, "I need to talk to Jillybean. Let me talk to Jillybean. We need to hear her idea, ok? Please?"

"No," Jillybean stated. "It'll get her killed and I know that doesn't concern you, but it concerns us very much."

Quick as lightning, Sadie shot out her hand and snatched the zebra from Jillybean's slack grip. The Goth girl then took a firm hold of the stuffed animal and started twisting Ipes' head around. "Tell me or else."

"I wouldn't do that if I was you," Jillybean said. Despite her cool words, her lips were tight against her teeth and her fingers were hooked into claws. "What do you think will happen to me if you destroy…my body? Do you think I'll go away? If there's nowhere for Jillybean to put me, I'll be forced to stay inside her, and there's not much room in there."

Neil stepped forward to come between them. "Sadie, don't hurt the zebra, and you, Ipes, there's a life on the line here."

"Yes, Jillybean's. All she ever does is give and all you guys ever do is take. If you cared about her, it would be different, but she's just the weird kid that hangs around, forgotten until it's time for her to bail you guys out one more time. She'll die for you, Mister Neil, even though you were the one who wanted to trade her. Who knows what craziness you have planned for her when you get to New Eden, another trade, maybe?"

"No," Neil replied in a weak voice.

"As for you, Sadie, all she wants is to be...to be..." It looked as though Jillybean had lost her train of thought or that she was trying to remember some key bit of information that was very important.

"Jillybean!" Neil yelled suddenly, making Sadie jump and Jilly blink.

"Yeah?" she asked. "What's wrong? Why are you yelling, Mister Neil? Why are you guys looking at me like that?"

Neil forced a fake smile onto his face, but tempered it with concern in his voice, "Jillybean, honey, there's something..."

Sadie interrupted, "Sorry, Neil, first things first. Jilly, we need to know your plan to help Nico."

Jillybean put a hand to her head, touching it like it had grown big or didn't feel the same. "Um...All that stuff you need? I think it's at the CDC," she said. "Miss Sarah told me they had a hospital and she told me everyone left in a rush, like in only a few minutes. There's no way they got it all out of there in time. So it's probably just sitting there."

"You're forgetting the germs," Neil said. "That's the reason people left in the first place. We can't go within a mile of that place."

"Maybe you can with that." She pointed at the gas mask. "I'd also get like a scuba-man suit and some gloves and some big rubber boots. All that stuff we can find easily. It'll keep the germs off of you and in all the doctor shows surgery stuff is sealed up in plastic. So that should be safe if we can wash it really well."

"Will this really work?" Sadie asked Neil.

He was slow to answer as his mind worked feverishly to come up with a reason why it wouldn't. Eventually he had to concede, "I don't see why not."

All that night he stretched his imagination for a reason why it wouldn't work. Unfortunately he couldn't come up with one, which meant he was stuck going into, what he considered was one of the scariest places on earth. With a feeling of dread like a cold boulder sitting in his belly, Neil got them going early and drove without stop to the CDC.

Chapter 27

Sarah

New Eden

The doors to the silo opened with a heavy creaking. It covered the sound of her swallowing, which was loud in her ears, as was her breath that ran in and out with gathering speed. Sarah couldn't feel her hands. It was as though she possessed ghost hands and the feeling, or rather the lack of feeling, was slowly spreading up from her wrists.

Behind the door were armed men. To her surprise one of her former traveling partners was among them, Sadie's ex-boyfriend, Mark. He was a big man and carried a big gun, however she knew that he was also somewhat of a coward. He was the slowest of the five to step forward.

"Whatchu two want?" one of the men demanded in a drawl. He had a bit of a gut and more than a bit of a swagger to him as he came to stand close to Artie. Sarah recognized him as the door warden from her previous trip to New Eden and she knew that he'd be thorough in his search of her. He'd find the pistol that sat clenched in one of her ghost hands down deep in the pocket of her coat.

Sarah cleared her throat and, pitching her voice a little lower than usual, said, "We're looking for the prophet Abraham. We heard…" Her mind suddenly became a complete blank as Mark turned his attention on her. He had been eyeing Artie but with the door warden staring down at the lunatic and clearly intimidating him, Mark looked closer at Sarah.

"Ya heard what?" the door warden demanded.

"That, that, y-you'd take us in," Sarah said. With Mark so close she couldn't stop herself and she dropped her chin, unable to look him in the eye. "We heard this was a place for *believers*."

The door warden bobbed his head at this. "It is and it isn't, dependin' on what it is y'all believe."

He was clearly looking for them to explain what it was they believed, but it was then that Mark touched her chin with one of his large hands; lifting it with gentle pressure to get a good look at her face. She tried tightening her lips, drawing them in so that they didn't look so full, and she let the Georgia sun strike her eyes so that she had an excuse to blink and squint.

Still, recognition was slowly dawning in his face when Artie spoke up: "I know we believe in beams, and the Father Almighty, maker of heaven and earth, and all that is seen and unseen...like the beams. And that the government is sucking us down and we believe that I'm the mayor of Easton and that I was fairly elected by one vote regardless of what dead Ponytail Bob thinks."

The men, including Mark glanced at each other and then at Artie. "What beams is that?" the door warden asked. His beard, large as it was, could not hide the fact that his lip was curled in manner that suggested Artie was distasteful to him. "What's he on about?"

"Only that we're from Easton," Sarah answered, quickly. "It's in Maryland near Baltimore. He's Artie and I'm Janice Sills. We heard that there was a prophet that took in good people if they believed and we wanted to see for ourselves this, uh, paradise."

"The beams can't get you underground," Artie added, tipping the door warden a wink.

"I get it, it's another one those shitheels," Mark said, abrasively, displaying his trademark toughness and courage when he was certain there was nothing to fear. The door warden elbowed him back.

"What did I say about y'all's cussing?" he barked before turning back to Sarah and apologizing. "Sorry 'bout that ma'am. He's still green, but for cryin' out loud he shoulda knowd better."

Before Sarah could say anything, Artie put in, "It's the beams. They're melting his brain. Why do you think *they* all turn grey? It's their brains melted out of their heads. Ask Janice, she knows. She knows and I know."

"That's 'bout what I figgered," the door warden said and then spat out a brown stream of chewing tobacco juice. "I think we all know what's going on. Miss, y'all can stop pretending."

Sarah could suddenly feel her fingers again. They were gripping the pistol dangerously tight, especially the index finger which had half drawn back on the trigger. "Me, pretending?" she asked. Her mind buzzed: How did he know it was her? Had she been that obvious? Did she still look so much like her old self that she had been recognized by a man she had only seen on two brief occasions?

"I think you have it wrong. I'm not pretending, I'm Janice…" She was in the middle of her sentence when Artie opened his mouth to spew more crazy. Sarah grabbed his hand, and looked at him sadly. "It's ok, Artie. I won't let them hurt you. You're going to be fine."

The door warden shook his head at this. "I don't know if'n he will be. Sometimes when the great prophet of the Lord cast out demons such as what's in y'all's friend, the poor feller up and dies. Like his body can't handle the presence of the Lord."

This talk of demons from out of nowhere made Sarah step back. "He casts out demons?" She was so surprised that she forgot to cast even the slightest of false veneers over her countenance. No one seemed to notice. Mark had stepped to the back of the group wearing a pissy look at being admonished. She went on, "Has he done a lot of this sort of thing?"

"It's becoming a right epidemic," the warden said. "Specially among all the new peoples that we has acoming through lately. The prophet of the Lord says that it's the devil hisself trying to destroy New Eden with infiltrators. I seed it too, people going all crazy and then the prophet he touches them and they calm. It is honest-to-God miraculous."

One of the door guards nodded in agreement and said, "Amen." This brought on an uneven chorus of *Amens* from the rest.

"Amen," Sarah said. She looked to Artie, hoping he would have enough sense to say it also, but he was mumbling under his breath. He would start in with his talk of beams and cell technology any second.

Sarah was clueless on how to proceed. She knew Abraham was a charlatan, and "casting out demons" seemed right up his alley, but the talk of people dying from it unnerved her. How did they die? Was that faked as well, or were the people killed on the sly and their bodies dumped where they could be "discovered?" Were there others in on it, or was it just Abraham working alone to increase his mystique?

The biggest question she had was how could she possibly bring Artie into New Eden knowing that he would likely be "diagnosed" as possessed and then even more likely killed? He was the perfect candidate; even then he was working himself up, his mumbling growing louder.

"We'll talk about the beams, later," she said, squeezing his hand. She was sure Artie would be one of the failures, one of those whose bodies couldn't handle the exorcism. But how would Abraham fake the whole thing? Getting Artie to "go all crazy" would be easy, but how would he get him to calm? She pictured an accomplice with a poison dart and a blow gun shooting him in the neck; however that would be ridiculously obvious.

What about poisoned sacramental wine? Or a hypodermic needle hidden in the folds of Abraham's linen robes? One of these last seemed most likely, which begged the question, could she really sacrifice Artie for her own gains?

She tried to feel the heat and the hate that, for the last month, had been brewing like hot bile deep inside her. Try as she might she couldn't seem to kindle that same rage. It confused her. What did it mean? Was she willing to turn back—*now*, when she was so close to her goal. So close to getting Eve back? Just like the bile, answers to these questions did not come to her.

She couldn't go on and she couldn't retreat which left only one alternative. "Will the prophet see us?" she asked. The warden started to nod and she went on before he could say anything. "Out here, I mean? I'm afraid for Artie. Close spaces make him worse."

The warden said he would ask, but could not guarantee anything. When he left, the two newcomers were asked to hand over any weapons in their possession. Reluctantly, Sarah handed over her pistol and allowed herself to be frisked. Artie was even more reluctant. He had to be wrestled to the ground, and he fought so hard that it took all four of the very large men to keep him pinned. They decided it was better to hold him there until the prophet arrived.

Unlike Sarah, Abraham had not changed in any appreciable manner since the night Jillybean had sunk two ferry boats and Ram had been killed.

The prophet swept out of the silo, his robes white as snow, his hair shining silver. He was flanked by two women who were dressed in azure robes. They were both somewhere in their thirties and very severe looking. Neither took much notice of Artie; their judging eyes were on Sarah who had been kneeling next to Artie.

"Hello," said Abraham, the prophet. "Good day."

Sarah could not bring herself to speak just then. Anger and hate ballooned in her with such sudden fury that she didn't trust her tongue. Nor did she trust her eyes. In what she hoped was a display of submission, she dropped her chin to her chest and sunk lower on her knees. To add to her display, she also grabbed hold of the hem of Abraham's robes as though she were groveling when what she really wanted to do was strangle him with the elaborately knotted cord he had tied around his waist.

"These are the two, my Lord," the door warden said.

"Yes," Abraham replied. She could feel his eyes on her and it was all she could do not to let a spasm of disgust show.

"They say you are a prophet," Sarah said, forcing out the words. "And that you can c-c-c..." The idea that he had some sort of real power to cast out demons was so preposterous that the word caught on her tongue. She cleared her throat and spat it out, "Cast. You can cast out demons from people."

"Yes, daughter of the Lord, I can," Abraham said easily. "For every ying, there is a yang. For every up, there is a down. The Lord chose the earth for his epic struggle with evil and he sent me to do his bidding, to challenge the imps and demons and all the hate-filled things that worm their way out of hell. Sadly, these are more prevalent now than ever before."

"Yes, my Lord," Sarah said. "But..."

One of the women, her right hand hidden in her robe, stepped forward, aggressively. "We do not question the Prophet of the Lord. He can feel the presence of evil in his midst and can send demons back to the depths of hell with just a touch. This is not subject to question."

"My child, my Amanda," Abraham said to the woman. "Can you love me too much?" He laughed and she blushed like a schoolgirl.

"I can't my Lord."

His laugh was lighter now as he regarded Sarah. "Perhaps we should let this woman..."

He paused to allow Sarah to introduce herself, but as he did he touched the back of her head and this time her body was rattled by a shiver. Fearing that he would realize her revulsion, she opened her mouth to respond and, unbelievably, came within an ace of divulging her real name!

She stumbled over a few nonsense syllables before finally saying, "S-S...it's, uh Janice."

No one seemed to think oddly of her nervous behavior. Abraham's smile even seemed to grow larger. Sarah guessed he enjoyed the intimidating effect he and his minions had on unarmed strangers.

Still with his hand on her bowed head, Abraham said, "Perhaps we should let Janice ask her questions. I'm sure she has a great many."

Sarah nodded, making sure to keep most of her face averted from Abraham. "I do. They say you can cast out demons, but what can you do for Artie? He's a good man and a good person. He loves the Lord, don't you, Artie?"

If the two women with Abraham were enraptured by his presence, then Artie was doubly so. He had his head canted up out of the dirt at a scary angle, maybe even an impossible angle. His eyes were filled with tears at the sight of the false Prophet.

"I love the lord," he said in a voice made strange by the angle of his throat. It was a creaking sound like a frog speaking.

"Yes, you do," Sarah said. She forgot herself then and looked straight up into Abraham's face. "See? He's a good man and a good protector and has done many good deeds in the name of the Lord, right Artie?"

"The Lord!" Artie croaked. "I love the Lord! He protects me from the beams and the blue electricity that speaks in tongues, *sssss*. He gave me victory in my election. He gave me Beth and now Janice..."

"Ok Artie," Sarah said, cutting him off before he could say something to endanger her alias. She turned her face up to Abraham, remembering this time to squint. "You see? He's not possessed, he just not, you know, thinking right. Some might say, uh, a little crazy."

Everyone looked at Abraham who had lost his gleaming smile. He stared at Artie with a bit of curl to his lip, but then burst out in his usual booming laughter. "Oh, Janice, the Prince of Lies spins his deception with such intricacy that mere mortals would confuse up from down if he wished them to. Do not be fooled by the flower and the butterfly for that which seems most pleasing to us may be the purest poison."

To this Sarah could only wag her head. Abraham chortled at her honest confusion and said, "Do you have the wit to see though the illusions of the devil himself?

Insanity has always been the perfect cover for demonic possession. Thank the Lord of Hosts that I have been given the ability to see through such...how should I put it? Amusements. That's all they are to me."

In other words, Sarah thought, Artie was doomed. She had hoped to plant the idea of Artie's insanity in their minds, but Abraham had countered her with his version of "logic."

Only he could judge if a person was possessed or not and only he could "heal" him. If he wanted Artie dragged inside for a little theatrical healing that would very likely kill him, there wasn't anything Sarah could do about it.

"That's why I brought him to you," Sarah said in a rush. She hadn't known she was going to say anything at all, the words just shot out of her. "Everyone knows your power...I mean we've heard of it up in Maryland and there were people who came south out of...Boston, who had heard of you, too." She had been close to saying New York, but stopped herself, not wanting to spark memories that could lead to her being recognized.

"Yes," Abraham said. "My fame has grown immensely, which is why we can be more selective about whom we allow to join us. Only those with the deepest faith are permitted into New Eden so that it may remain pristine. Is that you, Janice? Do you have great faith?"

Sarah groveled in the dirt, holding his hem, fiercely. "Yes, I do. I see it clearly how much the Lord, uh, loves you, his Prophet." Just then, she felt a certain pride in her acting skills, she had hit the exact right note, which was great for her, but not for Artie.

"Then I will help your friend," Abraham said, again touching her. He began to turn away, to lead them down into New Eden where Eve waited to be rescued and where Artie would soon die.

Sarah had known this moment would occur. She had brought Artie along with the sole purpose to be sacrificed one way or the other. But now that the hour had come, she hesitated, filled with regret and second thoughts.

"Wait, please," she said, holding the false prophet back by the hem of his robes. He waited with his pleasant smile slowly losing its pleasantness. Five long seconds ticked by.

With everyone looking at her, Sarah could think of nothing. Her mind was far too rigid in its thinking, far too linear for her to come up with a spur of the moment plan to save Artie. Her vision of the world was narrow, her paradigms hard and brittle as fired clay.

She knew facts: Abraham had begun to perform "exorcisms" in which some people died. New Eden had become more selective, yet Abraham was willing to bring in a clearly insane person. Abraham wouldn't just stand there for much longer. Sarah knew the answers to save Artie were in front of her, but they would not arrange themselves in her mind in a cohesive manner. She couldn't seem to figure out what to say or do. Her one thought was of Jillybean. What would she do differently?

Jillybean would change something. She would note the one thing that didn't seem right, the one thing that wasn't congruent, and she would turn it to her advantage.

What wasn't right in this situation? Sarah's first thought was: everything. Her second thought was more precise: Abraham was a snake, a charlatan, a kidnapper, and almost without question, a murderer. There was nothing pristine about him or about New Eden at all. The word "pristine" caught in her head. If New Eden was so perfect then...

"Artie can't go." The wardens were just getting ready to stand Artie up, but now they hesitated and looked to Abraham for guidance.

"Why is that?" he asked.

"B-because this was a mistake," Sarah said, thinking on the fly. "He can't go in if he's a demon. I couldn't think of anything that would be more blasphemous than to drag something so awful evil and dirty into New Eden. I don't want that on my head."

The false prophet beamed at this. "Your loyalty and faith in the Lord is overwhelming in one who has only just seen the light."

"And so is my faith in his prophet," Sarah said, pulling harder on the hem. "Please, if you see that Artie is afflicted with a demon, touch him now and free him. Do not let him suffer anymore." This was so wholly an unexpected request that Abraham drew back slightly and gazed at her with sharp eyes. Perhaps he was looking for the angle Sarah was playing but, more likely, he was taken aback, put on the spot, forced by his own words into action.

"You are most considerate," Abraham said at last. "And yours is a request from the heart. I will use the gift given to me by the lord."

Abraham knelt before Artie and put out his hands to him as a camper would before a fire. Sarah, who knew full well that only a snake such as Abraham could find a way to wiggle out of the spot she had put him in, held her breath in the seconds that followed.

Her fear was unfounded. Abraham ducked displaying his "powers" of exorcism simply by declaring Artie free of demons. He even mussed Arties hair, but then he grew sad. "He is not a vessel of Satan, and for that we should rejoice. However, his sin has been very great. His mind has been turned inside out because of it. I'm afraid he will not be able to join the family of Believers until his soul is right with God."

"Yes, my Lord, but...but what about me?" Sarah felt like a high-stakes poker player holding nothing but a pair of twos with her life on the line. She was afraid to move, afraid to swallow, afraid to look at Abraham and more afraid not to. What if he thought she was hiding something? Or worse, what if he saw that she *was* hiding something?

She sweated out the seconds, waiting for his answer, as the gritty sand bit into the bones of her knees and Georgian gnats began to form into a cloud above her head. Finally, he lifted her chin and looked her square in the face.

The two of them had never been this close before and his imperfections were obvious: there was a scar on his cheek under his left eye, the pores of his nose were large and deep, tufts grew out of his ears like weedy stands of

241

sage in a desert. Even his hair wasn't nearly as perfect as he wanted people to believe: it was flaked with dandruff.

Sarah was worse off and knew it. Her black and butchered hair bore no resemblance to the beautiful blonde mane she had once possessed and her once-smooth complexion had been replaced by peeling skin and fading bruises.

"You've seen some difficult days, haven't you, Janice?" Abraham asked. The part of her that feared getting caught relaxed, slightly. Inches from her face and still Abraham saw only Janice Sills.

"Yes," she said. "It's horrible out there. I-I don't want to go back."

"Is your faith strong?"

Sarah had all the faith in the world. She had faith that she would either get her baby back or kill the lying piece of shit in front of her. "Yes, I do."

"Your faith is your shield, dear Janice and it has saved you," Abraham cried with a flourish, standing tall and raising his hands to the heavens. "Come join the family of Believers!"

Chapter 28

Jillybean

Atlanta, Georgia

"Look at this," Jillybean gasped, gingerly touching the bright metal and letting the sharp point indent the skin of her finger. "A speargun! Do you think it's shootable?"

Ipes sat wedged between the Velveteen Rabbit and the crook of Jilly's left arm—the little girl kept her right hand free whenever possible, just in case. *Probably not,* Ipes said. *These sorts of things work with springs and rubber bands, I think. You can't keep them ready to shoot all the time or they'll break. But that's only a guess.*

They were a hundred yards from the dark waters of Carter's Lake, standing in Doug's Boats-N-Bait Shoppe, a fading building that wasn't much larger than a standard sized hut. From its walls and ceiling, hung nets, plastic lobsters, singing bass and so many other fishing-related decorations that Jillybean felt as though she had wandered into a *Red Lobster* restaurant.

"This makes me hungry," she had said when they first walked in. They had searched for food but found the speargun instead. In a shed next to the main "building" Neil and Sadie were thumbing through the assorted, rentable wetsuits, leaving Jillybean to explore as they usually did.

Sometimes she felt like an afterthought when they were busy with their grown up stuff. On a certain level she knew every kid probably felt this way at some point, however, as there weren't any other kids left in the world to play with, the feeling was especially acute.

At least she had Ipes. Yes, he had been somewhat overbearing lately, but who could blame him? His job, as he constantly reminded her, was to protect her, and that had kept him very busy in the last few days. Still, there was something about the zebra that worried her on a level that went very deep, so deep that it felt like only a rumble of nerves or the sensation like the sweaty ending of a barely-remembered nightmare.

...You need to stop listening to his voice in your head...that's what Sadie had said. Whenever she thought about it, she would feel queer inside and Ipes would be extra good for a little while.

He was in that mood now. *We could get it working, you know.*

"Get what, working?" She blinked suddenly, feeling like she had missed something. What had they been talking about?

The speargun, silly.

"Oh, right," she said somewhat distantly. Her attention was now on a clothes rack hung with pink bikinis; some were for kids. She pulled down the smallest and held it up to her rail-thin chest, thinking that if the weather warmed up anymore she'd like to take a dip in one the zillions of lakes and ponds that dotted Georgia.

"What do you think of this bikini?"

Ipes ruffled his mane, thinking. *I know what your mommy would say.*

"That I'm too young for a bikini, I know, but she isn't here and I don't think Neil or Sadie cares."

I don't think they do either, however that doesn't mean we can disregard your parent's advice. They told you no bikinis for a reason. Remember pedofilers? Remember stranger-danger? We have to be more careful than ever.

"I guess," she said, putting the hanger back on the rack. Stacks of shorts caught her attention next. "I can wear shorts in the water. I know that."

What about the speargun? Ipes said. *It can still be shootable. There are pulleys and a lever that you have to crank down. You may not be strong enough to use it, but the grownups are. And you know we could use more weaponry in this group. Of course a speargun isn't the best weapon. A gun would be better, but it sure beats running around with only a hope...*

Suddenly the sound of Ipes' voice became vague as though she was hearing him through a long tube. Jillybean shook her head to clear her ears as Ipes went on...*and a prayer. Sadie doesn't even have her bat anymore, which is crazy...*

Now his words were overlapped by a strange vision: she was kneeling, looking at a tiny gun, the one she had found back in the suburbs of Philadelphia. It sat in the thick grass next to a house, its metal twinkling up at her. She reached out her mud-daubed hand and covered the gun over so that it was hidden, and then, very oddly, the vision seemed to go in reverse. She brushed back the grass, gazed for a second at the shiny metal and picked the gun up. It was so peculiarly heavy...

Jillybean! Ipes cried, suddenly. *Look, a monster. Get Mister Neil, quick!*

She came up out of the vision rattled and alarmed but, true to her nature, she didn't jump or react in a panicky way. Instead, she slunk low, bending at the knees, ready to spring in any direction.

"W-where is it?" Her ears perked and attuned for the telltale signs of the monsters: the low moans, the shuffling feet, the objects clumsily knocked over. Nothing came to her.

Just outside, he told her.

Jillybean slowly raised herself and saw the monster in question; it was halfway from the water's edge and munching contentedly on rhododendron blossoms. "Oh that one," she said, relaxing. "I saw it before. Looks harmless enough, for a monster that is. So...what we were we talking about?"

Uh, the speargun.

She felt somewhat jumbled in her thinking and was sure it was something else entirely that had been on her mind, but it wouldn't come to her, especially with Ipes yapping.

You should try it out on the monster.

"You think so?" She took another look at the monster and noted the distance between them: ninety feet. "You've gone soft in the head, Ipes. There's no way the speargun will kill at this range. We're too far away, and besides, I never have shooted one of these before, I'd probably miss."

We should at least tell Mister Neil about it. You don't want it sneaking up on him. Everyone knows he's got worse hearing than a snake, and they don't even have ears.

She had to agree that Neil was about as out of tune with his surroundings as a man could be. A warning seemed reasonable, so they went around to the shed and found him struggling into a form-fitting, ladies-juvenile, neoprene wet suit. He was out of breath and pink in the cheeks from his exertion. His color matched the collar and cuffs of the suit nicely.

"There's a monster on the other side of the building," Jillybean said. "Just wanted to let you know."

Hurriedly, Neil picked up his ax and, due to the constricting nature of the wetsuit, waddled out to do battle. He came back, huffing to an even greater extent. "He's dead. You're safe now, Jillybean."

Although she had never been in any real danger she thanked him and then asked, "When we're done saving Nico, can we go swimming?"

"Maybe," Neil said. "I guess it depends on how long it takes. I've never done surgery before. But first we have to find a better suit. This one's too…girlie."

"Oh stop," Sadie said. "Who's going to see you? And we don't have time to be picky. Nico is fading." This was true although they were mega-dosing him with antibiotics and keeping the tourniquet on as long as they dared.

Neil agreed to the "girlie" wetsuit and was cheered slightly when he found a pair of size seven rubber boots in the boys section. Once he was suitably attired for underwater exploration, Neil folded himself in the driver's seat as the rest of them piled back into the Tercel where Nico was dozing in a damp sweat with the copper smell of blood around him like a cloud.

Because of his anxiety over the Russian's health, Neil went at a fearful pace. Though there seemed nothing to fear. The roads were relatively free of zombies, and there weren't any black Jeeps or Humvees spitting hot lead at them. There weren't even any white-robed crazies thumping their reworked and reworded bibles.

It was such an easy ride that Jillybean fell asleep in the front seat and didn't notice when Neil covered her with a blanket. She slept for the hour-long ride, using the very soft Velveteen Rabbit as a pillow.

"We're here," Neil said. "Wake up everybody." Jillybean came instantly awake; Sadie was slower and Nico, who had his head in Sadie's lap, could only find the strength to crack a red-rimmed eye. Neil took a shaky breath and pointed. "The CDC is just down the road. Hopefully I won't be gone long."

"Good luck," Sadie said. "Be careful."

"Yeah, good luck, Mister Neil," Jillybean said.

"Luck," Neil said, as though he didn't quite understand the word. "Ok, here goes nothing." He took out the gas mask from its carrying case and began to put it on.

Ipes practically went berserk. *Stop him! He can't get out yet.*

"Why not?" Jillybean asked.

Has he checked the strength of the wind and its direction? He could end up killing all of us if he's not careful.

"Oh," Jillybean said. She tugged on Neil's arm until he pulled his head back out of the mask. "You have to check the wind. If we're not up in the wind from the CDC the germs could get us."

Neil was red-faced and had been all set to be cranky at her, but now his eyes bulged as he looked about trying to see which way the wind blew. For the most part the air was stagnant and hot, but when it did blow it went from their left to their right.

Ipes didn't like it. *Tell him to leave the keys. We'll come back for him in an hour.*

"I don't think I will," Jillybean huffed. "Ipes wants us to leave you here, Mister Neil and come back for you, but I don't think we should."

"I know I won't," Sadie said. "First off, we're too far away for anything to really happen to us, and second, not all germs are airborne. Look at the zombies, they're doing ok." There were a few of the undead stumbling around, all of whom seemed just as horrible and grey as always.

That doesn't prove anything! They already have the Super-soldier virus in them... Ipes stopped when he realized Jillybean wasn't listening as much as she was glaring. *At least have him hide us. We can't just sit out here on the street. What happens if the bounty hunter comes strolling on by?*

This bit of common sense was something they all agreed to. Neil drove to a parking garage and found a spot on the highest level where they could see all the way to the CDC, a quarter mile away. Neil was ashen-faced and his hands shook as he tried to adjust the mask on his face.

"I can't see worth a darn in this thing," he said. His words came out muffled. From the backseat, Sadie tried to help adjust the straps, but the problem was more than just the fit and the plastic hood. Neil was hyperventilating. His own breath cast a fog over the lenses.

"Slow your breathing," Sadie told him. "Try to control yourself. It'll be alright. The clinic is in a different building from the lab; it's probably completely safe. Just get what you need and get back."

Neil took slow breaths and gradually he calmed and the lenses cleared. "I wish I could go with you," Jillybean said, when he didn't look so panicked. "You need someone to watch over you."

He smiled at this. She could tell because his eyes crinkled behind the lenses of the mask. "Honestly, I wish you could, but it's too dangerous."

"I can at least walk you down to the street so you don't trip on the stairs. I think Ipes is being too paranoia. That's what means being afraid of everything. I mean we were right in front of the main lab just a few weeks ago when everything was fresh and we didn't get sick, and it's not like this car is magical, you know? I don't think it's germ proof."

In the back seat Sadie's dark eyes grew larger. "Shit. I never thought about that."

Neil tried to glare but it wasn't all that noticeable. "Watch your language, please." He shifted in his seat, a laborious process in the extra tight wetsuit; the gas mask didn't help. "You can walk me down, but I don't think you should go any further."

Jillybean had no plans on going further. The idea of breathing in killer germs was unsettling, mainly because she misunderstood the concept on a fundamental a level. In her mind it seemed to be the same thing as breathing in poison and that she would die instantly. Another fallacy that skewed her thinking was that she expected the air to smell different with germs floating about in it.

After opening the Tercel's door she took an exploratory sniff. What struck her first were the odors of concrete, fading diesel, and the dusty smell of a garage. Beneath that was the scent of Dogwood blossoms drifting in from the west and the slight rank odor of zombie that underlied everything else. Big cities always had that odor.

Neil watched her pause and lift her little nose. When she gave him the thumbs up, he nodded and started toward the stairs that would bring them to ground level. He carried the shotgun in his left hand, his axe in his right, and on his back was an empty pack. With all this and a heavy mask on his face and hood that went from his eyebrows to his shoulder blades, he didn't seem to realize he wasn't being quiet in the least.

The little girl ran around in front of him and put up both hands and then put one of her fingers to her lips. "You're being too loud," she admonished.

"Ok," he practically yelled.

Jillybean lifted up the hood and said, "Just nod."

He nodded at this and she gave him a strained smile. She led the way to the staircase and, once the door was open, she paused again, sniffing and listening. When her senses indicated it was safe to proceed she started down the stairs with Ipes in one hand and a magic marble in the other. Neither was needed.

249

They got to the bottom and Neil patted Jillybean on the head with one of his gloved hands and then waved. She waved as well and since she didn't know a hand signal for good luck, she blew him a kiss instead. He returned it clumsily and then opened the door.

Fearful of both germs and zombies, Jillybean slunk back and this was why the man in green camouflage, who stepped out from around the outside wall of the stairwell and stuck the business end of an M4 right up to Neil's eye, didn't see her.

Run! Ipes commanded in a voice that was part Daddy and part Ram. The order came without the least panic, instead it held such authority over her that, against her will, she took three steps back up the stairs before she fought for control of her own body. It was a terrifying experience. It was as if her body belonged to someone else.

"No," she hissed through gritted teeth forcing herself to turn around; she moved as if she were loaded down with lead. "Ipes, I swear I'll drop you right here and leave you forever if you don't let go of me." Just like that, her body was hers again to use and move about, though at that moment all she could do was shake.

How had the zebra done that? It wasn't supposed to be able to do that.

I am just trying to save you, Ipes said, again using the Daddy/Ram voice, but this time softer.

"Don't you do that anymore," she warned under her breath.

Her whispers went unheard as the army man pulled the weapons from Neil's hands and yanked off his mask. The man paused and then exclaimed in a low dangerous voice, "You! You're that funky little pervert I caught back up in Maryland. What the hell are you doing here?"

Neil's answer was spluttery and practically nonsensical. "I-I, uh, the germs. M-my mask, I n-need it." Neil was standing in the partially closed doorway and Jillybean could see the army man wasn't the bounty hunter, which was a relief.

"What do you need a mask for?" the man demanded, again his voice was pitched low. "And the rubber suit? Were you thinking of raiding the CDC for some more little girl panties? Or…" his voice raised angrily, "Or were you after some good germs to sell?"

"Uh-uh," Neil replied. "No, I just need some supplies: f-food and medicine. That's all."

"Dressed like that?" the soldier asked before kicking Neil's legs out from under him and sending him to the concrete, first to his knees and then down to his belly. "You're a liar. No one dresses like this unless they plan on going down into the labs." The man stepped on the back of Neil's neck. "Now, you're going to tell me what you were after and who you're working for."

Please run, Ipes begged. *Go warn Sadie and Nico first if you want to, but you can't just stand there!*

That was the best bet; it was good ole' herd mentality: sacrifice one for the sake of the rest. Jillybean figured she could probably hide the three of them somewhere in the parking garage until the danger had passed. That was the safest move, the instinctual move. But it wasn't the move of someone with the precocious mega-watt brain power that Jillybean possessed.

Hiding meant Neil would probably die. And Nico as well; he needed help in the next few hours or he was doomed. The concept of *bleeding out* drifted through her subconscious, it meant certain death.

To save him was predicated on saving Neil. How could she accomplish that? Certainly not by relying on some simple misdirection with a magic marble. This soldier carried himself as Ram had done. He was quick and alert; he had recognized Neil despite the passage of days and his wild, pink-wetsuit-covered appearance.

The soldier was disciplined as well. He could have hurt Neil badly when he had tripped him, but he chose not to. Not only that, his right index finger had never once slipped down to the trigger of his rifle. It had sat straight along the barrel just above it, ready to kill, but only with purpose.

Finally, though he was one of the Colonel's men, he seemed to be a soldier with at least some honor. He had not robbed Neil when he had the opportunity to the first time they had met. He had also seemed angry that Neil might be a pervert, a word that was linked in some way with *stranger danger* and the reason why her mother had always warned her not to take candy from people she didn't know. Perhaps the soldier had a protective streak, again like Ram

So all this meant: what?

First off, the soldier may have been after Sadie and Nico, but he wasn't after Neil and certainly wasn't after Jillybean since he had no idea that she even existed. Secondly, he thought Neil was trying to get into the lab for germs. He didn't believe Neil was going for medicine, because Neil wasn't sick.

Ahhh! There it was; her solution for saving Neil, and hopefully, Nico as well. All that was needed was for Neil to produce someone, other than Sadie and Nico, who was sick. He also needed someone to vouch that he wasn't a pervert, but was in fact just a nice guy. Jillybean could handle both roles.

After a deep breath, she coughed. It was a little sound, not at all what she was hoping for. She tried again and had only just barked the first of what she had figured was to be a chain of coughs when the door slammed fully open and the soldier was there, crouched, using the cement wall to shield his entire body except for the edge of one shoulder.

Practically all she could see of him consisted of his rifle which was aimed dead on her forehead and now she coughed for real.

Chapter 29

Jillybean

The Centers for Disease Control Atlanta, Georgia

Against the gun pointed her way, all Jillybean had to protect herself with was her zebra, which she held up in front of her face.

Jilly, what are you doing? Ipes said, with a shaky little laugh. *I said I was sorry about that little mix up we had with me taking over your body. It won't happen again, so how about you put me down.*

In answer she coughed harder, really trying to dig deep and bring something up. It was her wish to emulate how Sadie had been coughing when she had pneumonia, something that turned out impossible to fake. Jillybean had to settle for a dry cough and pathetic look. The soldier seemed both unimpressed and unsympathetic.

"I'm sorry," she said. Without realizing it, the two words were a stroke of genius. Perhaps nothing else could have softened the man's hard look as well as they did. The army man had hazel eyes with heavy brows the same deep brown as the very short hair on his head. His jaw was strong and scruffy. Over all, he looked to be about as tough a man as she had ever seen, but at her apology that toughness eased slightly.

He crouched low, looking at Jillybean, this time not as though she were a target for his gun, but as a little girl. He then looked beyond her up the stairs, then again at her, scrutinizing her pink jeans with the dirt on the knees, and the crumpled yellow shirt that she had picked out days before when Sadie was finally getting better and they had made the decision to travel south.

Slowly he took his eyes from her and gazed out at the street, taking in every detail.

"What do you have to be sorry about?" he asked. When he talked his voice was so rough, Jillybean had to wonder if this was how rocks would sound like if they could speak.

She decided to cough again, before saying, "For making Mister Neil, go get my medicine. Is that against the law? Is he going to get in trouble?"

Neil had been shaking his head at her in a tiny way, but what he meant by it she didn't know. When she mentioned his name he stopped and creaked his head back to look at the soldier.

"I thought his name was *Norman*," the soldier said, quitting his crouch and coming to stand over Neil.

Jillybean hesitated only a second. "He told a fib. That's what means he didn't tell the truth, because he wanted to protect me. There are bad people out there and he keeps me safe."

"Is that right?"

"Yes," she said, adding a cough.

"He ever touch you?"

"Yes," Jillybean replied, misunderstanding the question. The second she did, Neil's blue eyes went wide in alarm. Quickly she added, "Not in a bad way. He patted my head before he left, that's all."

"Not even a hug?"

"No," Jillybean said with obvious disappointment. She hadn't had a hug since Ram died. For the longest time, Neil and Sadie had been sick and Sarah…Sarah thought she was a weirdo. These thoughts stung and she forgot herself. When she looked up at the soldier, he was staring at her and, in spite of their age difference they held each other's gaze almost as equals. She looked away first. It seemed to her that his eyes held some sort of unraveling power, that to look at them for too long would allow him to see through her veil of lies and understand her true self.

"So what do you need medicine for?" the soldier asked. Neil began to offer an answer, but was poked in the back by the rifle. "I was asking the little girl."

Now, she tried not to cough because she felt it would be too obvious, so of course her body decided it suddenly needed to clear its throat. After she did and after his hazel eyes narrowed, she answered, "Pneumonia. I need some sort of sillan. A-pennysillan I think it's called." She could tell that he wasn't buying her cute act.

"What's your name?"

"Jillybean. It's like jelly bean, but it's Jillybean and this is Ipes." He didn't seem to care about the zebra, which meant the feeling was mutual. Ipes wanted out of there as fast as possible.

"My name is Captain Grey and I have some good news and some bad news for you, Jillybean. Unfortunately, the CDC is cleaned out. There isn't a needle, test tube, or even a single aspirin left in the entire place. Even the germs are gone." He took stock of Neil's expression at this point: Neil looked confused and concerned and Jillybean was right there with him. She had to wonder, who would want germs and what would they do with them?

The only answer the seven-year-old could come up with was: bad guys would want them to do bad stuff with. "And the good news?" she asked.

"The good news is that you're cured," Grey said, eyeing Jillybean closely. "Your pneumonia has magically disappeared. What do you have to say about that?"

Jillybean had nothing to say to that, nothing that would be believed at least. Neil tried his own attempt at lying, "It's not what you think. We were going to sell the medicine…"

"Shut up. I was talking to her," Grey said, jabbing Neil in the back with the rifle a second time. Again he leveled his gaze at Jillybean. "I want you to tell me the truth and if you do, I'll go easy on your friend, Mister Neil. Meaning he won't get hurt. I'm sure you don't want him to get hurt so…why are you here?"

The truthful answer to that question would most likely end up getting Nico and Sadie killed. Jillybean hung her head, letting her brown hair fall in front of her face. Even Ipes was silent.

The captain breathed out, long and tiredly. "Alright, where have you been? New York? New Eden?"

Though the question seemed innocent enough, Jillybean kept her mouth shut. She didn't know what answers were "safe" answers and what ones weren't.

"You must be hiding something big if you can't even tell me where you've been," Grey said. "What is it, Jillybean? I promise you're not in trouble. Look at me. Look at me before I lose my temper. You don't want to see me lose my temper, do you?" The man's voice kept getting lower, sounding more and more dangerous. It began to work on her nerves, making her shake in fear.

"Why don't you let her go?" Neil shouted. "She's just a kid, alright? Let her go and I'll tell you whatever you want to know."

Grey considered this for a moment and then smirked. "You just want me to let her go? Out there with all the zombies?" He snorted at this and then demanded, "How many people are with you, Neil? Don't pretend you haven't got the foggiest idea what I'm talking about. You want me to believe you would let a little girl run away by herself? Hardly. There's more of you around here, but only one or two, am I right? I saw your piece of crap Tercel come putting right down this street and I'm willing to bet it's parked upstairs somewhere. I think we should go take a look at it."

Jillybean looked up to see Neil's defiance wilt. His face fell and tears jumped into his eyes. "Look, I can pay you… something. Whatever it takes, ok? Whatever the bounty is, I'll pay you more and that's the truth. It just might take some time, but I'm good for it."

"What are you talking about?" Captain Grey demanded. "Are you trying to collect on that bounty? Is that what's going on? Jillybean! You tell me right now, is Neil holding people against their will?"

Again the soldier and the little girl locked eyes. This time it was Jillybean who held the upper hand. In his passion he had opened up too much. "No. Sadie is his daughter and there are bad men after her, but I get the feeling you're not one of them."

"In that you're very wrong, Jillybean," the captain said. He reached down and with one arm lifted Neil up by the back of his rubber suit. "I can be very bad if I have reason to be. Let's go."

He marched them upstairs to the highest level, always keeping Neil in front of him and not at all worried about Jillybean. She could've left if she had wanted to, but not only was her fate tied to Neil and Sadie's, she stuck with her reading of the army officer as not as bad a man as he was letting on. When they reached the top, Grey brought the rifle up, sighting it on the Tercel.

"You don't need the gun, they're unarmed," Neil told him. "And Nico is wounded. He was shot three days ago by a bounty hunter."

"Three days?" Grey wore a strange look. "South of Hagerstown in a Ford Explorer? That was you?"

"Yes," Neil answered reluctantly. "But we didn't want to hurt anyone. We were just trying to get away and then there was shooting all over the place."

"You were lucky it was just one of you that got hurt. I didn't think any of you would live. We lost a good man in that fight, Jay McClellan. A good friend." He was quiet for a few blinks of his eyes and then he raised his voice and called out, "Sadie Walcott. Step out of the vehicle, now."

Neil tried to touch his arm, but Grey shrugged him off. Neil came around in front of the soldier, though not quite in front of the gun. "I told you I'd pay you more than the bounty. Ten percent more. How is that? Huh? Just tell me what it'll take. We're not bad people, ok? We weren't trying to get germs out of the CDC, only medical supplies."

Grey didn't say anything to this, instead he was nearly entirely focused on the Tercel and the black-haired Goth girl climbing slowly out of it. Sadie wore a look of utter defeat. "Hands up," Grey ordered. "And turn slowly." Her black jeans were tight and her t-shirt, form fitting. There was nowhere she could hide a weapon.

"I'm sorry, Sadie," Neil called across the forty feet of concrete between them. Grey took Neil by the pink collar of his wetsuit and pushed him forward, using him as a human shield until they were at the Tercel.

"Son of a bitch," Grey said when he saw Nico. "That arm does not look good." He opened the rear door and grimaced at all the blood. "I'm going to need my bag. Neil, my hummer is parked downstairs in the alley that runs behind this parking garage. I need you to get my med bag. It's in the back seat."

"What's going on here?" Sadie asked. Her emotions seemed to be fighting themselves. Fear versus hope. The tussle was playing on her face, making her muscles dance. "Aren't you one of the bounty hunters?"

"I think he's one of the Colonel William's men," Neil said.

"I'm not a bounty hunter," Grey said, with a look of disgust. "And I'm not with that jack-wad, Williams."

"But back in Maryland you mentioned saying something to the colonel about us," Neil said.

"You ever think there may be more than one colonel in the world?" Grey said. He set his M4 on the roof of the Tercel and began to take off his camouflage outer BDU shirt. "My commanding officer is Colonel Albright and his C.O. is General Jackson. We're out of Colorado."

"Colorado?" Neil asked in amazement.

"Yeah, it's one of the fifty states, you might have heard of it." Grey ducked into the Tercel and tried to peel back the first layer of Nico's black, blood-crusted bandages. This caused a fresh trickle of red to come seeping down from the lower edge.

Eager to watch, Jillybean climbed into the front and leaned over the seat. The blood didn't bother her at all, but the smell crinkled her nose. "So, are you a good guy?"

The captain shrugged. "I never really thought about it. I'm not a bad guy." He went back to exploring Nico's wound, while Jillybean watched and the Russian grunted in pain.

"Is sore like rotting tooth," Nico said, in a voice like sandpaper.

When Grey straightened he wore a look of concern. "Neil, I need that medbag ASAP. Go get it." Grey's ability to command lay in his voice. Its tone held such authority that Neil nodded and took off at a waddling run.

The captain then glanced around him at the parking garage and then at Sadie. "If you have sheets or blankets, I need them," he said. "Any bandages too and fresh water would be good as well."

As Sadie went to the trunk to get blankets, Grey pulled Nico out of the cramped interior of the car and laid him out on the concrete. Jillybean squatted down next to Captain Grey and declared: "Colorado is one of the square ones in the middle."

"Yep."

"So that doesn't make any sense," she said. "Colorado has mountains and eagles and bears, but no ocean. If you're a captain, where do you keep your boat?"

"I'm not that kind of captain," he said absently. His mind was clearly focused on Nico, who was doing his best to remain conscious. "I'm a captain of men, not ships."

"Is very cold," Nico said, the words coming out blurry and soft.

"It's going to be ok," Sadie said. She covered him with a blanket and then propped his head with a pillow, kissing him once.

"It's not cold," Jillybean said. "I think it's kinda hot. Do you think when we're done saving Nico, we can go swimming? Neil said maybe, but I don't…"

"Don't interrupt him," Sadie said, gently pulling Jillybean back. "Maybe you should go play with Ipes. We'll talk about swimming later, I promise."

Jillybean was far too interested in what was going on to leave. She watched as Captain Grey undid Nico's belt and untucked his shirt. He cut away the sleeve that was all bloody and ooky, and then propped the Russian's feet up on the Tercel's spare tire.

Neil came back, huffing and puffing in a major sweat due to the insulating nature of the wet suit, and the weight of the medbag. Grey didn't bother to thank him, instead he started an I.V. with, what to Jillybean, looked like a humongously scary needle.

He watched as the fluid ran smoothly into the drip chamber and then nodded, satisfied. "We'll let that one run wide open. Neil, get changed. You look like an idiot and that suit is only slowing you down. I'm going to need you to find lots of wood and water."

"But the germs," Neil said, touching his wet suit. "There was some sort of major accident at the CDC a while back. It's not too safe..."

Grey interrupted, shaking his head. "You don't have to worry about any damned germs. There wasn't an accident. It was all a set up, probably orchestrated by Yuri Petrovich if I had to guess. He knows germs and he's in the best position to gain by having the CDC shut down. Now, he's the only game in town when it comes to any sort of vaccinations."

Neil looked stunned at this. "Jeeze, that's awful."

"Yeah, it is," Grey said. "Now, if you don't mind, I need the wood and the water. Also find me a barbeque grill. One of those round, backyard ones should do. And some pots to boil the water in."

In an effort not to "look like an idiot," Neil threw a sweater vest over his wet suit. The captain snorted at this and then turned his attention to Nico. First he put on blue latex gloves, cut away the old bandage and inspected the wound, prodding here and there with the tips of his fingers. "That's not good," he said. "We have a little necrosis going, which, I suppose should be expected."

"Is that bad?" Sadie asked. Her eyes were dark and her hair black, which only made the extreme paleness of her skin seem even whiter. To Jillybean it looked as if she was about to faint. "Is it? Are you a doctor or something? Can you fix him?"

"Nope, not a doctor, but I've seen enough blood and guts in my time to qualify me for some sort of medical degree." He gave her a quick look and his eyes widened just a bit. "Maybe you should go help Neil. I can't have you falling out of formation when I start cutting away the dead flesh."

Her eyes began to float a little in their sockets. "Dead flesh?"

He took her by the elbow and led her a few feet away. "Yeah, definitely go help Neil, and take Jillybean with you."

"No, I'm good right here," Jillybean said. "Blood is ok with me so you don't have to worry about me fainting. I can even help. I just have to put Ipes in the car with the Velveeta Rabbit."

Grey watched Sadie walk toward the stairs, holding onto the parked cars as she went. He then eyed Jillybean, taking her measure. "In what way can you possibly help?"

"Ummm," she said as she considered things. "I can get things for you and I can tell you when the water bag is empty, which it is. See?" The I.V. had drained down to nothing and looked as flat and wrinkled as an old balloon. "And I can tell you if any monsters are coming and I was good in school."

"We'll test you first," Grey said. "Hang me another bag of .09% normal saline."

For other children this might have been a daunting and nerve-wracking request. For Jillybean it was only a matter of processing what she had seen already and using her native intelligence to replicate the captain's actions. Grey's medbag was very large and filled to over-flowing, but it was also extremely organized. The IV fluids were obvious, as was the writing on them. She simply picked out the normal saline, bit her way through the outer sleeve—Grey had simply torn open the packaging, but she wasn't strong enough.

Then she pulled off the old deflated bag in the exact opposite manner she had seen him put it on. At the end of the clear tubing was a sharp plastic "spike" this was poked up into the bottom of the bag in a special port. When the first was off and the second seated properly, the fluid started running immediately.

"Good," Grey said. "Let that one go full bore. With the next one we'll dial it back." She nodded, eager to help. He leaned over Nico. "How are you doing? Still with me?"

"Da, but I is still cold."

"Jillybean, another blanket," Grey ordered. "Wrap him tight, but make sure you don't cover the arm. Now, Nico I'm going to clean this wound out and it ain't going to be pretty and since it's going to hurt I'm going to give you some morphine for the pain and a little touch of Ketamine to knock you out." This he did by way of injecting the drugs into a secondary port on the IV tubing. Almost immediately, Nico's eyes rolled back and his face went slack.

Grey ripped off his gloves and then undid a heavy metal watch, which he handed over to Jilly. "Your next job is to monitor his breathing. See the second hand? The longer, fast one? I want you to count his breathing—in and out counts as one. Every few minutes I want you to let that second hand go all the way around and count his breaths. Tell me if they drop below eight per minute. Morphine can stop a person from breathing if they take too much, got it?"

"Yes."

"Yes, sir is the proper response."

"Yes, sir."

He then got down to business. First he scrubbed out the wound with sterile water and an orange solution he called Betadine. Then he re-gloved a third time and opened up different sets of sterilized instruments. One was a tiny knife called a scalpel which he used to cut away tissue that was necrotic; he explained this to mean it was dead. He then took forever to dig at the wound with forceps before coming up with a jagged, bent, sliver of metal.

"There's the problem," he said, tossing it aside. "That little sucker was cutting two different directions in there."

After that he began to sew up a major vein that had bled the entire time. He cursed and squinted in at the "slippery little bugger" until finally he got it joined together. Lastly, he stitched up the wound itself.

During all of this, Jillybean kept an eye on the IV, counted breaths, and replaced blood soaked sheets beneath the wound and, once, when Nico started to stir, she held down his arm down until Grey pumped in more of the Ketamine/morphine mix.

"Done and done," he said after wrapping Nico's arm in a fresh, white bandage. The whole procedure had taken over an hour.

Neil and Sadie had come back long before and had the water boiling and were busy re-sterilizing the instruments, keeping well back from the blood. "Is he going to be alright?" Sadie asked.

"Hopefully. I've started him on antibiotics through his IV. We'll keep that going until tomorrow and then we'll go to something a little easier on the system."

"Thanks a lot for everything, But..." Neil paused, looking small and easily broken compared to the fearsome soldier, "Um...what do you plan on doing with us?"

Grey gave him a shrug. "I hadn't planned on doing anything with you."

"Then why did you follow us all the way down here to Georgia?" Sadie asked.

"I didn't follow you all the way to Georgia as much as you preceded me here on your own. The truth is I'm here on orders. I neither knew nor cared where you were going."

"But you were asking for us in Maryland," Sadie said.

"And you chased us down in your Humvee after that," Neil added.

"My orders were to investigate what was happening in New York, including the extent of the slave trade and the rumors of bounties being placed on people's heads. I heard you were somewhere south of Philadelphia and since my team was in the area, I thought I would ask around to maybe warn you that there were people after you, but Neil, here did too good of a job lying to me."

263

Neil's face took on a bit of pink shame. "Sorry about that...but, but what about in Hagerstown?"

Grey shrugged. "We were tracking that bounty hunter and almost had him twice. The second time we had a sweet little trap set for him and then you guys got in the way."

"Did you get him?" Sadie asked, hopefully.

"No," Grey said. "The opposite really. That bounty hunter was too good. Mac bought the farm and Bull got holed a couple of times. He'll be alright though." He paused, shaking his head, slowly. "That just left me, and as much as I wanted to go after the bounty hunter, I received new orders. My C.O. wanted me to find out what the hell happened here at the CDC. The idea of another crazy virus leak has got what's left of the country freaking out."

"And you think the alarms and everything was staged?" Sadie asked. "Do you have proof? Because if you're wrong and there really is some sort of new super virus..."

"Not hard proof, but the circumstantial evidence is overwhelming. All the rumors say that the people fled from there in a panic; that no one was left within an hour of the alarms going off. But when I went in last night, every building had been picked clean, including the equipment in the labs, and the germs."

Neil folded his arms over his sweater vest, and said, "Maybe it was some scavengers looking for..."

Grey stopped him with a shake of his head. "It wasn't a few scavengers. If there were just some choice items missing I would agree with you, Neil, but it was everything. Only teams of men, organized and not at all afraid of germs, could have done this."

"Why would anyone want the germs?" Jillybean asked. She understood getting stuff, food and medicine and TVs, but getting killer germs seemed a dangerous waste of time.

Grey stood and stretched. He was a foot taller than Neil and looked twice as broad. "I hope they took them to keep them out of the hands of others, but with Yuri, who knows. He'd sell his own mother if the price was right."

"So you're going back to New York next?" Sadie asked. She was on her knees next to Nico and so had to cant her chin well back to look the captain in the face.

"Maybe after I finish my work down here," he said with a tired sigh. "Somewhere south of Atlanta, there's a bunch of fruitcakes following around some Charles Manson-wannabe. They call themselves the *Believers* and from what I've heard they're bad news. You know, the type of people who'll show up at your door wearing nothing but a suicide vest full of explosives and a smile. Sometimes I have to wonder about humans. We have so…" he paused at their sudden silence. "What's with the looks?"

"We're on our way to New Eden, too," Neil said in a rush. "They—they have my wife and my baby."

"This is crazy," Sadie said. "You've practically been with us this whole time. It's like fate was trying to bring us together. Do you believe in fate, Captain?"

He shook his head but with little conviction. "I believe in carrying out orders, and I believe that sometimes shit happens, but I'm not one of those guys who believes that everything happens for a reason. I'm sure God doesn't work like that." Whether he believed in fate or not, Jillybean could see the man wasn't nearly as cocksure of himself as he had been only a minute before.

Chapter 30

Sarah

New Eden

Artie had been freed to go back to Maryland, but Sarah didn't think he would make it. The land surrounding New Eden was so densely populated by zombies that a man on foot had almost zero chance of getting through alive, and a man, raving like a lunatic, had even less than that. Still, he was armed with his pipe and the .38 Smith & Wesson, something she had insisted on, more as a salve to her guilt than as a real hope that he would be able to fight his way home again.

The guilt she felt for Artie was as fleeting as a sunshower. She passed beneath the earth and into New Eden and, just like that, the guilt was gone, replaced by the knowledge that she had even less chance than Artie of ever seeing Maryland again.

The home of the Believers had undergone some obvious changes in the six weeks since she had been there. The first of which was the number of people going to and fro. It seemed as though the population of New Eden had doubled or tripled. What Sarah had previously thought to be vast windowless hallways, now felt small and cramped. Though to be sure, walking with Abraham did complicate things. Unlike before, the Believers now stopped and knelt on the white tile when he passed by, causing traffic jams at every intersection.

The second change that struck Sarah was the fear. Her own fear was literally palpable, as she could feel her pulse hammer in her temples, however it was the fear she saw in the Believers that struck Sarah as new. They eagerly dropped to their knees and eagerly put out their hands to Abraham and they eagerly cried *Amen!* at his simplest utterance.

They were too eager. Sarah saw clear as day, that they were afraid of being deemed *less than* in some fashion; less religious, less of a fanatic, less of a Believer. It made her wonder what would happen to anyone who was seen as *less than* in Abraham's eyes? Would they become "possessed" and would they be among those whose bodies couldn't handle the exorcism? The more Sarah saw the Believers bowing and scraping, the more she thought: yes.

This was all the more incentive for her to set her plan in motion and get out of there. Time was against her. Even if she could manage to fake worshiping a psycho like Abraham for very long, her appearance would give her away eventually. The last vestiges of her blisters and bruises would be healed completely in a day or two and her blonde hair would start to show through shortly after that.

But what exactly was her plan? So far, its outline was the very essence of simplicity: grab Eve and make a run for the doors. It was in the details where things got sketchy. Where exactly was Eve? And where were the doors? After five minutes below ground she was already lost, and this time she couldn't channel Jillybean. The little girl had what seemed to be a photographic memory, while Sarah had never been able to remember where she put her keys five minutes after walking in the door.

Even with her head in a whirl of plans and fears and identical looking hallways, Sarah couldn't help but react to the sound of her baby.

She had been following behind Abraham and his two female bodyguards and they had just come to another of the many bisecting passageways when, from around the corner, came the throaty, low chortle that Eve made when she was being tickled. Without thinking, Sarah stepped forward so that she was practically abreast of Abraham, something that was clearly a rule that was never to be broken.

One of the two women who flanked Abraham shoved her back, savagely, slamming her into the wall. There might have been hard words exchanged between them but then Sarah saw Eve for the first time in more than a month, and her mouth fell open, and she was struck dumb.

"There's my princess!" Abraham cried.

Because the words were so evil and so wrong, they hammered Sarah's eardrums and sent a spike of loathing right into her heart. She burned with such hatred yet, at the same time, the sensation barely registered on her.

There was her baby. There was Eve. That little child was the only thing pure and right in Sarah's mind. She stared at the infant and wanted to cry and laugh at the same time. Eve seemed so big. Her cheeks had rounded into baby perfection and her hair was longer than it had been, curling just at the nape of her neck. And she had teeth! Four of them right in the front. They were little, stubby things which hadn't been there before. Sarah was in shock. Her breathing came rapidly. Her hands opened and closed, and she did not notice right away when someone said the name, "Janice."

Her arm was shaken by a stranger. "Are you Janice?"

"Huh? Me? Right, yes I am," Sarah said, coming back to reality.

The woman who had touched her was small and a little plump. She was dark skinned with black hair, and she introduced herself as Tina. "We should not stare. We should keep our eyes down, yet also keep them aware, in case we are fortunate enough to be spoken to by the Lord's Prophet."

"Oh, right," Sarah said, dropping her chin, but still flicking her eyes toward Eve. Seeing the baby set up such a longing inside Sarah that she thought she would strangle on the air in her lungs if she couldn't hold her.

"You look faint," Tina said. "It can happen when you are around *him*. Come, I will show you to the preparation room."

"Preparation room?" Sarah asked, being pulled away by the little woman, feeling as light and empty as a kite. She tried to walk looking back at Eve, but in seconds the crowds had swallowed her up. She looked back to Tina. "What's the preparation room? What happens there?"

They took a turn down a hall that was far less crowded. Tina picked up speed, walking quickly on her short legs. "We will get you ready for tonight's ceremony: your baptism into the family of believers. It is the first step in becoming one of us."

"Great," Sarah said with sham enthusiasm. "Why are we walking so fast? Is it going to be soon?"

"No. We have a little over two hours until the service," Tina explained. "But dawdling is frowned upon, as is any expression of laziness. Idleness is a sin. *The Lord wills and we works*. That's the saying we have and it's a true fact that the people in New Eden are the most industrious in the world."

Sarah saw that Tina was very serious and believed every word, and yet they accomplished very little in the next two hours.

The preparation room was two levels down and on the same level as the very bottom of the inverted pyramid-like church. There was even a little hall that led from one to the other. The room was a square and contained nothing more than a bathtub, a full-length mirror, and racks of white linen robes. She went to these first and made to touch the fabric but Tina pulled her hand away.

"You're still dirty with the filth of the outside world."

Sarah's clothes were discarded without a thought or the least consideration, not that she had any special connection to them, beyond the fact that they *were* from the outside world. They represented something to her—a chance to go back. They were dirty but the dirt had come from a place that was free. New Eden, no matter how pristine, was clearly not a place of freedom.

Still, it had its perks. Sarah was able to bathe in steaming hot waters until her toes were wrinkled like prunes. After being toweled dry, she was given a robe and anointed with heavy perfume that had her blinking from its strength. She was then inspected by Tina who looked at her short hair and made a face; there wasn't much she could do with it.

"You are still pretty," she said.

Sarah looked into the mirror and saw that, unfortunately, Tina was right. The bathwater had washed away much of her disguise: the dirt, the ash, and the ragged remnants of her Goth make up. Even her skin was almost as smooth as ever, but it was the denim-blue of her eyes where she looked most like herself.

She tried squinting, which was better. She then added a nose-squinch to the squint and, although she looked as though she had smelled something nasty, she was practically unrecognizable.

"Why are you doing that to your face?" Tina asked. "Do you need glasses?"

"Yeah," Sarah said, grasping at the ready-made lie. "I lost mine."

"Well, try not to do that to your face for at least for the next half hour or so. It's almost time. See? Ten to six. We have service every night at six and every day at high noon."

Sarah felt her stomach heave with a case of the nerves. "So soon? I don't know if I'm ready. I didn't even know if he would take me. There was a rumor that he would only take people if they came in twos. When did that change?"

"The Lord makes the rules," Tina said, sharply. "They are handed down to the Prophet and they are not subject to our questioning, only to our obedience."

"Of course," Sarah was quick to reply. Inwardly noting that any rule was to be given her whole-hearted support regardless if it contradicted an earlier rule or maybe even a current one, if that was what Abraham wished.

Tina looked at her steadily until Sarah gave her a smile of apology, at which point Tina returned it as if nothing had happened. "Ok, I can hear the Believers coming in," Tina said. "Yes…there's the chanting. Just do what I do and be…enthusiastic."

Sarah pledged to herself that she would be enthusiastic to the point of crazy, but that was before she felt the walls of the preparation room vibrate with the thrum of hundreds of voices.

"What are they saying?" Sarah asked. It was a rhetorical question stemming from her surprise and fear. The chanters were singing:

My Life. My Death. For you.

"Enthusiastic!" snapped Tina. "Don't look so scared, Janice. Start chanting with the rest. It'll be ok. Just do as I do and try to smile for the Prophet. You are pretty, he likes that."

Tina started for the door and Sarah, who did not want to be thought of as pretty by a psycho like Abraham, scrunched up her face again. After Tina said the chant once, Sarah tried to join in, however the words cut so hard against the free will ingrained in her that she stumbled over them and sounded like a teenage boy whose voice was cracking as he hit puberty.

"Go with the flow," Tina said. "Become one of us. *My Life. My Death. For you.* Just like that."

Sarah tried again, "*My Life. My Death. For you.*" She felt like crying.

And then Tina opened the door that led to the church and the sound really struck Sarah. It was such a heavy noise that it draped on her like a weight and made walking through it like pressing into a side-slanting rain.

At her core, she felt threatened by the chant's fundamental insanity. She was about to be brainwashed. Here was where the process would begin and she knew better than most where it would end. In her mind she pictured Yuri's cruise ship in the East River and she saw the cabin where she had found Abraham a month before. She could see the hand grenade cradled by his follower Timothy. He had been so happy to die for him. He had been so absolutely crazy.

Sarah's feet rebelled when they entered the main part of the church. It was almost filled. There were so many more of them, and their robes were nearly blindingly white. They were like an avalanche of people waiting to come crushing down on her if she made the slightest mistake. Just like Tina, they chanted with *enthusiasm*, each vying to be the craziest of them all.

271

Tina reached back and grabbed her, chanting emphatically: *"My Life. My Death. For you."* She nodded for Sarah to mimic her. Sarah tried, though her voice was so lost in the din she ended up just mouthing the words in order to hold onto her sanity.

Then the chant grew louder as Abraham and his entourage of six sharp-eyed, stern women came down the center aisle. The people worshiped him. They reached out to touch him and he obliged those within reach of his long arms. He seemed part rock star, part politician and part demigod.

"Do what I do," Tina yelled into her ear. They were at the bottom of the main stair, right next to the shimmering pool of water. The smaller woman dropped to her knees and put her forehead to the floor. Sarah followed, afraid to even glance up to see what was happening. She didn't need to. Abraham passed right next to her, his long robe sliding across the back of her fingers.

He began to speak and instantly the crowd quieted. It was exactly as if a switch had been thrown. One second they were screaming their love and the next they were sitting on their hands with their lips zipped. Sarah marveled at this, wondering how a crowd could be so well trained, but then out of the corner of her eye she saw Abraham's escort of women.

They were the only ones not staring at the false prophet and hanging on his every word. Instead they each were watching a section of the audience and in their hands they held clipboards. Every once in a while one of them would jot a note and the people in that section would sit straighter and smile more broadly. They were afraid, but it was nothing compared to what Sarah was dealing with. She was very close to vomiting.

"Janice, please stand," Abraham said. Sarah was so disjointed and freaked out that she didn't react when her fake name was mentioned. Tina shot to her feet and pulled Sarah after; she was so scared that she forgot to squint or screw up her face.

"Yes?" she said. Abraham raised an eyebrow at this, while next to her Tina's breath drew in sharply. "I mean yes, My Lord?" she added quickly.

"Do not shake so," Abraham said, smiling now that his new slave was so desperate to please. "We lose our fear when we join the family of Believers. What do we have to fear here in New Eden? Certainly not zombies, and not hunger, or disease, or any pain such as is the everyday fare in the rest of the world. We do not fear because we believe!"

He had shouted this, which was the cue for his audience to go crazy again, but only for an allotted amount of time and then they quieted—eight hundred people went from cheering to quiet in one second. Sarah could not believe this level of mind control.

"Do you believe, Janice?" he asked.

"I do," she said, as loudly as she could without actually screaming.

"What do you believe?"

Sarah was shaken by the question. She had fully expected a repeat-after-me sort of oath and then a quick dunk in the pool. Giving an impromptu statement was another thing altogether.

"I, uh, I believe that…I mean I believe in the uh…"

She began to tremble even more. How could they expect a recitation of beliefs from someone so new? All she knew for sure about New Eden was that it was filled with a bunch of mind-numbed robots who believed this guy was some sort of prophet. Wait…that was something, at least.

"I believe you are the prophet of the Lord," Sarah said. What else did she know about him? "And I believe that you built New Eden with his, uh, guidance and love. And I believe you can cast out demons. And…and I believe that only you can keep us safe."

Abraham beamed at this and cried out: "She believes!"

Sarah felt the first wave of mind-conditioning kick in as she smiled back at Abraham, relieved that she had

273

pleased him and happy that she wasn't going to be punished.

"Come to the pool and kneel before it," he commanded.

She did so quickly.

The position she found herself in, kneeling with her head extended outward, made her feel like she was placing her neck into the yoke of a guillotine. Abraham knelt beside her and rested his hand on her back.

"With this water, the gift of the Lord, I can wash away the sins of your old life. No matter the sin, be it murder, adultery, idolatry…these were sins committed in ignorance. These were sins of the blind. Do you wish me to wash them away?"

"I do," Sarah said.

His hand gripped tighter on her neck as he asked, "Do you wish me to wash away the filth from your eyes so you have full understanding of the Lord and his Prophet here on earth?"

"I do."

"Do you understand that any sin committed from this moment forward will be committed in the light of understanding and will be permanently branded to your soul?"

Sarah hesitated, fearing she was about to agree to something horrible. "I-I do."

"Do you understand that the soul of a Believer can only be freed from sin through the purity of fire?"

"I do," she said not much louder than a whisper.

"Do you, Janice, wish to pledge both your life and your death to the Lord through his prophet, Abraham?"

Abraham's hand had been gently pushing her lower and now she was so close to the water that when she spoke it shook the image that swam on top. She saw her face, though with her dark hair and the shadows she looked more like Sadie than herself, and above her like a monstrous, angry, mythic god was Abraham.

His insanity lit his features and his evil could not be hidden.

"My life. My death. For you," Sarah said.

He grinned and his mouth and teeth seemed huge, as though he could take her head off with one bite of his giant teeth. She almost screamed at the vision, but then he plunged her into the water and held her beneath its surface until her lungs were about to burst.

Chapter 31

Sadie

The Centers for Disease Control Atlanta, Georgia

The top level of the parking garage was an odd scene: next to an ugly, teal Tercel there was a round grill sending up smoke like it was the fourth of July. In front of that, lying on the cool cement, was a man who was so pale and unmoving he could've been a cadaver on a morgue slab. The pile of fresh, bloody rags sitting in a heap right beside him didn't help the image. There was also a soldier whose arms bulged with muscle, a teenage girl with spiked hair and a Goth fetish, a small man wearing a sweater vest over a wet suit and finally a little girl in pink jeans who wouldn't stop twisting and hopping up and down.

"We can help you," Sadie said after Grey had quizzed Neil on everything he knew about New Eden. "Come on, Captain, we've been there. We know the way, we know the people, we know the layout of the place, or actually Jillybean does, but she'll tell you, right Jillybean?"

"I have to go to the bathroom," she said. "Real bad."

Neil held out his hand for her. "Come on. I gotta go too."

When they were gone, Sadie laid the back of her hand on Nico's cheek; was cool to the touch. She shot Captain Grey a quick look, seeing so many differences between the two soldiers. Nico was a young man, still with blonde fuzz instead of a proper beard. Grey was mature, though not yet grizzled. The muscles of his forearms looked like tree roots and his knuckles had been permanently scarred long ago.

They were both relatively quiet men, though in Nico's case it was because he wasn't comfortable speaking English in front of anyone but Sadie. Grey seemed to like silence. He rarely spoke for the sake of speaking and when he walked he made as little noise as forty-five pound Jillybean.

Sadie was irked by the necessity for silence. Life wasn't lived properly on tip toe. When she felt they had been sitting there quietly long enough she tried again to make her case: "Please? You have orders to investigate New Eden anyway. While you're inside you might as well see about our friend. We can help. Neil is, uh, versatile and I'm pretty fast, and Jillybean is..."

She paused, unable to describe Jillybean properly without making her sound like a freak. "She's very smart," Sadie finally said. "If there's anyone who can help you get into New Eden it's her."

Grey swigged from a water bottle in one long pull. He laughed once and shook his head. "You guys sure do have pluck, and courage and hope, and all that crap, but what you don't have is any chance at getting into New Eden. If it's how Neil described it only a professional can get in."

"Like you?" Sadie asked. "I'm willing to bet a million dollars you could get in and once you're in you could open one of the silo doors for us."

He sighed at this. "This sort of job is never like it is in the movies. I know that's what you're thinking. Everyone thinks it's always so easy."

Sadie gave a half shrug. "Movies are based on something, right?"

"In real life I would need a squad of trained men to back me up, not a trio of misfits. And I would need the right equipment. To start, I'd need real time satellite imagery or a UAV at the very minimum. I would need communication gear, probably C4..."

"What's C4?" Jillybean asked, suddenly appearing from around the Tercel suddenly.

Sadie jumped. "Dang, where did you come from?"

"The bathroom downstairs."

"I meant...I guess I meant you were awful quiet," Sadie said. "You scared the bejesus out of me."

"Sorry," Jillybean said. She went to stand directly over Nico's face and as she looked down at him she went on,

"Captain Grey said we were all too loud, so I decided to be quiet instead. What's C4? And what's UAV? Ipes says UV stands for ultra-violet. That's what means a certain kind of light. Purple-ish, I'm guessing."

Grey blinked at this and questioned, "Purple-ish?"

Jillybean looked up from Nico. "Yes. Violet is sort of a light purple, so I bet ultra-violet is a deeper purple. Like a purple kind of purple. But you know Ipes could've been mistaken. Maybe he meant ultra-violent. Violent is what means fighting and such."

"That's what I hear," Grey remarked.

"So, is Ipes right?" Jillybean asked, walking over to where Grey sat with his back to a concrete pillar. They were eye-to eye. "About the UV stuff, I mean?"

Before answering he swigged again from his bottle. "It's UAV. It stands for unmanned aerial vehicle. You'd call it a little spy plane and C4 is an explosive material."

She nodded at this. "And a squad? I know what a squid is, but I never heard of a squad before. Is it like a group of squids? You know, like a goose is to a gaggle like a squid is to a squad?"

Grey blew out, wearied by her constant questions. He even said as much, "You ever stop asking questions?"

"Me? Do you want me to stop asking questions?" Jillybean had retrieved Ipes and the Velveteen Rabbit at some point and now she consulted the zebra. "Ipes say that ignorance is for ignoramuses which I think is sort of like a hippopotamus. Either way they aren't too smart, and that's not good. So what's a squad?"

His wide shoulders slumped. "It's a group of highly trained individuals, without whom we have no chance at getting into New Eden. This shouldn't even be your first priority right now. Your friend needs rest and we need to find a secure location."

"Can we get a location with a pool?" Jillybean made a show of running the back of her hand across her forehead and blowing out loudly. "It's awful hot around here. Who knew that Georgia could get so hot?"

"Everyone," Grey growled.

When Neil returned, pink from the heat, he told the group that he knew of a place that would accommodate all of their needs.

Nervous of bounty hunters and bandits, they back-roaded it around the city. Neil and Jillybean traveled in the Tercel, while Grey, Sadie, and the still groggy Nico took the hummer. They drove beyond the suburbs to a home that was not only fortified against the zombies—its windows and doors were boarded over with inch-thick plywood and barred with steel—it also came with a little pond for swimming and fishing.

"Oh, this place!" Jillybean cried upon seeing the rectangle of a house and the pond. She jumped out of the Tercel before the dust had settled and was the first inside and then the first back out again after she had dropped off her *I'm a Belieber* backpack and kicked off her shoes. In one hand she had a fishing pole and in the other a stale-smelling towel. She didn't know what to do first.

Grey glanced at the sun. "Fishing is best at dusk. I'd go swimming now. Take care to keep an eye out for stiffs."

It was a surprise to Sadie that he seemed so utterly casual about the safety of such a tiny person. "That's it? Keep an eye out for stiffs?" she asked.

"She looks like a good soldier," Grey said swinging the heavy medbag over one shoulder. "I'm sure she'll be fine." For him the discussion was over with. He turned back to the Hummer, and with one arm lifted Nico out and leaned him against the vehicle.

Still pale from his blood loss, Nico swayed in place and attempted a brave smile that was mostly grimace. "I am fine. I am walk, thank you Captain. Thank you for helping. Is very nice."

"Uh-huh," Grey replied.

The remains of the afternoon passed quickly for all of them except Sadie. Nico lay on the couch, zonked out from the pain meds the captain had given him. Grey slept as only a soldier could: he dropped his gear, flopped into a recliner and was snoring within thirty seconds. Jillybean spent her time swimming, chasing frogs along the edge of the pond, hunting for salamanders beneath rotting logs, and catching more fish than anyone knew what to do with.

Neil pulled up a folding chair and sat with Ipes and the Velveteen Rabbit in the shade of a cottonwood. Ostensibly, he was guarding her, though in truth he was in more danger than she was. Whenever a zombie ambled by she would retreat to the safety of deep water leaving Neil, who didn't like to get wet if he could help it, to deal with the beast.

Sadie couldn't bring herself to leave Nico's side. She monitored his IV and his pulse. She fretted over the slightest seepage from his wound. She panicked if he breathed nine times a minute instead of ten, and by evening she was the most worn out of the group.

They enjoyed grilled fish for dinner. It was a tasty meal but strange. "That's Suszal," Jillybean told Sadie, pointing to her dinner. "She was very pretty before Mister Neil chopped her head off. Mister Neil is going to have Kissy, and Captain Grey, you have Chedrick the Second. That's what means he was Chedrick's son. Chedrick was a fish I caught the last time we came here."

"Uh-huh," Grey said before forking half of Chedrick the Second into his mouth. He then picked fish bones from his teeth, before finishing off the fish with another gargantuan bite.

Neil, fastidious as always, raised his eyebrows at Grey's caveman ways. His individual portions were precise, each designed to sit on his fork without the possible drama of falling off. He chewed, swallowed, wiped his lips and asked Jillybean, "What was your fish's name?"

The seven-year-old knew manners as well. She held up a finger as she finished chewing, turned slightly to produce an unwanted bone from her mouth, stuck it beneath the hidden edge on the near side of her plate and answered simply, "Sixty-eight. She died before I could name her."

Jillybean looked sad at this and Sadie was on the verge of saying something sympathetic, but Grey was quicker: "You gonna eat the rest of her?"

"We have extra, don't worry," Neil said, getting to his feet. "Jilly caught more than enough for everyone to have seconds." He scurried away to refill the Captain's plate while Jillybean pulled her plate closer, stuck a guarding arm around it and made an effort to eat more and talk less.

Sadie turned her gaze to the captain. "So? You were going to help us get our friend...my mom out of New Eden."

"I don't remember agreeing to that," Grey said. Sadie could tell he was eyeing Jillybean's stomach capacity relative to the size of the fish left on her plate. "Besides, you don't know if she's there. From what you say she could be anywhere. Even dead."

"She's there," Sadie insisted with more certainty than she felt. Grey said nothing; he only turned his head slightly and spat out a fishbone like he was flicking dirt from the end of his tongue. Sadie made a face at this but forced her lips to smile long enough to say, "This shouldn't be an issue. Aren't your orders to check out New Eden?"

Just then, Neil came in with more fish. Though there was enough for everyone to have more, only the captain had seconds. He cut the fish in half but before he could take another heaping bite, Sadie gave him a pointed look.

"My orders don't include rescues," he told her with his fork just in front of his lips.

"Did your orders include going after that bounty hunter?"

"I have some flexibility," he admitted, speaking slowly as though he was worried about trapping himself with his own words. "I'm to find out the exact location of New Eden, discover their numbers and their armaments and if possible their intentions. You've already given me most of that."

They needed his help badly and Sadie felt it slipping away. "So you have flexibility when it comes to doing the right thing? This is the right thing, Captain. Abraham isn't some gentle priest looking for religious freedom for his peaceful followers. He's a Jim Jones style kook. He's thinks the apocalypse was a gift from God for him to reshape the world and repopulate it with his crazy followers."

"I know all of that already," Grey said, lowering his fork. "I'd like to help but I don't see how I can. First, it doesn't sound like we can even get into New Eden, not without an army, at least. Maybe you don't realize it but I only have my M4 and a couple of grenades. I'm not packing an arsenal. Which leaves us with one option only: sneaking in. Even if there was a back door, I'd stand out like a sore thumb, and you guys are all on their kill list. We'd be captured before we knew it."

"Please?" Sadie said, going so far as to clasp her hands in front of her. When he shook his head, her face set into a hard frown. She'd tried cajoling and begging, now she went with anger. "So you won't help us? You know what? Before the apocalypse I used to have such respect for our soldiers, but now I realize you guys are all a bunch of mother-fuc..."

She stopped in mid-curse and glanced at Jillybean who was taking in the spectacle with her blue eyes flung open to their fullest. They weren't the beautiful, soft, denim blue like Sarah's, nor did they have the sweet, innocent quality of Neil's baby-blues. Jillybean's eyes were sharp, icy, and ferociously intelligent. She took in everything, body language, tone, pitch. She certainly knew what Sadie had been about to say and her wisp-thin eyebrow went up as a way of protest.

After that half-second glance, Sadie cut off her hot anger and turned cold. "Cowards, I should say. You're all a bunch of cowards, or worse."

Grey spat out another fishbone, this time without turning his head. Neil watched the bone fly and click off his glass. He didn't say anything. Grey seemed like a volcano, though, thankfully he didn't explode. He seethed, hissing, "You don't know what you're talking about. I've seen hundreds of soldiers die...literally eaten alive to save, lazy, ungrateful little shits like you. What were you doing during the apocalypse? Were you out there fighting for your family or for your country?"

Sadie, who had been robbing people to survive, couldn't bring herself to look into Grey's eyes.

Neil certainly didn't feel like adding his rather unheroic exploits which had consisted of him cowering inside his own house.

The silence spun out until the captain snorted. "That's what I thought. These soldiers you call coward fought until there wasn't a country left to fight for. We fought to save other people's families while ours were killed. We fought and we fought and most of us died."

"Sorry, we've had some trouble with soldiers," Neil said.

The excuse sounded lame in Sadie's ears and she figured the captain would unleash his fury, however his emotions took a u-turn and he only waved his hand as if shooing away a fly. "There are always a few bad apples. Look, Sadie, I never said I wouldn't help, but we don't know if your friend is even alive."

"Eve is," Neil said.

Grey gave him a tired look. "I'll do some recon work, ok? Tomorrow, I'll go at first light. Just know that I can't promise anything."

Chapter 32

Sarah

New Eden

The bedroom was a windowless ten-by-ten cell, furnished after the fashion of a soviet gulag. It contained only two bunk beds and a four-drawer dresser. The walls were stark white and the floors cold linoleum. The only decorations were a picture of the prophet that hung oddly high on the wall above the dresser and a list of rules that was tacked to the back of the door.

It was a very long list.

Believers will attend regular daily services which are held at 12PM and 6PM. Believers will also attend special services and exorcisms.

Believers will pray in the prophet's name a minimum of seven times a day.

Believers will attend mind-cleansing on a weekly basis. Do not deviate from the posted cleansing schedule.

Believers will not allow blasphemy in their presence and will report it as soon as possible.

Believers will not tolerate the questioning of the rules.

Believers will donate one third of their day in labor to the Lord.

Believers will donate one third of their day in labor to the Lord's prophet...

There were thirty-two rules in all. After Sarah read them she felt ill, not sick to her stomach, the feeling went far deeper. The rules were designed to destroy who she was, her humanity, her sense of self, her essence, perhaps even her soul. They were in place to cage the mind and crush the concept of personal freedom.

After half a day among them Sarah realized that the Believers had their rules so that thinking wouldn't be necessary.

Every minute in the stilting, cloying, suffocating dungeons of New Eden only served to reinforced what Sarah had suspected: that the Believers were being brainwashed on a tremendous scale. The mind control began with body control; each Believer was worked to exhaustion. Below the earth they excavated new tunnels like insects, bringing out earth wheelbarrow after wheelbarrow. They hollowed out chambers from rock and clay using nothing but shovel and pick. Above ground, they plowed and tilled and threshed all by hand.

The work was so strenuous that they were happy for prayer breaks and looked forward to the two daily services. Chanting was supposedly soothing and most of the Believers rocked in their chairs as they droned out the long prayers. To Sarah, the sound wasn't so much soothing as it was mind-numbing, and that too was by design.

All-in-all Sarah saw New Eden as a giant, humanoid beehive. At the top was the queen bee—the prophet who was catered to in every way imaginable. His one job, aside from interpreting God's word to mean anything he wanted it to, was to create new Believers out of old humans. The next strata in the "hive" were the *Brothers* and *Sisters*. These were generally the Believers who had been with Abraham the longest or they were those lucky few who were hand-picked because of their potential. For the most part they did little in the way of actual work.

The Sisters were the high priestesses to Abraham. Supposedly, they served him in some sort of religious capacity, however, judging by the jealous looks many of them had given Sarah, they served him in other, more salacious, ways as well. In addition to their "religious" duties, the Sisters had other official roles. Since only they could carry weapons in the lower portion of New Eden, they acted as body guards to the prophet. They also regulated the workers. With their ever-present clipboards and their judgmental looks, the Sisters kept the Believers scurrying around in an endless sweat.

The Brothers were thuggish and lazy. Unlike the Sisters, who had a hand in everything, their only job was to provide external security. They lounged around in the five silos that overlooked the valley from which New Eden had been carved, playing cards or swapping stories. It was rumored that each was a marksman of some ability and that with their scoped rifles they could see anything that moved in the valley. Whatever their ability, the silos were perfectly situated to repel attacks from any direction.

Beneath them in rank were the drones, the lowest of the low, the real Believers. Of these, Sarah had classified two distinct types: the robots who had ceased to be human and had fully accepted their new role as mindless automatons, and the soon-to-be-robots who clung to the last speckle of their personalities.

Sarah's roommates consisted of two of the former and one of the latter. The one soon-to-be-robot, a wretched woman of about Sarah's age, named Dinah, was dreadfully sad. The moment they met, Sarah could tell by the fullness of her eyes and the way her mouth parted that Dinah wanted to talk as any normal woman would.

She wanted to know where Sarah was from. She wanted to know if there was hope outside New Eden. She wanted to tell of her own adventures in the apocalypse. She wanted to share experiences because that's what people did. Sarah could even tell Dinah wanted to gossip about the prophet and, desperately, she wanted to make snide comments about the two robot roommates who slept on command, ran to mind-cleansing because they were so excited to rid themselves of impure thoughts, and who timed their shits to maximize how much of their day they could spend praying for Abraham.

However, Dinah held back.

Her lips quivered in want, her fingers would flare as a thought struck her and her mouth would come open, but she was simply too afraid to commit to more. Sarah didn't want her to. She wasn't there to make friends or commiserate about how bad things were. In her mind, Dinah was getting everything she deserved. She had traded a dangerous freedom for the surety of slavery.

Not only that, Sarah didn't trust her. She didn't trust anyone in New Eden. For all she knew Dinah was some sort of spy, whose job it was to ferret out those who were weak in their faith or who could be trouble in the future.

Sarah's other two roommates were less likely to be spies. Just after the lights were turned down—an automatic event since there weren't any switches in the room—one of the robot women suddenly said in a very loud voice: "Lord above please bless your beautiful prophet here on earth."

Not to be outdone, the other robot cried out louder, "Lord bless his perfect soul and grant him more of your wisdom for he is the wisest of everyone."

On the lower bunk across from Sarah, Dinah started making little noises as she tried to add something, "Uh... uh...Lord? Please, uh, bless his soul and his heart. The prophet is great."

Now it was Sarah's turn. She could sense expectancy from the other three women; the only problem was that she could only think of hateful things. She wanted God to strike Abraham down with a bolt of lightning. She wanted it to come down right onto his ridiculously perfect hair and split his head in two. She wanted to claw his eyes out and stomp his testicles.

As much as she wanted to, she couldn't pray out loud for any of that, but at the same time she was still a Christian. It didn't sit right with her to lie in a direct prayer to God.

Crossing her fingers, she prayed, "Lord, please bless the prophet's soul...judge it according to its deeds and reward it accordingly." Reward it with hell, she thought.

"That was a good one, Janice," the robot in the bunk above Sarah said.

"*Amen*," the second robot said pointedly.

"Yes, of course, amen," the first robot added quickly.

Dinah sounded glum, "Amen."

Within a minute the two robots had dropped off into sleep. Dinah, clearly wanting to talk, tossed and turned. Sarah lay there, trying her best to remember the floor plan of the tunnels. After the baptism, Tina had given Sarah a partial tour of New Eden, leaving off such restricted areas as the prophet's apartments, the Sisters' quarters and the armory.

Everything else was open. They visited cafeterias, kitchens, industrial-sized laundry facilities, machine shops, everything a community would need and a few things they wouldn't, like an exorcism chamber.

"You are number 894," Tina said. The room was circular in shape and tremendous in size. It had hardwood floors, much like one would find on a basketball court, except that instead of having free-throw lines and three-point arcs marked on the floor, it had numbers radiating outwards in growing circles.

Tina brought her to 894 and pointed at it. "This is where you kneel." She then lifted her chin to indicate an odd stair stepping alter, like a pyramid. It stood in the middle of the room thirty feet high.

Sarah felt her pulse quicken. "Are there that many exorcisms?"

"It is also used for soul cleansing. The fire of the Lord burns away sins." Tina looked up at the altar in awe, which was good because she didn't see how Sarah had gone pale.

Tina spoke no more on the subject and they left the exorcism chamber by the middle of its three exits. She brought Sarah to the next area that had no business in this, or any community: the mind-cleansing rooms. "Remember your times and your number: 894. You cannot switch either."

"894," Sarah repeated.

"Right. It's really easy. Just come in and sit in the chair. When the light goes green state your name and your number. Then just listen to your prompter, she'll guide you."

"A prompter? What kind of prompts are there?"

"The prompts will be like; how do you feel about the prophet? Or how much do you love the prophet on a scale from one-to-ten? It's nothing to worry about. Mind-cleansing is a way to rid yourself of impure thoughts."

"Oh, that's good," Sarah said with a little laugh, as though this wasn't the second craziest thing she had ever heard of—soul-cleaning by fire was going to be hard to beat.

Now, hours later lying in the dark, Sarah went cold at the thought of it. She tried to blink away the image of the pyramid. She had to force her mind back to the floor plan, but it was hard to picture.

The original size of New Eden, back before the apocalypse, had been relatively small, but, since the zombie plague, it had grown with every passing day. It obviously hadn't been designed by an architect or built by an experienced engineer.

Hallways went this way and that, crossing each other, changing direction or looping oddly. The chaos appeared baseless, however it was generally granite deposits, which the Believers found hell to cut through with their primitive tools, that was to blame. Sarah puzzled over the layout until she fell asleep, still thinking about the strange maze of halls. At five in the morning the lights flicked on and immediately one of the robots cried in a shrill voice, "Lord please bless our prophet's glorious soul!"

Sarah blinked in confusion.

The other robot wasn't about to be outshone. "Bless his great heart!"

Sarah smacked her lips and said, "Huh?"

"Bless his health and his soul," Dinah said as quick as she could.

Just as the night before, everyone looked at Sarah in expectation, but her mind felt like mud. It was a slog just to sit up. "Uh…and, uh, God bless his…" Her mind suddenly seemed almost completely empty. She could picture Abraham and the only thing that stood out was his stupid hair. "His, uh hair. God bless his hair."

She expected disapproving looks, but instead, the first robot nodded and said, "He does have great hair."

The other agreed and Dinah made it unanimous.

Sarah sighed under her breath and went to change out of her pajamas. Her one dresser drawer had come complete with a set of white robes for services, a pair of pajamas, and a one piece work suit that zippered in front. It also had a black case that held all the basic toiletries she would need.

"Shower first," one of the robots said, hurrying out the door still in her pajamas and toting her black bag. Sarah followed at a run. Everything seemed to happen at a run. In the bathroom were thirty stalls, thirty sinks, thirty showerheads, and one *Sister* in an azure-blue robe with her one clipboard. Her eyes were flat and hard as she watched the women. Sarah tried to blend in with the rest.

The bathroom held a hundred women all trying to get through their morning routine at once. It was remarkably quiet; eerily so. Sarah finished at the same time as one of the robots, mostly because her short hair didn't need anything more than for her to rake her fingers through it. They sped back to their room, dressed in less than a minute and left again. Sarah thought they were heading to breakfast instead they went to the temple to pray.

Despite her hunger, there was no turning back. She found her numbered seat and began to pray, but not to the evil prophet. She prayed to God that she would be able to find Eve and she prayed that they would be able to get out of there somehow. She also prayed for Neil and Sadie and even Jillybean. Sarah felt so horribly afraid and lonely that it hurt to think of her family. It was easier on her heart to keep it oriented on revenge.

Finally, she saw her roommate stand and head for the door. Sarah jumped up and ran after. "Stop," Sarah said, the second the temple door was closed behind them. Obediently the woman did. She had shoulder length dirty-blonde hair that she wore parted in the middle. She was plain to the point of being ugly.

"What is it? I don't want to be late."

"What am I supposed to be doing?" After Sarah's tour, Tina had dropped her off at her room and had left without a word. Now Sarah was somewhat stuck. She figured she could make it back to her room, but didn't know if that was the right thing.

"I don't know," the woman said. "I have to go."

Sarah was about to follow her and beg her for a glimmer of information, when she realized that this was actually a golden opportunity to explore. It would not be out of place for a newbie to be wandering around lost. The first thing she did was to jog back to her room so that she had a good starting point. From there she went out in an arc always coming back to a place she knew and gradually learning her way around.

Eventually, one of the blue-robed Sisters found her. "Are you 894?"

Fiction had caught up with reality. She had been reduced to a number! "My name is Janice and they assigned me that number."

"Where have you been?" The sister was small, almost all of them were, and thus she had to lift her chin slightly to look into Sarah's pretty eyes. "Were you wandering around lost?"

Sarah's nod was slight, displaying her embarrassment.

"That's what I thought. I am Sister Chastity, your *Lead*. I am the Sister for the eight-hundreds. You come to me with any questions and you will come to me with any reports of blasphemy. I set your assignments and I make sure you have everything you need. Do you?"

"I think so."

"No you don't because you don't know the first thing about New Eden." Beneath her clipboard was a folder, she handed it to Sarah. It read: *A Time of Becoming*. "This is your handbook. Memorize it. In three days I will quiz you on its contents and you will pass."

"Yes, ma'am."

"Yes, *Sister*, but that's in there as well." Chastity took a step back and looked Sarah up and down. "You are lucky I'm your lead. There are some who would be threatened by your looks, however I was clearly chosen for my competence and for my ability to note nuance. Our Lord's prophet has his eye on you."

"Really?" Sarah asked, feeling her guts begin to churn. Although it would get her closer to Eve, the idea of being anywhere near Abraham without a gun in her hand had her insides shaking. That thought triggered another: Was Chastity armed? Sarah tried to look for a hidden weapon without being obvious.

"Yes really," Chastity replied, frowning at Sarah, who hadn't been as discreet about inspecting the woman as she had hoped. If she was packing a gun it was a small one.

"I like your robe," Sarah said, feeling heat in her cheeks. "It's a nice color on you."

"Page sixteen: *Believers will wear white robes when not working.* Get used to the pure white. I doubt you have what it takes to become a Sister," Chastity said icily.

"Sorry."

Chastity grunted something that could've been an acceptance of her apology. She then began walking down the hall, her small feet tapping out a quick patter. "As I was saying, the prophet saw something in you. I noticed it at your baptism. He is not usually so *forceful*."

Sarah nearly choked, remembering how she had been held under the water for so long. For a few seconds, she thought Abraham had discovered her identity and was trying to kill her right there. And now this lady was trying to tell Sarah that the aggression had been a sign of affection?

"So what does it mean?" Sarah asked after a deep breath.

"It means the Lord has blessed you with beauty and me with brains. Together we can go far. Tell me, Janice, do you have any special skills? In a work related capacity?" she added quickly when Sarah blanched. "Something that would be useful, say near at hand."

"I was a stay at home mom," Sarah said, jumping at the chance. "There was a baby, yesterday in the hall. I'm great with kids..." She stopped when Chastity began shaking her head.

"No, that won't do. The Lord's prophet has many, many people already lined up for that position. I'm talking about something more professional."

"I was also a...pharmacist." Sarah had been a pharmacy representative, a pill-pusher, but she figured that wouldn't mean so much to Chastity. "I don't know if that's what you mean by near at hand."

"Every moment nearer to the prophet is a moment nearer to God," Chastity said. "That closeness is how any sane person registers their worth in New Eden. Let me set you an example: would you rather pull a plow in the fields or would you rather be on the hospital staff? Would I rather be the Lead for the eight-hundreds or would I rather be the prophet's personal advisor. We all have dreams. That one is mine."

"It is a worthy dream," Sarah said dipping her chin. "I would not like to pull a plow."

"Then let's see what we can do to get you on that team," Chastity said. "All we have to do is get the prophet to agree that a pharmacist is needed in New Eden, which won't be easy."

"You don't have one?"

"No. He has said the Lord either heals a soul or he does not and that man should not interfere."

"Then how am I going to change his mind? I cannot make a case that is greater than that." Sarah knew that she couldn't make any case to sway Abraham. She just didn't have enough knowledge in the field. Her sales ability had more to do with her looks that anything else.

"You will have me with you. Remember, I have the brains. Use the beauty the Lord has given you. Together, if it is meant to be, we will both be closer to our Lord. A very worthy cause, as you said."

Chapter 33

Sarah

New Eden

Sarah waited outside the doors to the prophet's apartments as Chastity went in. Things were progressing so fast that she forgot herself and smiled at the two women guarding the doors.

"Don't you have something better to be doing?" one of them asked. Her right hand was in a fold of her robe and Sarah guessed she was armed. The Sisters were all somewhat small—probably chosen in order to make Abraham look taller—and they were uniformly severe in their appearance. They wore their hair stretched upward into torturous-appearing buns, which did nothing to relax the lines of bitter authority that creased their brows.

"I'm supposed to be waiting here for Sister Chasti…"

"We know, we were right here when she went in. But what could you be doing instead of just standing there gawking?"

"Oh, sorry." Sarah was about to kneel in prayer, but then she remembered the handbook. Hoping that it might have some information she would find useful, she cracked it open. Within a minute she wished she hadn't. The handbook was simply a more detailed explanation of the thirty two rules that she had already read. There was also a long-winded and completely self-serving, "Bio" of Abraham.

It was enough to make her sick. It wasn't the right time to read the thing anyway. She had too much to ponder. She had to find out where Eve's room was. She had to figure a way to get her out of there without alerting any nannies and causing a huge ruckus. She had to find a way to get passed these two armed guards, then she had to figure out a way to get passed the other guards at the silos.

It seemed impossible and, out of foolish desperation, she looked around for a fire alarm, hoping she could use the trick that seemed to work in every movie: pulling the alarm so that everyone fled. Like all the hallways the walls were plain white paint over white drywall. No alarms. Above them, evenly spaced were neon light fixtures and every twenty feet or so there were small vents that moved air around the hallways. She peeked up at one of the registers hoping to see huge ducts that she could crawl around in, again like in the movies, however it seemed too small to fit even her slim body through.

"894, what are you doing?" Chastity had come back and was frowning at her. Judging by all the wrinkles around her eyes and around her lips, she frowned a lot.

"Me? I was, uh, praying and studying the handbook, sort of at the same time."

"Whatever works for you. Come and sign in." One of the guards held out a clipboard, while the other stood ready with her hand beneath her robe. Sarah put her number in the first column and then signed Janice Sills in the next. Chastity handed her a slip of paper. "Keep this on you at all times. It's a validation slip. Only a person summoned from within, is allowed into the inner sanctum. Not even a Brother is allowed in without the proper slip."

Together, they strode through what seemed to be a simple door like all the rest, however this one ushered them into a whole new world. Gone were the sterile white hallways that seemed to have been lifted straight from the innards of a mental institution. In their place were polished marble floors and hand-worked masonry. On the walls were works by Rembrandt, Monet, and Renoir, pieces that Abraham had "picked up" while in New York. Everything was gilded or beveled or flourished in such a way as to over-awe.

Sarah walked with her mouth open and again forgot herself by staring all around instead of concentrating on where she was. She had to be pulled to her knees by Chastity when they came to Abraham's reception room.

"So, my dear Chastity, I hear you wish to make an addition to our hospital staff." He sauntered over and came to stand right over Sarah. She could feel his eyes boring into the top of her head and she dared not look up.

"I do, my Lord. I was only just made aware that out newest Believer was a pharmacist before she was given to us as a gift from the Lord."

"Oh," he said with clear disappointment. "I was hoping for a surgeon." He walked full around Sarah, sighing as he did. "You know how I feel about pharmacy in general. The Lord has blessed us with the ability to fight germs and viruses, to heal our own wounds, to fight heart disease by regulating what we eat and by exercising, and to cure cancer with our positivity and prayer, not by poisoning ourselves with radiation. We are magnificent creatures as we are. Just look at Janice. Stand up Janice and turn around for us."

Sarah did, feeling the color rise in her cheeks.

"You see? Perfect. No makeup, no fake breasts, no face lift. God has created this beautiful creature. His great love shines outward from her soul and man has done nothing but harm this poor woman." He lifted Sarah's chin and stared right into her eyes and for just a second she was sure that he was on the verge of recognizing her, but then Chastity spoke.

"Yes my Lord. Perhaps that's what led me to suggest this new position. I don't have anything but plow work left for her."

"Plows must be pulled for food to be grown."

"Yes my Lord," Chastity said bowing her head.

That was it? That was all Chastity was going to say on the matter? What happened to her supposed brains? Sarah felt her chance at getting a permanent position so close to Abraham's inner sanctum, slipping away. She would be relegated to pulling a plow with a team of other women. She would be ground down by the work and baked by the sun. She would grow old before she had another chance to be this close.

Sarah canted her chin down just the slightest and stole a look at Chastity. The woman was on her knees with her hands clasped in front of her. Was she carrying a pistol beneath her robes? And could Sarah get to it fast enough if she lunged quickly, without hesitation? It didn't seem likely, however she felt she was in a now-or-never situation.

If only Abraham would turn away for just a second.

He didn't. Instead he went around Sarah and asked, breathing down her neck, "What do you think, Janice? Is man, with his pills and his syringes greater than God's healing hand?"

A shudder that was impossible to miss went down her back. "Never," she replied.

"What a great answer," Abraham said. "So simple, so direct, so absolutely perfect. Yet your job was trying to compete against the Lord, to show the world that man could heal without his power."

Sarah had no answer for that.

Chastity seemed to join Abraham's side. "Is that what you thought, Janice?"

"No."

"Did you think your hands in the lab were greater than God's in heaven?"

Did pharmacists even work in a lab? Sarah thought they just moved pills around, filling bottles like a warehouse worker filled orders. She shook her head.

The Sister went on, "Or did you think God worked through you? That you weren't competing with God but that he was guiding your hands?"

Would it be blasphemy in their eyes to answer yes? Would she kill her chances to get closer to Eve by answering no? Abraham took the decision out of her hands. He boomed out his laugh and raked back his silver hair.

"Chastity! Are you suggesting that God works through us, as if this is news to me? Of course the Lord uses his followers for the betterment of the world. That is not the issue here. The issue I have is when man tries to supersede the Lord. Do you know the purpose to a fever when one gets sick?"

He glanced at Sarah, but she didn't know, though she knew that a pharmacist should. She dropped her gaze, hoping that he would answer his own question, something that he frequently did. He didn't disappoint her. "It's to raise the body's temperature so as to kill the virus affecting it. But what does a pharmacist suggest doing? Take Tylenol to reduce the fever! And what is the purpose to something as simple as a cough? To bring up irritants that might cause infection. But what does the pharmacist suggest? Taking a cough suppressant! And we wonder why out society was so out of whack!"

"Yes, my Lord," Sarah said.

"Yes indeed!" Abraham cried, getting worked up. "The rationale behind pharmacological studies and advances clearly show the beauty of God's wisdom in our lives. It's in their day-to-day application where we fail as humans. We treat the wrong things at the wrong times. We create super viruses and then congratulate ourselves when we find the cure months too late. We make lotions to turn us tan and then need to find cures for skin cancer. We take drugs so we can enjoy life and then those same drugs ruin our lives. You see? A pharmacist can be of great value but can also be a great danger."

Chastity cleared her throat. "Surely the danger to your people would be less if the pharmacist could rely on your heavenly wisdom guiding her."

"I'm sure it would," Abraham said and then clapped his large hands together excitedly. "It's settled! Janice will be our new pharmacist. And you are right dear, Chastity, I will need to meet with her regularly. We'll start with tomorrow for dinner."

There was a pause as if she was supposed to thank Abraham, but Sarah couldn't speak even if she wanted to. Dinner with this vile, murderous, asshole? She wanted to be close, but that would be way too close.

Thankfully, Chastity spoke for her. "Your will, as always."

Minutes later, when the two women were back in the hallway Sarah made a show of grinning. Though it made her sick, she had what she wanted: frequent access to the prophet's apartments. Now she needed more. "Thank you so much," she said and then hugged Chastity awkwardly, making sure her body pressed against the Sister's body, especially on the right side.

Sarah was pushed angrily away, but not before she felt the gun at the Sister's hip.

"That is not allowed!" Chastity cried. "Our love is exclusively for the Lord and his prophet on earth. We do not waste it on our fellow Believers. Page four of the handbook."

"I'm sorry," Sarah said, though she wasn't. She had to hide the surge of excitement that blared in her soul. Chastity was the key to getting out of New Eden alive with Eve! She had a gun and when Sarah took it from her she would never see it coming. "I didn't know. But thanks again. You did it."

"*We* did it," Chastity corrected. "Now, I have other duties. You report to the hospital—down this corridor, take your first left, you'll see it on your right. Find out every medicine we have and everything we need. Don't let Doctor Gowdy bully you with talk of it being *his* hospital. He fills in as a surgeon, but he was only a periodontist before."

Just like that, Sarah was on her own. She went to the hospital and met with the four-person staff. Along with Gowdy, there were two nurses and a second doctor who wasn't a real doctor either, he was a chiropractor and he immediately tried to set Sarah up for a spinal adjustment.

"My schedule is wide open." He tapped one of two clipboards hanging on the wall. On it was a daily calendar, broken down by the hour. There were only two appointments for that day and a single one for the next. He seemed so exceptionally sleazy with his greasy smile and his roving eyes that it was no wonder he wasn't busy.

Doctor Gowdy's schedule was practically full. Sarah only glanced at it as a way to break eye-contact with the chiropractor, but immediately her attention was riveted on a single word: Eve. Her name was highlighted and starred. She was supposed to have a checkup on the following day. Sarah couldn't take her eyes off the name.

"So, where did you go to school?" the chiropractor was asking, putting his hand on her shoulder.

Sarah jumped, feeling her stomach knot instantly and adrenaline surge into her bloodstream. "Don't touch me! That's not allowed. Page, uh, four of the handbook. You can't touch me."

None of the hospital staff were of the ultra-religious robot type and Sarah's outburst caused them to step back —no one was safe from the rules. "I'm sorry," the chiropractor said, with his hands up. "I didn't mean it."

"It's ok. It's…I was just…" Sarah had to take a deep breath. The rape had cast a long shadow; the touch of any man no matter how innocent almost felt like an assault itself. "It's ok. I just freaked a little. Could one of you show me where you store the pharmaceuticals?" This she asked of the two nurses.

For the remainder of the day, when she wasn't faking her way through religious mania, Sarah thought about Eve and, to a greater extent, Abraham. She was certain that at dinner he would touch her and, since he made the rules, it would be allowed, and definitely encouraged by Chastity. The thought of this evil horrible beast of a man touching her, pawing at her, kissing her…

Sarah found valium among the cabinets and, with shaking hands, popped open the bottle and swallowed one dry. The drug helped, as did focusing on her daughter. She would get to see Eve! Picturing her baby was the only thing that got her through the six o'clock worship service, the rushed dinner, and the bizarre prayers in the dark after lights out that were an exact match to the night before.

When the lights came back on the next morning and the two robot roommates took turns beseeching God to bless Abraham, Sarah was still thinking of Eve. With a sigh, she forced the little girl's image away and started preparing for her confrontation with the prophet. After her shower and a filling breakfast, Sarah went right away to the hospital and started pouring through the latest PDR available.

The *Physicians' Desk Reference* contained information on every currently used medication. Sarah was hoping to find something in the barbiturate family that she could put into a hypodermic needle to "knock out" Chastity and or Abraham.

Unfortunately, she ran up against a hard reality that crushed her hopes: New Eden's stock of medicine was shockingly small, limited in both scope and quantity. The best she could find was Lortab—a pain reliever that, in high enough doses would cause someone to lose consciousness. It was not fast-acting, nor did they have it supplied in liquid form and she had no idea if crushing up a bunch of pills and stirring it into water would work in the way she wanted it to.

With tranquilizing not a choice, Sarah began considering lethal options and now she ran up against moral objections. She could kill Abraham; that was not a problem. However, could she kill Chastity? In cold blood? She wrestled with this through a quick lunch and then a long noon service of chanting: *My life. My death. For you.*

The vile chanting helped her come to the conclusion that if things were different and Chastity found out about Sarah, the Sister would kill her and gladly so. Any of the Believers would, from the bitterest Sister down to the newest convert, Dinah. It was a heavy realization and it helped with Sarah's decision: she would kill whoever got in her way. It turned her cold and made her feel tight through the chest up until Eve giggled and babbled her way into the hospital.

At the sound, Sarah's heart blasted her pulse throughout her body so that she could feel it in the soles of her feet. At the same time she became aware of the motherly part of her soul. It demanded action. It demanded that Sarah take her stand right then and there. It didn't care that two Sisters and a nanny accompanied the baby.

The nanny was none other than Sarah's old friend Shondra. The big woman fussed over the baby and Sarah approved. Unlike everyone else in New Eden Shondra smiled constantly and her warmth was like a fire on a cold night. She caught Sarah staring from around the corner and didn't even blink.

"You're the new person."

"Yes." Sarah used the excuse of looking at Eve in order to break eye contact with Shondra. It was strange that she wasn't recognized by a person she had spent time with every day for a month. It was one thing when Mark at the silo had seen a dirt covered vagabond, it was quite another when Shondra couldn't pick her out with the only real difference in her appearance being a different color and style of hair.

It was probably a combination of location and expectations. No one in the world expected Sarah to show up in New Eden. Still, Sarah kept her chin down and her voice low.

"She's looks like a good baby," she said, fighting the urge to touch the child. The Sisters flanking Shondra were not caught up in the aura of the baby. In fact they seemed extra vigilant as if they had seen something in Sarah's face.

"Bah-de, bah-da, bo-dah," Eve said, around her fist which she had wedged in her mouth.

"She's the best," Shondra said, bouncing her.

Doctor Gowdy stepped forward and cleared his throat. "We have our check up to begin, so if you'll excuse us, Janice."

Sarah hovered beyond the curtain of the first exam area, and fretted in an anxious sweat. Was this just an annual or was there something wrong? Was she going to get a shot? Would she cry or would she be a tough little soldier. Sarah didn't know which she wanted. What about her weight? What percentile was she in? Why did Gowdy say: Hmmm?

"Ok, everything looks good," Gowdy said after what seemed like an hour but what was in fact only fifteen minutes. "She's got a clean bill of health, so we'll see you again next month."

"A month?" Sarah blurted out. "Is there something wrong? I mean most babies don't see their doctor every month."

"This isn't most babies," Gowdy replied, giving Sarah a hard look and then tilting his head toward the door, suggesting that Sarah leave. She couldn't bring herself to do so. The best she could do was step back out of the way so that the three adults and Eve could walk by.

When they did, Sarah waved at the chubby-cheeked little girl.

"Ba-dah. Ma-ma," Eve said and raised a dimpled hand off of Shondra's back and held it out to Sarah.

Sarah couldn't breathe.

"Ma-ma," Eve said, louder, as the distance between them grew.

"She said, ma-ma!" Shondra remarked with a laugh. The black lady held Eve up over her head and smiled with great enthusiasm, but Eve was still looking at Sarah and Sarah was staring right back.

"Ma-ma," Eve said again.

Now Shondra looked back and her jaw fell open. There was no getting around it. Shondra had recognized her.

No, Sarah mouthed the word, shaking her head slightly, silently begging her friend not to say anything. Shondra didn't. She gave the slightest of nods and headed for the door.

"Ma-ma," Eve said again and then she was gone.

It took all of Sarah's strength just to make it back to the little room that had been designated as the pharmacy. She sat on a blue crate and cried. They were tears of joy—Eve had recognized her and called her Ma-ma! They were also tears of relief—Shondra had recognized her and not said anything...or so she thought.

The door to the pharmacy opened minutes later and one of the Sisters who had accompanied Eve was standing there. In her hand was a pistol which she leveled at Sarah."

"You're a Denier, a filthy Denier!"

Chapter 34

Neil

Southern Georgia

As Sarah was experiencing her first morning in New Eden, discovering that to the hierarchy she was nothing more than a number, Neil was puttering about the little house south of Atlanta in an increasingly tense mood. Captain Grey had left on his recon mission before first light and by noon everyone was scared that he had been killed or captured.

"This shouldn't be taking so long," Sadie said. She wasn't one for pacing, instead she stretched the lean muscles of her legs on the living room floor next to Nico who was laid out on the couch. The Russian was markedly better. He smiled now and was as awake and alert as his pain meds would allow him.

"Recon is slow business," he intoned as he had every time Sadie complained about how long the wait was. "Do not worry my *Kraslvaya*, it will be ok."

Neil walked to the kitchen to check on Jillybean—the girl had paused again. She stood slightly bent at the waist with her hand out as if she was about to pet a dog, only there was no dog. For three seconds she stood absolutely, unblinkingly still. Only her thin brown hair stirred at the mercy of a confused back and forth breeze.

The corners of Neil's mouth drew down as he stood there, hoping she would click back into place as she had the first time he saw her this way. That had been after breakfast. The next two times, he had watched her stand rigid until he couldn't take it and had called to her.

It was the same now. "Jillybean?"

She came back with a start, as if he had snuck up on her. "Yes?"

"Um, are you hungry?"

She glanced at the sun, puckering one eye. "Is it lunch time already?"

Neil had to force his mouth to keep its little smile in place; time displacement was another bad sign. Sadie worried Jillybean was suffering from post-traumatic stress disorder, Neil thought it was worse than that. When he had first met Jillybean, Neil had thought Ipes was a cute manifestation of what was a justifiable self-defense mechanism. In the last couple of weeks, however, he had begun to fear that she was borderline schizophrenic or was on her way to developing multiple personalities.

Now, after seeing the strange catatonic lapses he had to assume she was getting worse, if she hadn't already crossed the border into crazy-ville. The correct, proper, moral thing to do would be to let Jillybean rest somewhere safe for a few weeks. It would have to be somewhere hidden, a lake in the Ozarks, perhaps where she could leave her fears behind and just be a child. And Neil planned to do just that, *after* saving Sarah and Eve.

If Sadie knew the extent of the little girl's problems she would insist on *before*. She would claim they didn't need Jillybean's help, that they were just as smart as she was, and that they could save Sarah and Eve on their own. Neil knew better. Sadie was sweet, and her love and loyalty could never be doubted, however forethought and planning weren't her strong suit, as she was the first to admit.

When it came to rescues, Neil didn't trust her, but he distrusted himself to an even greater degree. Anytime danger had ever put him in the position to make command decisions, he had panicked, his mind crushed by insecurity. Looking back at the apocalypse he thought it was a miracle he had survived.

He didn't trust Nico either. The Russian was handsome, strong, and brave, yet he hadn't shown the slightest hint of anything other than ordinary intelligence. Nor did Neil trust Captain Grey. He was clearly a man with extraordinary skills, great intelligence and years of experience. He had proved himself capable of both taking a life and saving a life, but he was still a soldier. He followed orders without question and there was no telling what the full extent of his orders concerning New Eden were. Perhaps there was a diplomatic aspect to them. After all Grey was a representative of his general in Colorado; it wasn't far-fetched to believe this general would want to begin forming alliances among the other ragged bands of survivors, even with kooks like Abraham.

That left Jillybean as the only person Neil could fully trust...as long as she held it together.

Fearing that her odd catatonic episodes would lead to something worse, Neil kept her close to him all day and that meant playing with her as the afternoon plodded on. He was subjected to a seemingly endless tea party on the porch, and a game of chase that ended with them both running from a zombie. When she suggested they play dress-up, he took control.

"Since that zombie left, let's go skip some stones instead."

"Do you mean skip over them? Or do you, like, wanna play hopscotch. That has stones *and* skipping."

"No, I meant throwing them. What you do is...I'll just show you."

They went around the house to the pond and Neil found a stone and chucked it: *ploosh*.

"Was that it? That just looked like you threw a rock," Jillybean said. "Did you forget the skip part?"

"No, I just got the wrong rock," Neil said, bent over and wagging his head side-to-side, looking for a correctly shaped rock.

"There's a right rock?" Jillybean asked. She squatted with her knees splayed like a pink-legged grasshopper. "What do you do once you throw it? Do we have to fetch it?" She sounded excited at the prospect.

"No. The whole point is to make the rock skip. Like this!" Just as the first, this one went *ploosh* and didn't skip at all. "Son of a...I need a flatter rock." Neil tried a piece of slate that he whipped side-armed at the pond. It skipped three times before sinking with a *plop*.

"It bounced!" Jillybean cried, taking two steps into the water and pointing. "How do you do that? Rocks are aposed to sink, I know it."

Neil showed her which rocks to use and how to sling them just right. Jillybean was not a natural. At the start, she threw with her wrist instead of her shoulder and the rocks would drop into the water one after another each with a disappointing *ploosh*.

Meanwhile Neil was getting a good rhythm going. His rocks would skip, bound, and sometimes even seemed to roll across the flat surface of the pond. Jillybean loved it and, as it was the only "athletic" event Neil was any good at, he did too.

They threw rocks until Neil's elbow was aching and the zombies were creeping down out of the forest toward them. Although she could never get her rocks to skip more than three times in a row, Jillybean went into the house excited to tell Sadie all about it.

The Goth girl had been trying new recipes out with the food they had on hand which consisted mostly of aging fish and a bushel of apples. She had tried roasting, boiling and finally frying the apples. Fried apples were surprisingly good: tart and sweet in proper measures. Jillybean turned her nose up at the bass and ate a plateful of apples as her dinner. Neil ate the fish to be polite, but worried he would regret it later as it was extremely fishy.

Dinner was over and the last of the sunlight, a precious gold in a sea of deepening indigo, was pushing feebly through the trees when Captain Grey returned, bringing with him a man dying of the zombie virus. Grey had bundled him in a blanket and bound him with silver duct tape.

"Beginning of stage 5," Grey commented, jerking his thumb to the unconscious man.

Sadie lifted a shoulder and Neil shook his head. "What's stage 5?"

Grey gave them a look of incredulity. "What's stage 5? It's the final stage. He's probably got less than an hour left. Grab his feet, Neil." Grey took hold of the man's shoulders and with Neil's help they brought him inside just ahead of the stumbling zombies.

"Why...why did you bring him...here?" Neil asked gasping. "Why didn't you just help him on to the next life out there?"

"He's from New Eden," Grey snapped. "Why else would I drag his soon to be dead ass all the way back here?"

"Are you going to torture him?" Sadie asked, nervously. Grey rolled his eyes as if the question was far-fetched. Neil didn't think it was. The Believers were such fanatics that he wondered if even a hellish torture would get them to talk about the secrets of New Eden.

Nico grimaced himself off the couch and when the man was settled in his place, Grey did the opposite of torture. He cut away the blanket, exposing the man's head and one of his arms. Next, he force-fed him medicine to reduce his fever and started an IV of Lactated Ringers, adding a morphine drip.

"You think you can save him?" Neil asked. "Really?"

Grey sat back on his heels and ran a camouflage-painted hand across an equally green painted face. "That's about the dumbest question I ever heard. What's that smell? Apples? Do we have any left?"

While Sadie got a plate for him and Jillybean a bottle of clean water, Grey told them what he had discovered. "We're screwed. New Eden is locked up tighter than a frog's ass. Those silos might as well be called what they really are: guard towers. They have 360 degree views, gunports to cover every angle, and very likely, communication gear allowing them to call in reinforcements. I got up close, but you guys don't stand a chance."

"I can be pretty sneaky," Jillybean said. She stood next to him holding the bottle of water like a pale, female version of Gunga Din.

"Yeah? Can you sneak past ten thousand stiffs? There is a very active horde of them all around New Eden. I mean a freaking big horde. I found them hundreds deep in a belt around the perimeter. It didn't make sense why they were arranged the way they were until I found these."

From his pack he extracted a number of light fixtures. As Nico and Neil inspected them Grey inhaled his plate of apples and sucked down the entire bottle of water.

"They are lights," Nico said. "You say they attract zombies. How?"

"All I know is that they're strobe lights. I couldn't tell you why it attracts them since we've always been more interested in *not* attracting them. However I can tell you why the lights are being used. The zombies act as a first line of defense and as an early warning system. If I was to attack New Eden I would need a company of rangers and by the time we fought our way through, the loonies inside would be prepared for us."

As her water-bottle holding duties were no longer needed and the lights looked to be just lights, Jillybean had drifted over to the man on the couch and was inspecting him. He had begun moaning and now that he was being rapidly infused with fluids he was no longer cherry-bright with the fever.

"He's not from New Eden," she stated. "He's from another place."

"Wrong," Grey told her. "I found him a hundred yards from the southernmost tower. He was yelling at them to let him *back* in. All I could get out of him was that he still *believed.* He probably screwed up and they booted him."

Jillybean touched the man's sweat-beaded forehead and leaned in close to sniff him. "Nope. He's from someplace else. He's smells real bad. They have bathes and showers there in New Eden. Sadie said so. And look at his hair. He's like a cave man. We learned about them in school, they ate dinosaurs and pulled girls around by the hair. And look at his clothes. They are real all dirty and old; they dress clean, the Believers do. So that means this guy is from someplace else."

Grey sighed, preparing to give his rebuttal when the man on the couch opened his eyes. Jillybean leapt back in fright, but the man only seemed confused. "Where am I? Where's Beth?"

"I'm Jillybean."

This statement would confuse anyone and the man was no exception. He only blinked with huge, glassy eyes at the girl until Captain Grey nudged her away from the couch.

"Hi there. I'm Captain Grey. You're safe here, ok? We won't hurt you. Can you tell me your name?"

"Arthur Higgs," he said around a thick, dry tongue. He tried to swallow, but only made odd clicking sounds. "I'm the...I'm the...I thought I was a mayor, but I'm not. Right? Isn't that right? And Beth is dead isn't she?" None of them present knew and so none of them answered.

"She's dead," he whispered. "And I'm dying. I can feel it crawling inside me. Like the beams...wait, there aren't any beams are there?"

"None that can hurt you, Arthur," Grey told him. "Are you from New Eden?"

"No, I'm from Easton, Maryland. Can I have a drink? I'm so thirsty."

Jillybean ran to fill the water bottle and Neil came closer to the couch. "Hi. I'm looking for my wife, Sarah Rivers. Have you seen her? She's about my height, and has long blonde hair, blue eyes. She's very pretty. Have you seen anyone that looks like that? She was in a white Honda Accord. Does that ring a bell?"

Arthur only shook his head, his eyes losing their focus. Neil went back to the dining room table and tried not to let the tears come.

"Sorry, Neil," Grey said gripping his shoulder. "It wasn't going to work even if she was in there. We would need an army to break in. Chances are she is alive and well but stranded between here and Philadelphia looking for gas."

Neil didn't believe that for a second.

"Here you go, Mister Arthur." Jillybean held out the bottle. Arthur drank noisily. He blinked with each swallow. The movement was mechanical rather than human and more than a bit distressing to look at. Jillybean stepped back. "What are you doing way down here? Were you trying to get into New Eden?"

His head went one way and his words went the other. "Yes. I remember now. Me and my friend Janice were hoping to be healed or protected or something. But they only took her because I was..." He stopped with a confused look.

"Because you were bitted?" Jillybean asked.

"No, because I was crazy." His words were fading in strength and his eyes started to droop. "I remember it like it was a dream. I was so afraid of crazy stuff; beams and electric water. I remember raving all the time. I was crazy, crazy, crazy..." His voice faded to nothing but then he blinked as if being startled awake. "Not anymore, now I'm dying. Just like Beth. It'll be good to see her again. It's been so long. So, so long. So long since I could think straight. That's why they didn't take me. I couldn't think straight and I was a danger."

Jillybean's lips were pursed and cocked to the side as she listened to Arthur. "But they took Janice?" she asked.

"Yeah, they said she had great faith. She believed that guy was a prophet, but he was crazy. And the people were crazy too. I was crazy, yes. I thought I was the mayor of Easton, but they thought he was a god. Even...Janice thought that. Even..."

His eyes lost their focus and his lips stopped moving in the middle of forming a word. Captain Grey checked his pulse. "He's going pretty quick. Neil, let's move him to the garage."

"What's in the garage?" Jillybean asked.

Neil wanted to answer her, but his throat was too tight. Where the hell was his wife? Where in the world was Sarah Rivers? Had she got to New Eden days ahead of them or Arthur? Or was she stranded, out of gas in some piss-ant little burg? If so, which one? There had to be over a thousand little towns between them and Philadelphia. The thought of dragging Sadie and Jillybean in a dangerous search of each was overwhelming.

Sadie answered the little girl. "Mister Arthur is going to turn into a monster soon and I know it might be sad, but

Mister Neil and Captain Grey are going to have to stop that from happening. Do you understand?"

Jillybean nodded as Neil grabbed the blanket near the ankles and Grey the shoulders. "I get it, but it's not so sad. It's what he would want. That's what I think. I'm just glad he was able to tell us where Miss Sarah is before he turned into a monster."

Neil dropped Arthur's feet with a light thump. "What? When did he say that?"

"He didn't," the captain growled. "Now get those feet."

Neil ignored him. He rushed to Jillybean full of excitement. "What did he say about Sarah? All he mentioned were two people named Beth and Janice. Is Sarah one of them? It's Janice, right?"

"I think so," Jillybean answered. "Miss Sarah is real smart. She probably knew she couldn't go to New Eden as herself so she made up a name: Janice. And she can't go looking like herself neither, so she probably cut her hair or is wearing a wig. And she probably has eye-changeable contact things for her eyes. That's what means they can change your eyes to a new color. Before the monsters came, my Aunt Alice wanted to get them because her eyes were kaka-brown. That's what she said."

"There's an awful lot of *probablies* and very few facts in your theory," Grey noted.

"Yes Sir, I guess, 'cept I don't know what facts or a theory is," Jillybean said. "Does it mean I talk too much? My old teacher Miss Monfit said that, too."

"Don't worry about any of that, just tell us what you think," Neil said, turning Jilly away from Captain Grey to keep her from being distracted by the air of authority that built up around him whenever he challenged anyone.

She seemed unnerved by Neil's desperation and leaned somewhat away as she said: "I think Janice is really Miss Sarah. Mister Arthur said he was crazy for a long time and that he was raving, that's what means he shouted a lot. And he said he was a danger. I don't think anyone but Miss Sarah would go anywhere with him."

"Why not," Captain Grey demanded.

"Because everyone knows that shouting brings out the monsters. I would be ascared to go around with someone who shouts all the time, but Miss Sarah was...what's the word, Ipes? Desperate! She was desperate because the rules say you couldn't get into New Eden 'cept if you have a boy with you."

"Right, that makes sense," Neil said. He let go of Jillybean to point at Arthur as if he was accusing him of something. "And...and he didn't know exactly why they were going, remember? He said it was to be protected or something. Sarah must have talked him into going."

"Or this Janice person could have been an old friend," Grey countered, playing devil's advocate. "Someone he had survived the apocalypse with; someone with influence over him. Maybe she wanted to go to New Eden because she heard it was safe. That is the more plausible explanation."

Jillybean stared at Arthur thoughtfully for a few seconds before shaking her head. "No. That's an explanation but not the most likely one. Mister Arthur said Janice had great belief when she met the prophet. That doesn't sound like a normal person. When I met Abraham, I was curious and ascared."

"Me too," Sadie said. "If he had done something...I don't know, magical, I might have been able to believe, but he was just a guy spouting bible verses, although he did look the part of a prophet."

"Yep," Jillybean agreed. "And he acted it, too. But he was a big fat phony. That's why someone new coming up and showing 'great faith' and thinking Abraham was some sort of god doesn't sound, um, plausible. Is that the right word? Yeah? Anyway it sounds like fakery and Miss Sarah would know how to fake it."

Neil was quick to agree, as was Nico and Sadie. Captain Grey was silent, staring down at Arthur who had begun to tremble and drool. "So much is possible but what is most likely?" he asked, talking more to himself than anyone present. He then jerked his head up. "Jillybean's made some good points and if she's right it means your friend Sarah is screwed. I wasn't joking about needing an army. Between the five of us we have a couple of grenades a shotgun and my M4. It's not enough."

"I have my axe," Neil said feeling light-headed; hope and fear fighting for possession of his mind.

"And it won't do you a lick of good," Grey said. "Grab this guy's legs. "Let's get this over with."

It was two seconds before Neil stooped and took hold of the man's ankles. He felt he should be saying something. Making an argument. It seemed as though they were giving up on Sarah too easily. They had come eight hundred miles and now they were letting her go. He could see it in the way Sadie refused to take her eyes off the floor and how Nico looked relieved, but mostly it was in his own gut where he felt the sensation. He was empty inside. He didn't feel love or fear or worry. He felt dead.

Sarah was gone. She was beyond Neil's ability to help.

The soldier nearly tugged Arthur's feet from Neil's numb fingers as he started for the garage and he had to lurch forward to keep from dropping his end of the body. The garage was dark with a wet smell of earth and oil. A Buick sat beneath a perfectly even layer of dust. Seeing it, made Neil want to simultaneously run his fingers through the fine grains and at the same time, preserve the pristine nature of it.

Grey didn't give it a glance. He lowered his end of the panting body and then rolled it over so that Arthur's face smeared the floor with sweat and mucus that had gone to an ugly, congealed yellow. Without the least gentleness, Grey exposed the back of Arthur's neck and plunged a black-bladed knife into the joint where the skull met the spinal column. Arthur jerked once, his feet kicking a rhythm and then went still.

"You want to say something for him?" Grey asked, standing over the body.

Neil was bug-eyed by how easily Grey had killed the man. "Um, no. I don't think so. I didn't know him."

"That doesn't mean shit," Grey said in a soft growl. He bowed his head. "Lord, in your might and wisdom please bless the soul of your son, Arthur. Guide him in the afterlife and lead him to your glory. Amen."

"Amen," Neil said, feeling guilty. The thought of a prayer hadn't even entered his consciousness.

"We'll bury him in the morning," Grey said and left the garage and the body without looking back. He went to the kitchen to wash off his knife and when he turned back he saw that everyone had joined him and were watching silently. He walked past them into the living room but when they followed, he turned quickly. His eyes fell on Jillybean who was playing with one of the strobe lights.

"Out with it," he said to her. "I can tell you're trying to come up with some sort of angle to get us into New Eden. Trust me though, I've already thought of all of them: ruses, distractions, cons. Hell, I even contemplated a modern day Trojan Horse, but I always return to the issue of being outgunned and undermanned. It's something we won't be able to get beyond."

Jillybean nodded. "Right. You said only an army could do it. I know where we can get an army."

Neil was down on one knee before anyone could say a word. "What army? People from around here? Is that what you mean?" Right before she could answer, Grey sighed with such obvious skepticism that it was insulting. Neil shot him a tense look and then turned her bodily away. "Don't mind him. Just tell me, what army?"

"Ok. It's the…it's the army…the army…" Jillybean began blinking rapidly, looking confused all of a sudden.

Sadie grew alarmed and dropped down in front of the little girl. "Don't listen to Ipes! He's being bad. Just remember we're here for you. Try to relax and tell us, what army are you talking about?"

Jillybean took a shaky breath and put her hand out to Sadie. "I'm alright. Ipes was being bad again. He says that you like someone who abandoned us more than you like me."

"No, that's not true," Sadie said. "Don't listen to Ipes. We all care for you, Jillybean."

"I know…maybe he should go to time out."

She started looking around for a proper place but Sadie shook her head. "Not in here. Put him in the kitchen or he'll keep interfering."

After she took the offending zebra by the scruff of the neck and marched him out of the room, Grey dropped onto the couch. "That's who makes the plans for you guys? No wonder you're in such a sorry state."

"She's very, very smart," Sadie said, loud enough for Jillybean to hear through the swinging door to the kitchen.

"It's true," Neil agreed. "She sees things differently than you and me. If she says she knows where an army is then I'd trust her."

"I agree that she sees things differently..." Grey lowered his voice, "...because she may have a screw loose. Don't pretend that you don't know what I'm talking about. Chances are..."

Just then there came a heavy thump on the front door— it was a very familiar sound, one each of them had heard a hundred times before. Grey slid off the couch and had his M4 pointed at the door in a quick move.

"The doors will hold," Sadie said in a whisper. "They're very strong."

The door shook beneath the blows of more zombies. Captain Grey checked the lock and rattled the knob, satisfying himself with their strength. He then checked the black draped windows. Peeking out, he let out a curse.

"Son of a bitch. There's about a billion stiffs out there. I wonder why they...wait." Suddenly he dashed from the window and charged into the kitchen. The others followed and at first Neil failed to see what had Grey pulling at his hair; the kitchen was shut up tight; everything seemed normal. Then it dawned on him that Jillybean wasn't there.

"She hung a strobe light on the porch railing out front," Grey said. "What was I saying about her having a screw loose?"

Chapter 35

Sadie

Southern Georgia

Sadie had the reassuring weight of the shotgun in her hand and was heading for the back door when Captain Grey grabbed her and pulled her back. "You're staying here. Someone's got to keep an eye on Nico. Neil and I will go out. Time to put that axe of yours to some use."

Although Neil paled at the thought of heading out into the night of a million zombies, he did not back down. He wiped the sweat from his palms and picked up his axe.

"I should go, too. You don't know her like I do," Sadie said. "She's freaking smart and she won't be easy to catch, and besides I'm faster than both of you put together."

Grey pulled back the black felt that had been slung over the window. The zombies were ten deep and crowding closer. He shut the curtain with a snap. "Speed won't help you tonight. I have body armor and Neil is inoculated; we should be safe enough. Besides, what if Jillybean comes back? She'll need you. I can tell that she looks up to you like a big sister."

"But..." Sadie began only just then Neil hugged her and squeezed her hard enough to stop her breath.

"Please, stay here for me. I'm going out of mind enough with Sarah and Eve out there and now Jillybean too? I can't deal with more than that. Not tonight. Not with so many zombies out there."

Reluctantly she agreed to stay behind.

Captain Grey dug in his pack and produced two radios. He handed her one, explaining: "Keep it on channel 6 and use it sparingly. If you need to report in, begin your call sign with a color but only if you're safe. Like this: *Blue, come in blue this is green*—do you understand? If you don't start with a color, I'll figure that a bounty hunter or one of the Believers has caught you."

"Color equals safe. Got it."

The soldier nodded. "We'll do the same. She has only a five minute head start. Hopefully, we'll get her quickly and get back. In the meantime try to disable that strobe without getting bitten."

"How?"

"Improvise, adapt and overcome," Grey said over his shoulder as he strode out of the room with Neil in tow.

"What's that supposed to mean?" she demanded.

"I think it means figure it out," Neil said and then they were both out the back door and quickly lost in the gloom of the night.

Sadie came back to the living room. She sighed, eyeing the radio. Then she clipped it to her jeans and sighed again. Finally, after a third sigh she said, "I guess we need to figure out that strobe."

"I am try to figure out what I get into," Nico remarked from the couch. He was still pale and weak from his surgery of the day before, however he wore a little smile. "Next time I save pretty girl, I think twice. Here we are. Bunch of crazies, running all over country to save woman and baby, and we cannot save ourselves."

"Speak for yourself." Sadie went to the window and peeked out. "Son of a gun there's a lot of them out there. Blow out the candles, will you?" The banging on the door was starting to become unsettling and she had to remind herself that, just like the windows, it was reinforced and would take a lot more than a few zombies to get through it.

Thankfully the strobe light was drawing most of their attention. It was draped over a decorative knob of wood at the end of the stair railing and there was an entire gaggle of zombies around it. Sadie bit off another sigh and looked back at the now gloomy room, seeing Nico more like a spectral figure than a man. It gave her the heebie-jeebies to see him like that.

"Do you think it's called a gaggle of zombies?" she asked to lighten her mood.

"What is gaggle? Sound like much of women talking."

"What?" she asked astounded. There was a throw-pillow at hand and she threw it indeed. Nico swatted it away with his good arm, chuckling.

"I joke. I know not good name for most a lot of zombies. You are American. Is your language. You should tell me, not me tell you."

"I don't know…" A thought struck her in mid-sentence. Throwing the pillow had given her an idea. "Why don't you rest on the couch, I'll be right back."

Sadie went to the kitchen and by the light of a flashlight began gathering up an armful of the heaviest pots and pans in the house. She then went to the second floor and slid up a bedroom window that opened onto the porch roof. She seemed very high up.

"Just don't look down," she joked. She would have to look down in order to knock out the strobe.

A glance told her that hitting the strobe, which was smaller than a clock-radio, with a twelve-inch skillet from the angle she was at was going to be a near impossible task. That didn't stop her in the least. She threw the first of her small arsenal since she didn't have any other ideas and it was better than carting all the pans back down stairs.

Throwing a skillet was neither an art nor a science, it was actually fun. The skillet curved away from her target and rang off a zombie skull before hitting the walkway with a metallic *klonk*. She threw the next one slightly off target to compensate for the curve that the first pan had demonstrated, but for some reason this frying pan went straight, hitting another zombie and ending up in the bushes.

She went through the remaining six pans with equally poor results. She did manage to attract all the zombies' attention and piss off quite a few. They gathered below, looking up with hate in their dull eyes. "Be right back," she told them when she had run out of things to throw.

She ducked back inside and sent the beam of her flashlight around the room. It had been a boy's room, but the items in it were extremely dated. A calendar was pinned open to July of 1977 and on the wall was a poster of Farah Fawcett in a red, one-piece bathing suit. Even after thirty-seven years her teeth still gleamed brightly in the dark room.

"It's like a time capsule in here," Sadie said in hushed tones. With her Goth look and her brash ways, it felt like she was disturbing the spirit of the room, as though the room was unhappy in some way that a girl was in it. The dim glow of the flashlight and the moans of the undead outside the window didn't help.

"Sorry about this, but duty demands," she said, briskly, as her light flicked over the bed and dresser and came to rest on a twenty gallon fish tank sitting on a desk. It was bone dry but still heavy. She heaved it through the open window and then slid it out onto the roof. After aiming, she let the aquarium slide down the shingles, crying out, "Bombs away!"

There was a tremendous crash that seemed to ring out in slow motion as shards of glass went everywhere, each seeming to break a second or third time. In the house below, Nico was yelling in alarm, asking if she was alright.

"I'm fine," she called out as she crept to the edge to see her handiwork. The tank had struck the rail a foot away from the strobe. The light was untouched and sat there, blinking merrily, seemingly unconcerned at the close call it had just had.

There was so much glass everywhere that she didn't trust the rubber soles of her Converse sneakers to keep her feet intact. "So much for using the front door," she said, wondering if this was what Captain Grey had imagined when he had said improvise, adapt, and overcome. Probably not.

She went back inside the bedroom, which was no longer quite so somber feeling. The air was lighter as though the spirit of the boy would have appreciated such shenanigans. "You liked that, did you?"

Eagerly, she went for the next larger item: a thirteen inch black and white TV. It didn't look like much, however she grunted under its weight and when she let it go, bounding off the roof, it struck the sidewalk with the sound of an explosion. She had missed again.

Nico appeared in the doorway just as she was climbing back in the window. "Well?" he asked. The strobe was still going strong and so far she had only managed to attract even more zombies to the house.

"I'm working on it," she told him.

He dropped onto the bed and in the beam of light they could see dust billow madly. Nico waved at the plume ineffectually and then pulled off the top comforter and slung it to the floor. Beneath was a blue blanket that was folded back neatly, revealing sailboat sheets. Again, the "boy" feeling came back, but this time it was with a feeling of nostalgia that made Sadie smile.

"Time to break out the big guns," she said, eyeing the next item that would add to her night of mayhem: a squat, three-drawer dresser. It was going to be a complete bitch. In fact, after making a guess as to its dimensions she figured that she would probably have to break the window to get it out onto the roof. But first things first: she had to clear a path. The heavy comforter Nico had tossed aside was in the way. She grabbed it and slung it over a chair...

"Well I'll be," she said, amused.

"You be, what?" Nico asked.

"I'll be feeling stupid." Instead of risking a hernia trying to get the dresser out the window, she took the comforter and crawled out onto the roof. Seconds later it was draped across the railing, literally blanketing the strobe light. "Improvise, adapt, and overcome," she whispered. "I bet Jillybean would've seen that right off the bat."

Sadie stared out, trying to pierce the shadows, wondering where the little girl was and thinking that maybe it might have been better if she had left the strobe light going to light the way home. Sadie began to feel the lightness of fear in her belly. She pulled out the radio.

"Hello Neil? Have you found her? Captain Grey? Can you guys hear me? Oh, shit, I forgot. Blue this is green.

Come in Green. Hello?" No one picked up. She tried again and again as the feeling in her belly intensified.

"They're not answering," she said to Nico. The Russian had fallen asleep on the bed with his good, left arm tucked under his head. "Nico? Hey, they aren't picking up. I've tried them, like twenty times and…"

Just then her radio squawked and she jumped. "Green this is blue. Come in green." It was Captain Grey's voice; he didn't sound happy.

Sadie hit the send button: "Hi, this is green. Did you guys find her?"

"No we didn't and thanks to all your God-awful chatter you nearly got us killed!" Grey's anger came in loud and clear through the little radio.

"Sorry about that," Sadie said.

"I don't want or need you to be sorry. I need you to be smart. I need you to remember the rules to broadcasting over the mother-fucking radio. First rule: always remember that *anyone* can be listening. Second rule: don't use names! Third, don't use it like you're an idiot teenager with a cell phone. Only use the mother-fucking radio when you have something mother-fucking useful to say! Over!"

"Sorry," Sadie said, feeling the heat of her cheeks.

There wasn't a response for over a minute, but finally Grey came on, announcing his presence with a sigh. "Green this is blue. My companion thinks that I was too harsh and that I need to apologize. I'm sorry for yelling. We will be continuing our search and will contact you only if needed. Out."

"Don't worry about it. I guess I was being pretty silly and all. I got the strobe off, sort of. Oh, don't use the front door when you come back. There's glass everywhere. Bye."

She waited, listening for some response but the radio was silent. Nico told her that coming back on to say "bye" as well wasn't necessary and Grey wouldn't do it. "He is follow manual very good."

Sadie didn't think so. She thought Grey was being an uptight jerk and planned to tell him so when they got back.

It was hours before she had the chance. They came back tired and cranky, sporting red scratches from tromping through the forest at night. She didn't need to ask if they were successful at finding Jillybean, Neil's depression was evident the second he walked through the door. He plopped onto a kitchen chair and began picking at the thousands of nettles that had attached themselves to his sweater vest.

Grey was standing at the table where Sadie had opened cans of raviolis for them to eat—he had his can empty in under a minute.

"About the radio," Sadie said, trying not to falter when he turned his hazel eyes toward her. "I don't think we have to be so *by the book*, you know. No one is out there, and even if they were what would they hear? A bunch of blabber."

The soldier glared, but after glancing in Neil's direction he gritted his teeth into an angry smile. "First of all, I don't blabber. Second, these radios can be traced, very, very easily, and third, you are probably the most wanted person on the planet. Your bounty is worth five thousand. That means you cannot afford to take chances. You have to live with the concept, minute-by-minute, every single day that there is *always* someone out there! Always someone listening. Always someone searching."

"Oh."

"Damn right, Oh. Now clear this table. Neil, get me more candles." The captain spread out a map and stared thoughtfully for a moment. Sadie went to grab the empty can of raviolis but he took her wrist gently but firmly. "I'll need that." He marked their position with an X and then drew a circle around it using the can.

"The circle is five-miles in every direction from this house, what I believe is the furthest distance she will be able go before sunrise. The question is: where is she going? Sadie, you said knew her the best. Where do you think?"

She wanted to shrug, but stopped herself. It wasn't the time for indecision, but unfortunately that's all she had. "I know Jillybean, but I don't know Ipes."

Grey's brows came down sharply. "Wait...what? Ipes? The zebra? Are you saying that a stuffed zebra is controlling her? Like she has multiple personalities?"

This time she did shrug but it wasn't out of indecision. She just didn't want to admit the truth. Neil spoke for her. "We think so. Maybe it's an early case, but I don't know."

"It's getting worse," Sadie said. "The zebra used to make suggestions to help her out, but at least twice it's taken over her body. Three times, now, counting tonight. I don't know where he would go."

"Probably somewhere familiar, somewhere safe," Grey said. "The CDC? Would she go there?"

Neil shook his head. "I doubt it. She never lived there. It was never her home and was never really safe in her mind. My guess is that she'll make her way north back to Philly. Only she may not do it right away. She might go south first and then double back. We're not joking when we say she's eerily smart. She won't go waltzing back up I95. It'll be by back streets and through the woods."

"Could she drive?" Grey asked.

The best answer was: possibly. With Jillybean, everything was possible. Since further searching that night would be both dangerous and useless, the four of them went to bed with the next day's plans already laid out.

Sadie would be stationed at a junction of roads northeast of the house in the town of Jackson. Nico would go south to Forsyth, not twenty miles from Macon. Neil would find a good perch to the west in Griffin and finally Captain Grey took the north segment in the town of McDonough.

There was so much land to cover, over sixty square miles, that Sadie's heart wasn't in it as she climbed out of the Humvee just as the dawn was cracking its way between the dark earth and the darker sky.

"Channel 6. Use it only in an emergency," Grey said, speaking of the radio hooked to her pack. She traveled light. In her pack were two water bottles, an MRE, a map, and three magazines of 5.56mm ammo. "Lock and load," he ordered.

Sadie was familiar with weapons and the M4 was little more than the next generation M16 which she had shot on a few occasions. It should've been nothing to pull back on the charging handle, slap a magazine in place and drop the bolt, but this was Captain Grey's "baby" and he was watching her closely.

Though his gaze wasn't sexual she never felt more like a girl than just then. She cleared her throat and began. "Safe on, pulling charging handle...mag in, and let the bolt go. Done."

He shook his head. "You didn't check to see if the chamber was clear. Don't forget that next time. Now let's see your stance. Ok, ok...your feet are good but why do you have your elbows tucked? You keep your elbows tucked in only if you're clearing a room. Out here give yourself a firm base. Alright, I'll be back at noon."

The humvee kicked up dirt and was soon dwindled by distance to the size of a toy. Sadie looked around. There wasn't much to Jackson, Georgia: some mom and pop stores, a few gas stations, and a couple of supermarkets; certainly not much in the way of sky-scrapers that would give her a good vantage. The best she had was the Butts County courthouse which sported a three story tall tower running up one end of the building.

She headed straight for it, but had to detour in a sprint as a number of zombies were converging right at her. Sadie normally liked to run, but never liked to do it with a back pack bouncing up and down on what felt like her kidneys and a rifle in her hands keeping her from using the full extent of her sprinter's body.

Still, she was very fast and she was able to elude the zombies by running around the block and then back to the court house where another zombie in the shredded-up uniform of a county sheriff had been on its hands and knees, eating the white-heads off the clovers. It hadn't seen her before and she didn't see it, now.

She went to the front door of the court house—it had been beaten down. Sadie raised the carbine and stepped in. Not a second later she heard the moan of the zombie but because of the acoustics in the empty building she didn't realize it was behind her until it had a grip of her back pack. In whirl, she let the pack slip from her shoulders and, turning halfway around, fired the M4 one-handed like it was a huge pistol.

There was very little kick as she blasted a hole in the zombie's head. It flopped at her feet.

"Why wasn't Grey around to see that?" she wondered aloud. Hoisting her pack, she stepped over the still warm corpse and went for the tower, finding the door to the stairs destroyed as well. She feared more zombies, but there were none and soon she found herself in an open area at the top of the tower with balconies facing each of the primary points of the compass.

As she was only a few feet above the tree line, the views weren't great, especially when she considered the fact that she was searching for a girl barely three and half feet tall. A part of her knew she was wasting her time. Jilly would avoid towns such as this, at least at first. She would cross the fields of heather and slink among the forests of elm and pine.

Sadie took out her map and studied it for a long time until she realized it was of no help at all. There just too much land to cover and only four of them to cover it.

"Blue, radio check. Over." Sadie's radio said. She pulled it out of its flap as she heard Neil say in a nervous voice: "This is silver. Radio-checking over."

"Red, radio check, over," Nico said, trying his best to sound American. Captain Grey had smirked when he had assigned *red* to the Russian.

"Green, radio check, over," Sadie said.

"This is blue, maintain radio silence. Out."

Her shoulders slumped. She knew they were going to do the radio check and still her hopes soared at that first crackly voice that someone had spotted Jillybean already. Trying to stay positive, she went to the east balcony so that the rising sun would warm her. The sun wasn't up ten minutes before became bored. She went to the other balconies and looked out. Nothing moved but zombies and the occasional pigeon.

Two sighs later, she broke out the map that Grey had folded so precisely into a five inch square. By ten o'clock she was so bored that she had the map completely open, and was tracing roads absently. It was a Georgia state map and there wasn't a single location in its borders that Sadie thought would draw Jillybean in particular. She laid it out flat, aligned it with the sun and then stood over it. Squinting downward, she began to wonder if she was far enough east.

"Does it really matter where I am?" she wondered. "If I was Jillybean, or Ipes I should say, where would I go and why?" The first answer and really, the only answer was: home to Philadelphia, and the why was obvious, so that left the how. "How would I get home?"

It was a stinking long walk, one that would daunt even Jillybean.

Would she drive? Sadie was sure Jillybean could rig some sort of device that would allow her to run the gas and the brakes and steer at the same time. However Sadie didn't think she would drive even if she could. The trip south had been so harrowing that Ipes probably wouldn't chance it.

"And that only leaves what, biking it?" Her first inclination was to dismiss the idea because the trip was too far and just as hazardous as driving, however she knew that Jillybean and Ram had ridden a bike for part of the time on their way south. Whenever Jillybean talked about that time her face would light up and she would smile at how much fun they had or she would laugh at how awful a sailor Ram had been.

"Son of a bitch," Sadie gasped realizing where the little girl was going. Jillybean was heading east for the ocean, Sadie was suddenly sure of it. "Blue this is Green," Sadie practically yelled into her radio. "I am switching locations to…" she looked down at her map and saw the perfect spot. "To Mon…um, I mean, I'm switching spots to a position east of me."

She had almost blabbed out very dangerous information, going against rule one: someone was always listening.

"Green this is Blue. How far east, over."

Sadie consulted the map. She was heading to the town of Monticello. It was a virtual hub of roads and if Jillybean was going straight east to the ocean she would likely pass near or through it. "Five miles."

"Affirmative, out."

She didn't waste a second wondering what that meant. Sadie hitched her backpack, snugged it down tight on her shoulders and jogged down the stairs and out into the warm Georgia air. She ran straight down route 16. It was a two-lane blacktop, bordered by farms, fields, and forests. The scenery made for a pleasant run and she didn't pause once for a rest or a drink until she came up on the outskirts of the town of Monticello.

There she slowed trying to look in every direction and down every street, thinking that it would be hard to spot the little girl, and it was. However spotting zombies behaving strangely was easy. There was a group scuffling around a parked Volkswagen Jetta. They were so focused on the little car that they didn't see Sadie at all, and so, sweating up a storm, she slipped up behind them. From about fifteen feet away she saw a lump in the front seat covered by a sheet.

"There you are," Sadie whispered. Now all she had to do was kill four zombies.

Sadie raised the rifle and pulled the trigger. The bullet took the ear off one of the zombies and skipped off the top of the Jetta. "Shit," she murmured and then adjusted her aim. The next three bullets dropped three of the zombies, but her fourth shot missed high and the fifth made a gaping wound in the last zombie's throat as it charged her. It was still alive, but it went down and that was good enough for Sadie.

She walked around it and tapped on the Jetta's glass. "Alright kid. The jig's up. License and registration."

Jillybean pulled back the sheet and glared up at her. Her eyes were bloodshot and there were dark circles beneath. She didn't look well.

"You ok?" Sadie asked.

"Go away."

"You know I can't do that, Ipes. I want to protect her too, and if you ask me, tromping across the country alone is about the most dangerous thing you could do."

"More dangerous than breaking into New Eden? I really doubt it. By the way, that one monster isn't dead. It's getting closer."

Sadie glanced back. The bullet had done something horrible to it; it could only use one side of its body, yet it was dragging itself on, gnashing its teeth.

"Come on, Jilly, let's go. I don't want to waste a bullet on that thing."

Ipes shook Jillybean's head. "No. I'm not going with you. Sure you could try to force me, but that won't be good for her and I'll just run away again."

"Can I at least get in the car?"

Jillybean smirked as though she knew Sadie's mind better than Sadie did, which might have been true. Still she unlocked the door and scooted over. "Thanks...are you hungry?" Sadie asked, ditching the rifle in the back seat and opening her pack. "I have one of those MREs. It's got cheese and crackers, your favorite."

"Sure, and while I eat you can tell me how wonderful it is being with your little group of outcasts. You can tell me how much you care for Jillybean and how you'd never put her in danger."

Sadie had been unzipping her pack, but she stopped. "First of all, I never said you were going into New Eden and second, we do care for you."

The little girl laughed at this. "Here we go. Where do I start? Miss Sarah though I was such a strange little girl that she couldn't even look me in the eyes. Nico thinks I'm a tag-along brat. Mister Neil...he likes everyone, but he

329

doesn't love everyone. He's committed to his family. That's who he loves. He'll die for them but not for me. And that leaves you, my ole pal Sadie. Do you love Jillybean? If you can say it right now so that I'll believe it, I'll let her go. I'll let her make her own decisions based on what her heart tells her and not her head."

This was a terrible spot for Sadie. Admitting love was the single most difficult thing she ever did. Growing up, she couldn't remember once saying I love you, even to her own family and they hadn't said it to her, either. Love was a word that she only used in emergencies and though this constituted an emergency she knew she wouldn't be able to pull it off with enough sincerity.

Yet she had to try. Her mouth came open, she nodded, laughed a little awkward laugh, raised her index finger as if she was going to make a point, and all the while the word love refused to come. She wanted it to come. She knew she loved Jillybean but the word wouldn't pass her lips. Finally, in a fit of anger she said, "This isn't about love, this is about fear. This is about Jillybean and all the things she's afraid of. She has a powerful mind. It's so powerful that she can invent you to save her from everything that scares her."

"Of course this is about fear!" the little girl snapped. "Fear is an emotion, just like love, and with Jillybean her love is constantly being rejected, it's constantly being stepped upon. However, her fears grow with each passing day. Picture a sailboat. Her fears are the anchor that holds her back and love is the wind that propels her forward. Which is greater?"

"For you, Ipes, fear will always be greater," Sadie said. "It's because you don't understand love. You were born out of fear and so that's all you ever see. You don't see the love that's all around her."

"You love Jillybean?" she asked with a soft, golden eyebrow skeptically arched.

"I do," Sadie said in a whisper. It had taken a lot just to admit it aloud.

"Then say the words. It's been over a year since anyone has told her they loved her. How long has it been for you?"

Nico said it all the time and Sadie distinctively remembered Sarah saying it before she left. Neil only rarely said I love you, however his actions spoke louder than words and Sadie didn't doubt his feelings in the least. "A few hours, I suppose," she admitted. Jillybean wore a smug look that bothered Sadie. It turned the little girl ugly. "I think I know why I can't tell you that I love you. It's because I'm talking to Ipes. Let me say it to Jillybean."

"Maybe you shouldn't. She very perceptive and you'll only disappoint her and make things worse."

"If she's so perceptive, she'll know the truth," Sadie shot back.

"Then say it," the little girl said. "I'll be listening."

Suddenly Jillybean blinked in confusion and then started working her jaw as if it had been locked shut. "Where are we? This isn't New Eden."

"No, it's not. I need to tell you something." Sadie had to pause and an embarrassed smile crept over her face. "I, uh, just wanted to say…"

Bamn! The two girls jumped as a grey fist smashed against the driver's side window. It left a smeary streak as it pulled back. Sadie glanced out and saw the zombie she had shot—only now she noticed how terribly big it was. She began crawling into the backseat to get the M4 when the fist smashed again, this time breaking the glass. A hand grabbed her leg.

Jillybean screamed and then Sadie heard the passenger door open and her little steps flying away. "Shit!" Sadie grabbed the M4 and tried to turn around but she was being pulled out of the car through the window. "Shit! Jillybean!"

Sadie pointed the gun over her shoulder and fired, hitting the roof of the car with her first shot and the steering wheel right next to her leg with the second. If she could only spin around she would have a chance but the angle was wrong and the car too cramped. "Jillybean!" Sadie screamed and then she saw the little girl race back with a brick in her hand. There was a thump and Sadie was released.

Quickly she spun around and brought the rifle to bear just as the zombie raised its misshapen head once again. This time her bullet found its target and black brains showered the driver's side.

Shaken and partially deaf from shooting from the inside of a car, Sadie climbed out. Jillybean made a face at the zombie and then asked, "What were you going to say?"

Sadie stuck a finger in her ear and wiggled it around. The little girl's words had come with a ringing that wouldn't leave. "I was going to say I love you." Had she shouted that? Had the whole zombie community heard?

Clearly it hadn't come out as well as she had wanted to. Jillybean looked slightly confused and a little disappointed. "Oh."

Sadie stepped toward her and she stepped back. "Jilly?"

The little girl shook her head. "No. She appreciates it, but it wasn't good enough. And it wasn't good enough that she had to kill that monster for you. You would have died without her and you'll probably die now, sorry."

"What do you mean?"

As an answer she pointed a small finger, eastward, behind Sadie. When the Goth girl turned her breath stuck in her throat. Straight down the road a black truck was barreling right at them. It wasn't Neil or Nico or even Captain Grey—Sadie could see the familiar green camouflage of the bounty hunter.

Chapter 36

Sarah

New Eden

The handcuffs were very tight. After only two hours the skin at her wrists had chafed and parted. She had bled and for some reason this bothered Abraham far more than Sarah's "crime".

"That was a perfectly good robe," he said, disapprovingly—this was after he had told her she would be burned alive. His own robe was so satiny-white that the yellow light from the single bulb dangling above seemed to slip off its surface and gather at his feet.

"Sorry for your loss," Sarah said with heavy sarcasm. "I know how much you value robes more than people."

"Some people, that's true," Abraham said with a little nod, "You, for instance. Deniers are the lowest form of life and cannot be tolerated to live a second longer than necessary. I mentioned the robe because it is a fine metaphor. Everything man touches is destroyed if his hands are stained with sin. What was pure is now stained, irrevocably."

"Too bad. Maybe your zombie-brained bitch-pack shouldn't have tightened these cuffs so much. Then we both would've been happy. I bet if you think real hard you can find another useless metaphor to describe that."

Abraham's smile slipped just the slightest before he could restore it to its normal brilliance. "Why are you here, Denier?"

"I came for Eve. You know that," she said heatedly. "You know I'm her mother and after the little incident with the hand grenade you should've known I wasn't going to just forget her. Any garden-variety prophet should've been able to see that. I wonder why you didn't. My guess is because you're a fraud."

He ignored the insult. "And your friends? Where are they? Where are Sadie and the Russian? You didn't travel all this way with only a lunatic as a companion."

Sarah smiled, looking up at the ladder that Abraham had descended in order to get into her prison. Her cell was nothing but a ten-foot-deep pit with a trench at one end for her to crap into. Her smile turned into a chuckle. "Why on earth would I tell you where they are? So you could kill them? Here's what I will tell you, that you don't seem to realize: you're an idiot, a real fucking idiot."

"Lower your voice," Abraham warned. "Right now we're just having a conversation. If you push me, I could have the Sisters start filling in this hole with you in it."

"That doesn't scare me in the least." Compared to being burned to death, being buried alive didn't seem all that bad. Really, nothing she could think of seemed as bad as being burned to death. Every time fire or burning was mentioned, she felt her chest constrict in fear, though she did her best to mask her fear with a very real hate. She couldn't stop sneering at Abraham. Even when she had laughed it had been around a curled lip.

Abraham noticed, and just like the more subtle insults she threw his way, he chose to ignore it. "Yes, I suppose it is hard to scare someone who has a death wish, so I'll lay off with the threats. I do have inducements that you might want to consider."

"It doesn't matter what you offer. I won't give up my friends, so don't waste your breath. Besides, what could you possibly offer me? Once you tell someone they're going to be burned to death, there's not much more to say."

"Maybe," he said, touching the side of her cell, feeling the dirt. He made a face and wiped his hands together. "There are still things I can do for you. Eve, for instances. You could see her one more time."

Sarah's mouth came open like a starving man suddenly set before a feast. With a great struggle, she shook her head. "No, I won't give them up. What do you want them for? Especially Nico, he's not a Denier. Is it the money? Are you looking to cash in on the reward?"

He rolled his eyes. "Please! What would I need with money? The Lord has blessed me in ways beyond your ken, or to put it in a way you might understand, I have every worldly good available to me already. Were I to turn the two of them over to Yuri, it wouldn't be for the money. Unfortunately, the world is once again embroiled in politics and intrigue. The truth is I would use the pair as a gesture of goodwill to our friends to the north."

"Wow, that is noble of you, letting Yuri kill two innocent people as a gesture of goodwill. Let me think about it." She glanced up at the light bulb for half-a-second. "Naw."

Abraham's smile vanished. "That's what I thought. The hallmark of the Denier is extreme selfishness. I'm trying to bring two city-states together in peace but since you lack the vision to see that, I will sweeten the pot so to speak. I could make your *passing* easier."

"How?" Sarah asked, hearing the hope in her own voice. Immediately she felt embarrassed by her weakness, but just the same, she didn't retract the question.

"You may think that I am some sort of monster, but in truth, I do not wish to cause anyone pain, not even you. My wish is to free people who are trapped by sin to give them a chance at heaven. Sadly there are some who can't be freed with reason and must be freed through the purity of fire. That being said, since it is not against God's commandments, I will frequently give a Denier a hallucinogen before their purifying. You'd still feel the pain, but you'd be in such a state that you wouldn't care. As an example, one girl just watched as the fire ate her right up. It was chilling, but at the same time comforting to know she wasn't mentally there, feeling everything you or I would feel."

The picture Abraham had painted was stuck in her head and she knew it wouldn't leave. "You're a sick fuck," Sarah seethed. "You pretend the drugs are to help your victims, but I think it's just so you get a better show out of them. Did you claim that one girl who let the fire eat her was possessed? Was her bizarre behavior your proof?"

Abraham shook his head with so much faux-sadness that if her hands weren't cuffed behind her back she would've punched him. "Let us worry about you. The fire is a hard death. Think about it."

Another sneering laugh cracked Sarah's lips. "You should be more worried about your own death, *prophet*. History isn't kind to religious leaders when their time catches up to them. Will they crucify you upside down like they did Saint Peter? Or stone you to death? Or do you have some poisoned Kool-Aid ala Jim Jones?"

His eyes turned hard, but not before Sarah was sure she saw a touch of fear in them. "Laugh if you wish," he hissed. "Laugh right into the fire. But look around as you do. I am the Lord's Prophet. He has protected me. He has rejoiced in my presence here on earth. He has given…"

Now it was her turn to roll her eyes. "Blah, blah, blah. I'm not giving up my friends."

His eyes flashed once more before he was able to control himself. With a great sigh, he went to the ladder and leaned back against it, hooking one heel on the lowest rung. "So be it. They're probably at that little house we found Mark in not so many weeks ago. I shall send a team. When they're found, you're going to wish you had cooperated."

"I really doubt that's where they are," she said icily. Surprisingly, he only shrugged and then turned around to head back up the ladder. "That's it?" she asked. "That's all the blustering you have for me?"

"I think it's a little late for more blustering as you called it. I'm not angry since I never really thought you'd tell me. Did you expect torture?" Her facial expression spoke for her and he laughed in his big way. "How would it look if the *Prophet of the Lord* tortured people?"

"Not good, I guess."

"Finally, your wisdom has shown through your insolence."

"Are you expecting me to say thank you?" she asked as he paused after the remark.

"Since it was intended as a compliment, yes." He started up the ladder saying over his shoulder, "See you in a few hours."

"Wait!" Sarah hissed. There was a question inside that had been burning her guts for the last month. "Why do you want Eve so badly? You're not going to *do* anything to her, are you?" He paused on the stairs and she saw his eyes shift down and away. She'd never had a clairvoyant moment in her life. Nor was she any more intuitive than the next person, but just then she knew with every ounce of her being what Abraham planned for Eve.

"Don't you dare!" Sarah screamed. Abraham went up the ladder, considerably stiffer than when he came down. Because her hands were cuffed, Sarah tried to kick the ladder down. It was her intention to stomp him to death. "Don't you dare, you sick fuck! Get down here!"

Then he was gone, and the ladder was drawn up.

"Don't touch her, please." Sarah stood, begging up at the black hole above her. What Abraham was going to do to Eve was too much to bear. She fell into the shadows and cried until every drop of moisture had left her and she felt hollow and old.

The hours dripped by. At first her brain was too numb for her to do anything but lie on the hard-packed earth and moan in misery. Eventually, her throat cracked and her eyes were so bloodshot she could feel the veins in them like hot, red threads. When she realized that not only were her hands numb, but her arms all the way to her shoulders were as well, she picked herself up and tried to shake herself to get the circulation going again.

As she did she tried her best to plan and to plot her way into an escape, but her ability to channel even the least of Jillybean's intuition failed her. With the steel cuffs so tight, there was no getting out of her make-shift prison.

Next, she tried to force her tired brain into creating some combination of words that she could scream to Abraham's Believers before they set her on fire. Something that would get them to turn on him, to rise up and overthrow his insane rule. However, when she played

Devil's Advocate and took his side to rebut her own arguments, they melted like cotton candy in a storm.

Not only did he have "God" on his side he had the fantastic *fear* of God on his side. All she had were accusations and nothing else.

She was still racking her brain for an answer when an early dinner of ground venison and corn was brought for her by two of the Sisters, one of whom covered Sarah with a taser while the other placed a plastic plate on the dirt next to the ladder. Neither of the women spoke. Sarah glanced once at the food and then turned away. She was too afraid of what was coming to eat and the sight of it made her nauseous. After a few minutes she kicked the plate into the crap-trough.

It was nearly six p.m. by then.

She would be "purified" after the six o'clock service. That's what Abraham had decreed earlier in the day when she had been brought before him. Though Sarah had been shackled, she had been accompanied by four Sisters, all of whom were armed. They had pushed her to her knees in front of him and he only stared until Shondra, her one-time best friend came forward to identify Sarah and denounce her as a Denier.

Abraham's eyebrow twitched just a single time as he recognized Sarah, but he didn't rant or rave. He feigned sadness at her betrayal and called her Judas. *"Every great prophet of the Lord must bear this burden of a Judas in his midst. Pray there is only one denier amongst us."*

Obediently, the Sisters and Shondra had begun praying. Sarah had been too stunned to do anything more productive than to gaze around, hoping to catch sight of Eve.

Now, in her pit she strained to hear the frantic praying that would mean the service had started. The air was dead and fetid. It was heavy as well, like a weight that sagged her shoulders and bent her back. She leaned on the dirt wall and that was when she felt the vibrations through the earth.

My Life. My Death. For you.

She knew the words and began to mumble them under her breath. It was soothing in its way to be able to just turn off her brain and mindlessly chant. It seemed to go on longer than normal, but eventually it had to come to an end. The vibrations ceased and silence held sway in the earth.

Sarah began to shake uncontrollably.

Chapter 37

Sadie

Monticello, Georgia

Jillybean ran, disappearing from Sadie's peripheral vision. The Goth girl couldn't spare even a second to see which way she went. The black truck with the bounty hunter behind the wheel was going about eighty and it would be on them in seconds, if she didn't do something to slow it down.

Up came the M4 and she sighted down it, feeling cool metal press against her cheek. At two hundred yards, the truck was too big to miss. She started ripping lead into it as fast as she could while all around her feet hot brass danced and skipped with a merry jingle on the pavement. Silver-white stars began appearing in the truck's windshield, letting Sadie know she was on target.

The truck yawed hard to the side and stopped with a screech of tires. For a split second, Sadie felt a rush, thinking she had killed the bounty hunter, but then the black muzzle of his rifle appeared over the hood. She dove behind the Jetta as the air whipped and cracked around her.

After counting to five, she was about to leap up and return fire when she saw that the M4's ejection port was open—she was out of ammo! She started patting her pockets when she remembered the extra magazines were in her pack and that was in the Jetta which seemed to be disintegrating as the hunter kept her pinned behind it. She poked her head up for a second and felt the wind of a passing bullet.

"Holy shit!" she cried, ducking back down.

For a few more seconds the Jetta absorbed an amazing amount of punishment and then the tok, tok, tok of bullets thumping home ceased, it was replaced by the zip of them passing overhead. Sadie was confused; did he expect her to stand up?

The confusion didn't last long. It was startled out of her by the roar of a second engine. In amazement, she turned to see Captain Grey's Humvee charging. It blazed right past her, jinking hard, left and right. Without thinking of the consequences, Sadie jumped up and went for the extra ammo; she only had seconds.

Captain Grey was charging the hunter, virtually unarmed.

Neil had been armed with the axe. Nico, because of his bad arm had been given the shotgun and Sadie had been given Grey's M4. Grey was charging with only his Humvee and a knife.

Sadie yanked open the back seat of the Jetta, stuffed her hand into the pack and, like magic, a magazine was right there. In four seconds the rifle was ready to fire. She pulled herself back out only to see the black truck taking off in peel of rubber. Thankfully the bounty hunter didn't seem to realize that Grey's charge was all bluff.

Quickly she lowered her weapon. The last thing she wanted was to accidentally disable the truck; the bounty hunter would come out shooting and it would be quickly apparent that no one in the humvee was shooting back.

When the two vehicles disappeared around the corner, Sadie took off at a sprint, not after Grey, but after Jillybean. Things had transpired so quickly that the girl had maybe a twenty-five second head start, which wasn't much when Sadie's speed was factored in. In a full sprint she raced down the side street Jillybean had disappeared down.

As expected the girl wasn't in sight.

"Jillybean!" she called. No answer. Halfway down the block, Sadie slowed and tried using her brains instead of her legs. Jillybean couldn't match her in speed. She would hide or use a trick of some sort. The street off the main strip did not boast much: a used book shop with all its windows blown out, a rib joint, an antique store, and a dive bar advertising a three-lane bowling alley in the back.

To her right a zombie was lurching in her direction, seeming to have come from the book store. Did the beast have any significance? Had it just been attracted by all the shooting, or was it heading her way because of something Jillybean had done? Sadie was almost paralyzed with indecision.

Since it was coming from a book store that could mean that Jillybean had run in there, hidden, and tossed out a magic marble to get the zombie to leave. Sadie took a single step toward the book store. Or...it could be that's what Jillybean wanted Sadie to think. She knew that when Sadie saw the book store she would associate it with Jillybean. Would Jillybean employ a double-misdirection?

"Ugh! I hate using my brain," Sadie cried.

The zombie was still coming. It was a slow one, gimpy because it was missing most of its left foot. Sadie concluded that it had been moving even before she had run down the alley—which meant that Jilly hadn't included Sadie in her thinking when she had run away. Maybe. When Jillybean had started running away, she had to have thought the gun battle would last longer than it did, which meant the zombie was random.

"Good job, brain," Sadie said.

The zombie had originally been moving diagonally on a line that would have put it going down an alley across the street. Sadie dashed for the alley. It was short, barely fifty yards and the second she turned into it, she saw Jillybean at the far end crouched in a doorway. In one hand she held Ipes; she was waiting as another zombie was passing blithely by the alley.

She turned when she heard the slap of Sadie's Converse on the alley floor. "Leave us alone." Her voice shook and her eyes twitched.

"No, I can't. Let me talk to her, please. You didn't give me a chance before. You didn't let me finish."

Jillybean swayed, holding to the rough brick edges of the doorway with her free hand. "You tried. You failed. You can't make us stay. You know that."

Sadie went down to one knee and touched Jillybean's hair; it was going everywhere as usual. She patted it down. "I want her to stay because *she* wants to. Just give me a chance, let me talk to her."

"No. I know what you want her for. You want to use her. She's your little, trained monkey, but not anymore." She pulled away with a glare but Sadie grabbed her arms again, gentle but firm.

Jillybean blew out. "We are at an impasse. You have the strength to carry her back, but I have the will to run away again and next time I won't leave vehicles intact. Next time it will be much harder. So I suggest a deal. I'll tell you where you can find the army to attack New Eden. I'll even tell you how to attack it, but you have to agree to let us go."

"No," Sadie said flatly. "You're afraid of New Eden, but you don't have to be. I'd never let you step one foot in there. Neil and I and Captain Grey would go. You'd be safe."

Jillybean considered this for a second and then shook her head slowly. "What if you all die?"

"Let me tell Jillybean what would happen."

For some reason, Ipes agreed to this. He nodded Jillybean's head and then a second later she jumped as if a spider had dropped down her back. Sadie grabbed her thin shoulders and hugged her.

"Am I sleepwalking?" Jillybean asked. Her eyes were afraid. She looked around without comprehension. "I keep having this dream like I'm walking around talking to people. Like before, we were talking and then there were guns and now we're here. Is everyone alright?"

Sadie didn't know. The sound of the car chase had faded. "I dunno. I hope so, but…" She shrugged her left shoulder. "It's a dangerous world now and something could happen at any time. Right?"

"Yeah." Jillybean looked nervous all of a sudden as though Sadie was about to drop bad news on her. Instead the Goth girl stuck out her pinky, hooking it slightly.

"You know what this is?" Sadie asked.

"Pinky swear?"

"That's right. A pinky swear is a bond that can't be broken. Ever. Put out your pinky."

Jillybean's eyes went wide and she switched Ipes to her other arm and held out her pinky. Sadie snared it with hers so that the two were locked together by their little fingers.

"I swear I'll be your big sister no matter what happens," Sadie said, nodding solemnly.

Jillybean showed her little kid teeth in a big smile. "And I'll be your little sister. No matter what, too."

They stared into each other's eyes for a few seconds. Jillybean because she was so happy, Sadie because she was worried about Ipes returning.

"About Ipes," Sadie began.

Immediately Jilly's smile faltered and she canted her head as if listening. Then she grew grim and her lips pursed. "He says he's been bad and that we're here," she paused, looking around in confusion. "We're wherever we are, because of him."

"Yeah. He sort of took over your body. Can you stop him from doing that? I don't think it's good for you. You hear that, Ipes? You're hurting her."

Jillybean put her little hand to her mouth as though trying to hold something in. She pulled Sadie closer and whispered, "I don't know if I can stop him. He just does it."

"Then maybe we shouldn't give him a reason to do it," Sadie said, standing and holding out her hand. Hand-in-hand, they strolled back the way they had come, dodging around the gimping, slow zombie when they came to it. "I'll do my best to keep you safe. You won't have to go anywhere near New Eden. I promise. Ok? Come on, I have a radio in the car that you can call Neil with. He was worried sick for you."

At the car, Jillybean listened to the instructions about the proper radio procedure and followed them to a T. "Silver this is Pink, over."

"Ah, it's so good to hear your voice, Pink. Where have you been? We've been going out of our minds."

"Don't answer that, Pink," Captain Grey cut in. "Silver, this is Blue. Maintain proper radio procedures. We will rendezvous at position G. Out."

"Ok, got it," Neil said through the crackling radio. "Sorry about that. I was just…"

"Silver this is Blue. When I say *out* that means the conversation is done. *Out.*"

"Mister Neil is in big trouble," Jillybean laughed, handing back the radio. "So where are we, and what does rend-a-voo mean? And where is position G? Is that a town?"

Sadie had been watching her closely, rather than really listening. "What? Oh, we're somewhere in Georgia. And rendezvous means to gather together, and position G was my old position. G for green. I was looking out for you in this dinky little town called Jackson. It's about five miles away."

This last she said without much enthusiasm. She had just run those five miles and didn't really feel like doing it again. They contemplated hanging out, waiting for Captain Grey to see if he would come pick them up, however there were seven or eight zombies heading their way. A few moseying towards them from the direction they wanted to go.

"We'll have to go around," Sadie said. She allowed Jillybean to pick the best course back to the main east-to-west road. The little girl seemed to have a natural compass built into her. She went south, poking her way through an apartment complex and then snaked a route among the heaps in a junk yard.

They hopped a fence, leapt across a sodden drainage ditch, and then curved to their right. They came up on the road without a problem and it wasn't long before Captain Grey's Humvee came speeding down it. The army vehicle had seen better days. The windshield was gone, the headlights were destroyed, and the engine was smoking and smelled of harsh chemicals.

The man wasn't in much better shape. There was blood on his clothes and a long scrape that ran along one cheek. "She ok?" He asked of Jillybean.

"Doing better," Sadie said. "I think it's best if we keep the action to a minimum around her."

"Fine by me. Get in."

Jillybean was apologetic for causing so many problems, but she was loath to discipline Ipes. "I'd chuck him out the window if I thought it would do a lick of good," Grey told her.

"I can't do that," she said, dropping her chin. "He was only trying to protect me, but—but he says he won't do it again."

"Uh-huh, right. The way I see it, if he's still talking to you he's still a problem. Why don't you have Sadie put him away in her pack?"

She reluctantly agreed and then, not a minute later, fell asleep, resting her head on Sadie's lap. "Take your time," Sadie said to the captain. "She needs lots of rest. I doubt she slept at all last night."

They drove in silence, Grey barely doing ten miles-an-hour. He kept glancing back at Jillybean. "I know you think she's crazy," Sadie said, "but I could say the same thing for you. Why the hell did you go after the bounty hunter unarmed?"

For the first time since she had met him, Captain Grey looked uncomfortable. "You wouldn't understand."

She blurted out the first thought that sprang to her teenaged-mind: "What? Do you like me or something?" He laughed at the suggestion in such an honest manner that Sadie was almost insulted. "Ok, then what is it?"

"I guess you could say I made a promise. Now drop the subject."

She did, but clearly it was still on his mind and he regained his composure only very slowly. Changing the subject helped. "The worst part is I didn't get him," Grey said. "He's a slick one, that dirty bastard."

Sadie touched him on the shoulder, giving him a little pat. "Thanks for trying and thanks for saving me. I was really screwed."

"Yeah, well," was all he said in response. They were silent after that. When the Butts County courthouse tower came into view, Sadie yawned and stretched.

She shook Jillybean awake. "I see Neil and Nico. They've been very worried about you. They'll want a hug."

"Ok," she said blearily, her eyes only partially open. Neil came up smiling, but the captain held up his broad hand.

"Hugs can wait," Grey said. "We need to talk about this army you mentioned, Jillybean." Sadie's lips drew into a line and she began to shake her head. "Simmer down, Sadie. If I have an army I won't need Jillybean. She'll be perfectly safe."

"We just want to hear what she has to say," Neil put in.

"It's them," Jillybean said pointing at a couple of zombies, slouching their way from the courthouse. "It's the army of the monsters."

Grey's face went hard as rock. It was obvious he was holding back an angry tirade by the barest of margins. "They're not an army. You can't control them."

"Yes, sir, you can," Jillybean said. "Sort of at least. The Believers use the strobe lights to control where they go. You told us that. We can too, if we want to."

"Go on," Grey said.

"Go on, where? Oh, you mean you want to hear my whole plan? That's simple. We take the lights and line them up at the silo we want the monsters to attack. Then we use your hand grenades, that's what means bombs, and blow up the door to the silo and then we blow up the doors down into New Eden. They're not that strong."

"A lot of people are going to die if you do that," Grey said.

"A lot of evil people," Sadie said, jumping in. "Evil and crazy. We told you what happened to our friend Sarah. And look what they did to poor Arthur. They killed him. Letting a crazy man free to wander around zombie infested lands is a death sentence and one he didn't deserve. They are all guilty of at least aiding and abetting kidnapping and murder. I have no sympathy for any of them."

"What about Sarah and Eve?" Neil asked. "This plan seems really dangerous. It'll be a race to see who gets to them first, us or the zombies."

Jillybean was in the process of digging out the cheese and crackers from Sadie's MRE when she paused to say: "It's not as dangerous as you think. Miss Sarah isn't like the Believers. They have been living underground like mole-people, they don't know how to deal with the monsters, but she does. She's real smart and tough. I think the hardest part is not missing her as she makes her own escape."

"This plan has a gaping hole in it," Grey said. "First we have to get to the lights without getting shot or eaten alive. And then once we unleash the zombies, they'll be between us and Sarah."

The little girl squirted the soft cheese onto the cracker, pausing to lick some off her thumb. "Yes sir, but you're wrong. We will be dressed as the monsters so we can go where we want."

"Dress like monsters. Is that a joke?"

"Yes Sir, it is not a joke. We…"

The captain groaned. "Stop saying it like that. It's yes sir or no sir. Got it?"

Jillybean nodded. "Yes sir."

"Hey, come on. Lighten up, Captain," Neil said. "She's doing the best she can and I happen to think she's doing very well. This plan is good. We've all played zombie at one time or another, except for maybe Nico. I'm sure he'll pick it up quick."

"Not this time he won't," Grey said. "He's injured. He'll stay with Jillybean and Sadie outside."

"Me?" Sadie cried. "Why can't I go?"

"Because we only have two weapons between us," Grey said in a hard-as-rock growl. "Because I need someone up top I can trust to keep an eye out on our line of retreat. Because with this sort of job, too many cooks will cock-up the broth big time. And because two people is all we need. Two people go in, only! We stay together. We don't play the hero. We get the prisoners and get out. Now, what do we need to play zombie-dress up?"

"So this is happening?" Neil asked. He almost looked like he was about to laugh his smile was so big. "What made you change your mind?"

Again Grey got that uncomfortable, somewhat embarrassed expression on his face. He was slow to reply so Sadie answered for him. "He's made some sort of promise. It's a big secret, which I think he should share."

"Why don't you shut your trap?" the captain barked in that hard way of his, except this time it was tinged with embarrassment and Sadie only smiled impishly.

Chapter 38

Sarah

New Eden, Georgia

After the chanting came silence. This lasted hardly a minute and then came the unrelenting, machine-like tapping of teeth-on-teeth. Sarah's jaw quivered without let up. She didn't try to stop it. What was the point? All she had was her fear. It drove her into a queasy anticipation.

She stood in the grooved marks where the ladder had been and stared up until voices came, flickering in her ears at first, but then growing steadily. They were coming for her.

Reflexively, as though it would make her invisible, she scurried away and put her back to the furthest corner of the pit and crouched down.

"Shit, shit, shit," she repeated, striking a frenzied whiny tone until the voices were so close she knew they were in her tunnel. There was the metallic scrape of the ladder and then she saw it being lowered.

"Go away!" she screamed as the first of the Sisters came down.

Sarah had hoped to be brave when the time came. She had pictured herself fighting, using only her feet—breaking bone with each of her powerful kicks. She had been brave in her fantasy. She had seen the Sisters for what they really were: jealous, little shrews, armed with clipboards, holier-than-thou self-righteousness, and of course their pistols.

None of which she really feared, not at this late stage of the game. She knew they wouldn't shoot her; that would spoil all the fun of burning her alive. And what did Sarah care now about demerits or haughty looks? Not a whit.

But that had been the fantasy Sarah Rivers, the one who was brave. The real Sarah cringed and pleaded. Two of the Sisters carried tasers and they weren't for show.

"Turn and face the wall," one of them ordered. Sarah did without question. Her insides shook.

The cuff on her left hand was removed briefly and her arms were tugged in front of her where the handcuffs were reattached. She cried out in pain; her shoulders had been pinned back for so long it felt like the cartilage in their sockets had calcified. There was no pity on the faces of the Sisters.

They tugged her to the ladder where one of them pointed upwards and said with a twisted mouth: *Git.*

Sarah did her best to please the cruel women. She stumbled up the ladder, a three-step process—foot, foot, hands—foot, foot, hands—which she repeated over and over. Halfway up, she lost her breath. It wasn't that she was tired, she just couldn't seem to pull air into her lungs.

When she paused, feeling a panic attack grip her, she was punched in the back by the Sister just beneath her. The Sister barked: *Git, Git.* Sarah found it impossible to move, until one of them mentioned something about getting the "hook." Her imagination went wild and, when she pictured herself being hauled up by a meat hook shoved through her back, she began to pant. Only then was she able to continue on.

At the top were more of the Sisters who drew together and formed a kind of ceremonial guard. Three went abreast in front and three behind pushing constantly and whispering threats. In spite of that her feet dragged and she leaned back into them. What lay ahead of Sarah was a thousand times worse than a few nasty women.

Git, git.

I'll taze you, bitch if you don't walk.

The Sister directly in front of her reached back and grabbed the cuffs by the short chain and pulled Sarah along.

More than ever the halls of New Eden were a maze. Nothing looked as it had only hours before. They passed

351

the little hospital and for five steps Sarah knew where she was, but then they took a turn and she was lost again. Just as she began to wonder if they were leading her in circles, they took a side corridor that went steeply downhill at an angle.

"Where are we going?"

"We're bringing you closer to hell, Denier," a man's voice answered.

Sarah yelped and turned back to see that Abraham had joined them. He wore robes of velvet black that made his hair seem to ripple and flow like liquid silver.

"I didn't do anything. Please, you know that, Abraham."

In anger over Sarah's disrespectful tone, the Sister in front gave a yank on the cuffs and at the same time the one directly behind tried to hit Sarah in the right kidney. The effects cancelled each other out so that she only felt roughly jostled. Abraham smirked but said nothing until they reached a large double set of doors. There was a handle of pearl on each and the hinges were made of gold. Beyond was a cacophony of voices. It was complete babbling nonsense, but it was loud. The Believers were gathered and were trying to outdo one another in their praise for their vile prophet.

Sarah's legs failed her, the muscles became soft and the bones felt hollow. Like a ragdoll she dropped, limp to the floor. "I can't do this," she said in a whisper, her cheek resting against sterile white linoleum.

The Sisters dragged her to her feet and pinned her to the wall to keep her upright. Behind, Abraham sighed. "Carry her if she does that again."

Two of the Sisters went to the doors, one to each of the pearl handles and paused awaiting orders. "Wait!" Sarah screamed. "Please...m-my Lord Abraham. I need to confess." She had nothing to confess, but she was so afraid of going into the Exorcism chamber that she was willing to make something up.

His near-perpetual smile widened. He shooed the Sisters back and asked, "You'd like to confess? About your friends? The ones on the outside or the ones on the inside?"

Sarah's mouth came open as she tried to fathom what he was talking about. Friends on the outside she could understand, Neil and Sadie, but who could possibly be her friend in New Eden? Her confusion and fear mixed, addling her mind even further. She could only reply, "Huh?"

"Who are you working with?" Abraham asked, coming close. "I sent a team out today to collect Sadie and the Russian from that house, but the two of them just happened to slip away right before my men got there. They say the coals in the fireplace were still hot. That's a pretty big coincidence, them just leaving like that, don't you think?"

Though he still smiled in his smarmy way, Sarah saw that it wasn't quite so natural as usual. There was a tension to it as though at any moment it would snap into a scowl.

Sarah had no answer to his question; she started to shake her head and that was all it took for the smile to disappear. "Who are you working with!" he demanded, his spittle making her blink. "Look at me! Who told them we were coming? Who? Chastity? Shondra? Are you and Shondra playing some sort of two-faced game?"

"No, I haven't seen Shondra in a month." It had been all of ten seconds since she had decided to make "something up" but in her fear that was forgotten and all she wanted to do was please this evil man in the hope he would see her honesty and let her go.

"Then who is it and what are you up to?" He came closer so that his angry, hot breath was right in her face. "Remember how I said I could make your passing easier? Well I can also make it a thousand times worse. I control the heat and the smoke. I can slow roast you if I wish. I can keep you alive for an hour as your skin blisters and then peels away like a rotten banana."

"Please, please don't do that." She tried to think beyond the image he had stuck in her mind, but nothing beyond begging occurred to her. "Please don't, please."

"I won't," he said, his smile returning. It was the oily smile of a used-car salesman making promises he wouldn't keep. "All you have to do is tell me who's in it with you. And don't try to tell me there's no plan. You let it slip, my dear. Remember, you warned me about what happens to religious leaders. You were a little more certain of yourself then."

"I-I don't know. Really, there isn't..."

"Liar!" he hissed. The smile vanished again and now the tension in his face had gone over to hysteria. "It's Chastity, isn't it? She had access to me, and she tried to get you assigned to the pharmacy...probably so you could poison me or drug me." He started pacing, mumbling to himself, his paranoia growing. Sarah saw it in his eyes, blooming dangerously and she tried to shrink down to something insignificant to keep from being its target.

"Was it her? It had to be. The only question is how did she get a radio? Sisters can't leave New Eden..." he paused wetting his lips with a pale tongue. "...She's working with one of the Brothers. Now I see. Is it Mark? Or Jim?" He had pressed in close once more and they were practically nose to nose.

"No. I don't know what's going on," Sarah said desperately. "I came for Eve."

"That's just your excuse," he sneered. "You aren't even her real mother. Eve is the excuse you're using to distract me from the real issue. Last month it was Lenny and now, Chastity and who else?" He turned away from Sarah and snapped his long fingers. The sound summoned one of the Sisters. She rushed forward and dropped to one knee.

"Yes, my Lord?"

Gently, he raised her up by her arm and the two began walking back to where the other Sisters were kneeling. "Kelly, let's have the front row cordoned off again. I'll want to see Chastity, Mark, and Shondra, of course..." His voice trailed away with the distance. Sarah could only stand in the corner where the doors met the wall and hope they would forget about her.

Kelly and two of the other Sisters sprinted away at top speed and Abraham came back slowly with a thoughtful expression. "Your plan is doomed. And you know what? I think it's actually better you didn't rat out your friends earlier. Now I get to see the reaction on their traitorous faces when you confess in front of all of New Eden."

After a short while in which Sarah only stood staring at the floor and feeling her soul shrivel, the Sisters returned to say that the traitors had been rounded up. Abraham laughed in his booming way, however his smile was tight at the corners and the worry in his eyes never left.

"Time for the purification," he announced. "Time for you, Sarah, to sacrifice your body for the sake of your soul."

Sister Kelly raised her small hand and knocked loudly three times on the double doors. There was a pause and then a Sister went to each of the pearl handles and flung the doors wide. Sarah cringed, expecting her senses to be assaulted by chants or screams of religious passion, but the room and the nine hundred souls in it were utterly silent.

It was so quiet that Sarah could hear the *scritch* of pen on paper when one of the Sisters, down the next aisle, scribbled something on her clipboard. The only other sound was the soft tread of the ceremonial guard, its prisoner and her executioner.

She was marched to the strange pyramid; up close she saw that it was composed of hand-carved, white granite slabs. She was forced to take extra tall steps to get up its steep side. Two Sisters kept her moving, each with a vice-like grip on her arms.

At the top, they removed her handcuffs and tore off her robe, leaving her shivering in fright wearing nothing but her bra and panties, and on her feet, leather sandals. Her hands were then bound once more, this time in a set of shackles. These were one size-fits-all and rattled loosely on her wrists when she gave them a shake. Between the iron bands on her wrists was a three foot length of chain that went through a wide-mouthed ring set on a waist-high pole. The pole was welded in the center of a fire-blackened grate and below that was a stack of wood.

The smell of kerosene wafted up from the wood, making Sarah dizzier than she had already been. She had to hold onto the short pole to stay upright. At first she hung her head, however the closeness of the wood made her want to retch—it was right there, inches below her feet. She knew the fire would eat her up...

"Oh, dear Lord," she whispered and looked up at the ceiling, thinking there, at least, she would get a respite from the images assaulting her, however the ceiling was worse. It was black as hell, scorched and smoke-bit. Embedded in the charring were flecks of grey ash and what looked like bits of blackened leaves hanging and curled.

That's skin.

Her mind reeled. She forced her eyes to the people, searching for Neil. He had to be there somewhere. He had to save her. The faces, all of which were blurred by hate, were unrecognizable. Only the ones right below her were familiar: Chastity, Shondra, Mark, and the hillbilly-looking fellow who had twice let Sarah into New Eden. Next to them were the four members of the hospital staff as well as Sarah's roommates, Dinah and the two women she had dubbed the "robot twins."

All of them, with the exception of the mindless, drone-like robot twins, looked to be on the verge of shitting themselves. They had good reason to be afraid. One word from Sarah would mean their own horrible deaths.

Abraham had come to the top of the pyramid and now the two of them were alone. "Which of them are in cahoots with you?" he asked so that only she could hear.

His voice sent her into a panic. Uselessly she pulled back on her chain, finding that she was excruciatingly close to being able to pull herself free. Her hands were just a fraction of an inch too big to slip out of the shackles. She then yanked back and forth on the chain, again, in vain. If she pulled her right hand back it only sent her left hand forward to the post and vice-versa.

When she pulled back with both arms and grunted under the strain of trying to break an expertly set weld, Abraham scoffed: "There is only one way you're getting out of here: they'll scoop your remains up in a Hefty bag. But you can make it quick. Who is it? You can tell me now or tell me after your toes are burned down to the nubs."

Her terror-filled brain was barely operable at this point, yet she knew one thing with certitude: Abraham was going to make it slow no matter what she said. He'd had done this enough times to know that she would eventually turn over every one of the people in the little cordoned area—guilty or not. In her agony, she would cry out every name she knew and Abraham, possessed by his paranoia would believe each one to be his enemy.

Instead of answering, Sarah gave up. There would be no escape, no rescue, no redemption. She would die horribly and she would die alone.

Abraham said something to her, but she didn't hear. He pouted for a moment, like a petulant child, and then began his sermon. It was long-winded and self-aggrandizing. He laid blame everywhere for what was about to happen and took none for himself. He made demands of his Believers, saying they lacked faith and that because of this treason they would have to work harder to earn his faith, and thus God's as well.

It seemed, simultaneously to go on a long time and at the same time pass by in a blink. With a shout to the ceiling Abraham announced God's punishment for sin and lit the fire. It was not slow to catch. The kerosene jacked the flames which reached up through the grating and seared her legs and ankles.

"Oh God!" she cried and leapt back. Her feet were free; she could move them however she wished, but only to the extent the short chain, stretching through the loop, would allow; it wasn't much. She danced in place, each step more painful than the last, while her face sweated gleaming, liquid diamonds that seemed to shoot light. She could see that light reflected in Abraham's evil eyes. He smirked and she cried out.

Very quickly, the pain became too much and she pulled her feet off the grate and hung from her wrists, her body extended over the flames.

She screamed into the fire and the fire crowded higher. Sarah felt her lips crack and heard the hiss as her sweat and tears hit the grating. In seconds, she was unable to bear the heat baking upward and her body reacted on its own to the agony. With her feet still in misery she was left with only one choice: she spun in place so that she hung by her wrists, the heels of her blackened sandals resting on the granite, her face to the ceiling.

It took no more than a few moments before the skin on her back formed blisters. They were like large, wet soap bubbles that popped as she writhed.

To her ears it sounded like the whole world was screaming, that every one of the nine hundred Believers were shrieking right along with Sarah. But it was just her. The Believers knelt in silence, learning the lesson to never, ever, misbehave, not even in the slightest manner. Sarah was sure she cried out for help, but not a person budged.

Only she moved, going round and round like a pig at a luau. Just as Abraham had told her, she was being slowly roasted alive.

He squatted down next to her, his face aglow from the fire and filled with a happy cruelty. "Are you ready to confess your nasty sins?"

Chapter 39

Neil

New Eden, Georgia

As the evening was particularly pleasant, Neil's profuse sweating was due solely to a case of stage fright. Under a slap of make-up and wearing only rags, he was performing a one-man show that he called: *I'm a zombie, too. Please don't eat me!* His audience consisted of about three thousand walking corpses who wanted nothing more than to eat the lips from his still screaming mouth.

Thankfully, the first part of Jillybean's insane plan was nearly over with. In the light of day, with only a stray zombie or two walking about, the plan had seemed reasonable. Now, his hands trembled as he went for the last strobe he needed. They came with little metal hoods that allowed the strobes to act like the lights on an airstrip, pointing the zombies to go in a certain direction. Once he got this one, he would then replant each of them so they pointed directly at the silo they planned to attack. A mile away, Grey was doing the same thing at what they were referring to as the "decoy silo."

The five silos were arranged around the valley in such a way that from the air they resembled a smiley face—the two northern silos, the decoy and the one they planned to attack were the "eyes" while the other three to the south made up the smile. Each of these latter had been assigned an observer; Nico was furthest southwest, while Sadie, who could react the quickest in either direction, was in the middle and Jillybean was the closest to the attack silo. Save for a couple of axes these three were unarmed. Their job was to watch for Sarah and Eve.

It was expected that some, if not all of the Believers would try to flee from the silos and that Sarah would try to hide within their numbers.

Neil was sure it would be chaos.

"Oh damn," he whispered as the strobe he had been approaching flashed in his face. None of the zombies took note of the little noise. They were too busy stumbling toward the light—seconds later, and a hundred yards further on, another strobe flashed in the dark—the zombies turned their attention to it while Neil tugged up the closer one.

"Finally," he said, stowing the strobe away in his backpack.

One of the zombies must have heard the word and turned, reminding Neil he wasn't out of the woods yet.

"Uuagh," Neil moaned and then made a weird limpy step as though one of his legs was longer than the other while at the same time he leaned his head all the way over so that his ear rested on his shoulder.

The zombie came close and stared for a moment and then, satisfied as to Neil's undead authenticity, it turned away, losing itself in the night. Neil felt the need to congratulate himself on his acting ability. He wanted to brag into the radio but after his close call he went to work resetting the strobes instead. To save time he turned them on after he planted each. When he was ready to set the last he saw a flaw in his thinking.

Five strobes were pointing thousands of zombies directly at the attack silo, which was exactly where he was standing. How was he going to plant the strobe, a very human activity, under so many watchful eyes? He hesitated in fear for so long that he became surrounded by the milling beasts, one of whom took particular attention in him.

"What are you waiting for?" it growled, nearly making Neil shriek. It was Captain Grey, looking like a hulking and very realistic zombie, except for the eyes, these were far too intelligent and driven.

"I'm doing it," Neil whispered.

With a deep breath, Neil jug-walked in a circle, keeping his chin down and his eyes up, spying to see who or what was focused on him. The zombies were mindlessly milling about and the silo was a brooding dark totem, silent and grim. Someone could be staring right down at him for all he knew, but there was nothing he could do it except plant the strobe.

Quickly he dropped to one knee and, very much by accident, his thumb hit the "on" switch and it flashed right into his face, illuminating him for a fraction of a second for all the world to see.

Blindly he stuck the light in the ground and by feel he aimed it in the right direction, and then he was up again, walking into things and tripping over divots and chuck holes, feeling more like a real zombie than ever before.

A blurred outline of another zombie came up and snorted, "Nice move." It was Grey again and as Neil couldn't tell if other zombies were close by he didn't retort, though he did shove the big man—with little discernible effect.

Gradually over the next few minutes, Neil's eyesight returned. He saw that the evening had turned into an early, clear night; above, the Milky Way sprawled across the sky in an unwinding scroll of light. Closer, the horizon was a dark, uneven outline that seemed to be moving and moaning nearer.

Neil went looking for Grey and found him loitering near the silo along with more zombies than Neil could count. Grey was impatient and man-handled the smaller man into position ten feet to the side of the doors, he then lurched back and, without the least subtlety, pulled a stretch of duct tape across a hand grenade and slapped it right above the lock on the silo door. He then stumbled away, losing himself in the mass of zombies, leaving Neil to wonder if he had pulled the pin on the grenade.

KABLAM!

The explosion sent metal and black zombie blood everywhere, Neil blinked from the light and the sound and the spray, and almost forgot he had a job to do. He was supposed to make sure the doors stayed open so that the flow of zombies into the silo wouldn't stop.

With his ears ringing, Neil searched around on the ground until he found a scabby arm that had been blown off by the explosion. He wedged it under the door. Just as he stood the first shots were fired inside the silo. Neil stifled a grin. So far, the plan was going perfectly. The guards were firing out of panic or lack of discipline, and as both Captain Grey and Jillybean had predicted it wouldn't last. After a couple of minutes, the firing tapered off as their ammo began to get low and the number of zombies seemed endless.

Grey forced his way into the silo. Neil recognized him by his size and by the long hump on his back where he had his M4 strapped beneath his rags. Across Neil's own back was the 12 gauge, pump action shot gun that had taken him an hour to saw down to size. He itched to unstrap it and carry it like a real man. Without it he felt vulnerable and way too soft.

Grey didn't seem fazed by the fact that he was in a mob of zombies empty handed. He moaned and groaned, and elbowed his way to the banked set of doors that led down into New Eden itself. The man went to one knee and when he stood back up, Neil knew enough to cover his own ears.

Seconds later there was another great boom and again there was blood flying. The zombies surged toward the sound, a river of diseased flesh and Neil was borne along like a piece of driftwood. Above him on a platform, the guards made a desperate attempt to stop the zombies from invading the lower halls by firing as fast as they could, however they didn't have enough men, nor enough ammunition and the stinking mass of undead went on, unchecked.

Neil walked with his shoulders hunched and hurried to keep up with the crowd until he was down the stairs and out of range of the bullets. Only then did he slow, hugging the walls, letting the army of the zombies go first. There would be opposition by the Believers, though what form it might take had only been guessed at.

Captain Grey caught up to him after a few minutes and together they progressed in the main body of the horde for about a hundred yards, passing a number of intersections without seeing anyone at all. "Where the hell are all the Believers?" Grey whispered beneath the persistent moaning around them.

Neil shrugged and glanced down one of the empty halls. When he glanced over to Grey, he found that they had been separated by the awkward flow of walking corpses. Nervous to be so far from his friend he began to nudge over but just then a woman in a blue robe came racing around a corner and stopped dead in her tracks at seeing the halls teeming with undead. The beasts let out a mind-numbing shriek of hatred and charged. She let out her own scream and then instead of running away, she wasted precious seconds digging frantically in her robe. When the zombies were twenty yards away she finally freed a small black pistol and commenced firing. In her panic she barely aimed and the five bullets were wasted.

Thankfully, she didn't try to reload. She would have been mauled right in front of Neil if she had. Instead she ran off screaming. He breathed a sigh of relief and then a grey hand with a grip like iron grabbed his arm making him flinch back against the wall in a very unzombie-like manner.

"Come on," Grey said, pulling Neil along, leaving behind a smear of zombie make-up on the pristine walls.

"You got to stop sneaking up on me like that," Neil hissed.

"Uh-huh," Grey grunted.

The captain kept them close to the front of the pack just in case they came across Sarah or Eve, but he also made sure not to be too close. The zombies were their shields and proved invaluable minutes later when the woman in the blue robe returned with ten or eleven more women all dressed exactly alike and all shaking in fear.

They formed two lines across the corridor and began firing and none proved any better that the first woman had been. Neil and Grey dropped to their knees and crawled over the bodies of wounded zombies, taking refuge in a south-running corridor that bisected the main one. The two of them pretended to be dead and waited for the inevitable retreat of the women. Even Neil knew they wouldn't last. Their weapons were weak and their training even weaker.

"Do you know where this leads?" Grey asked jerking his head to indicate a side hallway where the flooring was white linoleum, its walls white and plain, and the ceiling made of white tiles with a neon light every ten feet. The hallway looked like every hallway in New Eden.

"Dunno," he said.

Grey made a face that was a combination of anger and disgust. "Do you at least know..." He stopped, listening.

Mingled with the gun shots, and the moans and the distant shouts of humans that had begun to pervade the background, was the very distinctive cry of a baby. The plaintive bleat was coming from somewhere in front and to the left in the maze of halls down.

Only seconds before, what had been empty corridors were now packed wall-to-wall with zombies. The zombies were entering New Eden in such numbers that they flowed like water in every direction, especially towards anything that looked or sounded human.

Neil was stepped on, and tripped over a dozen times before he could get to his feet and struggle forward. Grey had been quicker and was close to the front of the pack, the sound of the baby drawing him on. Aggressively he shoved and jostled his way until he was just behind the first few ranks of zombies.

He was a bit too close, as it turned out.

Neil and Grey came to another crowded intersection. The sound of the baby was to the left while to their right, eight more women in matching blue robes came racing up. They were straight up terrified. In one hand they each held a black pistol and with the other they reached out and grabbed the robe of the woman next to them, anchoring themselves in place.

At a word of command, they fired a ragged volley and a number of zombies reeled. Those that fell were replaced with barely a pause. A second volley had the same effect as the first, just as did the third, meaning the gunfire was practically useless. The women were firing far too slowly and methodically. They reminded Neil of a line of Redcoats from the revolutionary war right down to the commands of: Ready! Aim! Fire!

Their fourth volley was at point blank range since they had foolishly allowed the zombies to close in on them.

"Run!" one of the women cried. The line crumbled and their last shots before fleeing went everywhere. Among the sound of snapping bullets, there was a thud and a spurt of blood—red blood. Grey dropped like a stone. By chance all of the zombies directly in front of him had been shot or had tripped over the ones that had fallen.

He was hit twice. Neil saw the captain's hand go to his chest, he saw the spray of blood and he heard him grunt. Unthinkingly, Neil bashed his way through and over zombies to get to the soldier. "Are you alright?" he asked, leaning over the man. There was a hole in his zombie rags square in the center of his chest, while at his throat was a shocking run of blood. It was bright and gleaned greasy on his makeup.

Grey was making a noise. It was a jagged, hitching sound when he tried to breath. It looked as though he was trying to say something and so Neil leaned closer. Grey slapped him across the face and said in a voice that grew weaker with each syllable: "Shut...the fuck....up. You'll...get...us...killed."

Chapter 40

Sarah

New Eden, Georgia

The smell of her own roasting flesh had Sarah gagging. The skin on her back bubbled with amazing speed and when the blisters popped they sizzled like a steak on the BBQ.

If she'd had the strength she would've puked. It was hard enough just to scream.

"Who's in it with you?" Abraham asked, leering over her. She was lying over the fire, facing the ceiling with her heels on the white granite and her weight suspended by the chains at her wrists. She had pulled herself up as far as she could but the strain was becoming too much.

"Shondra!" Sarah screeched at the top of her lungs. It was a lie and a criminal one at that, but she was beyond the ability to fathom right or wrong. All that mattered to her was getting off that fire. "And Chastity. Please make it stop! Please it hurts so bad!"

"Who else?" Abraham asked excitedly. The names had fed his paranoia and he wanted more.

Sarah couldn't answer just then. The strength in her arms gave out and she sagged closer to the flames which were jumping through the grate. Another scream ripped out of her and, with a great effort, she spun to face the flames. Unfortunately the chain slipped and her left arm rattled right down to the grate with a hiss.

The pain was so immediate, she had to stand and when she got one foot beneath her and lifted herself she left a scald of stinking flesh behind.

"Who else!" Abraham thundered.

"All of them!" she cried pointing at the group of people in the cordoned off area and dancing in place. The leather of her sandals was growing blacker by the second while blisters began to form along her calves. "Now please," she whimpered.

He ignored her. His focus was on the betrayers, who wilted beneath his anger. "All of you are guilty of…"

He stopped as a soft thrumming ran through the walls and stirred the air of the exorcism chamber. Seconds later there was the distant pop, pop, pop of gunfire. "What is that?" he asked

One of the Sisters ran up the aisle and went to the main doors. She cracked them, peering out and then jumped back as another Sister raced into the chamber with her gun drawn and her face lined with fear.

"There are zombies inside!" she yelled. "Thousands of them are in the hallways. I think one of the silos is under attack." The Believers began to look back and forth, but only with their eyes. They were more afraid of Abraham than they were of a horde of zombies invading their home.

"Which silo?" Abraham asked.

"I don't know. Number four, maybe."

Abraham stared down at Sarah who was jerking all over the place, her feet leaping in agony whenever she put them back down onto the grate. He didn't seem to notice her at all. He had a faraway look about him.

After a few seconds as the entire room seemed to lean in towards him he began to blink, rapidly, and his chin started quivering. "Kelly!" he said, looking around for the woman with eyes that were bugged crazily. When he saw her he clapped his hands in agitation. "Arrest the traitors. Put them in the pits for the time being. Where's Mary? There you are. I want you to form five squads of Sisters and block off the main hallways. I want you to stop the zombies. Do whatever it takes. Everyone else, back to your rooms."

The orders were carried out simultaneously, meaning the room was thrown immediately into chaos. There were three exits which became jammed in seconds. People yelled and pushed, surging back and forth in the aisles. Orders and counter-orders were bellowed and some of the

Sisters began swatting people out of the way with their clipboards or brandishing their pistols.

And all the while Sarah burned alive. "Help! Please, help!" She shrieked for all she was worth, but she was ignored by everyone except for Abraham.

"You did this," he said, standing over her in a wrath, pointing in accusation with a long, shaking finger. "You deserve the fires of hell. You deserve everything that the Lord in heaven…"

The sounds of more guns firing followed by a wave of screams shut him up. He went from a pillar of holy indignation to a cringing man-child in the turn of a second and then in the next he fled, leaping down the stone stairs and vanishing in the mayhem.

It was a testament to the unimaginable misery she was suffering that Sarah begged for him to come back. He did not and she was alone at the top of the pyramid flopping about in agony, burning one part of herself at a time until she came to the realization that the only way to escape was to make a sacrifice.

With all her strength, Sarah pulled back on the chain with her right hand, this of course, meant that her left hand and arm were extended over the fire. The pain was immediate. Sarah pulled harder. The pain sent her mind to the edge of reason. Sarah pulled with a scream of rage building. The flesh on the back of her hand browned like a turkey on Thanksgiving. It then began to smolder and blacken.

The smell, and the sight of her arm smoking, and the pain were nearly too much. Her head began to whip back and forth, but still she pulled on her shackles. She pulled with everything she had.

Slowly, the shackle began to slide over her hand, collecting a sluff of blackened skin at the leading edge. Seeing it sent a wave of revulsion through her but she didn't stop pulling. Now her entire left arm was black and reeking. Her mind rebelled against the pain and the horror but her body didn't stop pulling until the shackle slid off altogether. It banged through the metal loop attached to the pole and Sarah fell back, landing on the cool white slabs of granite.

In horror, she stared at her left arm wishing she could chop it off. It was shriveled and nasty. It was a dead thing attached to her live body and she wanted it gone. Strangely, it didn't hurt anymore. The nerves had been burned away along with her flesh and muscle. Higher up, around her bicep where the skin was cracked and fake-looking was agony that dwarfed the pain skittering along her entire body.

Summoning every ounce of determination, she shut it all out.

Shaking like a foal, she stood, barely aware that her right hand was still shackled and trailed a length of smoking chain. There, on the first step was the robe that had been torn from her body. She put it on, uncaring that her touch had turned it black in parts and that it was ripped in others. Who would care what her robe looked like when she was such a monstrous sight?

Slowly, she began to work her way down the side of the pyramid and each step brought fresh pain, however she had experienced far too much agony already and it didn't deter her. She went up the aisle with a heavy limp—her entire left side had taken the brunt of the heat in that last minute and the skin of her leg felt ready to split down the middle.

She stumped on through the main door where she could hear the shouts and gunplay of a battle occurring not far from her.

Abraham's orders to his Believers to go back to their rooms ran contrary to anyone's ability to, and down one hallway after another there was a whirlwind of individual fights characterized more by ineptitude than in decisiveness. It was unbelievable chaos. The humans screamed and fought with anything at hand: potted plants, chairs, rakes, and even steak knives, while the zombies came on in relentless waves.

Sarah rooted for the zombies. Mostly the reasons were obvious but it was also in part because after her torture,

369

she actually resembled a zombie more than a human being. Purposefully, she lurched into the fray. In spite of the blood and the body parts and the anarchy, Sarah knew where she was and, more importantly, she knew where she was going: straight through the battle.

She was knocked into and struck and shoved all sorts of ways, but since she didn't attack anyone, no one and no thing attacked her. Her only stop was when she saw one of the blue-robed Sisters go down under the rending claws of a zombie. The woman was screaming loud enough to wake the dead and at same time was beating the zombie on the head with her pistol.

Sarah stooped and, one-handed, picked up a shovel that been discarded. In a great circular motion, she brought the heavy tool up and around and brought it whistling down onto the zombie's skull where it caved in the occipital bone. The beast slumped onto the Sister who struggled out from under it. Before the woman could stand Sarah brought the shovel around a second time and put a two-inch deep divot in the crown of the Sister's head.

There was some spurting blood which added to Sarah's "disguise", but she paid it no mind. She was after the pistol, which had to be pried from the dead woman's hand. It was empty and that wasn't unexpected. She tucked it away in her bra, and limped on, dragging the shovel through the gore.

It wasn't far to Abraham's apartments and when she arrived, she was pleasantly surprised to find the doors were unguarded. She guessed the reason: Abraham had issued too many orders to too few Sisters.

The doors were locked. She tried using the shovel like a hammer, but it was too big and awkward. The doors resisted her feeble attempts until she stood before it panting. "What would Jillybean do?" she asked herself in a scratchy whisper, the words eking out from a throat that was bone dry and felt to have been worked over with a razor blade.

Jillybean would take into consideration the tools at hand: one shovel, as well as the problem before her: a double set of doors that were locked. Sarah blinked at the doors and then pictured the little girl standing next to her with her tiny fists balled on her nonexistent hips. The imaginary girl tilted her head, first one way, then the other and Sarah did the same. It made her dizzy and so she looked at the one constant: the line between the doors.

"There's the answer, Sarah," she said. She stuck the blade in the crack and began to pry. Wood splintered on her first attempt. It wasn't easy, one-handed, but by the fifth attempt she had exposed the striker plate and one good heave later the doors swung open. Abraham stood just down the hall holding a brass-handled fireplace poker as if it was a baseball bat. He stared at Sarah in disbelief.

"Who let you out? Why aren't you still burning?"

Sarah strode forward letting the shovel fall on the expensive tile with a loud rattle. In response, Abraham held the poker higher, but it was all bluster that Sarah saw right through. His fear had rendered him pathetic and small. "Get out! These are my private quarters and you are not one of the Lord's chosen…"

The black pistol was its own argument and trumped anything he had to say. "I want Eve," she said, pulling it out of her bra and pointing it steadily. He began to shake his head and she thumbed back the hammer—her bluff only a single, useless squeeze away.

"No, please, don't. You can have her," he whined dropping the poker and holding out his hands to her. "Just…just don't shoot. I'll…I'll go get her. Wait right here." He jerked a thumb behind him and started backing up with his eyes glued to the gun.

"No, you'll show me where she is," Sarah ordered. She advanced and he retreated, though now he seemed just as disconcerted that such a hellish-looking person was tracking ash onto his carpets and smearing blister-pus on his doorknobs.

He walked backwards eyeing the gun and the mess in equal misery until they were at the nursery. It was beautiful, perfect for a little princess. Everything was shaded in pinks all save the white-painted crib where Eve

371

was lying. Sarah went to the crib and would have cried if she wasn't so close to system failure from dehydration. Instead her eyes turned bright red and her breathing took on a labored quality. From around the end of a bottle, Eve stared up at her mother without recognizing her.

"Hi, Peanut. Mama's here."

Eve blinked her giant blue eyes and then in one quick motion rolled over and then hefted herself up using the railings. The bottle she retained by gritting it between her new teeth. She looked confused as to what she was seeing and Sarah didn't blame her. She had passed by a mirror and had recoiled in shock. Her lips were deeply cracked and raw, while the skin of her face sported hundreds of tiny blisters, when she smiled they weeped a greasy looking fluid.

"It's Mama, I'm your Mama. Do you remember me?" Sarah asked. Eve replied by wiggling her butt and doing spastic knee bends. She even put out a hand and opened and closed her pudgy little fingers, always her way of asking to be picked up. "I can't pick you up just yet." She turned to Abraham who had retreated to the corner of the room. "I want her bundled in a papoose. Do you have one? I can explain how to…"

"We have one," he said.

It was more of a baby-sling, but it did the trick. Abraham bundled Eve and then stepped back. Sarah slung the baby and then covered her slightly with her robes. She then forced Abraham back the way they had come. At the reception room he balked, refusing to go any further and Sarah couldn't find the strength to make him.

"You're just going to get her killed," he said, pointing at the bundle beneath Sarah's tattered and befouled robes. "You'll die out there and so will she. I'm a good father. No matter what you think of me…*she* needs me."

"She needs you to sit down on the couch and don't make any moves."

Abraham did, watching Sarah with shrewd eyes. "You going to shoot me?"

"I'm not a murderer," Sarah said, backing into the hall that led out into the sterile-white sections of New Eden. Abraham's eyes narrowed.

"You're not going to shoot me? I would shoot you if our places were turned. I guess that means you don't have any bullets in that gun, do you?"

He stood and Sarah continued to back away. "I only have a few left and escaping takes precedent over killing you, but I swear I'll put a hole in your gut if you keep going."

His eyes shifted to the side as he thought about this. "I'd kill you. I know I'd kill you. Nothing could stop me from..."

Sarah turned and fled, hobbling down the hall, passing the Rembrandts, the lacquered wood, and the gleaming fixtures. Behind her Abraham came speeding, and just at the doors she had destroyed she turned, holding the worthless gun out; a last gamble.

"You don't have any bullets left," he said. For some reason he had stopped just shy of the doors, he seemed reluctant to come out. Sarah kept walking backwards.

"Come closer if you feel like gambling."

He took only a single cringing step forward and snarled, "It's no gamble! You're out of bullets and you're taking my Eve out there! If you ever loved her you'd stop right now."

She was thirty feet away from him now and the zombie sounds were beginning to pick up. Abraham swung one of the doors closed and jutted his chin around it. Now it was Sarah's turn to sneer, "And if you loved her you would come get her." She began pulling the trigger sending the hammer clicking on empty chamber after empty chamber. He flinched with each one, while his expression soured and turned petulant, but he didn't move from behind the doors. "I think Eve will be safer with me, than with a big piece of chicken shit like you." Sarah said and then turned to find a pack of zombies to lose herself in.

Chapter 41

Sadie

New Eden, Georgia

The bark of the pine tree bit into her ass, through her jeans, leaving strange, primordial patterns in her flesh, and this was ok with Sadie because her ass had gone numb twenty minutes before and she didn't have a clue.

Unaware, she began gnawing the shredded remains of a thumbnail. Had she been aware she would have stopped herself, she had gone through eight nails in the course of the afternoon and she was worried that she would start on her toenails next.

It was always like this when she was forced to wait on anything dangerous or exciting. She had zero patience— the afternoon had dragged on endlessly, and the evening wouldn't come. The sun appeared to defy physics by refusing to set. It came sliding down the sky but seemed to stop when it hit the horizon as though it just got comfortable and took a break.

Finally, the sun had set and then the pain of waiting intensified to an even greater degree. This was because her job was to sit around twiddling her thumbs and staring up at a silo. She groaned, a sound more or less indistinguishable from the groans of the countless zombies moving about in the night.

Across the valley, there was a flash of light and then, seconds later, a gentle rumbling noise let her know that Neil and Captain Grey had finally set off the first of the grenades. Now came a tense few minutes as the crackle of rifle fire came, followed by a second explosion.

"They're in," she whispered to herself, taking a glance up at "her" silo. She was half a football field away from it, sitting up in a tree, but despite that, she had heard what sounded like a cry or a shout from the building. Cocking her ear she practically held her breath as she waited for anything more to come from the silo, however it went back to being grimly silent.

She decided it was time for the radio check. "This is Green, begin radio check. Over."

There was a slight pause and then Jillybean's little voice came through the two-way: "Green this is Pink. I read you five by five. Over."

Another pause and then Nico said in his accented voice. "Green this Red. Five by five. Over."

Captain Grey had explained that five by five meant the best possible signal based on twenty five subjective responses. It was a complicated way of describing levels of signal strength and clarity. All Sadie cared about was that five was good and one was bad. She was about to give her response when Captain Grey broke in.

"Red, this is Blue. Signal strength extremely low. Repeat last transmission Red." Even over the radio the man sounded cranky.

"Blue, this Red. I read you five by five. What is my status? Over."

Sadie made a face at her radio. Captain Grey wasn't supposed to even have his radio on since no one expected the waves to penetrate below the ground and into New Eden. "Blue this is Green. You can hear us?"

"Yes all except Red. Red repeat last transmission."

"Blue this Red. Radio check. Over." Nico sounded put out and Sadie didn't blame him. Zombies were crawling all over the place and the idle chatter on the radio would only draw them closer.

"Red this is Blue. Advise move your position. Over."

"Da. Copy last transmission. Will move. Out."

"Say again?"

"Da. Copy last transmission. Will move. Out." There was a touch of angry sigh from Nico before he cut out.

In vain, Sadie squinted into the dark towards her left. The silo that Nico was staking out was three-quarters of a mile away and had been barely visible above the trees when the sun was out. Now, all Sadie saw was a dimly

375

etched horizon. But that didn't stop her from looking anyway, her thumb coming back up to her mouth.

She was just starting to nibble her way into needing a band aid when she saw a quick sparkle of light. It looked as though a signal was being passed, or fireflies had been amped up, but then the sound of guns firing followed, rolling down the valley coating the night in fear. Nico didn't have a gun!

"Nico are you ok?" she yelled into her radio. "I mean, Red. Come in Red, this is Green…Red? Come in Red? Red! Nico what just happened?"

Her radio remained silent. Before she knew what she was doing she was out of the tree and running west. Her entire body had gone as numb as her ass and she didn't feel the sting of branches whipping her face as she raced through the night forest. She probably would have run right into a trap but her radio clicked in her hand and, hoping against all reason that it was Nico, she stopped in her tracks and listened.

"Green this is Pink," Jillybean said, speaking very fast. "What's going on?"

The fear in her voice was coming in five by five. It set off a protective alarm in Sadie which allowed her to think through her fear for Nico. She spoke into the radio: "Listen very carefully, turn off your radio and hide! That wasn't Captain Grey. I-I think the bounty hunter is out there. He can find you if you use your radio. Don't move and don't use your radio. Out."

Sadie paused, expecting a response despite that she had just warned Jillybean not to use the radio. The little girl stayed quiet and smart. Knowing her, she had probably turned her radio off altogether so that it wouldn't give her away if danger was…

"I'm an idiot," Sadie whispered and then spastically started twisting the barely seen knobs on the radio until they all clicked over to the right, the direction she hoped was *off*. She then crouched with her hand on the rough hide of a pine, freaking out. Was Nico dead? Should she go find out? Or was the bounty hunter really out there waiting for her to come investigate? Or…was he coming for her?

Tears of indecision and panic filled her eyes and then fell from her cheeks. She longed to turn her radio on again just to see if something really had happened to Nico. Maybe he was calling for help right then! Maybe he'd only been wounded and now he was bleeding to death and calling her name over and over again.

Her fingers danced over the radio wanting desperately to turn it on again, but in her heart she knew better than to risk it. *He* was out there. Like a spider spinning its webs, the bounty hunter was out in the dark, waiting for her to screw up. Just then she didn't know if staying still meant screwing up or moving meant it. Always the runner, she felt that staying still was the wrong play. But where would she go?

To get answers.

Sadie tucked the radio into her jeans and began to run towards the east, towards Jillybean. Her fear for Nico sent a surge of adrenaline through her and she sped faster than was prudent. The danger in a sprint like that was very real. The forest was filled with deadfalls, rabbit holes, and zombies by the thousands, yet she was light of foot and lucky.

"Jilly?" she whispered three minutes later. Sadie had set Jillybean in a tree opposite the southeast silo, but that had been when there was still light to see by and now all the trees looked the same. "Jillybean, it's Sadie, where are you?"

There was a little sound to her left, like that of a squirrel dancing on a log. Sadie turned to it. Under the gloom of the trees the night was thick and the air muggy. She could see very little and had to pick her way forward slowly through a mesh of fallen logs, taking tall, gawking steps like a stork. Another sound to her right; again it was just *click-tick* among the trees. She went for it, her eyes wide like twin lamps.

"Jilly?" she called.

Practically at her elbow, Jillybean said, "You should whisper." Sadie jumped and had to swallow a squawk of fright. The little girl was crouched under the heavy branches of a spruce. "There's a monster over in that glade. It probably can't hear you if you whisper."

Sadie took a long quivering breath before saying in a lower voice than Jillybean's, "I heard something over to our right. It could be the bounty hunter."

"No, that was me. Ipes didn't think we could trust that you were alone or not being followed so I had you walk around a bit, chasing my magic marbles. Hope you're not mad. What happened to Nico? Were those gun shots? Is he ok?"

"I don't…" she wanted to say she didn't know, but that was a lie. She knew. Deep in her heart she knew. "I don't think he's ok." The words came out from very high in her throat. It felt like she was choking on them. "How on earth does that bounty hunter keep finding us? It shouldn't be possible."

Jillybean patted her arm and then stroked it gently, saying, "We're very really obvious that's what Ipes was trying to say before, and I have to agree. The bounty hunter knows us. Or really, he knows you and Sarah. He knows you came from the CDC so that's where he went to find us. But the CDC was all abandoninged, so what else does he know about you two? He knows Sarah's baby was taken from her by Abraham. Everyone knew that on the boat so he knows too, probably."

"And so he came to stake out this area, thinking we would come," Sadie said, seeing how easily they had fallen into his trap, yet again. She looked to the southwest where Venus was just starting to lose its brilliance in the night sky.

Sadie dropped her chin, feeling empty. "Why didn't you say anything before?" she demanded in a soft, accusatory tone.

"Ipes did try to tell you, amember? But nobody wanted to listen to him. He was very cranky about it."

"Yeah, I remember," Sadie said.

They were quiet for a few moments and then Jillybean shocked Sadie by asking: "So what do we do now?"

Sadie laughed. Even with her heart tearing itself apart over what happened to Nico, she chuckled at the question. The sound was filled with self-loathing. "You're asking me? You're always the one with the plans. I never can think of anything. I'm too stupid to think of anything. But I guess...I guess we wait and see what happens. If we stay real still and hide I don't think the bounty hunter can find us in the dark."

"What about Mister Neil?" Jillybean's little brows contracted as a thought struck her. "He won't stay quiet. When they find Miss Sarah and the baby he'll come out and start blabbing on his radio. He'll want to know where we are. And he'll give away his position. And if we answer, we'll give away ours!"

Sadie followed the train of thought and realized that even if Neil didn't use his radio he'd be caught. She could picture Neil blundering about in the dark searching for Sadie and Jillybean...and poor Nico. He'd be acting differently from the Believers or the zombies and the bounty hunter would know. "I have to go warn him or he'll die."

"Me, too," Jillybean said.

"No." She put her hands on the little girl's shoulders and squeezed gently. "It's too dangerous inside New Eden. You stay out here and be a mouse. You're the best at hiding. The bounty hunter won't be able to find you if you just keep still."

"Ok, I will. 'Cept, but what happens if I see Miss Sarah and the baby? Should I go get them?"

"Yeah, I guess so. Bring them back here, but don't expose yourself for nothing. Bring them here and stay put! Can you do that?"

Jillybean nodded and said she could. Satisfied, Sadie threw off her outer "zombie shawl," a ragged and multi-colored set of rags designed to fool the brainless undead, and then slid her backpack off. From it she extracted her mask and her hunting knife. The mask was Halloween fodder and depicted the leering visage of a ghoul. It didn't look much like a zombie but at the same time, it didn't look anything like a human either. In test runs that afternoon, carried out by Neil, the shawl and mask combo had fooled every zombie.

Beneath their shawls the three people of the "outer" team wore white robes lifted from a nearby catholic church. In the dark, they had hoped to be able to blend equally with either the zombies or the Believers depending on what the situation called for. Now Sadie was going to try to "pass" under the harsh lights of New Eden.

"Wish me luck," she said throwing the shawl back over her white robe. The pack she left sitting there. She liked to travel light.

Jillybean's own mask had been perched on the top of her head this entire time. She touched it as if to remind herself that it was still there before saying, "Good luck. Don't get caught. And don't get eaten. And don't get shot. I'll be right here…can I have a hug?"

The hug was fierce and tight, but also short-lived. Time seemed against them. Hell, everything seemed against them. Sadie couldn't remember the last time they had caught a break. And poor Nico…the misery inside of her threatened to erupt out of her chest in a great rush of tears and screams, but she reined it in, barely.

"Stay put," she warned the little girl and then left but only managed to take a few steps before she turned back. Sadie bent down and hooked out her right pinky. "Sisters."

Jillybean hooked it with her own. "Sisters," she said solemnly.

Now, Sadie left and this time she didn't look back. Without the pack she ran with the light steps of a doe and as she breezed past the zombies in the field, few took the time to even wonder what it was that shot by. Though some trailed after, none came close to matching her speed. As she neared the silo, she slowed down, dropped the ghoul mask over her face and began to moan and limp.

The zombies nearby, and there were many hundreds all around, didn't give her a second look, and she was able to squeeze between the door and the mob of putrid grey flesh. The smell in the silo was outrageous. It was the eye-watering stink of country-fried road-kill on a blistering July afternoon—triggered by the smell her moaning became real as was the terrible retching noise she made in the back of her throat .

The smell and heat left her weak. She kept to the wall for support, however, because of the difficulty in seeing through the eye-slits of the ghoul mask she slipped on a string of someone's intestines and stumbled, causing an avalanche of zombies to domino downwards into New Eden.

The undead formed a writhing carpet, and because she felt time pressing in on her with growing urgency, Sadie descended using the backs and, in a few cases, the faces of the undead as her stairway. At the bottom the chaos continued.

Sadie fake-limped to the first main intersection and paused trying to decide which way to go. From both left and right came screams and gunshots suggesting that there were at least two battles being waged somewhere in the maze of corridors. Further down the hallway in front of her smoke began to pile up at the ceiling making everything hazy.

Zombies went in every direction and with the smell of smoke and blood they seemed more enraged than ever. They attacked anything that was even vaguely human, including Sadie. She was knocked into by one and in order to steady herself she put a hand to the wall. It was a delicate hand, white with slim fingers and clutched in its grip was an eight-inch hunting knife.

Only humans carried things, zombies did not.

In an instant one of the beasts had a hold of her arm and before she knew it her forearm was in its mouth and its teeth were crushing down. The bite was vicious and painful, yet she kept her wits and switched the knife to her free hand. With a growl of her own she drove the blade into the dull yellow eye of her attacker and it fell at her feet.

381

Things went from bad to worse in seconds. More zombies came at her, knowing nothing more than she had human hands and carried human tools. It was enough to drive them to kill. Though she had killed the first with a soldier's eerie calm she knew she was no *Rambo* and so she did what she did best, she fled.

She raced for the smoke, hoping that some sort of base, natural fear of fire would stop her pursuers—it did not. They kept coming and their numbers swelled. She took her first right and then her first left stumbling upon more and more zombies. One she dodged. The next she threw to the side. A third grabbed her by the shawl. She gagged as it tightened around her neck like a noose. Somehow she twisted and turned until she wrenched it out of the zombie's grip.

Winded and shocked about how easily everything was falling apart, Sadie knew she had to get out of sight. Down the hall, there was a door and she ran to it and prayed: "Please God!" as she turned the knob. It was locked. She banged on it and screamed, "Open up! I'm human. I'm human!"

The zombies crowded from both directions and one was nearly on her when the door opened and she was yanked into the room.

Her ghoul mask had been knocked to the side and she couldn't see who was around her or what was going on, but she heard with perfect clarity: "It's one of them. Kill it!"

"Stop! No, I'm human, look." She pulled up the mask to show them. There were six Believers in the room and they all breathed a sigh of relief. Sadie did as well. Though none of them had guns, they were all armed in some manner.

"Why do you look like that?" a woman asked.

Sadie touched her shawl and then forgot the question altogether as she remembered the zombie bite. She turned her arm over…"Oh thank God." Because the nights were still chill, Sadie had worn a long sleeved shirt and a hoodie beneath her robe. Counting the shawl, she had four layers of clothes on and the zombie's bite had only gotten through three.

"Thank God?" one of the Believers questioned. "Don't you mean, thank the Lord's prophet?"

"Yeah," Sadie agreed while her eyes flicked about. She was in a long room with many desks, each aligned precisely with its neighbor. Upon each was a spinning wheel and spools of white yarn. There was a second door across from her; Sadie broke for it, leaving the Believers gaping.

They had been momentarily confused by the zombie attack and by her outfit, but she knew she was likely three seconds from being recognized, maybe not as herself, but definitely as an outsider. Perhaps out of instinct alone, they rushed after her, but she was speedy fast and was through the door with a ten foot head start.

They stopped at the doorway and would not go further, and for good reason: more zombies. Sadie booked past them, flying at an unnatural speed. One even had her dead to rights. It came from another corridor and was already moving at an angle that couldn't be cut, but she kicked into a gear she didn't know she possessed and scraped by with only the length of a fingernail separating them.

Her mask blew off the top of her head and without it her zombie-shawl was useless so she let it go. A door opened to her left and a man appeared looking both ways. "In here!" he cried, waving her in.

She was out of options and she rushed in, pulling her robe tight around her throat and sliding up the sleeves of her hoodie that were peeking out.

"Was there anyone else out there?" he asked. She thought about the group trapped in the spinning room, but she shook her head. They would have to take care of themselves. He glanced out from the protection of the door once more and then pulled his head back in looking dejected. "We're falling back to the Exorcism chamber… I'm starting to think we should never have left it."

"Oh, yeah," Sadie said, keeping her head down.

"Come on." The room they were in was for storage. He walked her to the back where another door stood open and from there they went down a wide hall. A number of believers were working at the end of it, stacking chairs and boxes and really anything they could to block it up. There was still a small opening at the side and they squeezed through—Sadie reluctantly.

She was supposed to be finding Neil, something she had foolishly assumed would not be that difficult. There was no sign of him, or Grey or Eve or Sarah. The only person she recognized was Abraham. The false prophet came storming down the hall surrounded by women in blue robes.

Sadie hurried past the barricade and found herself in a large open room whose main feature was a white stone pyramid rising up in its center. The room had a gut-churning, nasty smell to it.

"I have been betrayed," Abraham said in a carrying voice. He looked around the room, his eyes blazing and his fists clenched in outrage. The two hundred or so Believers that were there refused to meet his eyes. Every last one of them dropped their chins and stood looking down at the floor, quivering in fear of his rage. Sadie did as well, though she snaked looks left and right, hoping to see Neil and Captain Grey among the people.

"Betrayed and abandoned! Where are the rest of the Sisters? Why didn't any of them come to my aid?"

"They may be dead, my Lord," one of the Sisters answered. "The halls are being overrun. They probably didn't escape."

"They didn't escape? They didn't escape? I find that hard to believe. Look up there and tell me what you see?" He pointed at the pyramid. Sadie didn't see anything special, but the Sister's eyes went wide at what she saw. Abraham began nodding and smiling nastily. "That's right. *She* escaped. *She* slid right out of her chains and waltzed right to my suite and took Eve! She took my Eve and then she escaped!"

Sadie gasped at the news. Sarah had escaped with Eve, which probably could only have happened with Neil's help. That meant Sadie was wasting precious seconds listening to Abraham whine. As casually as she could, Sadie glanced back at the hall she had come in from—she couldn't go that way. It was mostly blocked and there were twenty people she'd have to fight her way through.

"Yes my Lord," the Sister was saying. "I'm sorry my Lord."

"Yes, you are," Abraham agreed. "You will all be sorry, for the Lord God has wrought this calamity upon you all for your lack of faith. That is *His* message! We shall stop these hell-spawned creatures and we shall rebuild and the Lord will demand more out of each of you. He shall demand sacrifice!"

"Amen!" the Believers cried. Sadie mouthed the word and then glanced to the other two exits. These were also blocked.

Abraham went on, strutting in front of his followers. "This chamber is to be renamed and rechristened. Henceforth, it shall be known as the Sacrificial Chamber!"

"Amen!" they echoed.

"Sins will no longer be forgiven or even tolerated. No longer will your soul be purified by fire. From now on your soul will be sacrificed for the greater good!"

"Amen!"

Amen? Sadie couldn't believe her ears. They just said amen to being sacrificed. She had to shake her head at the crazy that was all around her.

Abraham lifted his hands up high and said, "The sacrifice will begin now, with her." He pointed right at Sadie who thought that she had kept herself hid pretty well behind a tall man in front of her. "Who are you?" Abraham asked.

Sadie froze with her chin down, hoping that he had pointed to someone else, but she had been the only one moving, the only one glancing from side to side, the only one that stood out from the rest. People drew away from her as though she was diseased. Finally one of the Sisters came up with gun drawn and Sadie looked up at Abraham.

His eyes went wide. "You! I should have known. I should have…but, but it's ok. It all works out. You will be the perfect person to christen this chamber. Sister Jill? Go see if the fire is still lit."

His eyes shifted to the pyramid and now Sadie saw the smoke drifting up from its peak. Her knees gave out.

Chapter 42

Neil

New Eden, Georgia

Despite being shot twice, Captain Grey had enough energy left to slap some sense into his companion. His hand was hard as a rock and when he slapped Neil in the face, it had the same bracing effect as being hit with a canoe's oar. Neil blinked and wobbled his jaw around on its hinge and a headache began to thump in his temple, but he also shut up, which was the main purpose to the slap.

A human voice in the midst of so many zombies would spell the kind of trouble that no amount of vaccination could cure. If Neil had kept up his blabbing, as Grey always called it, the beasts would have torn him apart. Thankfully, the zombies were too preoccupied by the fleeing Sisters and charged after them in their usual reckless manner so that Neil only had to worry about getting trampled to death.

In the most realistic manner he could contrive, Neil moaned and forced himself to his feet. He stood over Grey, bracing himself against the wall and although he was small, he was coordinated and balanced, and managed to keep from being bowled over by the masses of undead.

They came on like a wave, the ones in back pushing forward relentlessly, but also mindlessly, reacting with all the forethought of a stampede of rogue elephants. At one point a zombie tripped, causing a massive pileup and for a moment the wave became a trickle. Neil took full advantage; he reached down, grabbed Grey's arm and pulled him across the corridor to one of the intersecting halls, leaving a long red smear in their wake.

A couple of dozen zombies watched this with something like interest. Here was what seemed to be one of their own, dragging another zombie. It wasn't in their version of normal and they charged.

"Oh shoot," Neil hissed. He pulled harder, his face turning red beneath the layer of grey makeup. There were a number of doors opening onto the hall and he went for the first one and once there demonstrated a very human action by reaching out and turning the door knob. The zombies, who had been befuddled at the concept of one zombie pulling another, let out a howl of rage and charged.

"Shoot, shoot, shoot!" Neil cried, hauling the very heavy body of Captain Grey into what was only a simple bedroom and then throwing his weight against the door, slamming it in the face of the zombies. The beasts raged against the door, trying to hammer it into pieces to get through. It shook with each blow, but it appeared well constructed and Neil turned his back to it and looked down at Grey.

His neck and left shoulder were covered in blood; his outer zombie gear was tacky with it. What worried Neil more was the hole in his chest and the way Grey's breath came out sounding like a series of weak hiccups. With fear growing like a branching weed in his chest, Neil dropped to his knees and ripped open Grey's zombie shawl. He unbuckled the clip to the M4 strap and then yanked Grey's BDU top open, sending green buttons flying and then he stared for a moment.

"Get...it...off," Grey said. The soldier was wearing a stiff, black armored vest that was indented right above the sternum. Neil fumbled the Velcro straps off the sides and then lifted the front plate section over Grey's head.

"Let me see," Grey demanded trying to lift his head up to see how badly he was hurt, but couldn't because of the wound in his neck.

Neil pushed his head back. "Just a second," he said, pulling out his knife and splitting Grey's undershirt up the middle. The man was so heavily muscled that he looked to have been chiseled out of stone, yet he was still flesh and bone. His breastbone was an angry red and there was a blue-black wheal dead center.

"Huh," Neil grunted.

"How bad?" Grey asked. Already his breathing was calming and his face looked less pale.

"Your chest isn't bad at all," Neil said, leaning over the soldier and inspecting his neck wound. There was a chunk of flesh torn away from the muscle that connected his neck to his shoulder. It was bleeding like a bitch, in Neil's medical opinion.

Grey tried again to look at his chest and again Neil pushed his head down. "It feels like my sternum is cracked in two," the soldier complained.

"Well, it's not." Neil cut away a strip of Grey's shirt and stuck it in the neck wound and then squeezed as hard as he could. The soldier glared. "Don't blame me." Neil said. "I didn't shoot you. I'm just trying to stop the bleeding."

"Uh-huh."

When his right got tired, Neil switched hands. A minute later he switched again, but not before peeking under the bandage. "Almost. You have to tell me what this promise was to get you to come down here. It had to be pretty sizable to go through this much pain."

"I promise I'll smack you upside the head if you ask again."

Neil laughed quietly. "I doubt you'll be smacking anyone for a while. Maybe if you had said you'd kick me…"

Gunfire out in the hall shut him up. The zombies stopped their pounding and seconds later someone began screaming. It went on for half a minute. Neil started to unsling his shotgun, but Grey said, "No. There'll be a hundred stiffs out there now and you only have five rounds."

Secretly relieved that he wouldn't have to put the delicate threads of his bravery to the test so soon after everything that had just happened, Neil went back to compressing the wound. It took a couple of minutes for the bleeding to stop and all the while Grey remained stoic. When the bleeding drew down to only a trickle, Neil,

389

directed by Grey, cut another strip from his shirt and tied it down over the wound, running it beneath his right armpit.

"It'll have to do," Grey said, with a grimace. "Man, I can still barely breathe. You should take the vest."

Neil was eager to, however he made a show of declining the offer to prove what a manly-man he was. Thankfully, Grey insisted and Neil put it on under his zombie outfit. He stood and stretched, getting a feel for the weight.

Grey was slow to get up. "Alright, we've sat around jerking off too long. Let's get moving, Hero."

It seemed rather insulting to be called "Hero" after Neil had probably saved Grey's life and he was just about to become indignant on the matter when he saw the steady look in the captain's hazel eyes. The man actually meant it!

"Yeah, let's uh…drop our socks and, uh grab our cocks," Neil said feeling his cheeks grow warm.

"You got that backwards," Grey pointed out. When Neil made to restate the old military saying, Grey put a finger to his lips and opened the door. The hallway was littered with blood and bodies.

"Which way?" Neil asked.

"We got a trail of body parts, which way do you think?" Grey led the way. He was once again buttoned up and dressed as a zombie, though his gait was now extremely stiff. He swung his right arm out from his body, while his left he kept tucked up tight, clutching his chest. He wheezed instead of moaned.

"I'll go first," Neil said in a whisper as he passed the soldier by.

They followed the human wreckage, seeing fingers and hands, a scalp, and a dozen corpses, but what stopped Neil in his tracks was when he looked down on a Halloween mask. "That was Sadie's."

Grey said: Humph. "I think those China-boys made more that one of these."

Neil wasn't listening. Instead he pulled up his shawl and pulled the two-way radio from his belt. "Sadie are you there? Sadie this is…" Grey snatched the radio from his hands.

After squinching his face from the pain of the sharp move, Grey said, "Did you forget everything I taught you? They can't hear you underground and even if they could you never use names. Please!"

"Fine, no names, but we still should try. This is Sadie's mask, I know it. Look on the inside. That's mascara. No one in New Eden uses makeup. To them it's like a sign of not being humble or something."

Grey saw the makeup. "Yeah, ok, but I'll do it. You're too emotional. Green this is Blue. Come in Green. Green this is Blue. Come in Green." He tried this for a minute before turning off the radio and handing it back to Neil.

"We have to hurry," Neil said, frantically. He was about to go running off when Grey took him by the arm.

"No, we go slow. We go steady. We go by the book or you endanger all of us. Now, stay behind me." Regardless of his words, Grey pressed on at a dangerous speed, passing slow moving zombies. With the carnage as a guide, there was no need to backtrack or stray away from the corridor and within three minutes they came up to a mass of zombies.

Ahead were shouts and screams and sporadic gunplay, indicating a battle was in progress. Neil caught Grey's eye and pointed at himself and then pointed ahead. He wanted to reconnoiter alone, but Grey shook his head. They both went, Neil taking the point because Grey couldn't use his strength without moaning in an all too human way.

The zombies surged forward and back like tides against a breaker and Neil was at the point of exhaustion when they finally got to the front. There they were confronted by what resembled a great pile of trash heaped into a mound. There were overturned desks and broken tables and mattresses, and what looked like a washing machine. And there were corpses, real dead ones, everywhere piles of them. The zombies were dying by the score, but there were so many that it would be anyone's guess who would win the battle.

The Believers had formed a human barricade around their prophet in the aptly named Sacrificial Chamber.

They were fighting as hard as they could, killing the zombies with grim efficiency as they straggled up and over the mound. Many of the Believers were dead and many more were injured and would turn into zombies in the next day or so but they fought on, sometimes with nothing but their fists.

Grey pulled Neil close and whispered, "We have to find another way around."

Neil shook his head and pointed with a trembling hand. In the center of the room was a white pyramid and at the top Sadie was being chained to a stubby pole. Abraham stood directing some of his Believers who were bringing up armloads of wood.

"They're going to kill her. Grey, we can't let them."

He had been loud but because of the fight only Grey had heard. Still the soldier put his finger to his lips. He then started to climb the mound. Neil tried as well but was waved back. Grey stopped at the top and took in the entire room in one long sweeping glance.

"Follow me," he said when he came back down. Wincing in pain, Grey pushed through the zombies until they were free and fast marching down the hallway alone.

"There are about two hundred of those crazy Believers in that room and each one will be happy to lay down their lives for Abraham. If we go in there we're going to die."

"But Sadie…"

Grey stopped and turned his eyes on Neil. He had never seen such a hard look on any one before. Even Ram would seem like a boy compared to this man. "Are you willing to die for her?"

Neil felt his guts churn but he rallied enough to say: "I'm here, aren't I."

"Good," Grey said and began his fast march once more. He took the first left he came to, and then began counting doors. "Here it is," he said at another hall. There was another fight in progress down this hall, though it was on a smaller scale than the last one.

Neil thought they would be going down the hall, but Grey took a right and then went in a big circle, taking three lefts in a row. At each turn he slapped his hand on the wall, marking the turns in grey makeup. He stopped when he reached the same hall they had started in.

Suddenly he smiled and looked embarrassed. "You wanted to know about my promise? It's simple. I swore an oath to be a hero."

Had they been sitting around a campfire roasting marshmallows, Neil would have laughed and razzed the big man. Instead, as this had come out of the blue, his mouth only came open and his top lip went up in a crooked, puzzled way.

"A hero?"

Grey smiled sheepishly. "Yeah. It was my C.O's idea. He thought that the world had stopped being good, you know? Like everything and everyone had turned to evil; even the military. We had fought without hope for so long that men just gave up. It was as though no one knew what honor was anymore. They just knew what survival was and getting theirs while they still had breath in their bodies."

"So are you like some sort of modern day knight? That's sort of ..."

"Weird," Grey said finishing his sentence. "Yeah it is, but someone has to be good. Someone has to do the right thing even if it's hard." Grey looked down the hall where the fight was ramping up. "If we go down there, we're going to die. It's really that simple. Do you still want to go?"

"I have to."

"Me too." Grey held out a hand to Neil. "If you shake it means you're promising to be a hero, even if it kills you."

Neil shook the hand and Grey clapped him on the shoulder. "Good man. Now here's my plan and I'm sorry but you get the brunt of the danger." Grey outlined a plan that relied on Neil's legs more than anything.

The first part was simple. They went down the hall to where sixty or so zombies were doing their best to scale another of the mounds that blocked an entrance to the Pyramid room. Grey went first. He pretended to fall at the base of the mound near a mattress but what he was really doing was setting it alight.

When Neil saw smoke coming up from it he called out in his loudest voice: "Yoo-hoo. Over here. Hey zombies!" They were so fixated on the dozen or so Believers trying to defend the door that they didn't all turn. That wasn't good enough. Neil ran at them waving his arms and screaming.

That did the trick. The zombies turned from the mound and charged. Neil scampered back still waving his arms, drawing them on. Only when the lead elements got close did he turn and run. He ran in the loop of hallways that Grey had marked earlier, always making sure to keep the zombies close. As he ran he heard Grey's M4 start to fire in quick succession—it had a distinctive crackle to it that was different from the pop, pop, pop, that came after.

Someone was shooting back.

"Oh please let him be ok," Neil said, puffing around the last turn. Now he sped up, going full sprint. He had to get to the mound and clear the best possible path through it before the zombies could catch up. Grey was still firing when Neil came up to the mound and started heaving chairs and old lamps out of the way. The smoke from the mattress fire came up in great billows making it very hard to see and harder to breathe through.

But that's why they had set it. As Grey said: *When you don't have the numbers, use chaos and trickery*. They certainly didn't have the numbers, unless the zombies counted. They came lurching forward just as Neil forced a table over. As a last item to remove, Neil grabbed a tall mirror. It cracked in his hands as if he had squeezed it too hard. Perplexed he tossed it aside and bent for a hunk of a chair, that was when what seemed like a bee zipped by his ear.

"Get down!" Grey was shouting.

It was only then that he realized that someone was shooting at him. The only problem was, that Neil couldn't "get down." Zombies were charging from one direction and people were shooting from the other. Grey was safe enough hidden by smoke and protected at the top of the pile by a filing cabinet. All around the front of the mound lay the bodies of the Believers he had already killed.

One wasn't as dead as she seemed and pointed a gun in Neil's direction. Neil ran, not knowing if he was shot or if the bullet missed or what. He ran into the room and the *bees* were again buzzing all around snapping the air. Right behind him, Jillybean's army came pouring into the room and now the chaos was nearly complete as a huge fight erupted.

Neil ran for the pyramid where the top was already aglow with an evil light. Abraham was up there looking tremendous in size, screaming orders, while Sadie, a few steps away, was snarling curses like a sailor. Neil began mounting the tall steps while at the same time he was trying to unsling his shotgun—the two actions almost canceling themselves out. Before he got to the second block of the pyramid a woman in a blue robe came running up.

She had a gun in her hand and could have shot him at any time but she seemed determined to shoot him in the face from a foot away. She came right up to him, her finger drawing in on the trigger, and as Neil lifted his hands to show that he wasn't armed, her head sagged inward on one side and blew out on the other sending a great sheet of blood cascading across the pyramid.

Neil was slow to react to the carnage right in front of him. The amount of blood and its very wet consistency and the fact that it was horribly bright made it all seem phony to him, like he was part of some sick game.

Just then the chaos hit its maximum. Grey's M4 was going nonstop, the Sisters were shooting the last of their bullets in all directions, and around the room, surging back and forth, the zombies were battling the Believers in horrendous hand-to-hand combat. Above it all Sadie screamed at the top of her lungs as the fire finally caught and Abraham slid out a black pistol he had commandeered from one of the Sisters, took aim at Neil and shot him in the guts.

The pain was immediate. He fell in slow motion, going head-over-heels, losing the shotgun which had been caught in his zombie-shawl but now disappeared. For Neil everything got quieter and quieter, all except Sadie. Her screams ramped up. Then he was lying on the floor of the room and her screams came up through the wood with growing intensity.

"I'll save you," he said, remembering his promise to be a hero no matter what. Before he got up however, he put his hand into his wound, knowing it would be wet and sticky, and knowing that if he felt his own liver he would puke.

But his hand found something hard as a board. "The vest," he said in amazement.

The vest had caught the bullet and had absorbed most of the impact. Yes, it still hurt like hell where he had been shot, but he wasn't truly injured.

Neil stood, wobbled, and then started up the blocks again. He was vaguely surprised to see that he had the shotgun in his right hand. When had he picked it up? And when had he thumbed the safety to off? He had no idea. Above him, Abraham was emptying the black pistol, firing across sixty yards of open floor to where Grey was crouched behind the filing cabinet.

The captain had drawn fire from every direction and thus Neil was able to climb right up to Abraham and blow his head off with the 12-gauge. It literally went bouncing down the steps spitting blood.

The sound of the shotgun was that of a booming, echoing canon and, for all intents and purposes, it signaled the end of the battle. There were zombies that still had to be killed and one of the Sisters used her last bullet to shoot uselessly in Neil's direction, while another used her last one to put a hole through her own heart.

Neil stepped up to Sadie and, shielding her with his body, blew off the chain that held her to the post. Immediately, she leapt off the grate and kicked off her converse, the rubber soles of which had melted clear away. He carried her to the bottom of the pyramid where she snatched up the pistol from the corpse of the Sister who had tried to shoot Neil.

"They were going to burn me alive!" Sadie exclaimed.

"What were you even doing here?" Neil asked as Grey came up. The three of them trained their weapons outward at the remaining Believers. Some looked fit to kill, while others just looked relieved, however most of them seemed too confused to grasp what had happened. Those who weren't fighting the zombies backed away afraid of the guns and the fearsomeness of Captain Grey's scowl.

"I was coming to warn you, but now Sarah...we have to find Sarah," Sadie said, her voice growing suddenly higher. "She's escaped with Eve, and...and...and..." Tears came to her dark eyes.

Neil grabbed her in his version of a bear hug, which was more like a koala bear hug in that he wasn't looking to crack ribs, but to let her know he was there for her. "What is it? What happened?"

"I think Nico's dead," she said, quietly. "The bounty hunter is out there. He tricked us into using the radios too much and he shot Nico."

"Then we have to go," Grey said, taking her by the arm and gently urging her toward the far left door. "My guess is that the bounty hunter is going to snatch up Sarah and use her and the baby to get to you, Sadie." There was too much truth to that than could be denied and they ran for the door.

Leaving New Eden was far easier than getting in. There were still zombies around every corner and down every hall, but the three of them made sure their disguises were in order and not a single undead beast challenged them. What Believers they ran into were directionless, confused people who ran from them in terror.

Breathing the night air was a blessing, however their danger wasn't over. Now, they were being hunted. But they had Captain Grey on their side and he used every trick in the book to get them safely back to the tree where

Sadie had left Jillybean. It was their hope that the crafty little girl had managed to get to Sarah first. Instead they couldn't find her either of them.

"Jillybean," Sadie hissed, going around the tree twice. "Jilly, where are you?"

The forest was still and quiet as the inside of a coffin. They began to spread out, searching and calling quietly. It wasn't long before they found the body. With night fully dark now, it looked smaller than it should and the blood splashed across its midsection was black as sin against the white of her robes.

Neil saw her first, lying with her legs lost in a myrtle bush and her torso turned and contorted. "Jillybean?" he asked. His voice quivered. Since the apocalypse he had seen too many bodies not to know the difference between a live one and one that was very much dead. This one was dead, pale and unmoving with the Velveteen Rabbit tucked gently against her cheek.

Chapter 43

Jillybean

New Eden, Georgia

Sadie left, jogging off with a swish of her robe, sounding like the wind passing through the trees.

From her perch in the tree, Jillybean glanced down at the backpack she had left behind. It sat open, but not inviting. The teeth of the zipper gleamed dimly as if they were real teeth attached to a squatting toad that could take her leg off at the knee if she wasn't careful. She had to blink away the image and remind herself it was just a backpack, and in the backpack...she looked away and tried not to think about the backpack anymore and what sat within it.

She wasn't supposed to have it. Sadie had taken it for Jillybean's own good. So instead, Jillybean scratched her nose and kicked her dangling feet back and forth beneath her. She sighed in boredom, meaning: she sighed loudly and often. After a while, she worked the wedgie out of her crack and after a bit more squirming, she had to repeat the effort.

Because the bounty hunter was out there searching for her she tried not to be such an ants-in-your-pants kind of girl, but she was bored. Really bored. Bored like Easter Sunday at church sort of bored. Usually she never got bored because she always had...

You might as well come get me, Ipes said.

"Not listening to you. I have the Velveeta rabbit to play with." Jillybean unzipped her own backpack with the fading picture of the boy with big hair and the peeling letters that spelled: *I'm A Belieber*. She dug out the rabbit and rubbed her cheek against its belly. It was very soft. Way softer than Ipes ever was, even after one of his infrequent baths.

Softer in the head, maybe.

"There you go again," Jillybean grouched. "You are always so jealous and sometimes your jokes are mean. And you know what? I *know* what you did before. You tried to take me over."

It was for your own good. They were going to get you...

Jillybean slid down from the branch in a wrath that Ipes could feel coming like a tornado. She went to the toad of a bag but wasn't afraid of it now. She was too angry to be afraid. "Taking me over isn't for my good at all! Do you know what means crazy? I do. Having a zebra talk out of your mouth is what means crazy and that's not good. Is it?"

No, but...

At the word "but" she zipped closed the backpack. It was mean since Ipes was very afraid of the dark, however he needed to learn a lesson. "That's how I felt when you taked me over. It was mean and not nice."

I'm sorry. His voice came through muffled.

"Uh-huh," Jillybean replied. She put her back to the tree and began to stroke the Velveeta Rabbit's ears. He really was the softest thing in the world, but he was also kinda dull like Ipes said. But at least *he* was nice.

I said I was sorry.

"Hush. You're in time out until you learn your lesson." Jillybean had a mind to scold him some more, because he really had been awful bad, when a she heard a little noise in the woods not far from her. She went *bunny*, slinking down to the base of the tree where the roots had erupted out from the earth and made a natural cove.

A man was out there, she knew it. Zombies were never this careful or quiet. It was a man who listened more than he walked, who stepped and then stopped, stepped and then stopped. He drew closer, cutting a line through the trees just on the edge of the forest; a line that kept him hidden but allowed him to see out into the valley; a line that Sadie had walked when she had settled Jillybean in the tree back when the evening had ousted the last of afternoon from the sky.

Closer.

Keep still.

Jillybean refused to budge, refused to look around the bowl of the tree to see who it was. She knew already. Any other kid her age would have looked and any other little kid would have been caught.

The man—the bounty hunter, who else would it be— passed her by. She listened as he drew further away and as she did she petted the rabbit's velvety ears. *Keep still* might have been bad advice, ok it was the most useless advice that could have been given at that point, still it was something. The rabbit hadn't said anything at all.

It's because rabbits are as dumb as they're soft, Ipes remarked.

"There you go making fun again," Jillybean said in exasperation.

You want the truth? There's nothing special about him. He's just a toy, while I'm your protector. Your daddy picked me to protect you and only I can.

Jillybean said, "Humph," to that. "I don't think you're as helpful as you think. You made me look crazy this morning. And I felt crazy, too." Having Ipes move her around had been more weird than anything. It felt like she was being rocked to sleep, and when she touched things there was always some sort of fuzzy barrier in the way, as though she had on giant, woolen mittens.

What really scared her was when he made her lips talk. She didn't know what she was saying, she only knew it was wrong. It made her feel like someone had stuck a hand up the back of her shirt and was using her like a puppet.

It was for your own good. Now can you get me out of here? It's really stuffy and I think Sadie left some old socks in here.

The little girl was halfway to the bag before she knew it. "No. No, I won't. I'm the boss of you. That's the way it's apposed to be and if I say you stay in time out then you gotta stay there."

But I'm not being bad, now, Ipes whined.

401

"You were very bad, taking me over, and I bet you'd do it again." The fact that Ipes said nothing to this confirmed the idea as fact in her mind. She started to get the shivers but stopped them, clenching her teeth. It occurred to her that the best way to stop Ipes was to figure out how he was taking her over.

"Look, there's some people coming from the silo. Sarah may be with them."

Don't go. You can't risk it. And besides the bounty hunter isn't after Miss Sarah, he's after Sadie. I'm sure Sarah will be fine on her own, without us.

"We can't trust the bounty hunter. He could do anything. So I guess that means I'm going. Miss Sarah needs me."

No she doesn't! Ipes cried from inside the bag. *You said you looked crazy before, now you're acting crazy. Sitting in a valley full of monsters and whacky Believers is crazy and now there's a bounty hunter? No, you can't go. I forbid it.*

"That's what I thought you'd say, but you can't forbid me because you're not daddy, so bye."

No!

Ipes was not subtle. His personality grew like a dark, smothering cloud and Jillybean felt her fingers fade, and her toes and knees were somewhere down below her but she couldn't tell if they were holding her up or if she was floating. In seconds her body was that of a ghost's and it was a struggle to retain any awareness.

"Where are the people you were talking about?" Ipes asked using her lips and her tongue and the breath in her lungs.

There are no people. Not yet at least, Jillybean said. It felt as though she was whispering in her own ear.

"Then why did you tell me there was?" Ipes asked uneasily.

To trick you. To see how you take me over—you do it because you think I'm ascared.

"You are scared otherwise I wouldn't be here," Ipes said, walking to the backpack and pulling out a toy zebra. It had a deflated air and, strangely, was like a corpse.

Uh-uh. I'm not ascared, Jillybean said. *There's no danger now and so you can't go running my body. So get out. You know daddy wouldn't want you to do what you're doing.*

Ipes laughed in Jillybean's high, little girl laugh and said, "You are more afraid than you realize. The reason you don't think you're afraid is because I take all your fears and I hold them for you. I sift them for you. I keep some back and only give you what you can handle. This is what you'd be like without me."

Suddenly, Jillybean felt a rush of static run up her limbs, her face twisted, her jaw working on its bone-hinges. Her control was coming back and with it came a frightening chill. She came awake and knew things...or perhaps now understood what she already knew:

There were monsters in the forest, some very close by. They would kill her if they found her. They'd eat her face as she screamed, or they'd open up the soft skin of her belly and pull out ropes of intestines, or they'd...

"Stop it, please," Jillybean whimpered. She cowered from her own imagination, shaking all over with Ipes and the Velveteen Rabbit crushed to her chest. Her cheeks had gone pale and, beneath the zombie shawl, she felt cold and clammy.

There's a lot more to be afraid of, Ipes whispered in her head. *The bounty hunter. The slavers. Those stupid Believers who'll kill you for no reason at all...the fact that your mom and dad are dead and that in reality, you are all alone in this world. All alone, except for me.*

Ipes began taking control again. Everything about her became sluggish. The night blurred into one big shadow and the stars slurred into smudgy points. Even her new fear lost its edge and grew stale.

"I'm not alone. I have a family," Jillybean insisted through lips that felt to have plumped up like sausages.

"Remember this?" From far away, she saw her right hand come up; the pinky was extended up and was hooked.

I remember, Ipes said. Now it was his voice that came up from the deep.

"Sadie is my sister," Jillybean exclaimed, her words crisp, coming off her tongue with a snap. "You're going to have to get used to that idea."

But Mister Neil is not your daddy. Your real daddy gave me to you to protect you. He would not want you putting yourself in danger for...for them.

"I know my daddy better than you," Jillybean said, her eyes glaring at the zebra. "He wasn't a coward. He fought for his family and I think he'd want me to do that too. I bet."

Ipes was quiet for a moment and then Jillybean remembered something that she couldn't have remembered: she was sitting in a home in Philadelphia, the one with the doll house. Sarah was with her. *Have you considered Jill?* she heard herself asking. *She needs a proper mother and father.* Sarah had grunted: *She's not my baby. I don't love her.*

"When...how?" Jillybean could barely form words, stunned by this new memory. "You taked me over before? And Sarah...doesn't..."

She doesn't love you, Ipes said, finishing her sentence. *She doesn't want to be your mother, that's what she said.*

Jillybean was confused and bewildered but also furious. She was hurt by what Sarah had said, but the betrayal by Ipes was too much. In a fury she began to stomp toward the nearest silo. People had begun to emerge. They stood outside of it huddling close like sheep in the rain.

Stop, Ipes said. *That bounty hunter is out there. He's going to expect exactly this.* When she wouldn't stop he tried to dominate her mind, however her anger was such that she was able to throw him off, mostly. She stumbled and went dizzy. There was a moment when she found herself pointing the wrong way. Ipes didn't feel like a zebra. He was more like a turtle all caught up in his shell, bunchy-like, as though he was outgrowing it and needed out.

As Jillybean was about to break from the cover of the forest and head into the narrow valley, Ipes changed tactics. Fear struck the little girl like a fever. She went *bunny*, dropping into a crouch, too afraid to go forward or back. Behind, the woods came alive with all sorts of sounds: clicks and cracks, and snapping branches. In front, the land was flat and bathed in starlight. She knew she'd be seen for certain if she tried to cross the fields of grass.

More Believers began to come up from the silo and some tried to run from the huddled mass. Only one left in a lurching stagger. It had to be Sarah.

She was only a shifting shadow moving in a line about a hundred yards from Jillybean. In a rush, the little girl darted along the edge of the forest, cutting Sarah off, but as she drew close, Ipes sent more horrible visions into her head and she couldn't bring herself to call out or even to move. Sarah walked on by.

Jillybean shook and shivered, more afraid than she had ever been, except in those early days when her dad had left and her mom had wilted into death. She was perfectly paralyzed in fright and would have remained that way except she heard another human. It was the hunter!

Stoked by the unnatural fear, Jillybean, didn't consider the fact that the hunter could not have seen her, crouched as she was in the dense under brush. Like a startled pheasant she broke from cover and ran in a panic straight for Sarah, hoping for the protection of an adult.

Sarah spun, holding a gun, but her arm dropped when she saw Jillybean. "Jillybean? Is that..."

Too late Sarah saw the bounty hunter. He was dressed head-to-toe in black and looked more like a shadow than a man, all except for his face. In the dark, his face looked like an insect's. Instead of shady pits where his eyes should be, there was some sort of contraption across his head.

Night goggles, so he can see in the dark, Ipes said—not to her, but to himself. Jillybean's fear had reached epic proportions and she had dislodged herself from reality. Ipes was in control.

"Drop the gun," the bounty hunter ordered, pointing his own.

Sarah's gun hand started to rise. It came up midway and her mouth came open as if she just remembered something. She let the gun fall.

There was a small thump in the dirt which generated another of those chaotic memories within Jillybean's confused mind. She was standing next to a house and in her hand was a tiny gun that just might fit her hand if she really needed it to—she pulled back some grass and hid the gun there and then stood. She stood, looked at the overgrown grass for a moment, and the knelt back down...

"Sarah Rivers," the bounty hunter pronounced in a voice as dry as dirt. "And Jillybean. You got the baby. Very impressive."

"You can't have her!" Sarah hissed.

"I can have anything I want and what I want now is Sadie Walcott. Where is she?"

Sarah started to shake her head and stopped when Ipes spoke: "Down in New Eden. I can go get her for you." Jillybean read Ipes' true intentions: he wasn't going to go into New Eden, he was going to run away. He was itching to run even then. His fear was as strong as Jilly's, in fact it was the source of Jillybean's fear and it was tremendous.

"No. I don't think so, Jillybean," the bounty hunter said. "You've proven to be a little too resourceful, a little too cagey for my tastes. But that doesn't mean you can't help me. Your body will send just the right message." The hunter in his black garb, brought up the black gun and pointed into Jillybean's chest.

For Jillybean, the progression of the night stopped. Time stood still as she realized that he was going to kill her.

"Don't look," Ipes said. The words were spoken aloud, but they were meant for Jillybean. Her eyes closed and her connection to the world became so tenuous that she could no longer feel her galloping heart or her panicky-breath whistling in and out of her lungs. The only thing she could really feel was Ipes' regret. It drew down her soul, making it heavy.

In the end, he had failed her, and he had failed her daddy. He had done everything he could to keep her alive, everything and more, however it hadn't been enough. The night sounded with a click as the hunter thumbed off the safety and then there was the infinitesimal pause as he began to pull the trigger...

Sarah leapt in front of Jillybean. "Wait! No don't."

Fear, like black pus or rancid, burning bile had been building steadily in Jillybean's heart, it seemed to ooze from every pore, but the second Sarah put herself between Jilly and a bullet, the fear vanished. Just like that, Jillybean blinked her own eyes and felt the ground beneath her sneakers with her own feet. She breathed air and felt her cooling sweat like a line of ice down her back. Ipes was gone.

I'm not gone. I'm right here. The little zebra was in her arms the way he was supposed to be. He swiveled his ears and looked about. *But where is here? Where are we? This is like the forest in Hansel and Gretel. It's freaky weird.*

"Shh," Jillybean said. Her world had suddenly snapped back into place and she was desperately trying to make sense of everything, foremost of which was the question of why Ipes' had stopped controlling her.

Because maybe I was never controlling you to begin with, he answered. *That was all you being cuckoo for coconuts. You were afraid and you tried to use me as a scapegoat.*

And why had Sarah jumped in front of her like that?

Because she's a better mommy that she thinks she is. I think she loves you as much as she can.

Love? A better mommy...Sarah was right in front of Jillybean holding her back with a hand that was black and ugly smelling. Her face was scarred, her skin was rent and ragged, and her body sagged to the left. She looked used up, but she wasn't backing down or whimpering in any way.

407

Sarah had her good hand held out to the barrel of the gun. "There's no need to hurt her. If you need a message sent, I'll do it." There was a sling across her shoulders; inside it was Eve swaddled and sleeping soundly. Sarah gently lowered the baby to the ground and then stepped forward with her hands up. "Just don't do anything to Jillybean, please."

The bounty hunter must have heard the pain in her voice. He flipped up his night vision goggles and inspected Sarah. "Shit, you wouldn't fetch a nickel in the markets. Crap." This last he murmured in disappointment before he brought the rifle back up and fired.

He fired without warning or preamble; the bounty hunter was too efficient for that sort of nonsense. He pulled the trigger and was done with Sarah Rivers. She stood for half a second, said, "No," in a sad, quavering voice and then, as her muscles came unwound, she fell to the black dirt.

Jillybean dropped down next to her and didn't feel a sharp stick cut into her knee, or the cool of the leaves sticking to her shins, nor did she feel her tongue as she asked: "Miss Sarah?" The explosion from the gun, like a great rock splitting, was a shock to Jillybean however it was the bullet slamming home with a dull thud that took her to the brink of insanity once again.

The bounty hunter came to stand over Sarah. He was going to shoot her again. He was going to punch holes in her and pin her to the ground with bullets. Jillybean knew it, and cared, but she found herself falling, falling into the deep void of her own mind where fear ruled. She was fading into that protective numbness and might never have come back, but she was pulled from the edge.

Sarah touched Jilly's hand. It wasn't a grasping desperate hand, afraid of what would come in death. It was a soft hand. It held Jillybean's with warmth.

"You'll...b-be...ok," Sarah said.

The words, the hand, the love in the last consciousness of her mind were, in the vastness of the world, tiny things. It was all Sarah had to give, and it was enough. Jillybean could handle pain, and danger and even fear, but she couldn't handle them without a reason to. Sarah gave her that reason.

"Not yet," Jillybean said to the bounty hunter. She gave up the Velveteen Rabbit, placing it against Sarah's cheek and rubbing it gently against her skin until the woman closed her eyes.

"That's a good touch," the hunter said. "They'll know I have you and the baby. Now, get back before you get splattered."

Jillybean didn't. She felt Sarah's hand slipping and hurriedly recited the only prayer she knew all the way through: "Now I lay me down to sleep; I pray the Lord my soul..."

"Oh please," the hunter scoffed.

"...to keep. If I die before I wake, I pray the Lord my soul to take."

Somewhere in the brief prayer Sarah Rivers died. Her hand slid from Jillybean's and fell upon her own breast and her head turned gently to rest on the Velveteen Rabbit. The bounty hunter saw it too. He slung the rifle and picked up Eve who had begun making little noises of fear. "Come on," he said to Jillybean. "Get up. We're leaving."

Slowly, she got to her feet and was pushed along by him, numb in body and soul, but not in mind. Her mind was again picturing a hidden memory: the house back in Philadelphia, and the tall grass and the little gun that just might fit her hand if it had to. She remembered hiding that gun because it scared her so much, but now she realized she had thought better of it at the last second. *Just in case*, she had whispered as she stowed it in the deepest part of her worn out *I'm A Belieber* backpack. Now she knew why she had never replaced it with something prettier.

You can't do it, Ipes said. *You can't kill him. The hunter is too good, even Captain Grey thinks so. We should just run.*

Running would only save her own life. What would happen to Eve? What would happen to Sadie and Neil? They would all die or be sold as slaves. The hunter would set a trap with the baby as bait and they would fall right into it.

Because he's too good, Ipes repeated. *Do I have to remind you that you aren't a gun fighter?*

That was true. She wasn't quick like a gunman from the Old West, which meant she would need an excuse…or an accomplice. Eve didn't like the rough handling she was receiving and had begun to make the warning noise she used right before she got really angry.

Jillybean turned as she walked. "I have a binky for her if you want it. Do you know what a binky is?"

"Yes." Somehow he managed to be menacing in that one word, only Jillybean wasn't menaced. She was too focused on the dangerous job at hand.

"Sorry. You don't look like the kind of person who would. I also have formula. That's what means fake milk. Do you want it?"

"The binky, for now," the hunter said. His eyes were flinty and sharp in the night. When Jilly stopped and turned her pack around on one shoulder, he seemed to be looking right into her and when she reached into the pack she knew she was caught. He had read her correctly and now she read him: he wanted to catch her and he wanted to punish her, he wanted to cause her pain. Her hand came out of the pack and the hunter was right there gripping her wrist, hurting it.

"Ow, no, ow," she whined, her face twisting in pain. He squeezed until she was down on her knees in the dirt and he saw what she held.

He relaxed his grip, slightly and looked at the pink binky somewhat puzzled. "I thought…"

"It's just a binky," she gasped. 'Let go, please. It hurts."

The bounty hunter gave her wrist one more tweak before taking the binky. He gave it a look of disgust and nudged into Eve's mouth. When he looked up from the swaddled baby Jillybean shot him in the armpit. She had originally had the gun in her wet palms, but because of his knowing look she had left it at the top of the pack and pulled the binky instead.

Now, it was in her hands where it fit just good enough to do the trick. Her first bullet went through both lungs and lodged in the intercostal space between the fourth and fifth ribs. When his knees hit the dirt he was face-to-face with Jilly. She shot him in the right eye and that bullet ricocheted around the inside of his skull, running tunnels through his brain.

Although he died instantly, he teetered just long enough for Jillybean to take Eve from him before his face slapped into the wet earth. She stepped across his body, heading deeper into the forest, crooning softly, the gun still in her hand and the zebra tucked between her thin chest and the baby. She walked without purpose or direction.

Jillybean was numb again; her mind adrift in sorrow and fear and heart-breaking pain. Added to this was the guilt of killing another human. She made excuses about how he was a bad man and how he deserved it, but they slid off the side of that new guilt, leaving it untouched and undiminished. She wandered in tears, reliving every aching day of stress since the apocalypse had begun. They felt like bricks that kept piling on and on and on until her psyche broke and she became nothing.

She felt like a ghost in a world of ghouls, right up until Eve spat out her binky and smiled at Jillybean, showing all five of her teeth. Only then did the little girl stop and marvel at what she had saved and only then did she forget all the pain and fear. Only then did she remember that she was loved.

Look at all that slobber, Ipes said making a face of horror. *That's scarier than any monster or bounty hunter.*

"Don't be jealous," Jilly chided, hearing her own voice like an echo in her skull. It grew more firm with each word. "This is our little sister you're talking about."

Epilogue

Sadie

Georgia

Sadie did not run with her usual speed or grace. Her lithe body was hobbled by pain, but she went on nonetheless with gritted teeth and barely audible curses. Her feet were blistered from the fire yet she was in better shape than Captain Grey whose sternum was the darkest of purple and whose face was ashen and pale from too much blood loss.

And she was in better shape than Neil who was so overcome with grief that he had blundered about the night forest in tears until he had become so exhausted he couldn't even stand .

So it was up to Sadie to go get the Humvee. Her feet weren't the only thing slowing her down. Despair and depression had her wholly in their grip—she couldn't seem to take a proper breath and her chest ached with misery and grief.

Nico was dead and now Sarah as well. The woman who had been the best mother a girl could ever want was dead. That was shock enough, yet it was the mutilation of her body that kept coming to Sadie's mind every time she blinked. Sarah looked to have been tortured over a fire pit. Her left arm had been a blackened husk and the smell...

Sadie couldn't think on that. She had to shut that out. To think on that would mean she would have to stop again and cry. It was only two miles to where the vehicles were hidden and already she had stopped twice to bawl her eyes out.

"No more of that," she hissed. She knew pain and grief, but also anger: the bounty hunter had Eve and Jillybean, and Sadie was going to get them back! Anger helped. After each bout of sadness, anger burned its way through to get her mind focused. She would find the bounty hunter and she would cut his balls off and…

"Sadie?"

In midstride, Sadie turned and raked the forest with her eyes, pointing the pistol she had picked off the body of a Believer. At first there was nothing to see but the night and the deeper shadows beneath the eaves of the forest, but then Jillybean stepped from behind a sycamore tree. She was holding Eve with her back bowed and it was no wonder, the baby looked to have grown five inches since she had been kidnapped and seemed half Jilly's size.

"Jillybean? Where's the hunter?" Sadie asked moving behind a sycamore of her own and peeking out from its cover.

Jillybean's face drew into lines: her forehead sprouted three across, her lips a dozen each as they pursed. "He's dead. I…I…he's dead. So is Miss Sarah. He killed her. He shot her. I don't know why, I really don't, but he did."

"And who killed the bounty hunter? Was it Ipes? Did Ipes make you or did he help you?"

"Huh?" Jillybean looked down at the zebra and shook her head. "No, Ipes is just…he's very small. He can't hurt anyone. It was m-me. I did it. He was a very mean, bad man. Maybe he was like a evil man, too. I keep saying things like that as a excuse but it doesn't feel right even though it's true. Is that wrong?"

Sadie had her own share of guilt. Ram was dead, and Julia, and now Nico and Sarah. There had been the black man who had tried to help her in New York and of course Cassie…there'd been so many deaths that she was having trouble remembering them all. And yet she still lived and for some reason it made her feel guilty, as though she should've done…something.

She understood, on some level, what Jillybean was going through. "I don't think you were wrong to do it. To kill that man, if that's what you're asking."

"Sometimes, I'm also glad I did it and that makes me feel all ascared in my insides, like I shouldn't be happy, but a part of me is."

413

The baby slipped in Jillybean's arms and she held her up with a knee. Sadie hurried forward. "Do you want me to take her?"

"Yes. Ipes keeps being all ascared she's going to stick one of his ears in her mouth. So...so what about the others? Is Mister Neil ok? Please tell me he is."

"Yep. He's got some scratches and so does Captain Grey. I'm not sure anything can kill him. They're going crazy looking for you. We should really..." she paused looking at the baby. Even in the dark she was beautiful. Her big eyes glowed and her little bump of a nose was red with the chill night air. She grabbed hold of Sadie's spiked hair and a line of drool fell from her lower lip.

"She's perfect," Sadie said, deciding at that moment, that their pain and grief had been worth it. Preserving life, especially in this hard world, was always worth the risk.

Jillybean agreed. "She is perfect. Neil will be glad to get his little girl back." When she said this, she held her face just so: delicate, brittle.

Sadie dropped down so that they were practically nose-to-nose. "He will be glad to get both his little girls back. Remember we are sisters." She stuck out her little finger and Jillybean hooked it with her own. "Without Sarah to watch out for him he's going to need all three of his daughters to keep him safe."

"Really?" Jillybean asked, trying on a real smile for the first time in days.

"Oh yeah," Sadie said, standing and taking Jillybean's hand. She didn't move to the Humvee just yet. She was drained and tired and sad, but there was also a little part of her at peace knowing that Sarah had done the right thing. A mother had to protect her babies. She nuzzled Eve's cheek and then looked down at Jilly.

"Yeah, Neil's going to need us, especially if we're going to Colorado. He might fall off a mountain, you know."

Jillybean giggled. "What's in Colorado? Why are we going there?"

Sadie lifted her left shoulder as a shrug. "Good people. That's what Captain Grey says about them, that they're good people. I don't know about you but I need to be around good people."

"I guess I do, too," Jillybean said, with a little smile. She then turned a nervous eye up to Sadie and grew very serious: "Though I'll need to know how they feel about zebras before I can say yes. Ipes is worried that they eat zebras up in Colorado."

The End

*

Author's note:

The story continues with The Apocalypse Fugitives, but before you run off to the bookstore to snatch up your copy could I ask a favor? The review is the most practical and inexpensive form of advertisement an independent author has available in order to get his work known. If you could put a kind review on Amazon and your Facebook page, I would greatly appreciate it.

Peter Meredith.

PS If you are interested in autographed copies of my books, souvenir posters of the covers, Apocalypse T-shirts and other awesome Swag, please visit my website at https://www.petemeredith1.com

*

The Apocalypse Fugitives

Beaten and battered in mind and body, the fugitives limp west, unaware that the human world is fading all around them, unaware that the last remnants of the goodness of man is being ground under the heel of evil at every turn.

When confronted with that evil, fight or flight are their dire choices, only Neil's small group is forced to take on more refugees who come to them empty-handed, unarmed, and hungry.

Neil is faced with the disturbing prospect of guiding them across two thousand miles of zombie-plagued-land, only to stumble at his first hurdle: the mighty Mississippi has become a river of death and, like the fabled River Styx, the only way to pass is to pay the river man his fee.

His price: warm bodies.

What the readers say about The Apocalypse Fugitives:
"I would rate this series as among the BEST in zombie fiction…"
"I love Jillybean! Jillybean for president!"
"This series, by far, is the most compelling, well-written zombie series out there."

Fictional works by Peter Meredith:

A Perfect America
Infinite Reality: Daggerland Online Novel 1
Infinite Assassins: Daggerland Online Novel 2
Generation Z
Generation Z: The Queen of the Dead
Generation Z: The Queen of War
Generation Z: The Queen Unthroned
Generation Z: The Queen Enslaved
The Sacrificial Daughter
The Apocalypse Crusade War of the Undead: Day One
The Apocalypse Crusade War of the Undead: Day Two
The Apocalypse Crusade War of the Undead Day Three
The Apocalypse Crusade War of the Undead Day Four
The Horror of the Shade: Trilogy of the Void 1
An Illusion of Hell: Trilogy of the Void 2
Hell Blade: Trilogy of the Void 3
The Punished
Sprite
The Blood Lure The Hidden Land Novel 1
The King's Trap The Hidden Land Novel 2
To Ensnare a Queen The Hidden Land Novel 3
The Apocalypse: The Undead World Novel 1
The Apocalypse Survivors: The Undead World Novel 2
The Apocalypse Outcasts: The Undead World Novel 3
The Apocalypse Fugitives: The Undead World Novel 4
The Apocalypse Renegades: The Undead World Novel 5
The Apocalypse Exile: The Undead World Novel 6
The Apocalypse War: The Undead World Novel 7
The Apocalypse Executioner: The Undead World Novel 8
The Apocalypse Revenge: The Undead World Novel 9
The Apocalypse Sacrifice: The Undead World 10
The Edge of Hell: Gods of the Undead Book One
The Edge of Temptation: Gods of the Undead Book Two
The Witch: Jillybean in the Undead World
Jillybean's First Adventure: An Undead World
Expansion
Tales from the Butcher's Block

417

53911519R00232

Made in the USA
Columbia, SC
23 March 2019